THE DARK BROTHERS: BOOK 2

BOUGHT TO BREAK

KYRA ALESSY

Copyright 2021 by Dark Realms Press

All rights reserved.

No part of this book may be reproduced in any form or by any electronic or mechanical means, including information storage and retrieval systems, without written permission from the author, except for the use of brief quotations in book reviews.

This work of fiction licensed for your enjoyment only. The story is the property of the author, in all media, both physical and digital, and no one except the author may copy or publish either all or part of this novel without the express permission of the author.

Credits:

Edited by Catherine Dunn

Cover by Deranged Doctor Designs

ALSO BY KYRA ALESSY

Sold to Serve:

Book 1 of the Dark Brothers Series

www.kyraalessy.com/sold2serve

One woman enslaved. Three callous masters. Secrets that could destroy them all …

Kept to Kill:

Book 3 of the Dark Brothers Series (Pre-order Now!)

www.kyraalessy.com/kept2kill

A cursed woman kept in a tower. Three elite mercenaries leading an army of killers. They'll use her for their own gains if she lets them. But is she strong enough to preserve her future?

For more details on these and the other forthcoming books in this series, please visit Kyra's website:

https://www.kyraalessy.com/bookstore/

IF YOU ARE IN ANY WAY RELATED TO ME

Put this book down. Don't read it. Burn it. It'll be better for everyone.

If you do not heed this warning, never ever speak of it. I don't want hear anything about this book from your lips. You will literally ruin my writing mojo if I know you read it. For real.

CHAPTER 1

LANA

'I know you're here. You're always in here. I know you're hiding from me. When I find you, do you know what I'm going to do to you?'

Lana gritted her teeth as a bit of straw brushed against her nose. She pinched it shut, willing herself not to sneeze. She was crouched in a small hollow space amongst the hay bales. He couldn't see her, but she couldn't see him either. A horse snorted and stomped and the others followed suit. They didn't like him here anymore than she did.

She heard him swear. He was very close. He'd hear the smallest sound from her, no doubt about that. If he found her now … she shuddered … losing her only hiding place would be the least of her worries. She held her breath, praying to the gods for deliverance, and, finally, she heard the door bang closed as he left.

Lana breathed out slowly and extricated herself from her hiding place. The stable was quiet and the horses calmed as soon as she appeared. She began her usual duties; feeding the mares and rubbing them down after their long day. Some she'd known since she came here. They worked the fields during the day and came in at night. Others belonged to travelers who were passing through. All were doted on, though, whether she knew them or not. Lana loved horses; always had, even as a child. She remembered that her mother had had high hopes for her stud farm once Lana took over when she was older, but they had never come to fruition.

After an illness had ravaged her dear mama's body for three long weeks, she'd finally succumbed in her sleep. Lana had been thirteen and her stepfather had sold her to Dirk, the stablemaster, long before the pyre was cold. Her mother's property was the most valuable in the area and, if he'd waited until she was of age, he would have had to relinquish it to her. That was the law and a freewoman of property was a force to contend with. So he had quietly exchanged her for a horse early one morning. Knowing her master Dirk, he'd probably still been drunk from the night before – and that was that.

It had been eight long years since that day and, though she was old enough to inherit, Lana was a slave. She had no rights to property unless she was freed and she knew Dirk would never give her the Writ of Ownership. Her stepfather was a dangerous man and no one wanted to be on the wrong side of him.

So she tried to make the best of her life. Dirk wasn't a bad fellow really. He was fair when it counted and he didn't hate her, just his life. His son, Ather, was the real problem.

Lana felt her ribs, still bruised from the last time Ather had found her. They hurt, but the black masses had turned to light purple and yellow now. New ones would take their place sooner rather than later. Of that she had no doubt. He liked to beat her for imaginary wrongdoings, and lately he'd been looking at her differently – in a way that made her skin itch, as if he'd just remembered she was female.

She hid her body under shapeless rags as much as she

could, but he'd noticed all the same. And he wasn't the only one. The men in the tavern leered and grabbed at her whenever Dirk sent her to get him a flagon. She hated it when she had to go, and she'd taken to rubbing stinking mud over her skin and hair to try to put them off.

Finishing her duties, she was about to curl up under the straw in the corner to sleep when she heard movement outside. Fearing it was Ather coming back, she leapt for her hiding place, but the door swung open before she had taken two steps, taking her by surprise.

Two monstrously large men trudged in, leading two of the biggest ink-black stallions she'd ever seen. Both men and horses looked like they'd been out in the wilds for a good long while. They were all hardened and worn, dusty and rugged. The men wore dark clothes and had thick black cloaks for the season. Both had dark hair and eyes, and their handsome faces alone were enough to guarantee neither of them would want for female company while they stayed at the inn.

At that thought, Lana blushed and hoped her face was still dirty enough to hide it. Their great horses stomped impatiently with their enormous hooves, their breath coming out of their nostrils like smoke in the winter air. It made them look like beasts from a dark realm and she imagined these men were just as wild as their mounts. She shook slightly. Village lads and farmers were one thing, but the last time men like these were in her village, they had simply taken anything they wanted; food, supplies – and more than one woman was now growing with a child that was not her husband's. Lana still had bad dreams about the raids though she had hidden herself well each time they had come and they hadn't been back since the end of the summer. The local lords had run them off, she'd heard.

Lana continued to survey them. No, she wasn't used to

men like these. They must be warriors of some sort though. Yes, that was right. She had heard talk earlier in the day from travelers who had come via the north road. Mercenaries had been seen journeying south to the ports, travelling to where their services would be best paid for. These men were part of that sell-sword army, the feared Dark Brothers. She must have made a sound, because she was suddenly the focus of their piercing gazes.

'Where is the master here?' one of them ground out.

She opened her mouth, but, to her mortification, no sound but a tiny squeak passed her lips. The one who had spoken looked impatiently at her and the other, amusedly.

'Are you mute, girl?'

'Leave her alone, Viktor. You're frightening her.'

Viktor smiled slightly. He was enjoying her discomfort, and her eyes narrowed at him.

'I am not frightened!' she sneered.

Viktor's grin widened. 'Are you sure of that?'

He took a step towards her and she took two back.

'You look terrified to me. Tell me where your master is before I become impatient.'

He was playing games with her. Ather did that as well, but whereas Ather's games always ended in her receiving a sound beating, these men had no reason to harm her. They had no reason to even think of her, so far was she beneath their notice, she mused.

She looked Viktor in the eye and stood up straight. 'The sun is almost down. He's no doubt asleep.'

A look was shared between the two men. 'Bit early in the day to be abed.'

'He's a drunkard,' she said simply. 'But he never comes to the stables anyway. If you want your horses taken in, there's room in the last two stalls for the night. A silver. *Each.* They'll be well tended. You have my word.'

'You'll see to them yourself, girl?' the other man asked, looking her over, somewhat oddly.

Unable to help herself, she barked a small laugh. 'Do you see anyone else, sell-sword?'

They both raised their brows in surprise. Perhaps they weren't usually spoken to like that by slave girls.

The one not called Viktor produced the coins and held them out to her while the other simply watched the exchange. She edged forward, afraid one of them was going to grab her as such things had begun to happen with alarming frequency over the past months. But they both stayed still, as if afraid she'd flee if they pushed her.

She took the coins gingerly from his open hand and looked him in the eye while she did so. She was no quaking waif. She'd have been the richest girl in the valley if her mother hadn't died. He looked like he was trying to suppress a grin, and she had to stop herself from rolling her eyes at him. She'd been punished for less in the past.

The coins secreted away in her rags, she made to take the reins from them, but they stopped her.

'These are not docile farm stock. They're war horses, girl,' Viktor sneered. 'They'll bite, kick and stomp on you as soon as look at you.'

Lana simply shrugged. Less work was fine by her, so she left them to take care of their own mounts while she brought the coins to her master. Ather was nowhere to be seen, so hopefully he'd gone to the tavern and she'd be safe until tomorrow afternoon when he woke with a throbbing head and in a foul temper.

She found Dirk staring into the flames in front of the fire instead of passed out into oblivion as she'd expected.

'Master,' she said softly, 'two men have housed their horses in the stable for the night.'

He didn't look until he heard the clink of the money as

she placed it on the table next to him. He turned his head to look at the silvers.

'How many years have you been here, girl?' he asked after a moment.

'Eight, Master.'

'So long?' Dirk leant back in the chair, still staring at the coins. 'And your da never came back for you,' he murmured, half to himself.

Lana frowned, wondering if his mind was finally going soft. 'He's dead, Master, remember?'

He snorted and glanced up at her. 'Your ma told you that so you'd stop asking about him after she married Garrick. She made him go.'

Heart pounding, Lana sank into a chair. Her da was alive? Why had he never come back for her? Did he not know her mother was dead?

'I don't understand. Why are you telling me this now?'

He shrugged. 'Thought you knew. He disappeared for a while, but heard the other day he's made his fortune in Kingway.' He gave her a measured look. 'I know you were dealt a bad hand. Your stepfather … I'm sorry, girl. In truth I took you when Garrick came to me because I thought I could keep you safe until your kin came for you and bought off the Writ. But he never liked you and he's a spiteful bastard. Had to treat you as a slave, he said, and he checks up you know. If it's not done proper, he'd force me to give up the Writ and take you back.' Dirk looked her up and down despite her awful appearance. 'And you could guess how that would go now you're grown.' He heaved a deep sigh and put his head in his hands. 'And then no one came. I know how my boy treats you, don't think I don't. None of it sits well with me, girl, but …' He looked up, shame in his eyes. 'I don't have it in me to stop either of them. I can't help and this place will be the death of you.' He patted her hand. 'Next time you have the chance, flee to your da in Kingway. But don't get caught. Garrick will take it out of your flesh any way he can.'

Lana stood up, her mind reeling. Escape? She'd thought about it before, but she'd had nowhere to run to. Her mind started to turn. She'd need food and supplies before she could flee this place. How far was Kingway, even? It would be difficult and dangerous, but for the first time since she'd become a slave, she felt hope blooming in her chest. If she could get to her da...

Dirk's gaze returned to the coins on the table and her thoughts of fleeing were halted for the time being. She thought he might give them to her for when she got away, but, as his eyes glittered, her heart sank. 'Get me a flagon, girl.'

She closed her eyes with a short prayer to the gods. She was still a slave for the moment, and she had a very bad feeling.

'Yes, Master.'

CHAPTER 2

VIKTOR

Viktor watched the girl leave the barn from the corner of his eye. She was unkempt and dirty and the rags she wore stank of horse shit. He missed the north. Even slaves washed themselves up there, and he knew of none who wore rags in such a sorry state. Her dark hair was plaited untidily down her back. It looked dark, anyway. It might be golden as ripe wheat under all that filth for all he knew.

Viktor saw to his horse and looked around while Sorin tended to his own. There didn't seem to be much more than a few houses, a stable, a shop or two, but they'd just finished a tedious job at the local keep and this was the nearest village. They'd be able to get a bed for the night before they journeyed on. Thank the gods there was a tavern in this backwater at least.

They walked the short, muddy distance to the inn, finding, to their good fortune, that a roaring blaze and a hot meal could be found. At least they wouldn't have to beg, threaten or steal for a meal tonight.

Inside, they found a few men. Some were eating their

suppers, others having a quiet chat over a tankard and minding their own businesses. There was a group of bawdy young men nearest the hearth. They were uproariously drunk and guffawing over a story one of them was relating complete with flailing arms.

Viktor rolled his eyes as he sat with his Brother at a table in a murkier corner. A sizeable wench sidled over. They ordered ales and whatever food there was from her ample chest and both surveyed the room in silence, more out of habit than the actual possibility of a threat.

Viktor had no interest in the group of men per se, but he kept an eye out as he glanced over at Sorin. He expected his Brother to be watching them as well, but his attention had been grabbed by something over Viktor's shoulder. He turned and immediately noticed the ragged slave girl slipping through the room, keeping to the wall as much as she could with her head down, trying not to be noticed.

His eyes narrowed as he observed her. Stupid girl. Didn't she know that every man's eyes followed her? The more she tried to hide, the more they were intrigued.

He saw one of the wenches thrust an earthenware jug into her hand with a pitying expression and try to usher her back outside quickly, but the drunken group had spotted her. One of them approached while the others looked on, their eyes predatory. The wench intercepted him with a smile, pushing her tits into his face, and murmured something meant to entice, but he pushed her away hard and grabbed the slave girl she was trying to protect.

Interesting.

'Where were you when I came looking earlier?'

'I was at the shop for your da,' she said meekly, not looking at him.

'Why aren't you at the stable where you belong?'

'Your da asked me to get him this.' She raised the jug, still staring at the floor.

One of his friends piped up from the group. 'Thought you said you'd fucked her, Ather. She doesn't look well-pleasured. Give her to me for the night. I'll give her back to you with a smile on her face.'

'I'd give her a bath!' said another, and they all laughed heartily.

Ather's face turned bright red with anger, hers with embarrassment.

Viktor took a long swig of his ale. Why couldn't he stop looking at her? He glanced at Sorin. His Brother was the same.

'The next time I'm looking for you, you'd better be where you should be. Understand, slave?' Ather sneered.

'Yes,' she answered and turned to leave.

He grabbed her and wrenched her back hard. 'Did I tell you to go, you little bitch?'

She stifled a cry. 'No.'

'Sit with us.' He pulled her towards his friends.

'I must get this to your fa–' she began, but he interrupted her.

'My da will be dead to the world by now.'

She struggled in his grip and he grabbed the front of her rags. There was an audible rip and Viktor could see a large expanse of fair skin. She covered herself in an instant and fled, but Viktor felt himself inexplicably hardening all the same.

Ather went back to his friends, laughing off his embarrassment at the girl's expense.

Viktor looked at his Brother and raised a brow.

'Flesh white as freshly fallen snow,' Sorin breathed. 'And certainly not so young as she appeared.'

'She's not as filthy as she looks, either.'

Sorin nodded as he gazed at the door thoughtfully.

Viktor knew that look. 'There won't be time to make a conquest of her. The job is done now that that girl's decided to stay at the keep with Mace and the others. Kane will be expecting us. Besides, this one doesn't seem interested in men.'

Sorin waved a hand. 'These provincial boys learn how to fuck from watching farm beasts. What do they know about pleasure? Ten gold bits say I have her screaming my name before we travel on.'

'Twenty.'

Sorin's eyes gleamed and Viktor almost felt sorry for the lass. His Brother loved a challenge.

CHAPTER 3

LANA

The next morning, Lana awoke to sun streaming in through the door of the barn. It was cold but, she was nice and cozy, nestled in the straw beside one of the horses for warmth. She stretched and yawned.

'Thought you'd make a fool of me, did you?'

She froze, her eyes snapping open in terror.

Ather grabbed her and pulled her up easily, hauling her from the stall. She was reminded of how strong he really was despite his hours of leisure – and how heavy-handed with the lash.

Before she could utter a sound, he wound his fingers through her hair as he grabbed his favorite crop hanging on the wall. He pushed her over a hanging saddle and brought the whip down on her back.

She cried out at the blow. 'No, Master! Please!'

It whistled through the air and this time landed on her arse cheeks. She squealed and he laughed cruelly.

'I'm going to give you such a beating you won't be able to sit down for a fortnight. Then,' he leaned close, 'I'm going to fuck you. After what I got a glimpse of last night, let's see what else is under all this cloth.'

She struggled as he began to pull at her rags, but he held her dirty plait tightly. With a loud tear, she felt her clothes fall away. Hearing and feeling nothing from Ather, she opened her eyes to look back at him. He was staring at her nakedness as if he couldn't believe his eyes. Then he smiled coldly. 'If I'd known what you were hiding, I'd have taken you long before now, slave.'

Lana wanted to scream her name at him, remind him that their mothers had been friends when they'd still been alive. Tears came to her eyes. She should have run last night without the supplies she needed.

She whimpered, digging her nails into the leather of the saddle. He kept up the beating until her back, arse and thighs were on fire and it took all of her will not to give him the satisfaction of her cries. He stopped. Was it over? Had he tired himself enough that she'd get a reprieve?

Then he kicked her legs apart and she felt the crop grazing her inner thigh, travelling upwards. A coldness settled in her stomach. Her breath was coming in short pants and the world was spinning. Why, oh why hadn't she slept in her hiding place?

He slapped her private place with the crop twice in quick succession and she jumped with a scream. She heard him chuckle and began to sob as quietly as she could. She couldn't stop her tears as she felt his hand where the crop had been, his fingers digging into her. She'd never been touched like this before. In her younger, naïve years, she'd imagined her husband would be the first on her wedding night – but it would be now. Here, in this barn as the horses looked on, by Ather, a man she hated. She felt like she was finally dying inside.

'We've come for our horses, boy.'

A voice cut through the fear and the pain. She recognized it but, she couldn't remember who it belonged to.

Ather stopped what he was doing. 'Come back later. I'm busy.'

'We'll take them now.'

Ather's punishing grip left her, but she stayed where she was, knowing it would be all the worse for her if he noticed her move before he was finished with her.

'I said I'm busy! Who do you think you are? This is my–' Ather fell into the hay next to her, clutching his jaw with a yell of pain.

This was her chance. She sank to the ground, grabbing her clothes and straightening in one fluid movement. She flexed her muscles, getting ready to flee, though she was shaking awfully. She spun and leapt for the door, but a large arm attached to a towering man caught her before she'd even made it halfway.

'Not so fast, girl.'

Then she remembered the voice. The Dark Brothers from yestereve. She began to struggle in his grasp, but he subdued her easily. Tears flowed down her cheeks as she looked up into his face. It was the one not called Viktor.

'Please let me go. I beg you. Please.'

He didn't release her. Instead he looked at his Brother and something passed between them.

'No.'

Then the man turned her around in his arms so she was looking at Viktor, and she knew he was looking at the marks made by the crop. Her face burned with shame as she clutched her ruined clothes to her front, fresh tears forming in her eyes.

'Get the stablemaster, boy,' Viktor demanded, not even bothering to look at Ather, who scrambled up and ran like the demon horde of a dark realm were at his heels, leaving her with the two mercenaries.

She was pushed – though somewhat gently – to Viktor. Then her clothes were prized from her hands. She gave a small cry as she was left with nothing to cover her body. She tried to conceal herself with her arms, but they were pulled to her sides.

'Leave them there.'

She did as he ordered, shaking so hard her teeth were chattering. Were the sell-swords going to take up where Ather had left off? Were they both going to rape her? Remembering the screams of the women caught in the open during the raids, she took an unsteady breath and yet more tears slid down her cheeks. A hand forced her chin up until she was looking into Viktor's face.

'What did you do to make him beat you, slave?'

She blinked slowly, trying to clear the blur of tears from her eyes. 'He said I made a fool of him.'

'That's all?' He sounded suspicious.

She felt an odd bubble of laughter rise up from her chest. 'What else does he need? I'm a slave and he's a boy who wants to feel like a man.'

Viktor took off his cloak, and she tensed. But he simply settled it over her shoulders, shrouding her body in a thick, fur-lined tent of black. She had never felt so grateful for anything in her short life as this small kindness.

The stable door opened and Dirk stumbled in, looking much the same as when she'd left him drinking the wine she'd brought in last evening.

Before he even had a chance to demand to know what was going on, the other Brother had thrown a bag of coins at his feet. 'For your slave. Bring us the Writ.'

Viktor swung her up into his arms. What was happening? They were buying her from Dirk? Why?

Just like that, she was handed to the other Brother to sit in front of him on his horse as if she weighed no more than a dormouse, Dirk disappeared and came out a moment later with a paper in his hand – and then they were leaving. She saw Dirk's stricken face and Ather's furious one as they left the barn and she was grateful and terrified all at once. Why did they want her? What would they do with her? Should she thank the gods for their mercy or pray to them to save her from these men?

CHAPTER 4

SORIN

Sorin cursed silently as the girl in front of him squirmed, trying to find a comfortable position in the saddle. She must be in pain from the beating, he mused. She was covered in welts, and he'd seen other bruises on her body as well. She'd been used badly; the lot of a slave sometimes, to be sure. It was the same in the north, of course, but there a girl with her beauty would hold court in the highest brothels, have maids to attend her, choose her clients and, in time, buy herself free – usually so rich by then that she sailed away to the cultured and beautiful islands of the east to live out her life in comfort and security. The south, provincial backwater that it was, didn't work like that, which was a shame. Slaves like her should be treated well, not abused and worked to death.

Sorin didn't speak to her, wasn't sure what to say, so he pretended to ignore her as he maneuvered his horse, though she was the only thing he could focus on properly. They rode in silence, slowly, away from the village and into the wilds. They would journey all day, not stopping until nightfall.

'What will you do with me?' asked a small voice in front of him after a few hours of silence.

He glanced at Viktor, who rode by his side. Neither said anything.

'Why did you buy me from Dirk?' she persisted.

This time, Viktor answered and Sorin was surprised when he told the girl half the truth. 'We didn't like what we saw.'

There was a moment of silence before she spoke. 'Aren't all slaves treated this way?'

'Not all.'

She turned to look at Viktor, her hair brushing Sorin's skin. He ached to run his fingers through it, tangled and dirty though it was. He was drawn to her somehow. He'd never felt anything like it before. He knew Viktor was as well, though he was trying to hide it. Though he didn't understand it, neither of them could have left her to her fate back in that barn.

'But why–?'

'Hush, little bird; you're safe enough with us,' Viktor said as they neared a fork in the road, brooking no further comment. Instead of taking one or the other direction, they led their horses off the road and into the trees between them. Not far away was a deep thermal pool next to a small clearing. They knew it well. This was where they would make camp for the night.

Viktor helped the girl down from Sorin's horse and set her on the ground. He walked off with his bow to hunt for their dinner. Sorin dismounted and sorted the horses, unsaddling and feeding them. Though he stayed alert should she try to escape, it was some time before he turned his full attention back to her. She hadn't moved, just kept glancing at him and the space in the trees where Viktor had disappeared.

Sorin chuckled. 'Are you going to run, girl?'

She shook her head.

'Are you not afraid?'

She blinked at him. 'Less afraid than I was when I woke up this morning.' She smiled very slightly. 'Although that's not saying much.' She looked back at the forest.

Sorin regarded her while her eyes were elsewhere. She was too well spoken. That was rare for a slave – unless she was a house slave from one of the wealthy families trying to emulate her betters, which she was most assuredly not if her appearance was anything to go by.

'Where are your parents?'

She didn't turn back to him. 'Dead.'

Sorin finished with the horses. 'Were your parents owned by Dirk as well?'

Viktor emerged from the forest at that moment with two rabbits caught in record time, and Sorin's interest was diverted to preparing dinner. He didn't realize until later, after they'd made a fire and roasted the meat, that she'd never answered his last question.

SHE SAT on the forest floor, the cloak a tent around her as she watched their movements. When the food was cooked, he offered her some, which she tentatively took from his hand. She scuttled away from them to eat it.

Viktor shook his head at Sorin, mumbling about manners and feral slaves. 'Want some more, girl?'

She nodded.

'Then come here.'

She came back slowly, gripping her borrowed cloak. Just thinking she had nothing else on under it made Sorin want to rip it from her delectable body and get a proper look at his leisure. He'd seen her in the barn that morning, of course, but his focus had been on her injuries. He shifted as he sat, and Viktor gave him a knowing look.

She reached Viktor and looked down at the ground.

'On your knees.'

She looked frightened but did as he said and sank down before them. Viktor offered her some meat, but when she reached her hand out, he pulled his away. 'What is your name, little bird?'

'Lana.'

'Lana,' Viktor tested. He held out the meat again. 'Come closer and you can have it.'

She stared at the food and then at Viktor. Sorin thought she'd refuse, but hunger won out, and she shifted forward until she was kneeling just a hair's breadth away. She plucked the meat from his fingers daintily.

Sorin surged to his feet, unable to watch anymore, he was so hard. He ached to push himself into her, feel her tighten around him in ecstasy. He walked to the pool and put his hand in the warm water, splashing it on himself. But it wasn't enough. He shed his clothes, not caring if she saw, and dove into the deep spring. It was hot as a bath in the middle and he floated just under the surface for as long as he could, trying to relax himself. What was wrong with him? Had it just been too long since he'd had a good fuck?

When he finally came up for air, the girl was still kneeling in front of his Brother, looking uncertain.

Viktor caught his eye and gave an uncharacteristic grin. He wasn't unaffected by the girl either. He stood, bidding the girl to do the same. Then he swung her up into his arms. She cried out at his sudden movement and struggled to get away from him, but he just hushed her. He strode to the pool and, with no preamble, ripped off the cloak and threw her in. There was a scream cut off by a splash and then she was next to Sorin, thrashing naked in the water.

Sorin groaned. This wasn't what he'd had in mind, but he wasn't going to look a gift horse in the mouth.

'Please! I can't swim!' she gasped, thrashing to stay above the water.

Sorin grabbed her and she clung on to him like a sodden kitten, clutching at him wherever she could reach. She was breathing hard and whimpering quietly as he took her in his arms. There was another splash as Viktor joined them.

There was a rock in the middle of the pool that she could stand on, but Sorin decided to keep that information to himself. He liked her body wound around his even though she was trying fervently to keep her distance.

'Well, you smell a bit better, at least!' Sorin chuckled.

She glared at him and he grinned. Their little bird had talons. He pulled her closer, being careful not to hurt her back. The cuts there weren't mortal, of course, but they needed tending. Unfortunately their healing supplies had run very low. He didn't like leaving the wounds, but until they replenished the salve on the morrow, there was little he could do except make sure they were clean.

He felt her breasts brush his chest, her hard nipples grazing his skin. She gasped and pulled away. He released her with a playful chuckle and she sank beneath the surface immediately. Viktor hauled her back up a moment later, coughing and spluttering.

'You're ours now. Submit or learn to swim,' Viktor growled in his typical, harsh tone.

She flinched but didn't struggle from his grasp as he pulled her through the water towards him and took hold of her arms.

Viktor nodded and Sorin moved behind her, trailing his fingers down her shoulders and cupping her breasts. He squeezed them, plucking at her nipples gently. She made a shocked, little sound and turned her head to look at him. He expected to see arousal in her eyes but, to his surprise, he saw only fear. His brow furrowed. Surely this felt better than whatever that boy had done to her countless times.

Viktor did something under the water that Sorin couldn't see and she gave a strangled cry, her head whipping round so quickly that her long, dirty hair slapped Sorin in the face.

Not like this. Sorin let his hands drift to her waist, only helping to keep her afloat. He tried to catch his Brother's attention, but Viktor's eyes were closed as his hands wandered over their new slave's body. Then Lana began to struggle. Viktor's eyes opened lazily.

CHAPTER 5

VIKTOR

When he saw her panic, Viktor's gaze hardened. 'You'd let your old masters fuck you but not us?' he growled.

She shook her head, not looking away from him. He grabbed her to him in a sudden movement and she recoiled with a cry. She was terrified of them, he belatedly realised.

With that sobering and thoroughly *softening* awareness he swore loudly, let her go and clambered out of the pond. Let his Brother calm her. Sorin was much better at that sort of thing than he was. Sorin wooed who he wanted. Viktor didn't bother these days. If they wanted him, he took them. If they didn't, he threw gold at them until they did. Slaves? He didn't know. He'd never owned one. Though clearly, she'd been taken against her will before. She was slight; he could so easily …

He growled in revulsion, disgusted with his dark thoughts as he threw on his tunic. He didn't even bother drying off, ignoring the chilly air. Instead he lay by the fire in his blanket, quietly freezing his bollocks off as he fumed.

He listened to the sounds of Sorin and Lana leaving the

water, Sorin giving her back the cloak she'd worn all day. They settled next to him, Lana between them both for warmth, and he drifted into slumber.

He woke at sunrise to an empty space where she'd been. He jerked up, surveying the camp and ready to jump to his feet to go after her when he spied her. She was by the pool with both their horses. The warning he was going to shout at the foolish girl to back away from them slowly before they attacked died in his throat.

She spoke to them softly and the giant, monstrous war beasts bred to kill – that Viktor had seen bite men's hands off with nary a warning – were nuzzling at her and playfully nipping at her cloak as she hefted their saddles onto their backs and deftly buckled them. Who was this girl?

Next to him, Sorin sat up and rubbed his eyes, yawning. When he saw Viktor's face, he followed his gaze. It landed on Lana and his mouth dropped open like a shocked boy.

'Gods,' he breathed. 'Well … you don't see that every day,' he said lamely as Lana kissed one and then the other's nose and the horses stood docilely as ponies while she fussed over them.

Viktor shook his head. There was more to their little slave than he'd realised yesterday, but he still didn't understand this strange feeling. He wasn't sure what they were going to do with her yet. They *should* destroy the Writ and free her. He looked over at Sorin who was still staring at her with a keen interest. No, they wouldn't be letting her go. They were too drawn to her, but she didn't feel the same pull to them as they did to her, that was certain.

He stood with a huff in one quick movement. 'It's time to go,' he announced.

They gathered their belongings and rode on, Lana with

Sorin once more. Viktor knew he wouldn't be able to have her in his lap and not touch her, even if she was unwilling, whereas Sorin seemed to have more restraint.

They reached the town they'd been aiming for to replenish their supplies from one of the Army's caches and left their horses at a stable nearby.

Lana looked amazed by everything; the shops and storehouses, the cobbled main street. She'd clearly never been outside her village. Viktor's anger had dissipated now, and he was left bewildered by her behavior in the pool. He and Sorin were Dark Brothers. Their army was feared, it was true, but they had saved her from her masters. He'd expected a bit of gratitude if he was honest.

Perhaps she'd never had more than one man at once. In their unit, they shared everything, even women – especially women – but she was not from their world, after all.

Or perhaps her former masters had hurt her worse than the bruises and welts on her skin. He frowned. Women could have pain if they'd been taken too roughly in the past, he knew.

He came to an abrupt stop, an idea coming to him. Sorin halted next to him, a brow raised in query.

'The alchemist will look at her.'

Sorin nodded. 'We need to visit him anyway. We brought that lichen he asked for last time.'

'I'll take her.' Viktor glanced behind at Lana, who followed them closely, still in her borrowed wrappings. 'You go to the supply stores and don't forget a new healers' bag. And find her something to wear besides my fucking cloak!'

CHAPTER 6

LANA

*L*ana watched Sorin go, wishing he had stayed with her, not Viktor. They both frightened her, but Viktor was by far the more fearsome of the two. He never smiled; he always seemed angry. Sorin, on the other hand, tried to make her laugh, and he'd stopped what he was doing to her in the water when she'd been afraid. Viktor hadn't, not at first. Their touches had felt nicer than anything Ather had ever done, though. And they didn't seem vicious. They definitely weren't the monsters the stories portrayed them to be. She chuckled softly as she followed Viktor. They were pleasing to look upon, too.

Viktor led her through a nondescript entrance and into a dimly lit room. Shelves filled with bottles lined the walls, intermittently interspersed with books and colored stones. A thin man in blue healer's robes sat in a chair by a small fire, reading. He looked up with the closing of the door.

'Ah, it's you. I wondered when you'd be this way again. Did you bring what I asked for?'

Viktor pulled out a small bag and tossed it to the man, who caught it after a short fumble. He opened it, glee spreading over his face as if he was receiving a long-awaited present.

'And was it where I said?' he asked as he pulled out a lump of what looked like dried moss.

'High in the mountains of the north, through the cloud bank and close to water. Exactly as you said.'

The man stood. 'Excellent. Excellent. What do you want for it? A potion? Coin?'

Viktor unceremoniously dragged Lana in front of him. 'Sorin and I bought ourselves a slave in a nearby village yesterday.'

The apothecary nodded as he surveyed her. 'Who was your master, girl?'

Lana realised that she knew this man. He had come to see her mother while she was ill once or twice. He didn't recognize her, though, and she was glad of it. She didn't want her new masters to know any more about her than they already did.

Thankfully, Viktor answered the question for her. 'Just some stablemaster.' He pushed her forward slightly. 'I want you to examine her. Thoroughly.'

The apothecary nodded and his eyes roamed boldly over what little of her he could see.

'Come to the back. Do you want to stay?' he asked Viktor.

'Yes. And my Brother will be here soon.'

They passed through a curtain and into some sort of examination room. There was a table and a chair and various tools and implements.

'Take off your clothes and climb onto the table,' the apothecary said to her with no hesitation.

Lana felt her face heat and she turned to Viktor, her eyes pleading. He shook his head, his expression shuttered. 'Do as he says.'

She felt her eyes fill with tears as she fumbled with the

clasp of the cloak and it fell to the floor. She wiped her eyes with the back of her hand and climbed onto the cold stone table, shivering.

She didn't need to look to know both men were staring at her body appreciatively. Her arms were taken and manacled. She gave a small cry, which got her a rebuke. 'Quiet, girl. I need silence to work.'

He did the same with her ankles, bending her legs at the knees and attaching each to a loop at opposite sides of the table until she was spread wide.

He ran his hands lightly up and down her body, checking her skin, eyes, ears, nose and mouth. 'Hmm, not a very well-behaved slave, I see,' he said when he saw the fresh bruises and wounds on her from Ather's beating the day before.

She said nothing.

'She looks healthy enough,' he finally informed Viktor. 'No maladies or rashes that I can see, though she's had a fair few beatings recently with a switch or a crop.'

Lana winced at his words. *A crop*, she wanted to say. It was always a crop.

'They shouldn't scar, though, if you tend them properly and they don't fester. I can give you a salve.'

'No need. Sorin is refilling our supplies as we speak.'

The apothecary chuckled. 'Of course. The Army's got a cache in town now. Never far from one of those these days. Suppose it's a necessity in your line of work, eh?'

'Mmmmm.'

Ignoring Viktor's lack of reply, the apothecary took her breasts in his hands and kneaded them slowly. This was not in the same way and with none of the excitement she had seen in Sorin's eyes the evening before in the pool.

'No growths that I can feel.'

He moved down and his fingers pulled her nether lips apart, and she lurched in surprise. He snickered.

He licked a finger and moved it up and down her slit, feeling her, his touch lingering here and there. She squirmed and gasped in unwanted pleasure as he applied pressure to certain areas, and then she flushed in embarrassment. How could her body be enjoying this when her mind was utterly revolted?

She vaguely heard the door open in the other room and his hands left her. Then Viktor was by her side. He caressed her face, almost kindly. 'Almost finished, Lana.'

She couldn't help but turn her cheek into his hand, wishing he'd unfasten her and stop letting this strange man touch her. He looked as surprised by her actions as she was, though his mouth curved into a hint of a smile.

'You're just in time,' the apothecary said, stepping through the curtain. He was followed by Sorin, whose eyes widened as he took in the scene before him.

'Gods. So I am,' he murmured.

Viktor gave him a questioning look.

'I got her a dress, but the cache was closed. I'll go back later,' Sorin answered his Brothers' unspoken question, his eyes not leaving her.

He made his way to her feet, watching what the apothecary was doing between her spread thighs. Something cold and thick nudged her entrance and she tried to move away, but she was too tightly bound. She felt it enter her shallowly and retreat. In and out, in and out, and then it went in a little further. She made a noise as it began to sting and it was removed immediately. Then the same was done to her back passage, though he coated the instrument with something slippery before he pushed it in. It still hurt, though, and she squirmed in discomfort until it was taken out.

She jumped as he gave her thigh a final, impersonal pat as one would a horse's flank, and he turned to the Brothers.

'So did you find anything?' Viktor asked, eyeing her body

as if she was going to immediately succumb to illness in front of them.

The apothecary grinned, his eyes flicking back to her. 'I don't know how much you paid, but I'm willing to bet you got a bargain.'

Sorin and Viktor both looked confused. 'What do you mean?' Sorin asked.

'It's impossible to be certain, but I believe she is untouched.'

Viktor shook his head. 'What?'

'A virgin, you fool. He means she's a virgin,' Sorin snapped with a roll of his eyes.

They both stared down at her.

'But when we came to the stable, your master …' Viktor finally began.

Lana longed to sink into the stone table. 'I made sure he never saw my body. I wore rags and rubbed mud over myself. He only ever thought of me in *that* way when he was drunk, and I had a place to hide whenever he came looking for me. When he caught me yesterday,' she closed her eyes, 'it was the first time he'd intended to do more than beat me, and you took me away before he could do much more than that.'

~

Sorin

SORIN ITCHED TO TOUCH HER. Partly because she was bound so helplessly and at their mercy, which stirred his own predilections, but also, he found to his surprise, he wanted to hold her in his arms, show her that not all men were cruel. He couldn't remember ever wanting to do such a thing before.

At least they knew now why she hadn't enjoyed their attentions in the pool the previous day. She was a scared little maiden – and she was theirs. If the apothecary wasn't here now, he had no doubt that both he and Viktor would be putting her fear to rest with pleasure.

As if the gods knew his thoughts, the outer door to the shop jangled open and the apothecary disappeared through the curtain. As soon as they were alone, Sorin couldn't help but begin playing with one of her nipples, taut and hard from the cold air of the room. She gave a small whimper as her eyes fluttered open.

Viktor drew closer to her legs, one hand travelling upward. At first, she tried to struggle, but only at first. She gasped as his finger drew up and down the wide-open apex of her thighs and began to tease her entrance.

'I saw you blushing, little bird,' he murmured so only they could hear, 'when the apothecary was putting his fingers here and testing you with his instruments. You were afraid, but I think you liked it as well.' He eased a finger into her slowly and gently, and she gave a small moan.

Sorin's cock tightened even more and he groaned. 'Let's go.'

Viktor nodded but didn't stop what he was doing. 'Tell me you like it, Lana. Tell me how much you enjoyed being bound; on display for us. Do you want him to use this on you again?' He held up the smooth, glass tool the apothecary had inserted into her. 'Shall I use it on you?

He kneaded Lana's entrance with it. She tensed as he eased it into her tight channel and began to move it slowly and gently. 'Tell me how much you like it.'

She moaned again, this time more loudly, and Sorin grinned. 'Tell him, Lana. Or he'll stop.'

Viktor ceased his slow movements and she whimpered, her hips straining towards him. He chuckled.

CHAPTER 7

LANA

'Please ... please, Master ...' she whispered, though she couldn't bring herself to beg him to continue.

'Tell us how much you're enjoying this.'

'I ... I don't want to, but I am.' She couldn't help it. What was wrong with her? She'd never felt like this before, never felt a pull to any man, and now she was being drawn to two. *I don't understand what is happening.*

'Neither do we,' one of them answered truthfully, and she realised she'd spoken aloud. They both hovered over her, looking equal parts bemused and concerned.

Her legs and arms went slack and she realised they'd released her. She was eased up to a sitting position and Viktor's cloak was draped around her once more. Sorin picked her up, carrying her out of the apothecary.

She didn't struggle, didn't do anything save close her eyes and curl her body into his with a sigh. It had been years since someone had touched her with anything near affection, let alone held her in their arms. Only a day had passed, she realised. Had she really only known them one day and night?

She was beginning to feel safe with two of the most

dangerous men she'd ever heard of and that, she found, was more terrifying than anything Ather had ever done. She was pulled to them in every way and probably would be even if they were cruel to her, which was pathetic but true. They wanted her body, and she knew being bedded by them would be as enjoyable as she'd been told it was by the tavern wenches – though she'd doubted them. But she was finding herself yearning for something more that masters did not give to slaves – affection, even love. She'd never had thoughts like these. Never. She didn't like it.

She didn't know where she was, but Dirk had said her da lived in Kingway. If she could escape the men, she could find the town. She could begin anew. She wouldn't be a slave anymore. She could perhaps find love and have a family of her own. She'd never considered such things before. But she'd never before left her village. Today she'd had a glimpse of the outside, and it was filled with possibilities. It was true that if she tried and failed, they would probably kill her. But she had to try to get to her father, she thought, as she let sleep take her.

When she opened her eyes, she was in a comfortable bed in a small room, resting above the covers and, thankfully, still wrapped in the cloak. She could hear the light hum of conversation through the thin walls. Distant doors opened and closed – the tell-tale sounds of a lodging house. Lana sat up. The room was clean but worn. The rugs were threadbare and the wooden floorboards rough and stained. The casement was closed, so the light was dim, but she could make out a full, steaming bath. She got off the bed and tried the door, her recent plans on her mind. It wouldn't open and she found when she unfastened the casement that the room was too high to climb out that way.

The light now shining in from the outside fell on the Brothers' packs. She paused for a moment and looked around at the closed door. If she truly wanted to find her father…

She searched through the bags, finding a large purse of gold coins and various weapons and clothes as well as the usual travel supplies. She hesitated. There would be no turning back if she did this. The punishment for a slave's thievery was harsh. She didn't want to do it, but she couldn't very well leave with nothing but the clothes on her back. She'd never survive. She grabbed a few coins and a small dagger, all of which she wrapped tightly into a bundle of cloth and stowed under the bed.

Her gaze returned to the tempting bath. She was alone. She couldn't escape at this very moment, after all, and it had been so long since she'd been truly clean. Making her mind up, she let the cloak drop to the floor. She grabbed the cake of soap resting on the table and gingerly stepped into the deep, hot water. She sat slowly, moaning in pleasure and then hissing as her welts burned, and leant back as it drew all the aches from her. She scrubbed her hair and body thoroughly, over and over before she relaxed, resting her head on the side. How lovely it was to be clean! She frowned. In hindsight perhaps she should have remained dirty. It was the best way she knew of to keep men at a distance.

But she would have missed out on her first, real, hot bath in years. She gave a long deep sigh just as she heard the door being unlocked. She sat bolt upright, realised that her breasts were showing and sank down just as the door opened. Sorin and Viktor entered. When they saw her, both froze.

'Your hair,' Sorin finally said. 'It's red.'

She touched it as she looked down at the water self-consciously. 'Yes.'

'It was so dirty even after the pond I thought it was brown.' Sorin grinned. 'Found the soap, eh?'

She nodded and couldn't help but smile at him. He was easy to like.

Viktor was different. She liked him as well, mostly from the rare moments he showed emotion and she could see his true nature. Now he didn't smile or even look at her. Just closed the door and went to a chair turned away from her, sitting down heavily.

She wondered if he was angry, but Sorin didn't seem bothered by his Brother's mood.

He got a blanket from the bed and held it up for her. She shook her head and didn't move from the water, and he rolled his eyes at her. 'We've already seen you, Lana.'

She blushed. *That was an understatement*, she thought as she rose, the water splashing around her. She stepped out and Sorin wrapped her in the cover. He led her to the table and told her to sit.

There was a knock at the door and Sorin went to answer it. He turned back a moment later with a tray in his hands. 'Hungry?'

Sorin set the food on the table in front of her and she began to eat slowly, savoring each bite. She'd had little more than kitchen scraps as Dirk's slave. When she looked up, she found Viktor's eyes on her, watching every movement. Heat began to creep over her skin. She didn't think the hunger in his expression was for the stew.

She finished quickly and stood. 'May I get dressed?'

'No,' was Viktor's immediate reply, and she bristled.

Sorin gave Viktor an imploring look. 'Yes, of course, but your injuries need proper attention or they could worsen.' He held up a small pot.

'I can do that myself.' The thought of standing in front of them naked for their scrutiny again was too much to bear so soon after being on that table. She didn't even care if they beat her for her insolence.

'You can't reach all of them,' Sorin pointed out. 'You can keep the blanket around you; just let it fall a bit at the back so I can reach them.'

She let out a small huff. 'Fine, but I am keeping the blanket, and when you're finished, I am getting dressed!'

Inside her head, a part of her screamed at her to be quiet, that she was going to get herself punished for her impertinence, but she ignored it. She was tired of being ogled like a prize mare and never being in charge of her own fate.

But Sorin didn't look angry with her, just amused. 'I promise. If you still want to get dressed by the time I'm finished, you can, of course.'

There was something about his words that made her suspicious, but he turned her so that her back was to him. The sooner he was finished, the sooner she could cover herself in the green dress that she'd noticed draped on the bed – assuming it was for her. She loosened her hold on the blanket, keeping it clenched to her front in case he tried to pull it from her, but he didn't. Instead he kneaded her shoulders gently, telling her the muscles were tight. She opened her mouth to say that this wasn't what they'd agreed, when he stopped. Something cold drew a gasp from her and she pulled away.

'Sorry, sorry, the salve is cold.' Sorin laughed as he touched her lightly, running his fingers down the length of the marks. He swore softly as he went further down. 'That boy really put his back into it.'

Lana shrugged. 'He was always heavy-handed. The horses hated him.'

Sorin turned her gently towards the light. 'There are older marks here. How often did you get the lash?'

'Twice a week, perhaps. Sometimes more. Depended on

how much he drank and when he could find me,' she said as she suppressed a shiver.

Sorin was silent, but she could tell something was passing between him and Viktor again. She felt his fingers lower, following the marks down her arse, and flinched. He hushed her and told her to loosen the blanket so he could reach the lowest marks on the backs of her thighs. She did as he asked, feeling his hands move down. She began to feel a peculiar sensation between her legs, though his hands were nowhere near, and she shifted slightly.

Sorin's hands massaged her skin, relieving the aches from the whip as well as from the horse-riding she wasn't used to, and she sighed, her eyes drifting closed as she relaxed.

'Did you enjoy your bath?'

'Yes,' she murmured dreamily. 'It was lovely. I hadn't had one of those since I was a child.'

'A child?'

She yawned. 'Before my mama died.'

There was a brief pause before he spoke again. 'I thought that would have relaxed you, but you're still very tense,' he said softly.

She felt his hand drift up the inside of her leg and, without meaning to, opened her legs slightly for him.

'Very good,' she heard him say. He teased lightly and delved into her slit. To her mortification, it felt wet, and she clasped her legs together, her eyes opening. His hands left her, but he picked her up and deposited her lightly on the bed. He pulled the blanket gently from her grasp and parted it, looking at her with open enjoyment. Then he lay next to her. He licked a nipple and bit it softly, causing her to arch off the bed.

'What are you doing?' she breathed, her eyes closing again.

'Helping you to rest,' he murmured back. His fingers were

gentle as they moved, finding the place that Viktor had before that made her moan in pleasure.

'I don't think this is helping.'

He chuckled. 'It will.'

His fingers teased her entrance and he plunged one inside her. She gasped and instinctively opened her legs wider as he moved it in and out, stretching her just a bit. She opened her eyes to look at him and instead locked eyes with Viktor, who was now standing beside the bed. She thought he might do something, but he didn't – just watched.

'Do you like what Sorin's doing, little bird?'

'Yes,' she said, trying to stifle a moan.

'Don't close your eyes again. Look at me, Lana,' Viktor ordered, every bit a battle commander that made her shiver in anticipation.

Sorin's finger began to move faster and she felt something begin tightening within her with every thrust as she stared into Viktor's eyes. Sorin's thumb began to move over that part he'd found before and her body went taut. She couldn't help it; she closed her eyes and screamed Sorin's name as a wave of pleasure washed over her.

Sorin's finger left her and she opened her eyes just in time to see him put it to his mouth and suck. Her eyes widened and he grinned. 'Good girl,' he cooed.

Then he stood, wrapped her in the blanket again and lay back on the bed with her. He drew her into his arms and she sighed.

She rested her head against Sorin's chest, feeling it rise and fall with his breath. 'I'm sorry.'

'What for?'

'I called you by your name. I didn't mean to, Master. It just came out.'

She heard the door and looked around the room. Viktor had left.

Sorin cupped her chin, forcing her to look at him. 'Call us by our names. "Master" doesn't suit us.'

LANA WOKE with a start alone in the bed once more. Sunlight streamed through the closed casement. She looked around the room as she replayed the evening. What had Sorin done to her? She cringed. Had she told them about her mother? She put her head in her hands. What was happening to her? How did they make her lose her faculties so easily?

She sprang from the bed, washed in the now-cold bath and donned the clothes Sorin had procured for her. The forest green gown was serviceable and, luckily, easily laced up the front so she wouldn't have to ask one of the men for help getting dressed. She grabbed her stolen bundle from under the bed, checking the coins and dagger were still inside before tying it far beneath her skirts, tightly so it wouldn't jingle. She was determined to escape them – and their crafty wiles.

CHAPTER 8

VIKTOR

Viktor had already been up for hours as he neared the lodging house and found Sorin readying his horse. 'I thought we were going to wait.'

Sorin shrugged as he buckled the saddle. 'I didn't fuck her.'

Viktor ran a hand through his hair in exasperation. 'I know what you did. I was there, Brother, and we had decided to go slowly.'

'What's the problem? I didn't go behind your back. What's bothering you is that I did something with her first.' Sorin turned to face him. 'Besides, you could have joined in if you'd wanted. She was perfectly willing.'

'Of course she was willing!' Viktor exploded. 'But she never even felt a woman's pleasure until last night. Did you realize? No, you were too busy congratulating yourself for getting past her defenses!'

'I was not –' Sorin stopped and his expression hardened. 'You're right. I didn't think about it being her first time for everything, not just … you know. Do you think she's all right?'

Viktor growled. 'You'd better hope she is.' He ran a hand through his hair again. 'There's something about her. We both feel it. We may not understand it, but she's important. Go and get her. We're leaving before we run into any other units. There will be others in the area so it's only a matter of time, but I'd rather no one knows about her yet so close to the campaign. Besides, we're due to meet Kane in three days.'

'What if he doesn't feel this thing, whatever it is?' Sorin asked.

'He will,' Viktor said simply. *He has to.*

Sorin left him to find Lana, and Viktor sighed. Watching her with Sorin the night before had left him needing a dunk in a cold pond. He'd already run the perimeter of the town twice, hacked at posts with his sword and everything else he could think of, but he was still hard. He closed his eyes, seeing Sorin's long finger pushing into her while she writhed on the bed with her legs wide, confusion in her eyes but inevitably succumbing to the pleasure he was giving her. Taking out his cock, Viktor worked himself as he thought about how she'd looked bound tightly to the apothecary table, her body straining at the ropes as he and Sorin had touched her, as the phallus had moved in and out of her. She had been so exposed and her channel so tight he'd only been able to fit one finger inside her. His hands quickened and he spent in the hay with a groan. It wasn't nearly enough, but it would have to do. For now.

He finished readying his horse. Lana would ride with him today. He'd be fucked if he'd let Sorin have that pert little arse rubbing against him all day again.

He mounted just as Sorin came into view, Lana following him in that green dress his Brother had found that left just enough of her chest on display for them. She also now wore her own black ermine-lined cloak.

Sorin lifted her up to Viktor with a knowing look that he

ignored as he settled her in front of him. She sat ramrod straight as if she were trying not to touch him any more than she had to. Her face was as crimson as her beautiful, red hair, and he almost smiled. He'd bet anything she was remembering him watching last night and trying to fathom why she'd liked that so much.

He let her tire herself out, knowing that by the afternoon she'd be leaning into him with fatigue.

Viktor was right. By the time they stopped to make camp in the evening, his arms around her were the only thing keeping Lana on the horse. When they stopped at the ruins in the middle of the forest, she perked up, however.

'What is this place?' she asked as she hefted her leg over to dismount.

Sorin helped her down, gliding his hands up her body as he did so, Viktor noted. 'It's a ruin of a castle or some such.'

She looked around in wonder.

'Stay close to the camp though. There's a portal around here somewhere.'

Her eyes widened. 'To a dark realm? There was one close to my village before it collapsed, but I never got to see it.'

Viktor chuckled. 'And you won't see one now either. The bridge rarely opens when the moon isn't full and its waning now.' He slid off his horse and landed on the ground, grabbing his bow from the saddle. 'I'll find us some dinner.'

Sorin began his usual task of unloading the horses when Lana stopped him. 'I can see to them if you like.'

Sorin shrugged. 'Are you sure you're strong enough?'

She made a scornful sound that made him smile in spite of himself. 'I may not have arms like yours, but I'd gamble my back is as strong.' With that she hefted the saddle bags off Sorin's horse like a seasoned traveler and stuck her tongue out at them both. This time he allowed himself a chuckle. She looked at him in surprise.

Sorin made a gesture of surrender and took up his own bow and quivers. 'Very well, I'll go with Viktor and get us some food. I'm a better shot, anyway.'

Viktor snorted. 'Care to make a wager, Brother; most kills wins and the loser dresses the meat?'

'I'd take that bet any day.'

Lana laughed. 'So long as I don't have to do it. I'm no good with skinning.'

She turned away and got on with seeing to the horses, and Viktor felt a warmth flow through his chest as he observed her. He glanced at Sorin and saw the same feeling in his face. He couldn't remember the last time he'd laughed, yet here he was in such an *agreeable* mood.

Shaking his head, he followed Sorin into the trees. They stayed together, watching for movement. Their blood began to pump as they stalked through the brush. They loved the hunt almost as much as they loved a good battle.

In the end, Viktor shot a small boar and Sorin killed two rabbits, so they called it a draw and hiked back to camp to prepare their feast. But when they got to the clearing, the horses were still saddled and there was no sign of Lana.

'Where is she?'

'Lana?' Sorin called.

She was nowhere to be seen. Viktor looked at the marks in the dirt. Most were theirs, but someone else had been here too. He drew his sword with a growl and Sorin did the same just as they heard a loud yell and then a scream from the ruins. They raced under the broken arches and through forgotten rooms and cloisters overgrown with fauna towards the sound.

They came upon three men. Dark Brothers. One was on the ground, unconscious, and the other two were in front of

Lana. She was pressed up against a stone wall, a knife at her throat.

One of them said something to her they couldn't hear.

She spat at him, her face defiant, and for a moment Viktor's heart swelled in pride. She was theirs.

'Back away from our woman,' he snarled.

Both men turned their heads and Viktor saw who they were. Uth, Kilroy, and the one on the ground was Fen. In battle these days, they preferred to hang back from the actual fighting and appeared for the pillage and rape, he recalled. He stalked forward. 'I said, leave our woman alone.'

'Your woman?' Uth sniffed the air. 'I don't smell you strongly on her. You know the rules; if you haven't claimed the female, she belongs to the Camp.' He grinned nastily.

'That's *in* the Camp, fool.' Viktor slammed the pommel of his sword into the closest man's face. Kilroy screamed in pain and went down without a fight. *Pathetic.*

With no one's attention on her, Lana had edged away from Uth and his dagger and ran behind Sorin.

Uth glanced down at his two fallen Brothers and his lip curled into a snarl. 'The girl practically invited us to take her.'

'That's a lie!' Lana cried from behind them.

'Quiet, girl,' Viktor spat. 'Your unit is down. Is she worth your life, Uth?'

'Bah! You keep the high-and-mighty bitch. You're welcome to her.' Uth sneered. Kilroy got to his feet with a moan, blood streaming from his broken nose. They grabbed the still-unconscious Fen and hobbled off in the opposite direction.

Viktor let out a breath and turned on Lana. He stalked towards her, but she held her ground, staring up at him. 'Do you invite everyone to maul you, you stupid girl? We leave you alone for less than an hour and you throw yourself at the first men you–'

She slapped his cheek with an angry cry – hard enough to make even his weathered skin smart. She stared at her palm and then at where she'd struck him as if she couldn't believe what she'd done. She was shaking with fury.

'I have never invited any man to touch me,' she said through clenched teeth. 'I have never wanted any man to touch me save y–' She took a shuddering breath, turned, and fled in the direction of the camp.

Sorin sighed. 'Fool,' he muttered at Viktor.

Viktor breathed out and closed his eyes. Even the idea that she would want anyone besides them was enough to make him insane with rage. He'd known her only days. What was happening to him?

'Well.' Sorin inclined his head towards where she'd disappeared. 'What I did last night was nowhere near as bad as that.'

Viktor let out a snarl, but he'd never before agreed so wholeheartedly with anything Sorin had said. 'Come on.'

'Where?' Sorin asked.

'Back to camp. We have to talk to her.'

'We?'

Viktor didn't reply. He ran quickly through the ruins to the horses, finding her sitting on a log with her back to them. Sorin was on his heels.

'Speak to her,' he ordered Sorin.

Sorin shook his head. 'This was your doing, Viktor. You fix it. As for me, I'm going to start a fire and sort dinner.'

He took himself off, saying something about gathering wood, leaving Viktor alone with her.

He walked slowly to the log where she sat hunched over, hugging her knees. 'Lana.'

She stiffened but didn't acknowledge him.

'I'm sorry. I didn't mean–'

'Are you going to have me publicly beaten or kill me?' she asked in a small voice.

'Neither.' Viktor walked around the log and crouched in front of her. 'Why would we do that?'

'I raised my hand to my master. I know the law.'

He grasped her chin and tilted her head up to look at him. 'The Brothers' laws aren't quite the same.'

He leaned forward and kissed her. Her mouth parted slightly as she gasped, and he slipped his tongue past her lips to taste her. Her eyes widened and he broke away, leaning his forehead against hers.

'You've never kissed a man either?' he muttered.

She gave her head a tiny shake and he groaned.

'How are you so innocent?' He pushed her unruly hair back from her face, his thumb caressing her cheek. 'I'm sorry for the things I said. I was angry and afraid they had hurt you.'

She didn't speak for a long time, and when she did, it wasn't what he expected. She pulled away from him. 'I wasn't always a slave.'

'What?'

'You asked why I'm so untouched. I wasn't born a slave.'

Viktor's brow furrowed. 'You were taken then.'

She gave a wan smile. 'Not quite, but this is the south. You must know how it can be here. Sometimes all it takes is a bit of bad luck.'

Viktor shifted and sat on the log next to her. 'Go on.'

'My mother was a freewoman.' Lana gave a small, brittle laugh. 'Not only that. She was the richest one in the valley.'

She stopped talking and Viktor took her hand in his. 'What happened?'

'My mother made my father leave us when I was very young. I don't know why. She told me he was dead. The one she married after him, Garrick, wasn't the sort of man she thought he was.'

'And he sold you?' Viktor guessed.

'I was thirteen when she fell ill and died,' Lana said matter-of-factly. 'Garrick took me to Dirk the day after her body was burned.' Lana turned towards him. 'No one ever touched me except Ather. No one ever really showed any interest in me that way except Ather, and,' she shook her head, 'it was only to prove to himself that he was my master in all ways.'

Viktor gritted his teeth at what he was about ask, but he forced out the words. 'Why did no one ever … take advantage?'

She shrugged. 'I suppose they thought my kin would come for me one day. No one ever did, but most people didn't try to be cruel to me. I think they felt sorry for me most of the time.'

Viktor was silent for a while. It was one thing to be made a slave in war or be taken from your home to become a slave in another land, but she'd been a freewoman until she was half-grown and then sold to a neighbor amongst people who had known her and her family as equals. The south truly was a different land to the north. He'd never thought on it before, but he supposed that enslaved free folk from the south were taken to the north as well though.

He glanced over at her. She was staring off into the forest at nothing, lost in her own thoughts.

'I wasn't always a Dark Brother,' he blurted out. He cringed, wishing he could unsay it.

She looked back at him with sudden interest. 'You weren't?'

He took a steadying breath. 'No.' He looked abashed. 'I was a farmer. I had a homestead in the far north. I had a wife, children.'

She cocked her head. 'They died.'

'Yes.'

Her hand tightened on his. 'How?'

He swallowed hard. He never talked about this. 'An attack. A fire. Afterwards I found some of the men responsible and I killed them all. Then I joined the Dark Army.'

'I'm sorry.'

They were both quiet for a while. They heard Sorin making a fire and sorting the horses, as Lana had been interrupted.

'They were Dark Brothers too,' she said. 'They're gone, aren't they?'

'Yes. They didn't hurt you?'

Her hand in his trembled. 'No, but they were going to. Two of them came upon me here and I ran, but there was another one waiting for me in the ruins. I hit him on the head with a stone, but the other two cornered me.'

She stood up and he followed, putting his hand on her shoulders. 'They're gone,' he promised.

'Are you sure? What if they're out there,' she gestured at the forest, 'just waiting?'

'One of us will keep watch all night to be safe.'

She relaxed under his hands and he drew her to him.

'Viktor?'

'Yes?'

'There were three of them. Why aren't there three of you?'

He grimaced. 'There are.'

'There's another?' She drew back.

'Yes. His name is Kane. He returned to the Camp after our last mission to meet with our Commander. We're travelling to meet him.'

CHAPTER 9

LANA

Something in Lana's chest fluttered as she gazed up at Viktor. *Another Brother?* Everything about this life was so new – better than her old one in many ways, but she wasn't sure how she felt about this new development.

'Why isn't he with you?' she asked.

'He had business ... elsewhere after our last job was done, but we'll meet up with him and the others soon,' he said cryptically, not easing her disquiet at all.

Others? She stepped away from him. 'What others? Gods, how many of you are there?'

Viktor chuckled. 'In our unit? Three Brothers and at the moment we have a few soldiers.'

'Who aren't Dark Brothers,' she inferred.

'That's right.'

She squinted at him. Getting even small amounts of information out of this man was frustrating. 'So, you have an army.'

He hesitated before he spoke, tilting his head slightly to one side and then to the other. 'More of a tiny unit of semi-loyal men to help where needed, but we are part of the Dark Army. Surely you know this already.'

Lana swallowed hard. She didn't want to ask her next question – was afraid of the answer, but she had to know. 'Will I have to … will you make me … with the others?' She stopped, shaking her head. *Just ask!* 'Will your soldiers want to lie with me?' she blurted.

'Oh, they'll definitely want to, little bird.'

Her stomach sank.

He grabbed her chin, the abruptness of the action startling her. His eyes were dark with an emotion she didn't really understand, a violent possessiveness that scared as well as soothed. 'But you aren't theirs. You belong to us. From now on, anyone else who touches you dies.'

'You'd really kill someone for that? For me?' She wasn't sure she liked that. No one deserved to die over her. *Well – maybe Ather.* She tried to be good, but she wasn't a priest of the Mount.

'All three of us would.'

But Kane hadn't even met her yet. She didn't understand the Brothers' world. She wondered if Viktor was getting tired of all her questions. She had so many, but now there were some that burned brighter than all the rest – what was Kane like? She got the impression that he was their leader, if the three Brothers could claim to have one. Would he want her as Viktor and Sorin did? How would that work and how long for?

Having three deadly mercenaries protecting her in her old life would have been laughable, but this was a new world, much more dangerous than the one she had left behind, she was starting to realize. Perhaps having real protection was a good thing. At least until she was able to flee. She thought back to the three men who had attacked her this evening and shuddered.

'Viktor?'

'Yes?' he answered her as he hefted the bags off his horse – the job she had started doing before those men had appeared with their vile threats and chased her into the ruins.

'When Uth was speaking to you, he said he could smell me. How?'

Viktor's hands stopped what they were doing. 'I hoped you hadn't noticed,' he muttered.

He finished unbuckling a strap and turned to her, catching Sorin's eye as he did so.

She frowned at him. 'Stop exchanging looks with each other and tell me.'

Viktor gave her an apologetic glance and led her to where Sorin now had a merry fire crackling away. He sat, pulling her down to sit next to him on the soft moss.

'What is it?' Sorin asked. He turned the meat that was now cooking on the fire, and Lana's mouth began to water. Viktor was silent for so long that she thought perhaps that was the end of their conversation for the night, but then he replied.

'She's asking about Uth.'

Sorin grimaced and glanced at her from the other side of the flames. 'Ah. You caught what he said, did you? Should have known you would.' He shrugged. 'She's going to find out eventually. Might as well tell her now.'

Viktor nodded solemnly. 'Very well, but, Lana, you mustn't speak of it. It's only rumored outside the Brothers and the Army wants to keep it that way.'

What did that mean? 'I won't tell, I promise. But I don't understand.'

'Brothers usually come in threes.' He looked around as if he was afraid someone was listening and lowered his voice an octave. 'Sometimes you get a Brother in a unit who's different.'

'Sometimes two,' Sorin piped up as he worried the meat with a stick.

Viktor rolled his eyes. 'It's rare. Most of the time there's just one in a unit and he has a ... well, a sort of gift.'

A gift. 'What kind of gift?'

Viktor leant forward and turned the meat on the fire himself. Sorin let out an audible sound of outrage and slapped his hand with the cooking stick. Viktor ignored him and answered her. 'It varies.'

'Some have travelled from Dark Realms to join us,' Sorin interjected. 'Sometimes they're from our world but they're ... different.'

Viktor gave Sorin a look that made him go silent before continuing. 'He means some aren't fully human. They have heightened senses or superior strength, transform into creatures. That sort of thing.'

Lana sat dumbly, staring from one man to the other, their impossible words going around and around in her head. *Heightened senses? Creatures?* When she finally spoke, all she could do was parrot Viktor's words. Her voice had risen to almost a screech. 'Transform into creatures?'

'Yes. Some. Uth is sometimes a bit more ... wolfy.'

Lana couldn't help it. She jumped to her feet, her mouth hanging open. 'That man who had a knife to my throat – who told me he was going to cut me into pieces after he and his friends defiled me – turns into a *wolf?*'

'A scraggly, mangy one,' Sorin cut in again. 'He's not very impressive. I once knew a Brother who could turn himself into a great, Dark Realm beast.' He gestured to his horse. 'Bigger than my steed, he was. Now that was something to see. Uth – well, the beast is like the man – uninteresting. But he does have a keen sense of smell.'

Men who could turn into beasts? Monsters roaming the lands? As much as Lana's interest was piqued, there was just too much to unpack in one night. She continued on their current vein. 'So Uth could smell that you hadn't ... *claimed* me?' Lana asked.

Viktor patted the ground where she'd leapt from and she sat down again. 'Don't worry, Lana. If he ever meets you in the future, there will be no confusion,' he murmured into her ear, and she felt her face grow hot as Sorin snickered from the other side of the flames.

They ate in companionable silence while Lana mulled over everything they'd told her. Everyone knew about the portals of course, but she'd never given them much thought. There had been a portal not far from her village, it was true, but she'd never seen it and it had collapsed some time ago. What were the other realms like? Who lived there? Were there just monsters? And these gifts the Brothers had, what others were there besides taking the form of an animal? She was burning with curiosity as she always did when she was met with something new, but doubted they'd tell her much more at the moment. Neither of them seemed much inclined to talk anymore.

After finishing their meal, they all lay beside the fire, with Lana in between Sorin and Viktor.

'Do any of you have one of these gifts?' she asked.

'Kane,' they both said in unison, sounding bored.

'What can he do?'

They were silent.

'You'll find out soon enough,' Sorin said cryptically from behind her, and she turned her head to scowl at him. He had the audacity to grin at her, and she swatted the leg that was draped over hers.

His arms came around her and she thought he was going to cuddle her to him, but instead his hands began to tickle.

She shrieked loudly, unable to help herself as she tried to grab his hands to stop him.

'No! Don't! Stop!' she laughed, and then she was on her back, her skirt bunched around her hips, and Sorin was straddling her. He stopped tickling and grabbed her wrists with one large hand, holding them over her head, lust in his eyes. She could feel that his cock was hard beneath his clothes at the juncture of her thighs, and her smile faded. Her tongue darted out to moisten her lips, and his eyes flicked down to her mouth.

'What do you want, Lana?'

'I don't know,' she breathed.

He ground his pelvis into hers and she moaned. 'I think you do.'

His fingers skated across her stomach and down to her mound, his touch light, skimming the skin so she could only just feel where his fingers were. They delved between her legs and she jerked, her legs parting for him. The wetness he found made his eyes take on a feral gleam as he withdrew his hand and brought it to her lips. 'Taste.'

Eyes wide, she opened her mouth and wrapped her lips around his finger. She sucked, devouring her own desire.

Beside her she heard a groan and realised that, as usual, Viktor was observing. She turned her head towards him.

'Is that all you do? Watch?' As the words left her mouth, Lana wondered where they'd come from. In that moment she'd been so courageous, but her bravery fled as she saw his eyes narrow at her challenge.

'No,' he growled.

She yelped as he wrenched the laces of her dress apart, causing her breasts to spill free. He ripped the dress away, leaving her completely naked while both of them were still clothed. Her breath hitched as she watched them. They were large men and she so small compared to them. She found she liked that. Viktor pinched her nipple hard and then let go. She whimpered.

Sorin moved to the side of her, sucking gently where Viktor had caused pain, and she gasped at the pleasure of his mouth. Then Viktor was between her bent knees, pushing them wide. He knelt between them.

'Does it look like I'm simply watching now?'

Lana shook her head as she felt his hand graze her inner thigh, travelling upwards towards her core. He slapped her mound and she gasped.

'Speak aloud!' he commanded.

'No!' she cried loudly as he pushed a finger into her, stretching her tight entrance.

Viktor smiled. 'Good girl.' He pumped in shallow strokes, using his thumb on that other part that made her writhe under him.

Sorin kneaded her breasts, kissing and suckling them, and then his lips were on hers, hard and demanding, his tongue caressing hers in strokes that mirrored Viktor's hand. She moaned as they toyed with her body, somehow knowing exactly what to do and when to bring the most pleasure.

Next to her, Sorin was fisting his cock while playing with her breasts. When he saw her watching him, he moved higher and groaned as she took him in her hand, moving it the way she'd seen him doing. Up and down, she stroked him. His breathing grew labored and he kissed her hard before pulling away from her. Feeling bereft, she huffed at him, and he grinned before leaning down and putting his mouth between her legs.

Shocked, she tried to struggle away as Sorin's tongue licked and Viktor's finger moved within her. Her body hummed with sensation.

She twisted and squirmed, part of her wanting to escape them and what they made her feel, but Viktor had her gripped tightly. That feeling began to grow within her, coiling tighter and tighter, building steadily, higher and higher until she could bear it no more.

'Please. *Please*,' she pleaded, but she wasn't sure what for.

Her hooded gaze locked on Viktor as Sorin teeth scraped her, pushing her over the edge. She screamed as wave after wave of pleasure made her legs shake and her body turn boneless.

When the shudders had finally eased, she felt herself being gently dressed and the Brothers lay next to her, both cuddling her sated body. She lay looking up at the stars in a half-awake bliss. Then she frowned. Again, she had been given pleasure and they had taken none. Why?

∼

They travelled south for three days, stopping to rest only at night. Oddly, the Brothers didn't touch her again save accidental brushes of their bodies while they slept, nor did they speak again about the Brothers' *gifts*. They also made sure that one of them was always with her, so her plans for escape stayed at the back of her mind. She still planned to leave. She had to find her da. All she needed was the chance. Though this was a far cry from life as a slave in the village, it couldn't last. And Viktor and Sorin had already begun to worm their way into her heart. What would happen to her when the Brothers resumed their lives in an army of mercenaries? Surely she wouldn't travel around with them; the little woman mending their clothes. It was laughable.

Though the weather was fair and the air relatively warm considering it was full winter, by the end of the second day Lana was miserable. Her legs and back hurt from their break-neck pace and she was nervous about meeting this third Brother, Kane.

She didn't know much about him save what little Viktor and Sorin had said, especially about this *gift* he supposedly had, and she had been left with an anticipation bordering on fear. After the evening at the ruins, any questions were met with silence, which made her worry more. What were they hiding?

On the morning of the third day, after riding for half the night, they came upon a crossroads. Lana's heart began to pound as she read the name of the town on the old wooden signpost. *Kingway.* The Brothers had brought her almost to where her father lived. They continued past the turnoff, but she was so close! If she wanted to get to him, she had to flee soon.

NOT LONG AFTERWARDS, they reached a camp close to a wide river. There were clusters of small tents around a larger one. Lana counted seven men around the two fires, eating their morning meal. Most greeted or nodded to the Brothers, and no one seemed surprised at their sudden arrival. Sorin lifted her from Viktor's horse and set her on her feet, but, to her chagrin, her legs immediately crumpled from the many hours on the horse.

Sorin grabbed her and Viktor tutted. 'Have to get you used to riding, little bird.'

'She can practice on me, Viktor!' called one of the sellswords, and some of the others laughed loudly.

Lana didn't look at them, knowing her cheeks would be flushed and entertain them even more. Sorin gave them a quelling look as he lifted her effortlessly into his arms. She began to wrap her arms around his neck, but then froze.

'They're only having their fun, Lana, but they'll treat you with respect. We'll make sure of that.'

'Thank you,' she said stiffly, 'but it isn't ... put me down, please. My legs will hold me.'

Inside that tent was Kane, and something told her that it was important to meet him on equal footing – so to speak.

Sorin set her down with a light, reassuring squeeze to the back of her neck and, thankfully, her legs didn't collapse under her. Viktor and Sorin walked in the direction of the large tent and she followed them slowly, willing herself not to shake. Why was she so anxious?

They went through the flap and it closed behind her, plunging them into a gloom that so contrasted with the brightness outside that it took a long moment for her eyes to adjust. What she saw when they did made her gasp quietly.

To say that the tent was opulent was an understatement. There were furs lining the floor, sheer curtains hanging from the ceiling to give a sense of multiple rooms, a table heaped with food, and several large pallets and cots. Various weapons, so large she doubted she'd even be able to lift them, were littered about. At a massive desk, an equally large man sat, bent over some parchments in front of him.

'You're a day late,' he said, not looking up.

'We were delayed,' Viktor said indifferently, walking towards the table, where a vast array of meats and fruits were piled on large plates.

'Clearly.' Kane shuffled through his papers.

Lana glanced at Sorin, who rolled his eyes at her with a grin.

He cleared his throat. 'Kane.'

Finally, the third Brother looked up from his desk. If it was possible, he was even more beautiful than Viktor and Sorin, but they looked remarkably civilized next to his rugged features. He had a few days' stubble and a long, thin scar running down one side of his face that disappeared into the dark hair of his unshaven cheek. He was dressed in black, like the others, and his eyes were a piercing blue.

His eyes narrowed when they locked on her, and his lip turned upward into a sneer. 'What is this?'

What, not who. Lana swallowed hard, her stomach a knot of dread. She wanted to turn and run, but Sorin was just behind her.

'This is Lana,' Sorin answered and propelled her to the fore with a hand at the small of her back.

She stepped forward only because she'd have fallen otherwise, but every fiber of her being shouted at her to run from the man in front of her. He looked at her like she was prey, and Viktor's words came back to her. *Some of them could transform into creatures.* Her hands shook, and she tried to hide them in her skirts as she stared at him. He knew she was afraid, she could see it in his beautiful, wicked eyes, and he was enjoying it. She tried to push the fear away. That was how she had dealt with it all those years as Dirk's property – just remembered who she was and where she came from – a source of pride. She was not some mewling, downtrodden, pathetic slave girl.

But it wasn't enough in front of this man, this force of nature. Even anger seemed to evaporate in his presence, leaving only terror. She wanted to turn and escape his gaze; either that or cower before him. She didn't even know how she was still on her feet. Something told her that she must not obey this command, wherever it was coming from. She had to stay where she was. She had to.

He stared at her, almost as if he was willing her to do something.

'We leave at dawn tomorrow. Not nearly enough time to play with her,' he said quietly. 'No matter how *delectable* she appears to be.'

'That's not why we brought her here,' Viktor growled from the table, and Kane smiled coldly.

The urge to run grew, but she held her ground. He wanted her to flee, she realised. This was some sort of test, and nothing good would come of failing – although nothing good might come of prevailing either, she supposed.

She drew in a ragged breath.

'What did you say her name was? Lana?'

She forced herself to nod, though he wasn't speaking to her.

'Lana.' He stood up from his chair, finally addressing her – *had he really not been standing before?* – and moved to the front of his desk. He leant against it. 'Take off your dress.'

Her hands moved before she realised they had. They began to pluck at the knot where the laces were tied and she couldn't stop them. Her eyes flew to his and she suddenly knew with a dawning horror what his *gift* was. He could *make* people do things. Things they didn't want to do.

She willed her hands to halt, but they continued to try to untie the strings holding the dress together, and she thanked the gods that they had twisted and gnarled into a secure knot while she'd been riding.

She felt a tear slip down her cheek and cursed her weakness. She could hear Sorin yelling behind her, but she couldn't hear properly through the roaring in her ears as she fought past the compulsion to do as Kane had commanded. Her hands slowed and she took a steadying breath. She looked back at Kane. He hadn't moved, but Viktor was standing between him and her. He looked furious. She slowly cast her eyes back down to her hands. It felt as if time were standing still, or at least moving very, very slowly. With all of her will, she told her wayward fingers to stop and move back to her sides. Miraculously, they did, and when she looked back at Kane, she registered surprise, even shock.

'Stop. It,' she ground out, and the pressure disappeared. She fell to her knees, breathing hard. She felt Sorin catch her as darkness claimed her.

Lana woke up some time later on her side on one of the massive cots, still in the tent. Sorin hovered nearby; she could hear him murmuring to someone. He appeared in her view.

'Are you all right?' He looked so concerned, she almost laughed. He and Viktor had put her in Kane's hands. They must have known what would happen, and he had the gall to be afraid for her?

'Why did you bring me here?' Her voice sounded so feeble and broken, she had to close her eyes so she couldn't see the useless sympathy showing on his face. 'Was it all a trick? Buy a slave, give her a taste of freedom so when you rip it away, she will truly be broken?' She felt tears wetting the pillow next to her cheek.

'Oh, Lana, *no*. Please believe me. We didn't know he was going to do that to you.'

Liar.

A hand caressed her face and she flinched away from it. It was false. All of it. It would have been kinder for them to have left her with Ather that day, and she said as much.

'I'm sorry, love.' *Love?* 'What he did was wrong. He knows he took it too far. He will make amends, I promise.'

She didn't acknowledge his words. She cracked her eyes open a tiny bit and watched him leave the tent a short time later. Outside, it was dark, and she was alone for the first time in days. She sat up quickly and pulled the knife she'd stolen from its hiding place. Perhaps she should thank the third Brother. He'd made this very easy. Gods, that first night with them seemed a lifetime ago now.

She found her thick cloak first and fastened it snuggly around her shoulders. Then, she went to the back of the tent, knelt down and slowly cut the threads of a seam, forming a small hole just large enough for her to squeeze through. She peeked out into the black and, finding no one passing, darted out into the shadows of one of the smaller tents. The sky was dark and cold and the wind was picking up. Not the best night for an escape with a storm probably coming in fast, but this might be her only chance. She would not survive here.

Kane could make her do anything. Anything he wanted. It was enough to drive anyone mad. Had they done this before to other people? To other women? She clenched her jaw. Well, she would not let it happen to her. If she were strong enough, she would kill Kane to ensure he couldn't do it again to anyone else. But she wasn't.

How odd it was that her reasons for wanting to flee Viktor and Sorin were completely the reverse when it came to escaping the third Brother. She would miss them, but only as a moth yearning for a flame. They had brought her here, after all, to the lair of the beast. They didn't care about her really. The taste of affection they'd given her had been a way to keep her pliable. That was all, and she had fallen for it like the naïve child she was. She felt a pang in her heart and her eyes filled with tears, but she dug her knuckles into her eyes and willed them clear. It was time to leave, not to cry.

She made her way to where she knew the horses were roaming. The sentry was asleep against a tree, a wineskin resting on his knee, and she thanked the gods.

She peered through the darkness at the camp. Fifteen men were gathered around the fires, including the Brothers. She watched them silently for a moment. They were arguing quietly amongst themselves. Perhaps they were disagreeing about what misery to inflict upon her next.

Sorin got up and stalked angrily away from the fire, and

her stomach lurched. If he went to the tent, he'd find her missing. But he just walked to the trees a short distance from the others for a piss. Viktor and Kane were still exchanging words. Kane fell silent, looking out into the gloom. Directly at her!

He couldn't see her, could he? She held her breath, and after a moment he shook his head as if to clear it and rejoined the argument. Lana dared not tarry any longer. She grabbed the reins of the nearest horse, whispering to him, stroking him calm as she led him into the trees. He came with her as docilely as a gelding.

When she was far enough away, she hefted herself – not without difficulty – onto his back and slowly circled around to the road, back the way they'd travelled this morning. From there she urged him into a canter just as the rain, thunder and lightning descended, but she didn't care. Cold and wet were nothing. She was truly free and she would do everything in her power to keep it that way.

CHAPTER 10

KANE

Kane stared again into the darkness of the forest past their camp, something niggling at him. But there was no one there, he was sure of it.

'... and when she wakes up, you will beg her forgiveness for what you did to her.' Sorin was droning on again.

'So you've told me at length, Sorin. I don't see why you're both so enthralled by her, truth be told. She's no more special than a pretty whore as far as I can see.'

'We aren't enthralled!' Viktor all but shouted. Then he lowered his voice. 'But there is something that we *feel* about her. Perhaps if you can take your head out of your own arse, you'll feel this thing too.'

'Feelings? What has happened to you? We're fucking Dark Brothers! Whatever you see in our future, this girl is not there.' Kane waved his hand. 'But I can see you won't be told. So be it. I'll apologize to the lass for making my little trial a mite difficult.'

Inwardly Kane cringed. He'd known at the time, watching her body tremble as she tried to fight what she couldn't see, that he was being too rough with her. When he'd first laid eyes on her, he had indeed felt this *thing* that Viktor spoke of. He had no idea what it was, but it terrified him. He'd made her suffer for that. He'd used his full strength on her, compelling her to run because he wanted her as far away as possible, but also so that he could pursue her in some primal urge he'd never felt before. He'd never met her like.

But when she'd faced him down, his fear had quickly turned to anger. He had wanted to hurt her. He would destroy that pride he saw and make her beg for her life. He'd thought it would make him feel in control, but the look in her eyes when she'd understood the power he had over her body ... he'd never felt so feeble and pathetic.

It had been years since he'd been kind to anyone save his Brothers. He knew how to hurt and kill, and he liked doing it. He hadn't had a woman in a very long time; hadn't missed them. But a fire had ignited as soon as he'd seen her. Even now it raged within him. He needed to see her.

He stalked from the fire and back into their tent. The others would want to follow. They were oddly protective, but he didn't intend to hurt her this night. Though he'd said the opposite to the others, she was indeed special. And, despite his comments, he'd been shocked at her ability to resist him. No one could, save Sorin and Viktor, and that was only because they were bonded to each other as each unit in the army was.

As soon as he stepped over the threshold, he knew she had fled. That was what had been bothering him. She'd been watching them from the forest. He smiled. Perhaps he would get his hunt after all.

He went back out to the fire. Both Sorin and Viktor eyed him with ill-concealed anger as he approached them.

Sorin stood up. 'Well?'

Kane shrugged. 'Well, nothing. She's gone.'

'What?'

They both ran for the tent. Viktor emerged a moment later just as the dark sky lit up with lightning. A clap of thunder followed in the distance. He ran a hand through his hair and strode to where the horses were tethered. 'There's a storm coming in fast. We have to find her!'

Kane snorted and followed him slowly.

'Fuck! She's taken my horse,' he heard Viktor mutter in the shadows. 'How did she even get out of that blasted tent without us seeing her?'

Kane heard a groan as Viktor kicked the man on watch awake.

'Dorn, you fuck, get up! What did I tell you would happen if you fell asleep on watch again?'

'I'm sor–,' the man began and then fell to the ground with a gurgle as Viktor plunged his knife up under his ribs. He wiped his dagger clean absently, looking out into the forest as if the girl would simply reappear.

Sorin came up behind Kane. 'Who's on watch?'

'Dorn *was*.' Viktor spat on the body.

'She used a knife to cut through one of the seams at the back of the tent.'

Viktor growled, running a hand through his hair. 'Where'd she get a blade? The weapons in the tent are all too heavy for her to lift.' Suddenly he was in Kane's face. 'This is your fault! You and your fucking mind games, Kane!'

Sorin sighed. 'The knife from your saddlebag is gone, Viktor. Some coins as well.'

Kane smirked. 'It looks to me that your own negligence is the problem here, Brother.'

Pain exploded in his jaw as Viktor's fist connected with bone, and he stumbled, laughing aloud before regaining his balance.

Viktor was pacing in front of him, ignoring him now, his

anger replaced by bewilderment. 'I can't believe she stole from us.'

'I can't believe you didn't notice.' Kane tutted. 'A Dark Brother being taken advantage of by a slip of a slave girl. Pathetic. Clearly you were both wrong. She's nothing more than an opportunistic slave, and now she's got our gold and a very valuable mount.'

Kane had the satisfaction of seeing Viktor's fury return just as Sorin stepped between them.

'Enough, Kane.' He glanced at Viktor. 'He's goading you, for fuck's sake, Viktor. She's simply afraid. We can trust –'

'Can we?' Viktor snarled. 'Perhaps she was playing us all along. Waiting for the right moment.'

Sorin waved a hand in dismissal. 'We've spent time with her. We know her.' His eyes narrowed. 'Don't let Kane get into your head. You know he's just amusing himself.'

'What do you propose we do then, Sorin?' Viktor sneered.

'We find her and bring her back, of course.'

'And the penalty she'll pay?'

Sorin hesitated. 'I don't know,' he said finally.

Viktor's eyes narrowed. 'If she had been bound to us and claimed it would be different, but, at the moment, she is a slave who has stolen from the Dark Brothers and escaped. You know it cannot be left unpunished.'

'No. It can't,' Kane said darkly as he stifled a smile. 'You're both too close to her to do what must be done. Besides, you've been ordered to the Commander within the week. You don't have time to go wandering after ... *wayward property*. I'll find her.'

'You?' Sorin scoffed. 'You'd kill her as soon as look at her – after taking your fill of her, of course.'

'Oh, Brother. You always think the worst of me.' Kane winked and watched Sorin's face contort. 'I may take a taste, but it's no more than you two have had.'

'Your *gift* won't work on her. You saw that before.' Sorin gloated.

Kane smiled. 'Perhaps I'll seduce her the old-fashioned way. Or,' he leaned in close to Sorin, 'perhaps I'll just force her the old-fashioned way,' he whispered. Sorin rounded on him, just as Kane had known he would, and he danced away with a laugh.

Sorin calmed himself, his hands curling into fists with the effort. 'You won't be able to hurt her, Kane. You think she's just a girl you can coerce and subdue, but I would pay to see the havoc she wreaks on you. When we next see you, you'll be a shadow of yourself, *Brother*.' Sorin left, walking back to the fires and Viktor followed.

'Find her,' he called back to Kane. 'We'll meet you at the camp by the coast before we sail.'

Kane returned to the tent and flopped down on one of the beds, deciding he would leave in the morning after the storm had abated. Already he could hear the rain thudding on the roof. He smiled coldly in the dark. He also wanted to give his quarry a head start. Listening to the downpour, he imagined her hiding in the forest – cuddling the horse for warmth, shivering in the darkness, unable to light a fire in case it was seen, her wet dress plastered to her skin, her nipples ... he groaned and then chuckled to himself. Perhaps Sorin was right. But he would never admit it.

He closed his eyes and willed his body to relax. It hummed in anticipation of the morrow. He hoped she didn't make it too easy.

CHAPTER 11

LANA

'Come.'

Lana walked slowly towards the voice. She recognized it but wasn't sure from where.

'Take off your clothes.'

She shook her head.

'Do it or I'll rip your dress to pieces and make you beg me for a new one.'

She shivered and let it fall to the ground. She heard a murmur of appreciation behind her, but when she turned, there was no one. Then his hands were on her, caressing her shoulders, cupping her breasts, molding themselves over her belly and moving lower. Her breath hitched and she made a sound of annoyance when the hand stopped moving and left her skin. Her body felt bereft.

'Touch me, please. I beg you,' she pleaded, her voice sounding far away.

A hand caressed the top of her thigh, but it didn't go to that place where she wanted it to. Instead it continued down the front of her leg and up the back in a large circle. She whimpered and he chuckled.

'So impatient.'

The hand moved towards her core once more, but again it veered away. She groaned in frustration. 'Why do you torment me?'

'Oh, sweet girl,' he said in her ear, 'this is not torment.' He nibbled at her. 'The torment starts when I find you.'

Lana woke with a start, her eyes darting all around her, but there was no one. *Kane!*

She looked down and realised one of her own hands was playing with her breast through the cloth of her dress while the other caressed between her legs. She snatched them both away with a shocked gasp and pulled her still-damp dress down to her ankles. She'd never touched herself in such a way before, nor ever had such a *sordid* dream!

She breathed out slowly, as *that* part seemed to pulse, and it took all of her strength not to let her hand drift down to continue what it had been doing while she slept. Instead she stood on wobbly legs. She was still in the forest where she'd stopped during the storm the night before. She took stock of her surroundings. The sun was only just up, the gloom of early morning still lurking where the undergrowth was thick. The sky looked relatively cloudless today now that the storm had blown itself out, though the air definitely had more of a crispness to it. She'd taken shelter beneath a rocky outcrop, and Viktor's great steed stood not far away, regarding her indifferently.

Using a large stone this time, she mounted him at once, drawing her fur-lined cloak around her despite its dampness. Kane was coming, and she couldn't let him drag her back to the Brothers. She stayed in the trees, following the road through the forest from a distance and not letting other travelers see her. At around midmorning, the woods gave way to farmland, and that quickly turned into the outskirts of a town. *Kingway!*

Before long she was in the center of a bustling market. She stowed Viktor's horse at a stable and paid his board for a few days. She knew she should sell him and get more gold to aid her in her flight, but she just couldn't do it. As she gave him a departing pat, she hoped they would find him. He was a war horse, after all. He didn't belong with the other nags ploughing fields.

She found an inn that looked inconspicuous in a poorer part of town in case it took some time to find her father. She got a room, food and even a bath. She felt guilty for using her ill-gotten gains for such a frivolous thing, but as she slid into the steaming water, her chilled, aching body finally relaxed and she realised this too had been needed. For her, it was as necessary as a hearty meal. After soaking until the water started to cool and feasting on a thick mutton stew with fresh bread, she washed her soiled clothes and hung them by the crackling fire. Then she lay on the bed and closed her eyes.

She woke sometime later. It was night and all was quiet. At first, she didn't know what had awoken her, but then she heard it – a scratching noise at her door and whispers. She scampered off the bed and donned her still-damp dress quickly. Then she looked around the room, her heart hammering. What should she do? There was nowhere to hide and it was too dangerous to climb out of the window in the dark. Remembering the knife, she grabbed it from the table. If there were more than one, she wouldn't stand a chance. She looked about wildly. There was only the bed. She darted back to it and lay down, closing her eyes just as the door creaked open. She feigned sleep and willed her breathing to slow, the dagger clenched by her side.

'There, on the bed. She's asleep. For fuck's sake, be quiet,' a man whispered.

'I am being quiet. You're the one who took so long to pick the lock on the fucking door,' a second answered.

She wanted to see them, assess the danger she was in, but she didn't dare move a muscle.

'Look for her coin purse,' the first one said.

So they were here to rob her. She doubted they'd find it. The first thing she'd done was find a loose board and stow the coins under the floor. They were silent as they searched her room. It didn't take long.

'He lied. There ain't no gold.'

'We need to go back to him with something, or he'll slit us open from throats to cocks.'

'Do you think …?'

'What?' asked the first one.

'Well, look at her. She's pretty. Worth something.'

There was a pause before the other one sighed. 'Well, I reckon she's better than nothing.'

Lana tensed. They were going to take *her*! She opened her eyes, gripped the knife and leapt up, swiping the air. The blade connected and she heard a grunt of pain. Her wrist was grabbed and squeezed. She screamed as loudly as she could, hoping someone would come to her aid, but it was cut short by a blow to her stomach that left her winded. She fell to her knees, gasping, and the knife clattered to the floor. She heard voices outside the room. So did the two men. The largest one gave a growl and hit her face with the back of his hand, making her fall back.

'Little bitch.'

He kicked her in the side and then they were gone.

Lana thought someone would come then, but no one did.

After a while lying on the floor, she lifted herself up with a whimper and limped to the door, closing it firmly. She sat in front of it, clutching her side, and sank into oblivion.

LANA WOKE LATE the next morning with a groan. She got to her feet. Nothing seemed broken, but her stomach and side were badly bruised. Though she wanted nothing more than to stay in bed, she set out to search for her father as soon as she had the strength. The Brothers would be looking for her, and it wasn't as if she'd gone far. Her only protection would be her father. She walked slowly as she inquired around the market but had no luck until later in the day, when she happened upon a merchant who said he knew who she spoke of. He directed her to a large house in a wealthy area. She found it easily enough, and, as she stood on the doorstep, she took a deep breath and knocked on the thick, wooden door.

CHAPTER 12

KANE

Kane prowled around the room slowly. The innkeeper had said that a young woman with red hair had paid for a night and then left. The morning after the storm, he hadn't even bothered following her tracks through the forest as soon as her trail had turned towards the road. He'd just made the half-day's journey to the nearest town. When he'd found Viktor's horse easily at the first stable on the main road, he'd known she was here or had been very recently, and, truth be told, he'd been disappointed that she hadn't hidden the mount better. Perhaps he'd overestimated her.

Locating the inn had been more difficult. It was a sizable town and she had chosen a place down a tiny alleyway in the poorest area, which he hadn't expected given the amount of gold she had stolen. It had taken him two days to find it. And over those days and nights he'd begun to have visions whenever he slept; vivid dreams about her and what he was going to do to her, with her. He clenched his fists. How she was doing it, he didn't know, but every time he closed his eyes, he saw her, taunting him. His cock began to harden and he swore, trying to focus on the job. He had to locate her first, but once he did, he was going to make her tell him how she was worming her way into his mind, and then he would punish her for it by doing everything she'd made him see in his dreams.

After inquiring with the innkeeper, who Kane assumed ran more dubious businesses than his semi-respectable inn, he was sure he'd found her. She had already moved on, though, or so he'd thought until he'd found the knife she'd stolen, bloodied and discarded under the bed. That didn't bode well, but there was no other blood anywhere else in the room. There may be no cause for concern. She didn't have experience with much else besides horses, according to Sorin and Viktor. She may simply have cut herself. It was a stretch, but it was possible.

A floorboard creaked under his weight as he moved around the room, and he froze. All the other boards had been silent. He pried up the wood. There, nestled in the dust, was a tied cloth filled with gold. He frowned at it. She wouldn't have left it willingly and he'd been watching this place all day. Where was she?

A curious feeling spread through him, which he was shocked to discover was worry. He sat on the bed. What was wrong with him? He'd scarcely said five words to the girl. He hadn't *worried* about someone in a very long time, not since well before he'd joined the Brothers.

He stood again, abruptly stopping the line of thought. He stowed the gold and the small dagger at his belt. Time to speak to the innkeeper. Kane had noticed the small, round man's demeanor change from friendly to uneasy when he'd realised who Kane was asking about, though he'd tried to hide it, of course.

He found the man where he'd left him, sitting in a chair in his taproom downstairs, nursing a tankard.

'The girl with the red hair. Where is she?'

The man's eyes darted around and his tongue flicked out like a lizard's to moisten his lips. 'It's as I told you. She paid for a night and was gone by daybreak.'

Kane's eyes narrowed. 'I don't believe you.'

The man's beady little eyes widened as Kane forced him to drop his tankard on the floor and splay both his hands out on the table.

'You know what I am. You've heard the rumors about us.'

The man nodded, drops of sweat starting to form on his ruddy skin.

'Then I'll make it simple. You're going to die. It's up to you whether it happens quickly or not.' He took the small dagger from his belt and stuck it through the man's smallest finger on the right, digging it into the table and severing it at the second joint.

The man's eyes rolled back in his head, but Kane wouldn't let him scream, nor move anything else at all.

'I can do this for as long as it takes.' He pulled the dagger out and slowly brought it down to rest on the next finger on the same hand. 'Do you have anything to say?'

The man opened his mouth and everything came tumbling out. *Ridiculous.* 'Please, sir. It's as I said. She came here and was gone by daybreak. But she was looking for someone – a man. I knew who she meant as soon as she said his name. But he ain't a man you cross, so I didn't tell her nothing. He owns a house by the river. If she found him, she'll be there.'

Kane growled and brought the knife down, neatly severing the next finger. 'That's not all, though, is it? And who is this man she was looking for?'

'Please, stop. *Please!*' The man's body shook, even held immobile as it was. 'No, that's not all; you're right, of course. She had gold. Could be someone else saw and decided to take it. There's a feller who works this area. Dunno his name. But he'll be drinking at the inn three streets over. If you hurry, you'll catch him. Big feller, dark beard, and he'll be with another one. Small, skinny.'

Kane snorted. 'Bet he gives you a cut, eh, you fucking prick? And the man she sought?'

'He's a merchant, but he's got shady ties. Dangerous.'

'Where?'

'By the main street, near the bridge. The biggest one.'

'Good. Now,' Kane held out the knife to the innkeeper's good hand. 'Bury this in your stomach as many times as you can.'

Kane left without a backwards glance. The innkeeper would follow the order until he physically couldn't anymore. He couldn't not. Only Lana had ever resisted him and he had no idea how that was possible. He went to the tavern and found the men easily. From a table, he watched them, but he soon realised they knew nothing of where she was. They were simply thieves. Not worth his time.

Kane ordered a dram and thought about his quarry. She was going to be very entertaining. He couldn't wait to teach her why she shouldn't have fucked with his head. Viktor and Sorin wouldn't like it, but he was the leader, after all. It was his right.

He struck up a conversation with some merchants to learn more about this man she was looking for instead. It didn't take long once their tongues were loosened by drink, and he began to learn some very interesting things. He wondered why Lana had gone to him. Did she know him? Who was he to her? Did she believe he could protect her? He smiled coldly in the dim light. She'd soon learn how wrong she was.

CHAPTER 13

LANA

Lana had been waiting for a while. Books lined the walls and comfortable chairs circled a large table. A fire burned warmly in the hearth. The house was well furnished, opulent even. Her father certainly had become a successful merchant.

The door opened and she stood quickly as a man entered.

The brown hair was greyer now, the tunic and breeches better quality, and there were more lines on his face, but he still looked like him.

'Da?'

The man froze, turning his head slowly to stare. 'Lana?' he finally said. He looked dazed.

She choked back a sob.

He opened and closed his mouth several times before he stepped forward and enveloped her in a hug. Tears flowed freely down her face. He hugged her more tightly and, at her wince, he let her go.

'I don't understand,' she hiccupped.

'Is it really you, child?' He stepped back and really looked at her. 'I thought … they told me you … What happened to your face?'

'Two men who broke into my room last night to steal …' She faltered at his furious look. What few memories she had of him painted him as a doting father. She didn't remember him ever being angry.

'Go on,' he said coldly.

'I tried to fight them off, but they … then they were scared away.' She gave him a wan smile.

Her father scowled. 'Two men, you say? One large and the other small?'

'Yes, but how–'

He interrupted her, speaking to a guard whom, she only just noticed, was waiting by the door. Why did her father even need guards?

'Find those two idiots. Now. They've inconvenienced me for the last time.'

Inconvenienced? Him? She almost snorted. But she kept silent and her gaze low.

'Da, please. Mama told me you were dead!'

Her father took her hands. 'You were very young, child. Your mother and I … She told me to go. I heard she'd remarried. But,' he shrugged apologetically, 'she was a freewoman with property. She did what the law allows.'

'But why didn't you come for me?' She tried not to sound accusing but saw by his grimace that she'd failed.

'Oh, my child.' He took her hands in his. 'I did come back not long after I heard your mother was gone, but they told me at the stables that a fever had taken you.' He bowed his head. 'I left in grief. I never went back.'

'Who would tell you such a thing?' But she had a feeling that she already knew.

'Oh, I don't know,' he said with an impatient gesture. 'A boy. The stablemaster's son, I think.'

Lana's good hand clenched in anger. Was there no end to Ather's malice? 'He lied. I was sold to Dirk. I was his slave.'

'Alora's husband?' Her father's eyes narrowed. 'What kind of slave?'

Lana frowned. 'Does it matter?'

'No, no, of course not. I simply meant ... Did he force himself on you, child?'

'No.'

'Did anyone?'

She wondered at this odd line of questioning but answered. 'No, Da.'

He seemed to relax then and rang a bell on his desk. 'I'm so glad you're here, my dear. It truly is a godly intervention. You've no idea how much you can help me. Let me have you taken to a room upstairs where you can clean up. I'll send my personal physician to attend you.'

She nodded, leaning into him for a hug. 'Thank you.'

He caressed her cheek. 'We can talk later, once you've rested.'

'I can't believe I'm here,' she said as she hugged him close again. 'I can't believe I've found you.'

A woman appeared.

'Take this girl to one of the guest chambers. See that she is given clothes, food and anything else she requires.'

'Yes, my lord.'

Lana was brought up another staircase, the woman leading the way. If the servant was surprised that she was taking care of a strange, bruised girl, she didn't show it. She opened a door off a long corridor and bade Lana go inside, saying she would have a bath prepared and send food and clothes up shortly.

Lana gazed around the lavish room as the door clicked

closed. The large bed was on a raised platform in the center. There was a copper bath in the corner and a balcony that looked out onto the river. She sat on the bed and tried to collect her thoughts. How much had happened since the morning when Viktor and Sorin had bought her from Dirk. She would go back one day, she promised herself, and she would make those who'd wronged her pay.

There was a knock at the door and a line of servants trundled in with ewers of hot water. They quickly filled the bath and departed, leaving her alone again. She undressed and submerged herself in the water quickly. She washed as best she could with her bad wrist, which now sported a black bruise shaped like a blobby hand. Her ribs and stomach were mottled and discolored already, so no doubt they'd be the same in a few hours. Everything hurt horribly. She sighed as she wrapped herself in a blanket to dry, wondering when her father would come to talk. She had so many questions about him and his life over the past ten years.

She caught her reflection in the looking glass and jumped, not recognizing her own face at first. To be fair, it had been a long time since she'd seen it in anything other than the surface of a horse trough, but the swollen cheek made her look like someone else entirely. Her lip was split as well.

Someone opened the door, and she turned to see a thin man who reminded her of the apothecary who'd examined her that day when she'd been tied to the table and the Brothers had ... She shivered at the memory and then felt a pang of regret. She'd never see either of them again. Even if they found her now, her father would simply pay them handsomely for the Writ of Ownership, she supposed. He clearly had the wealth to do so.

The physician smiled at her, his kind eyes making Lana relax at once. 'Well, my dear, I understand you fell down some stairs.'

Lana blinked, not sure why her father had chosen to lie. 'Um. Yes. I'm so clumsy.' She laughed lightly, hoping it didn't sound too forced.

'Well, we'll soon have you sorted out, young lady, don't you worry. And well in time for those nuptials. Congratulations, by the way. Your father was positively brimming with joy.'

This time Lana's mouth hung open. *Nuptials?* 'Oh, uh, yes,' she mumbled. 'Thank you.'

She did as she was directed by the physician, moving this way and that while she was poked and prodded. He applied salve to her face and then to her wrist, bandaging it efficiently, but when he asked if there was anything else, she didn't tell him about the other bruises. She just wanted him to go so that she could seek out her father and ask him what was going on. He bid her a good day and left as quietly as he had come.

She clad herself in a red flowing dress that had been left on the bed. It matched her hair so well that it looked garish, she thought, but it was all there was. It was also a bit too tight and too low-cut in the bosom area for her liking. Still, it was a nice gesture, and her other one seemed to have disappeared. Her shoes and cloak were gone as well.

She shook her head and tried the door, half-expecting it to be locked, but it opened easily and she peered out into the corridor. There was no one there.

Well, she remembered where her father's study was. She hardly needed an escort in his house. She set off down the stairs and soon found herself exactly where she wanted to be. The door was slightly ajar, and she'd just raised her hand to knock politely when she heard voices inside. She lowered it at once, not wanting to disturb her da.

She bit her lip and listened harder. She didn't like to

eavesdrop, but she was getting an odd feeling that something here was amiss.

'… and those two idiots?' her father's commanding voice asked.

'I had their throats slit and their bodies thrown in the river,' the guard said, his speech slightly muffled.

'Let me know as soon as we hear back from Boone. I want them joined quickly. If this works, my territory will triple. It's as if the gods themselves sent her to me so our two families could be united.' There was a pause before her father spoke again. 'I just hope my daughter is as virginal as she claimed, or he's liable to murder her in the marriage bed and then come for me as well. None of us will profit then.'

'Do you think she'll be any trouble?' the guard asked.

Her father chuckled. 'If she is, I'll give her to you for half an hour so long as you don't spoil her face any more than those two fools did. He won't take her if she's too damaged, but a bruise here and there won't be commented on.'

Lana covered her mouth in shock. How could her father have such awful plans for her? So quickly? How could he do this? They'd only just found each other again.

Feeling like she couldn't breathe, she backed away, turned and ran as quickly and as quietly as she could up the stairs, closing the door to her room silently. She went to the balcony first. She'd been given the highest room, she realised with a sinking feeling; a gilded bower that might as well be a cell in the dungeon. There was no way out of here.

Then she had an idea. It was dangerous, but no worse than trying to get out of the window. She reached for the bell-pull, rang it once and then picked up a useless vase that sat on an equally impractical table. She hid behind the door. It opened a few moments later.

'Did you n–'

Lana swung the vase down on the servant girl's head and

she fell to the floor with a thump. Lana grimaced, feeling slightly ill and very guilty as she turned the woman over and began to remove her uniform. She put it on over her own clothes and donned the silly cap, hiding her red hair beneath it. The shoes were a problem. Hers were gone and the servant's were much too small. She'd just have to make do barefoot.

She pulled the girl out of sight and padded to the door. Taking a deep, calming breath, she walked at a normal pace into the hallway and down the stairs. At first, she wasn't sure where to go, but then she spied another servant and simply followed at a distance up another hall and down more steps until she found herself in a bustling kitchen. Everyone was too busy to notice her, so she bundled a few handfuls of food scraps into her apron and made for the open door.

'You. New girl.'

She froze and turned. A cook was pointing at her with a wooden spoon and she swallowed hard, getting ready to flee.

'Take these as well,' the cook said, gesturing to a pile of potato peelings on the side.

Lana nodded and scooped them into her apron without a word. Exiting the kitchen into an alleyway, she walked quickly to the main street and, when she was out of sight of the house, picked up her pace. She ran until her ribs hurt too much to breathe, and only then did she slow and find somewhere quiet to hide.

She left the maid's clothes in a small passage between two large buildings despite the impracticality of the thin gown she was wearing underneath, and set out at a brisk, warming pace back to the inn where she'd left her gold, glad now that she hadn't taken it with her. Assuming it was still there, she could still get away. She tried to ignore the sad, hopeless feeling that now enveloped her. Nothing had changed. She had had no one this morning, and that was still true.

She stopped abruptly as tears flooded her eyes so quickly that she couldn't see to walk. She groped blindly for the wall that she'd been walking beside and leant against it, sinking to the ground and feeling very tired. She gave in to the tears, sobbing quietly and trying to marry up happy childhood recollections with the cold, evil reality. How could her da have had such little regard for her? How could he have been so opportunistic as to sell her in marriage within hours of finding her alive? Had he ever cared about her at all? Had anything he'd said been true?

She felt rather than saw the shadow loom over her. She looked up with a gasp, thinking it might be one of her father's other guards. It wasn't.

CHAPTER 14

KANE

Kane stood in the shadows outside the large house. The man Lana had been searching for was powerful in this town, so it was best to tread quietly. She was in there. He could feel it somehow. There was a balcony door open on one of the upper floors. He was about to start the climb when a maid emerged from the kitchens. He stepped back out of sight to wait, but as she passed, he saw a wisp of tell-tale red hair and smiled. The girl must not have received the help she'd wanted.

He followed her at a distance, watched her take off the maid's dress and couldn't help but gape at the one underneath. Gods. The gossamer matched her hair exactly and clung to her like a second skin all the way to her hips before flaring out to the ground. He made himself look away for a moment to get himself under control. Had her friend dressed her thus? If so, he could guess at their *relationship*.

They walked to the poorer area of town. She was trying to get back to the tavern for her gold. Of course she was. She wouldn't get far without it, after all. His eyes narrowed.

They'd need to make an example of her, the little thief. No one stole from the Dark Brothers.

She stopped

and slid to her knees. His brow creased. He approached slowly, wondering what she was doing. As he got closer, he saw she was weeping and rolled his eyes, not in the least bit moved. He wouldn't put it past her to know he was watching and be putting on a show to try and wrap him around her finger like she did to him in those fucking dreams.

She looked up and he saw her face for the first time. Her cheek was swollen, the side of her jaw bruised and her lip cut deeply. She didn't try to run, just quietly stared at him.

'Who did that?' he asked before he could stop himself.

'Two men trying to rob me,' she said dully as she slowly got to her feet. 'I think they're dead,' she added, as if she knew by the tightening of his fist that he wanted to kill the two bastards for hurting her – despite his earlier promises to himself that he would do something similar.

He frowned. 'You might as well come without a fuss – unless you want to go back to that house.'

Her shoulders slumped and she shook her head, not meeting his eyes.

He turned and started walking, and she followed meekly. He glared back at her. What was this? He'd expected some fight, argument, something other than this submissive assent. He noticed she favored one side and her arm was bandaged, but he didn't ask. He'd see for himself later. He led her to the stable, intending for them to leave the town without delay.

'I'm glad you found him,' she murmured, gesturing to Viktor's steed.

He sat astride his horse without a word to her.

'Um ... the gold.' She had the decency to look ashamed, he noted. 'It's at a tavern where I took a room.'

'I found the horse as well as the gold, thief. It was *very* easy,' he sneered, adding the last to dent her pride.

She flinched at his tone but said nothing more. Her gaze flicked to Viktor's mount.

'If you think I'd trust you anywhere but riding in front of me, you must have been hit harder than you thought,' he snapped, more angrily than he'd intended, but his hands were gentle as he reached down, picked her up and settled her between his legs.

She made a small gasping mewl that she tried to cover with a cough, but Kane had heard it all the same. His little captive was in pain, but now wasn't the time. He would deal with that once they were back in the forest.

Then he made a discovery. 'You walked through the whole town not wearing anything on your feet?' he asked incredulously, examining them both for damage and then wondering why. What did he care if the soles of her feet were cut?

'My shoes were taken.'

'Your cloak as well?'

'Yes.'

He snorted and clicked his horse to a walk, pulling Viktor's behind. Before long they were on the forest road, heading south towards the coast. The sun was high and there were still hours of daylight for journeying. By all accounts they should have made the next town by that evening, but as the afternoon wore on, he could see that she was too injured for a hard ride. Her hand kept pressing into her ribs and her belly when she thought he wasn't looking, and before long she couldn't sit upright, covertly leaning against him for support. Not that he was complaining.

They stopped in the late afternoon and he made camp a little way from the road while she sat on one of the large boulders that littered the ground, staring into nothing. He offered her ration biscuits and some fruit, which she devoured hungrily.

He sat by the fire and watched her, huddled on her rock, until the light started to go. In their first encounter, she'd had much more spirit.

Finally, she looked back at him.

'You're hurt,' he said.

'Just my face and wrist. A physician saw to them. They're fine.'

'So you're a liar as well as a thief.' His words found their mark as her eyes blazed for an instant before they became shuttered once more.

She said nothing.

'Come here.'

She looked startled and shook her head.

'Do it of your own will or I'll make you do it,' he threatened, betting that she didn't know that his gift wouldn't work on her.

Her lower lip quivered for a moment, and then his gamble paid off as she set her jaw and climbed slowly to the ground. She came to stand in front of him.

'Take off your dress.' His words from their first meeting came back to him, and inwardly he recoiled at his poor choice of them now.

The girl just stared at him for a moment, her eyes showing him nothing. Then she looked past him, ignoring him as she began to unlace. He held his breath as the dress loosened and he could see the tops of her breasts. She drew it down from her shoulders and he could see her chest in full. Her nipples were raised in the cold air, begging for his attentions. He didn't make a sound, afraid she'd take flight like a deer surprised in a glade. She shimmied it down lower, and his eyes went down with it and he swore softly at the sight he saw. Her stomach and lower ribs on the right were a mass of bruises.

'Those two you mentioned before?'

She still didn't look at him, just stood stiffly as a flush began to mottle her skin. 'Yes.'

'You said they're dead?' Kane asked, his voice cold.

Her eyes darted to his in alarm. 'Yes.'

'Tell me the rest of it.'

'Like this?' She gestured to her state of undress, shivering.

He wanted more than anything to say yes. She'd do as he said, so afeared was she of his power. But the air was cold, and the last thing he needed was for her to catch a chill on the way down to the coast. He supposed he'd have to loan her a cloak. The gossamer dress pushed her breasts up nicely but wasn't very practical. It would offer little protection from the elements.

He delved in his bag for the salve the Brothers used to heal themselves quickly between battles. He brought out the small pot and his arm snaked out slowly, giving her ample time to step away, but she didn't move. It wound around her narrow waist, drawing her closer to him, and he heard a small gasp. He peered up at her from his seated position. If he didn't know any better, he'd say she was ... no, she couldn't be *aroused* by him. She was afraid, he reminded himself, just afraid.

His fingers smeared the salve over the bruises, holding her firmly as she twisted slightly from the pain of it, gentle though he was trying to be. He didn't have much practice with this sort of thing, after all.

When he had finished, he wound a bandage around her torso and tied it off. Then, his cock all but screaming at him to desist, he helped her on with her dress and laced it – though tighter at the chest than before so her breasts spilled out of the top slightly. That much he could do.

If she'd been scared of him before, now she looked almost bewildered.

'Go on, then.' He signaled for her to sit down next to him by the fire, which she did.

'Will you promise me something, please?'

Inwardly he scoffed. *So innocent.* As if he couldn't break a promise. When was the last time he'd pledged anyone anything? He knew at once. He'd sworn to Lily and Toman that they'd be safe and they'd both been torn to pieces in the arena that same day. He shoved the thoughts away. 'I already know what you would ask. For me not to compel you.'

She nodded.

He didn't answer her. 'Tell me what happened after you stole Viktor's gold and his horse. He is very angry with you, you know.'

She cringed. 'Is that why the others aren't here?'

'No.'

When he said nothing else for a few moments, she began to speak. 'I took a room in the tavern. That night, two men came to rob me. They couldn't find the gold, so they decided to take me instead. I fought them and I screamed. The big one hit me and kicked me, I think. They ran off after that.' She shuddered, and Kane was seized by a notion to put his arm around her.

He stood up instead. 'Go on,' he barked.

'I went to a friend, but ... he couldn't help me, so I left.'

Kane's eyes narrowed. There was more to her story, but the hour was getting late and she needed rest for their ride on the morrow. She could keep her secrets until he forced them out of her later.

He spread out his only bedroll by the fire and lay down upon it. 'We have a long ride tomorrow.' He patted the space in front of him.

She didn't move.

He sighed. 'You can do it your way or mine. The outcome is the same, but you'll feel better if you decide to do as I say on your own terms.'

She took a long look at the bedroll and then lay down in front of him slowly, trying not to touch any part of his body with hers. He grinned behind her as he took her uninjured wrist and manacled it to his own.

She pulled at the irons with a small cry. 'What are you doing?'

'You've proven yourself to be untrustworthy. This way I know I won't wake up tomorrow alone, both horses gone and my bags stolen.'

'I wouldn't do such a thing,' she muttered.

He snorted and lay back. After a few moments, he felt her relax in front of him, her breathing steady.

He wondered what had really happened to her in the house. It took more than a single beating to break a person, man or woman, but broken she was. He found to some surprise that it gave him no satisfaction. He'd spent days thinking of what he was going to do with her and now she was here, thoughts of all the plans he'd made to torment her were as ash in his mouth.

Observing her sleeping form before him, he shook his head in confusion. A newfound conscience wasn't good for a man who made his living killing for money. Perhaps it would have been better if he hadn't found her. With a long sigh, he closed his eyes. This journey was going to be very, very long.

SHE GASPED as he took her wrists, her naked body writhing as she struggled, but he forced her arms above her head easily, dominating her, stretching her lithe form beneath him. He opened her roughly and his hand felt between her thighs. His fingers came away slick and he chuckled. 'Pretend I don't excite you all you like. Your body doesn't lie.'

She moaned as his hand returned to her folds, teasing and caressing until she strained against him, whimpering, silently begging for more with her movements.

He kissed her neck, biting and suckling gently before doing the same to one pert nipple, his other hand still holding both of hers captive.

Her body was so responsive to him. Her innocence was plain, but where that might have bored him in the past, in her he found it to be a potent aphrodisiac.

He let her hands go and gripped her tightly as she undulated her hips against him, seeking contact with him wherever she could find it. Her hands now free, she moved them over him, caressing his arms, chest, and down his stomach to his cock. Her hand closed over it and she made a sound of contentment as she rubbed her thumb over the tip, spreading the bead of wetness she found there before bringing her thumb up to her mouth and tasting him. He growled and his lips descended on hers, deep and insistent, and she returned the kiss just as intensely. He threw her back on the bed, his arms holding hers above her head once more.

'Leave them there,' he ordered.

She looked like she wanted to protest, but her half-closed eyes were enthralled. She liked his command of her. She just didn't like that she liked it.

She did as he said and he moved down her body, pausing to kiss, lick and suckle wherever he saw fit as she squirmed under him. When he reached the juncture of her thighs, he bent her knees and spread them wide, flicking his tongue between her legs. He licked up and down her slit, slowly but firmly, before fastening his lips over her bud. She moaned so softly with every breath, as if she were ashamed of her pleasure. He wanted to tell her that he loved the sounds she made, loved what he could make her feel.

He plunged two fingers inside of her and she cried out, bucking wildly as that sent her over the edge. Her body shook as it was engulfed by waves of ecstasy and she melted back into the bed, boneless and sated, her legs quivering with the aftereffects of her pleasure.

He grinned at her and positioned himself at her entrance, and then he noticed a manacle running from her wrist to his and frowned. That hadn't been there befo–

He opened his eyes at the same time as she did. He was on top of her, her dress unlaced and bunched around her hips. He held her knees. They were bent and her legs were spread wide beneath him. His breeches were undone and his cock was pressed against her entrance. He could feel her silken heat. She was so wet, so ready, but the shocked look in her eyes made him roll away with a curse only to roll back over her again a moment later.

He took her by the shoulders and shook her. 'How are you getting into my head like this, woman? How do you invade my dreams?'

She drew back as far as she could. 'I'm not doing this.'

'Lies,' he accused.

She was breathing hard, looking at him with an adorably confused and wholly innocent expression. She shook her head. 'I'm not. I swear it.'

She took in the state of her dress and began to try to wriggle out from under him, pressing against his groin in little strokes that made him want to continue what he'd been about to do in the dream. He grabbed her hips with a groan.

'By the gods, stop moving! You can't go anywhere, anyway. You're still chained, remember?'

She stilled at once. 'Please.'

'Please what? Let you up or fuck you?'

She swallowed hard and closed her eyes. 'I – Why is my head so muddled?'

'How should I know?' he growled.

She looked up at him. 'Are you really not making me do this? Making me dream these things? Every night you're *there* and …'

'And what?' he asked, eager to hear more.

'I like it,' she said so quietly he almost didn't hear her.

He breathed out slowly, his cock throbbing, painfully unsated. 'What do you like?' he couldn't stop himself from asking.

'The things you do to me and the things I do. I don't want to, but I do.'

He leaned over her, taking in her swollen lips and bare breasts. He looked at his fingers, wet with her arousal, and grinned. Her eyes widened.

'Seems silly to stop now,' he murmured.

He moved over her, positioning himself at her entrance once more. She didn't stop him; instead a hand fluttered up to stroke the stubble at his jaw.

Kane forgot to breathe as he felt her caress. He'd never been touched in such a way. His lungs began to burn and he took a deep gulp of air.

Then he heard the baying of dogs in the distance and cursed loudly.

'What is it?'

'Hounds.'

He put his very unsatisfied organ back in his breeches quickly, promising himself they'd continue this later, and deftly unlocked the manacle holding them together.

'Put yourself to rights. They aren't looking for us, but it

won't be long before they're upon our camp, so unless you want them to get an eyeful, cover yourself.'

She did as he told her and got to her feet. 'Actually,' she said, touching his arm, 'I think they might be looking for us.' She avoided his gaze. 'Well, for me, anyway.'

CHAPTER 15

SORIN

Sorin stood at attention next to Viktor. Both had their eyes forward and were motionless except for the slow rise and fall of their leather armor as they breathed. They'd arrived at the main camp of the Dark Army that morning, a week earlier than the Commander's missive had ordered, as they'd found out when they got there.

Sorin wished Viktor and he had just gone after Lana the night she'd escaped. Instead they'd taken Kane at his word and he had lied to them. They'd left that very night to travel south instead of going after their captive because he had told them they had to be with the Commander in a few days when really they'd had a full sennight.

Kane had a penchant for making his quarry run before he closed in for the kill, so to speak. Sorin hoped Lana got under Kane's skin and made him regret his little chase as soon as he found her. His Brother was vengeful and dangerous and the bad in him far outweighed the good, but there had been times, rare though they were, that Sorin had seen quite another man lurking behind Kane's dark eyes.

Sorin had seen him save a small child from the river once

and another time spare a quivering farmer and his family as their town was ransacked and their neighbors murdered. Kane didn't know he had seen, but when Lana was caught, he hoped it would be that Kane and not by the man who was known as one of the cruelest of the Dark Brothers.

Sorin couldn't remember the last time he'd felt something like peace within himself, but he was terribly close since Lana. He hoped being around her would do the same for Kane.

After having time to reflect, Sorin believed he knew why they were drawn to Lana. It was a rare thing these days, but a unit of Brothers sometimes found another they were pulled towards. There were at least two he'd heard of recently; one in this very camp so perhaps it wasn't so unusual anymore. If Lana was their Fourth, that would explain why they'd been compelled to take her with them, why they couldn't let her go.

But it didn't explain the peace they felt around her. That wasn't because he was drawn to her as a Fourth. That was something else and he was afraid he knew why that was as well.

There were stories as old as the Army itself, muttered by Dark Brothers in the dead of night. Tales of witches that had almost brought about the fall of the Army. The legends said that their numbers had been many at the beginning, when the Dark Brothers were the sentinels who protected the realms instead of mercenaries who now only served for the clink of gold. He would have to search through the texts in the archives for more though. Facts were hard to come by from that time. They were rare, but what if Lana was one? It would explain how she was able to get past their defenses so easily.

'You're early. Good.'

Ousted from his reverie, Sorin simply nodded to their

Commander respectfully and saw Viktor do the same from the corner of his eye. The General's hair was greying, and any skin not covered was crisscrossed with scars of battle, but although he was advancing in years, the size and strength that marked them all as Dark Brothers was very much still with him. The Commander appeared as robust and virile as he always had been, which was lucky for him because as soon as his ageing body showed any sign of weakness, he'd be challenged for the leadership of the Brothers and gutted.

'You summoned us, Greygor.'

'Aye. So I did.' Greygor walked behind his desk and regarded them thoughtfully. 'I received a bird from a Brother two nights ago.' He sat. 'About you two.' A look of annoyance marred his features as he watched them. 'Can you not imagine what it was about?'

Sorin turned his head toward Viktor slightly, a horrible idea dawning. Greygor had the eyes and ears of many, but surely he couldn't already know about Lana, could he? Viktor just stared straight ahead.

Sorin kept his face carefully blank and hoped Viktor was doing the same. 'Who?'

'Uth.'

Sorin couldn't help it as his lips curled into a snarl. 'It wasn't Uth's place. We were coming –'

'Silence!' Greygor boomed. 'You were not coming to tell me yourself. I summoned you on another matter. But this we will talk about first. Have you or have you not got a girl travelling with you?'

Viktor cleared his throat. 'We do, sir.'

'Where did she come from? What does she know?'

'She's but a slave. Nothing.'

'Nothing,' Greygor mimicked. 'Nothing?' He slammed his fist down, causing his wine goblet to overturn and spill its contents over the parchments that littered his desk. He paid it no mind. 'You are part of my best unit and we are days away from an invasion that has taken years to plan and will make you wealthy beyond your dreams. She could have been sent by the Island Citadels to spy; they're certainly powerful enough these days. Did you think of that? No, you were too busy thinking with your pricks. Where is she now?'

'She–' Viktor began.

Sorin interrupted Viktor with a meaningful look at his Brother. 'She is with Kane and our men. We travelled light to reach the Army sooner.'

The general's eyes lit with a feral gleam that made Sorin's stomach churn with the suspicion that Greygor was playing a game with them and had yet to tell them the rules. 'No matter. I will have Kane bring her to me when he arrives and we will see if she is what you say.'

'If you believe she could be a threat, then so be it.' Sorin feigned indifference, but inwardly his mind was racing. The last thing they needed was for her to be brought here to where the Brothers were amassing. Being an unclaimed woman in their midst wasn't safe at the best of times, but if anyone even suspected what she was, they'd kill her at once. Sorin shuddered. It didn't bear thinking about.

Regardless, as soon as Greygor saw their unusually beautiful slave, she would be taken from them and used, if not by their Commander, then by other Brothers he wished to gain favor with. Now Greygor's years were waning, he needed all the support he could get, and he would use her as a pawn in his power games. Greygor would have summoned Lana no matter what they had said and was probably disappointed that she hadn't travelled with them. Uth's dispatch must have been very detailed in its description of her.

'Fuck off, the both of you. I have no wish to include you in my other plans now.'

BOUGHT TO BREAK

They both bowed their heads and left their Commander's tent.

As soon as they were out of Greygor's earshot, Sorin turned on Viktor angrily. 'You were going to tell him about the gold,' he accused. 'You would have made her a fugitive of the Dark Brothers, a target for any Brother who found her.'

'Yes.' Viktor's eyes held no remorse.

'She fled in fear and only took what she needed to survive.' Sorin turned away from his Brother with a growl. 'She isn't Greta, you fucking prick,' he muttered.

Sorin fell as Viktor tackled him from behind with a roar. He fought his way back to his feet, catching Viktor in the head hard enough for the bigger man to pause and shake it to clear the stars from his vision.

'You don't know what you're talking about,' Viktor snarled at him.

'Your wife's decisions cost her life and those of your children,' Sorin shot back.

In that moment, his Brother looked so lost that Sorin softened. He put a hand on Viktor's shoulder and spoke quietly. 'Lana is not her, and you must stop these bitter thoughts before they put her in more danger. Do you not see, Brother?'

Viktor looked at him blankly and Sorin sighed. Viktor was so focused on Lana's thievery that he hadn't even thought.

'Look around.' Sorin gestured to the tents that surrounded them, the camp of three thousand Brothers and sell-swords. 'Greygor's command is that Kane bring her here.'

Viktor shrugged. 'So?'

Sorin sighed, pinching the bridge of his nose, and spoke slowly. 'We haven't claimed her. She's no different from a woman taken in a raid.'

Viktor swore and looked around as if only just realizing they were standing in the middle of the Camp of the Dark Army. 'Kane can't bring her here. Fuck. Greygor will give her to one of the other units or let her be used in the pleasure tents.'

'I think she's our Fourth and it's worse than that. I believe she's a –' Sorin's eyes darted around, making sure there was no one near.

'A what?'

'A witch as well,' he whispered.

'A witch,' Viktor said with a sneer. 'She's no more a witch than I am!'

'If not a witch, then what? I felt different around her. You did too. What do the stories say other than that they were hunted by the Brothers and their numbers dwindled after the Army became mercenaries? We aren't just drawn to her, we are two sides of the same coin, she makes the darkness in us recede. I need to look through the scrolls and the old books from the archives, but she is one. I'm sure of it.'

Viktor still didn't look convinced. 'Whether she is or she isn't, she cannot be brought here.'

'What can we do? You can bet we're being watched. We can't leave to warn them, and they won't let us near the birds to send a message. But Kane is no fool. He must realize that she needs to be claimed at least by him before they set foot this side of the river.' Sorin began to walk in the direction of their unit's tent.

Viktor caught up to him with a few long strides 'But it's Kane. When was the last time you even saw him with a woman? After what he did to her in the tent, we shouldn't have left her for him to find. He arranged it so we thought we had to leave or face Greygor's wrath so he could chase her down himself. What if he brings her here on purpose, knowing what the Commander will do to her? I know you think he has another side, Brother, but he's cruel, brutal. That's why he's Greygor's second in command. His loyalty is to us, then Greygor and the Brothers, not to Lana.'

Sorin rubbed his eyes. 'That's what Greygor is counting on, but Kane knew the moment he saw Lana that she was different. By the time he gets here, he will feel as protective of her as we do. He won't be able to put her at risk even if it puts him at war with his nature. I hope.'

'And what about her punishment? She stole from the Brothers. The soldiers will start talking as soon as they arrive. The whole camp will know within a day, and Greygor will insist the law be followed as a matter of pride.'

'If she's claimed by us, the law should be void, but you're right. He might demand it regardless. For now, though, we can only wait.'

CHAPTER 16

LANA

Lana's hands shook as she pulled her dress down and plaited her hair. She could feel Kane's eyes boring into her back as he quickly packed up his supplies and she couldn't help but flush. She'd spent years avoiding men wherever possible and now her body was betraying her and she wanted three of them! When had she become so wanton?

After her da, her mother had taken a few lovers before settling on her stepfather. Although it may have been remarked upon, no one had really thought much about it. Lana was a slave. It was a given that she would be used that way eventually, but she wasn't supposed to enjoy it. What would people say? But then she wasn't in her village anymore. Who was there to judge her but herself?

Kane pulled her up onto the horse. Her ribs twinged, but the pain was nothing like it had been the previous day. The Brothers' salve did indeed heal quickly. He settled her in front of him, and she could feel his hardness prodding behind her like an unsatisfied beast. She tried to move away, but he put his arm around her waist and hauled her flush against him with a growl.

'Tell me the rest of it, woman.'

'I have a name. It's Lana,' she said curtly.

'Very well. Tell me the rest of it. *Lana.*' He said her name in barely a whisper that she felt on the back of her neck, and she shivered.

'My friend didn't want me to leave,' she began but stopped when she heard him snort.

'I know who your friend is, woman. No more lies and half-truths or I'll take a whip to that round little arse of yours at the camp.'

Lana gasped in spite of herself and twisted round to look at him. 'A whip?'

'Perhaps, as its your first time, I'll go easy on you and use my hand.'

'It's hardly the first time I've been beaten,' she said flippantly, though in truth the thought of it made her stomach revolt.

'The way I do it, it will feel like it,' he promised, his arm around her tightening.

She swallowed hard. 'The man from the house … I was searching for him.'

'Go on,' Kane urged.

She closed her eyes and grimaced. 'He's my father. I thought he was dead,' she continued hurriedly. 'My mother told me he was dead.'

Kane was silent and she realised that she'd surprised him. He was probably not a man used to that.

'And?' he finally asked.

Lana sighed. 'When I found him, I thought that I was safe. But I overheard him speaking with his man. He was going to make me marry as soon as it could be arranged. He doesn't care for me; he only wanted to use me.'

'Who?'

'What?'

'Who was your father going to make you marry? You probably would have been better off staying with him than being a slave.'

Lana tried to remember. 'A man called Boone,' she replied finally.

Kane snorted. 'Never mind.'

'Why? Who is he?'

'A powerful man; a warlord in the far north. He's known for his violence. He kills his slaves frequently during his rages.'

Lana looked away as a fresh pang made her want to cry. Her father would have sold her to a beast. She'd made such a mistake coming to find him, thinking he would help her. Everything was so much worse now.

Kane said nothing more as he weaved the horse through the trees and into a stream to mask them, but still the sounds of the dogs got louder and louder. Finally, he cursed.

'The fucking things have our scent. We won't be rid of them now.'

'What are we going to do?'

'Ride out and meet them. I have better things to do than waste all day riding around this fucking forest.'

Kane turned his horse in the direction of the baying hounds and, true to his word, began to maneuver the beast towards them. It didn't take long until a cry rang out as they were spotted. Kane jerked the reins and his mount halted at once.

As men came out of the trees around them, Lana shrank closer to the Dark Brother at her back. She couldn't help it. He was strength where she felt so feeble. If he was surprised, or indeed felt anything at all, he didn't show it. He sat regally, not even looking at the men surrounding them. She felt a flash of pride – as if he were hers – and her brow furrowed in confusion.

'I'll take my daughter now, sell-sword.'

Lana's father sat on a dapple-grey, extremely docile-looking mare behind his men and, though she was scared, Lana smiled at a sudden memory.

'What are you so happy about?' Kane murmured behind her.

'My father's horse. I just remembered he's a terrible rider. My mother was always –'

'Natter my ear off about it later, woman. Just now we have problems.'

Lana scowled at him. 'Can't you just ... you know ... tell them all to leave or something?'

'Or something,' he said ominously. Then he spoke loudly for her father to hear. 'I'm no sell-sword, and the woman is mine.'

Her father was silent. His eyes surveyed Kane, reassessing the threat he posed. 'My apologies. I did not realize you are one of the famed Dark Brothers. I just want my beloved daughter. I'll pay for her, of course. A bag of gold? Two? You need only name your price.'

Kane picked up a piece of Lana's hair that had fallen from its bindings and played with it casually. 'My price would beggar you. I find I quite enjoy your beloved daughter.'

Lana snatched her hair away from him. 'Stop playing games. Stop goading him.'

'Goading him?' Kane leaned closer. 'What if I stripped you to the waist here in front of all these men and fondled your tits while you struggled? Would that *goad* him?'

Lana felt him growing hard once more. 'Stop it! It would provoke any father to see such a thing done to his daughter.'

Kane snorted. 'Even one such as he? You already see he

would buy you from me like a brood mare, sell you to a worse man for his own gain.'

Lana's lip quivered at his harsh words and she struggled to stop the tears from forming in her eyes. 'I s-suppose it would be more a matter of pride for him than true affection for me,' she conceded.

Kane's fingers tangled into her hair and pulled her head back to survey her face. A flash of something crossed his features, confusion or fear perhaps, but it was gone too quickly, and his usual mask of indifference settled back over him. He let go of her plait.

'I grow tired of these games. Brother or no, give me my daughter or my men will attack.'

Kane's eyes narrowed. 'You think to threaten me with your motley soldiers, you old fool?'

Lana's skin began to tingle, making her feel like she was back in that tent when she first met Kane, and she gasped, hugging herself and pushing back into his body. The irony wasn't lost on her that she was trying to find comfort in the belly of the beast, literally. What did give her pause was that the beast's arm settled around her and gave her what could be considered a reassuring squeeze.

'Kill the man next to you,' he commanded, his voice carrying through the trees.

Her father's men didn't hesitate. Each turned to the nearest man and struck him down, killing their comrades until there was just one, breathing heavily and looking around disbelievingly at the carnage. It was finished so quickly, Lana looked around them in shock.

Lana tore her eyes from the bodies, swallowing hard and feeling dizzy. She glanced back at Kane. The man was smiling darkly. His eyes shone and he looked so pleased with himself, entertained even. Disgusted, she looked beyond the scene.

Her father gaped, his eyes searching for anyone else in his employ to help and finding no one there because all but one were dead.

'You. Last soldier. Kill the old man and then yourself.'

'No!' Lana shrieked, grabbing Kane's arm, but it was already too late. Her da fell from his horse, a bolt from the soldier's crossbow in his chest. The final deed done, the soldier drew a knife and slit his own throat from ear to ear.

'You killed my da. You killed him,' she wailed.

He said nothing, just turned the horse away as if nothing had happened.

She twisted in the saddle and began to pound her fists into his chest, his arms, anywhere she could reach. He let her for a time before taking her hands prisoner in his own with a curse.

'I hate you!' she said vehemently, and he shrugged. 'You may not touch the blood, but your hands still run red with it, sell-sword.'

'A Dark Brother is not a sell-sword,' he rumbled.

'I see no great distinction,' she spat, no longer caring what he did to her.

His arms picked her up and turned her to face him in the saddle, except her legs got stuck on one side, so in essence he was now cradling her like a babe.

'You should be thanking me for getting rid of one of your enemies for you. For a little slave girl, you certainly have enough of them.'

'What does that mean?' she demanded.

'Whatever the fuck you want it to mean. I care little. My camp isn't far. We'll be there by midday and I'm running short of patience. Mind your tongue, slave, or I'll give you to my men to entertain with your pretty virgin body until I have use for you.'

'Sorin and Viktor may be angry with me, but they'd never let you do such a thing,' she said with confidence.

'They aren't there,' he sneered.

'Where are they?' she asked in concern.

'Would you care if something had happened to them?' He seemed surprised at her worry.

'Of course. I – I'm fond of them.'

'Then you're a fool because you're worth less than nothing to them.'

Not giving credence to his nasty words, she looked away from him into the trees that still lined their path, hoping he couldn't see the tears in her eyes.

He was silent for a time. 'They've simply been called away,' he finally said.

They reached the camp by noon, as Kane had predicted. He took her off the horse and carried her into his large, luxurious tent, barking orders at his men. Sitting down on one of the beds, he held her as his soldiers came and went, fetching and carrying whatever he commanded.

Lana's eyes became heavy and she closed them. 'He wasn't a bad man, you know. Not before,' she whispered.

'What?'

'My da. I have memories of him being a loving father.'

'People change.'

Lana opened her eyes and looked into Kane's. 'I will never forgive you for what you did today.'

'I wouldn't expect you to.' He began to unlace the front of her dress.

She blinked back tears. 'So now you ravish the maiden after felling her father before her eyes?'

Kane's expression gave nothing away. 'Nothing so sordid, I'm afraid. There's water for bathing, but I won't be leaving you alone in case you try to escape again. I also wouldn't trust many of my men to watch you and not fall on you like a rutting animal.'

'I can undress myself.'

'Shh. I won't hurt you.'

After today she shouldn't believe him, but she was so tired, she let him do what he willed.

He set her on her feet and pulled the dress down until it pooled on the floor. She looked away from him, a blush rising even as she berated herself for letting him anywhere near her after what he'd done. So what if her father had been planning to marry her off to a brutal warlord? He'd loved her really. She might have been able to bring him around. Now she'd never find out. Because of Kane.

And yet despite her loathing, even now her body responded to his touch. The lightest brush of his fingers on something as innocuous as her wrist was enough to make her yearn for him to put his hands on her, his fingers in her. She shuddered and he asked her a question. She ignored him.

He led her to a steaming basin and began to wash her. Slowly and methodically, he traced up her arms to her back and chest before doing the same to her legs with a cloth. When he reached the apex of her thighs, he paused, his eyes searching hers. Resigned, she breathed out slowly and widened her stance for him to wash her.

Someone came into the tent and Kane shielded her body with his immediately.

'Get out.'

'I'm sorry, sir. A bird from the Commander.'

'Leave the message on my desk and fuck off.'

The sell-sword left and Kane led her to the bed. He didn't dress her in anything, just laid her down and tucked her under the blankets bare. She closed her eyes, feigning sleep, and heard him go to his desk. Tears began to fall, and she was glad she was turned away from him.

She wondered at his gentleness. Was he feeling regret? She wouldn't have believed that a man who killed so happily would feel guilty afterwards. He clearly didn't believe killing her father had been wrong. She squeezed her eyes shut. She should never have gone with Kane, should have tried to escape him when she had the chance, though she couldn't think of when there had been such a moment. But she should have fought harder. At least her father might still be alive, not lying in a forest, his body to be ravaged by animals.

She turned and looked over at the Brother responsible; terrible and beautiful. Why could she not control her reactions to him? Like Sorin and Viktor, she was drawn to them all. What was happening to her?

CHAPTER 17

KANE

Kane busied himself at his desk with the many documents and plans that had been awaiting his return – since days before he'd gone after the woman. The raid of the Islands was imminent, but much had to be done to ensure their success. The Commander was being less than useless, as per usual these days, and, as his second, Kane was picking up the pieces. He hadn't even been given the full details of whomever was paying the Brothers' Army for their support, though it must be someone obscenely wealthy for Greygor to entertain a campaign that could go so wrong. The invasion itself wouldn't be difficult with their numbers, but the Islands had powerful allies. They might end up fighting battles on multiple fronts in the future. It was a risk and one that wasn't worth the spoils as far as Kane was concerned.

The old man was getting on in years and it was beginning to show. Another Brother in his position would already have challenged his leadership, but Kane had never wanted that mantle. He was content to work from the shadows and carry on his own smaller, private wars. Greygor knew that, which was why he'd chosen Kane in the first place and, at least in Kane's personal endeavors, success was more or less assured. Soon the culmination of his, Sorin's and Viktor's work since they had become a unit would be realised. Revenge would finally be theirs, and they could afford no distractions.

His eyes fell on a tiny parchment on the edge of the desk. The bird from the Commander. He'd forgotten it. He looked over at the woman, admiring her sleeping form on the other side of the tent – but still in his line of sight lest she try escaping again – and frowned. *He'd forgotten it.* Because he'd been too busy trying to comfort her, though he had not the first idea of how to do such a thing. He'd neglected his duty because of her. That couldn't happen again.

He read the short note and sat back in his chair, staring at it. It simply summoned him. She wasn't mentioned, but Kane knew Greygor. He would have no reason to meet again so soon. Greygor must be aware of her and, this close to the invasion, he would be suspicious of anyone joining them suddenly. Such people could be spies, after all.

His Brothers would have kept her existence a secret until after the Islands had been secured. They wouldn't have said a word, which only left Uth, a Brother who had been a thorn in his side for years. Uth craved power but, like so many, would have no idea what to actually do with it. However, perhaps this time he'd done Kane a favor. He looked over at her again. *A distraction.* As far as he was concerned, she'd been nothing but trouble. He should have simply killed her and been done with it, but he couldn't. He hated that he couldn't. What was this power she had over them? It was dangerous, whatever it was.

If Greygor wanted her, he could have her. She wasn't claimed, after all. Once it was done, Viktor and Sorin could do little about it without his agreement. They'd thank him in the end.

He got up and silently walked to where she slept. Her eyes were red, as if she'd cried herself to sleep, though he hadn't heard her. He ignored the strange sensation in his chest, had no idea what to make of it. It was a hollowness, an ache. His fingers twitched with a powerful urge to pull back the blanket he'd tucked her under, knowing her dress was still on the floor near the wash basin where he'd bared her fully to his gaze. He hadn't been disappointed.

Just fuck her and be done, a voice inside him coaxed. By the gods, how he wanted to rip off that cover, spread her legs wide and take her the way Dark Brothers took everything they wanted. He'd make her scream his name even as she struggled to be free of him. Kane's cock grew painful against his breeches and he turned away with a curse. He had been hard almost from the moment he'd met her. With any other woman he would already have had her, but there was something about this one that warned him away. She was different, in his thoughts, and he was losing the tight control that had kept him alive when others had died. Yes, this girl was dangerous.

He went to the basin, stripped and washed in the water that had long since gone cold, hoping it would help. When he was finished, he looked over at the sleeping woman. He watched her for a moment and realised she was only pretending to slumber. Her eyes were open, just a fraction, but enough to see. She was watching him bathe. A part of him was shocked and another part shocked that he was shocked. It had been so long since anyone had surprised him as often as she was able to. He pretended not to notice her as he dried himself slowly. Then he took his thick rod in his hand, still hard as a rock, and began to stroke himself. He heard her gasp and smiled to himself when he saw that her eyes were now tightly shuttered.

He strode towards her bed, making his mind up. 'Were

you not enjoying the spectacle, Lana? Look. You're missing the best part.'

Her eyes opened and widened as she took him in. 'I'm sorry. I didn't mean to–'

'To what?' he asked smoothly. 'To watch me or to enjoy what you saw?'

She said nothing, but the tongue that came out to moisten her lips as her eyes fluttered about was his undoing. He pulled the cover from her and ordered her up.

She complied immediately, and inwardly he groaned. It was as if she truly wanted to please him, and he wasn't one to look a gift horse in the mouth. She stood in front of him, gloriously naked and quivering slightly, her gaze on the floor in front of her.

'Look at me.'

She raised her eyes slowly until they came to rest on his.

'Kneel.'

Slowly, she dropped to the fur-covered floor.

'Do you know what I want of you?'

Still looking up at him, she nodded hesitantly.

'Speak aloud.'

'I think so, but I – I'm sorry. I don't know how.'

'You've never taken a cock in your mouth?'

She shook her head.

'Open,' he ordered, 'and gods help you if you bite me.'

He pushed the tip past her lips and waited as she grew used to the intrusion. 'Use your tongue.'

He felt a tentative lick and groaned, resisting the urge to grab her head and thrust himself down her throat. He was large and she was untried. He wasn't a complete monster, he discovered. He pushed in further.

'Suck,' he ordered. 'Use your hands here.'

He showed her where to touch him at the base of his shaft, the pressure to use and how to move, and soon he was

BOUGHT TO BREAK

pushing into her mouth as she took him in her fist. He found he liked her inexperience, enjoyed her hesitation and resolve to please him. He even liked that she couldn't swallow him fully. She instinctively began to quicken her pace and his fingers laced through her long red hair as he thrust into her hot, wet mouth. He came, harder than he ever had before, throwing back his head with a roar as his seed spurted down her throat. Surprised, she tried to tear herself away, but he held her fast until he was finished.

'Swallow it,' he growled, and she nodded with wide eyes.

He helped her to her feet, unsure what to say. He felt sated as he hadn't in ages, perhaps not ever. He wanted to thank her for allowing him to be the first, tell her that he'd never felt such pleasure. Instead he told her gruffly to get back into the bed.

He didn't meet her gaze as he turned away, but he knew she wanted reassurance. He shouldn't give her any, shouldn't encourage this, but he made the mistake of looking back at her and saw confusion and distress. For some reason the idea of leaving her in such a state was distasteful. In the past, he would have done that and worse – and reveled in it. Now, he cupped her face gently and traced his thumb over her mouth.

'You did well,' he said softly, tucking her under the covers.

He went back to his desk and worked far into the night. He gave the orders that the camp was to be packed up at dawn to make the short journey to where the rest of the Army was waiting. Then he called in his most reliable man, Henrick, and gave the care of the slave to him. He couldn't be near her any more than was necessary. What had happened had proven as much. He dozed in his chair the rest of the night, not trusting himself any closer to her.

. . .

IN THE MORNING he woke to the screams of the soldier who'd interrupted him the afternoon before. Orders were orders and he was to be obeyed. A good flogging once in a while kept the others in line. He splashed some cold water on his face and set his clothing to rights.

The woman began to stir. Kane picked up her dress from the floor and tossed it onto the bed where she lay, not looking at her.

'Get dressed unless you want to travel naked,' he said coldly, striding from the tent. Outside, he barked at Henrick to see to her and walked into the trees for a piss. Already wanting to be back in her presence, he swore. It was going to be a long three days before he was rid of her.

CHAPTER 18

LANA

Lana donned her dress just in the nick of time as an older man she didn't recognize walked into the tent. He was one of the Brothers' soldiers, that much she could see, but his presence made her eyes dart this way and that, looking for a suitable weapon in case he attacked. Her panic must have been evident because he put his hands up, didn't come any closer and introduced himself as Henrick. He told her that he would see to her needs until they reached their destination and she need only ask him for whatever she willed. He pointed at the table, which seemed to be constantly stocked with fresh food, though she never saw anyone bring any, and told her they'd be leaving before the sun shone through the trees.

She ate some fruit hurriedly, saw to her ablutions as quickly as she could and was waiting for Henrick when he came to collect her a little while later. He escorted her outside just as the main tent was beginning to be dismantled. Everything else had been packed up with military precision, she noted. Everything had its place and everyone had a job to do. Everyone but her. She frowned as she was led to a horse.

She hadn't been truly useful in weeks. She'd been a slave for years and she'd always had work to do. Now there was nothing, and it was starting to bother her. But then, a lot of things were bothering her. That was perhaps the least of them.

She was helped onto a gelding's back, then Henrick left her to mount his own stallion. She was to ride alone and had been given a docile 'lady's horse' that couldn't outrun one of theirs – as if she had anywhere to flee to. If she'd learned anything over the past few days, it was that she was woefully ill-prepared for the world outside her village. And utterly alone.

They began to move. Their travel was quicker than she'd anticipated, as they left the wagons behind to travel at their own slower pace. Henrick rode next to her in silence. She found his company oddly soothing. Perhaps it was because he was older and didn't look at her with lust in his eyes the way the other soldiers did. She tried to ignore the men, but their covetous looks her way and whispers to each other made her uneasy. Fortunately, whenever one of them got too close, Henrick gave him a pointed stare and he receded back into the ranks.

They travelled long into the day and stopped in the mid-afternoon by a river. Some of the soldiers made fires while others went to hunt, and Lana was reminded of Viktor and Sorin. Where were they and, in fact, where was Kane? She hadn't seen him since that morning. Her cheeks heated as she thought of how she'd watched him in the night. What had she been thinking? And then what she'd done afterwards … He hadn't even coerced her. After all that had happened the day before – Gods, her father's corpse hadn't even been cold and she had still wanted to please the man who'd caused his death. What did that make her?

An old woman had come to their village selling love charms once. Was Kane using something like that, or perhaps a subtle compulsion born of his horrible *gift*? Surely these things she felt weren't real. They had to be some trick or sorcery, didn't they?

But they so closely mirrored her odd feelings for Sorin and Viktor. What did it mean? She hardly knew these men, and so much of what she had seen of them was dark and violent. They killed with no remorse and, in fact, with pleasure, it seemed. Their world was so far removed from hers. How could she care for such men? It was true that Sorin and Viktor had seemed to have a soft spot for her. They had treated her well, after all. But they were angry with her for her thievery. Would they treat her cruelly when she saw them again? She sighed in confusion and frustration. There was no way out of this that she could see. Again, she could only wait and see what fate had planned; leave everything in others' control. The way a slave's life was, she supposed.

Henrick had her sit on a rock by the river away from the men but still close enough that she didn't stand a chance of escaping again. So she sat, her arms wrapped around herself, shivering in the cooling late afternoon air. She watched as the soldiers came back with their kills sometime later, roaring at each other and guffawing as they drank deep from their wine skins. It was a contest, she realised. The man who came back with the most meat was the winner, much like the one Sorin and Viktor had played that night by the ruins.

In this case it was a large, bearded mercenary who beat his chest and howled, and she smiled in spite of herself. Unfortunately, he turned at that moment and noticed her regard, puffing up his chest and letting his eyes drift over her boldly. She looked away at once, but Henrick was already there.

'You'd do well not to call attention to yourself, girl,' he scolded. 'I've been given the task of seeing to your safety, but even I can only do so much if they mutiny with none of the

Brothers here. I'll leave you to your fate, girl, just see if I don't. You're not worth dying for.'

She looked down, chastened. 'I'm sorry, Henrick. Truly, I didn't mean to.'

He threw something on the ground at her feet with a snort. A cloak. He must have seen her shivering. She'd had to leave her other one in her father's house and the gossamer dress was definitely not made for winter travel. She was afraid she was beginning to get ill. She felt tired most days, even after a good night's sleep.

She donned it quickly and looked up, intending to thank him for his kindness, but he'd already moved to one of the fires. Once the meat was cooked, he brought her some, and by then the wagons had caught up. Short work was made of erecting the tents, though the large one of the Brothers' was nowhere to be seen. By the time darkness fell, Henrick led her to one of the smallest ones and ushered her inside, telling her he would be close by if she needed anything, though she got the distinct impression that any requests before morning would not be met with friendliness. She finally asked him where Kane was, but he simply shrugged and left her, tying the flaps tightly behind him.

The next two days passed in the same fashion, the hours so indistinguishable that Lana began to question how much time was passing. Kane didn't appear. Henrick rarely spoke to her and the others never did at all, she supposed on pain of death. It was as if she was behind an invisible wall, closed off from everyone. Even the dreams of Kane at night had stopped. She began to feel lonely and isolated, which she told herself was silly. She'd spent years as a slave with no family or friends, though it had been different. She'd always had the tavern girls to talk to. Though not friends per se, they'd been close in their own way, and they'd always been kind to her when they were able.

At the end of the third day, they reached a ferry to cross the river. The men began to go across in groups with their horses, then the wagons, one by one. When it was her turn to go with Henrick, she froze as her hand touched the railing of the large raft. The other side of the river looked the same as the one she was on, but there was something frightening, menacing. The ferryman complained about her taking too long, and Henrick prodded her forward.

'Where is Kane?'

Henrick shrugged, his usual response to a question he couldn't – or wouldn't – answer, she had learned. He pushed her again, but she refused to budge.

'I will not go a step further until I see Kane,' she declared.

'By the gods, woman, what is it?' asked an impatient voice.

She turned to find the man himself on his mount behind her.

'Where were you?' was all she could think to say as she was met with his stupid, ridiculous, handsome face.

He didn't answer her. Instead he gestured with his head towards the boat, questioning.

'I don't know.' She looked back at the other shore where the men and wagons waited.

Kane rolled his eyes at her. 'The ferry is nothing to fear.'

She heard Henrick board, saying something under his breath about silly women being afraid of stupid things. She ignored him as she looked Kane over. Finally, he was here. She hadn't realised how wound up she'd been over the past days until now, as her muscles began to relax. Why would his presence comfort her in the slightest? He was a ferocious brute, she reminded herself crossly. He pretended to be a man, but he wasn't at all. He was a monster who took pleasure in death – not whatever her silly girl's mind was trying to turn him into.

'It's not the ferry. It's something else.' She looked into his eyes and saw a flash – remorse, resignation – and her heart sank. She took a steadying breath and her eyes turned pleading. 'What's going to happen to me on the other side?'

Kane actually met her gaze. At least there was that. 'Our Commander wants to meet you. That's all. You worry for nothing. Viktor and Sorin are there as well.'

She forced a nod and some semblance of a smile, turned, and walked with leaden feet onto the boat. Kane dismounted and boarded after her, and the craft set off along the thick rope that guided it to the small jetty opposite. She clenched the wooden rail, her knuckles white. She couldn't explain it, but she knew with certainty that when they got across the river, Kane would show that brutish side of himself and betray her, to what or whom she couldn't say.

She turned her head slowly. Neither Kane nor Henrick was watching her, and the ferryman was focused on the journey. She turned back and looked down into the water. Dark and deep. It wasn't the best escape, to be sure, but perhaps drowning here was preferable to what awaited on the other side. At least she could choose something, control something, even if that was her own death.

Making her mind up, she climbed slowly onto the rail, hoping they didn't notice her actions as she stretched out her arms. Looking up at the open, cloudless sky, she leant towards the water. Everything seemed to happen so slowly as she pitched forward and felt herself tumbling over. She vaguely heard a yell behind her, but it was too late. Hitting the cold water was a shock that made her limbs freeze, but the darkness quickly enveloped her. She didn't try to thrash or kick, just let the current take her. The water was murky and the light disappeared quickly. She closed her eyes and tried to ignore the screaming of her lungs as they were starved. She tried to be at peace as she floated, the cloak and skirts of the dress weighing her down. Her limbs grew heavy and she let out the last of her breath, the bubbles tickling her nose as they sped to the surface.

Something grabbed her and began to pull her, up and up, and she didn't have the strength to resist. Her head broke the surface and she gulped in a breath. She coughed up water, spluttering as she tried to breathe. Her limp body was dragged through the current until it felt land. Then she was picked up and set down on a blanket of what felt like moss. She finally opened her eyes. Kane lay next to her, looking equal parts furious and relieved. They were on the opposite shore.

'Why did you save me?' she croaked.

'Why did you wait until the boat to try to escape, you little fool?'

She looked away from him and let her head fall limply to the ground. 'Because you're a fucking liar.'

He said nothing.

She turned her head towards him. 'And I wasn't trying to escape.' She closed her eyes and snorted softly. 'I can't even swim.'

He rolled on top of her in a sudden movement and she squeaked as his mouth crashed down on hers. She struggled under him for a moment as he parted her legs with his in a practiced move and pulled up her sodden dress.

His mouth left hers as he pulled at the bodice of her red gown. Freeing a breast, he descended on it like a starving man, licking and sucking the tip, making her arch into him with a whimper she couldn't contain.

'What are you doing?' she asked, her mind in a fog.

He didn't answer. Instead he pushed a thick finger into her dry channel, and she whimpered as he freed his cock with the other hand. It sprang free of his breeches. Her hands went to push him away but, of their own volition, grabbed his black tunic and pulled him closer instead. With a growl, he captured her wrists and held them over her head as he lined himself up to sheath his rod inside her. She felt sudden wetness gathering at her entrance and made a sound of impatience, aching for him to fill the emptiness that clawed inside her.

'The Commander is waiting,' a voice drawled.

The man on top of her stilled immediately, his breath ragged. He didn't move for a moment, swearing softly as he tried to master himself. She felt him tuck her breast back into her dress and was thankful as she opened her eyes and saw they were surrounded by two massive Dark Brothers she'd never seen before and a handful of soldiers.

'I'm sure he is.' Kane's voice sounded relaxed and slightly bored as he lifted himself away from her. As he stood, he bent down and grabbed her around the throat. His grip was gentle as he nudged her to her feet, but to the men watching it would look rough and uncaring, she realised. Her brow furrowed. What was the show for?

As soon as she was standing, he pushed her forcefully at one of the other Brothers with a chuckle. 'Get her out of my sight.'

Stung, she looked up into the hard eyes of the Brother now holding her. He was watching her intently with an expression on his face that scared her. She suspected she'd be more than just afraid soon enough, and it made her tremble.

CHAPTER 19

KANE

'And bind her hands,' Kane continued. 'She's a slippery one.'

With a shrug, Quin tied Lana's wrists behind her tightly enough that she made a sound of discomfort. Kane didn't meet her eyes as she was led away from the river. He followed closely with Quin, feeling like he'd just made a terrible mistake. His mind raced. What had he done?

'Not like you to let your lust get the better of you, Brother,' Quin remarked next to him.

Kane forced a believable laugh. 'You know how eager the new ones can be, thinking a good fuck will get them special treatment.'

Quin guffawed. 'Aye, that's true enough. She'll understand her life here after a night in one of the pleasure tents.'

He saw Lana stiffen and steeled himself against her. If he could convince Greygor to let him and his Brothers keep her for themselves, then this would all be over soon. If not ... He cursed himself, all of a sudden seeing everything he'd tried to deny with clarity. Sorin and Viktor cared for her more than he'd seen them care about anything or anyone. They'd never forgive him for this. Their unit would destroy itself from inside. Kane should have claimed her before, if not for himself, then for Sorin and Viktor. Now it was too late. She'd already been willing to drown herself rather than come here, and she didn't even know what 'here' was yet.

They entered Greygor's tent and Kane instinctively donned his mask of indolence. Greygor was a cunning bastard. If he knew Kane wanted something, he'd make him pay for it.

The soldier who held Lana pushed her forward and she landed on her knees in front of the Commander with a cry. The others left them.

Greygor looked down at her with a look of practiced disgust. 'This is your new slave? She looks half-drowned and smells like a latrine.'

Lana said nothing, just stared down at the floor. Greygor grabbed her chin and forced her to look up at him. His eyes narrowed.

Kane gritted his teeth, reminding himself that for once violence wouldn't help and neither would his gift. He couldn't erase memories, so whatever he made Greygor do would be remembered later and there would be a reckoning – unless he made the older man kill himself in an accident of his own making. Kane discounted the thought almost as soon as it emerged. A dead Greygor meant Kane would become Commander, which would put an end to his unit's plans. The revenge they lived for would never happen, and that would be worse than death.

Instead, he leant against Greygor's desk and yawned behind his hand. 'You summoned me. I assume it's because you heard about our little acquisition. I understand your thinking, but as you can plainly tell, she's just a slave girl. She's pretty and she'll warm your bed well enough, but look at her. 'She's no spy from the Islands. Whatever Brother told you of her misled you.'

Greygor spared him hardly a look. 'You know it was Uth. Don't play your childish games with me, Kane. She's clearly no spy. But you're right, now I look at her she is pretty – a rare beauty in fact. You've brought me something that could be very useful at a difficult time, Kane, and I thank you.'

Three men stepped into the tent as if on command: Ryon, Torin and Bull. It took all of Kane's strength not to let anything slip in his expression. Ryon and his unit had voiced their dissent on the Brothers' imminent plunder of the Islands on more than one occasion. They'd been garnering support from others in the Camp, and Kane knew without a doubt that Lana would not be leaving with him. She would be ensuring their support and Greygor's command.

'Ah, meet your new masters, girl. After seeing you, I'd love to keep you for myself at least for a bit, but you have a higher purpose.' Greygor addressed the newcomers. 'I assume she meets with your approval?'

Ryon circled Lana slowly as the other two hung back. Her head was bowed again. He cut the ropes that bound her hands. 'Get up, whore.'

Lana rose slowly, looking tiny compared with Ryon and the others' large frames. They could crush her in an instant and they weren't known for their amorous skills. In fact, they were banned from the pleasure tents because so many women did not survive encounters with them.

'She belongs to my unit,' Kane drawled.

Greygor waved a hand. 'Not anymore. You know the rules, Kane. If you wanted to keep her, you should have claimed her. I have it on good authority that you haven't. But I'll make it up to you. First spoils of the Islands will be yours.'

Kane hid a scowl. There was nothing else he could do

here now. It was done. 'Very well. The very first, and the very best.'

'Good. It's finished then.' Ryon grabbed Lana's red dress by the bodice and ripped it off her in one swift jerk. She shrieked in shock as her gown fell to the floor in shreds and she was bared to their eyes. 'You don't mind if we examine the goods?' he asked, his eyes roaming over her as she tried to hide herself. 'Our whores don't get luxuries like clothes. Going soft, Kane?'

Kane's very being burned with fury, but he chuckled as her eyes found his. They were wide with horror. Ryon would pay for touching what was his – theirs. For every moment of her fear, Ryon's unit would be punished, Kane promised silently.

Greygor caught Ryon's shoulder and pulled him back from Lana. 'Take her if you will, but I want your support or I'll see yours and the others' throats slit while you sleep, no matter the cost.'

'Agreed.' Ryon smiled nastily. 'Now, my unit and I will be indisposed for a while.' He saluted Kane insolently and grinned. 'You should have claimed her before you crossed the river, Brother.'

Ryon took her by the back of the neck and pushed her to the two others. They grabbed Lana's arms and walked her out. They would parade her before the camp first, showing their prize before they took her to their tent and began their depravities. Kane didn't have much time.

Uth barged in. 'You promised she was to be given to me!' he snarled at Greygor. 'We have a score to settle with the bitch. Why is Ryon marching her around the camp? She won't last the night with them.'

'Hold your tongue, dog, or I'll cut it out,' boomed Greygor, and Uth was silent at once. 'Leave us.'

Uth's mouth opened and closed. Then he whirled around

and disappeared. Kane made himself shake his head in mock surprise. 'If I'd known the slave was going to be this popular, I'd have asked for more payment. Gods, I don't understand it. She's nothing special.'

Greygor shrugged. 'Some women have their uses.'

'Indeed. If you'll excuse me, I'll need to break the news to Sorin and Viktor. They were taken with her, but a trip to one of the pleasure tents will see them to rights.'

The Commander nodded and Kane strode nonchalantly from Greygor's tent. Once he was clear, he ran for his unit's, tearing open the flaps and finding no one inside. He swore loudly and turned just as the other two arrived.

'I didn't claim her,' he blurted. Viktor and Sorin didn't reply. They made no sound or movement for what seemed like ages. Then Viktor came forward and hit him so hard that he fell. But he didn't retaliate. He deserved this.

'Where is she?' Sorin snarled.

'With Ryon's unit.'

CHAPTER 20

LANA

Lana hung by her arms, limp. Everything Ryon and the other two had done so far echoed through her body. After her clothes had been ripped off and she'd been thrown to the proverbial wolves – at least she hoped they were proverbial. With the Brothers' gifts, a person didn't know, after all – the trio had walked her through the rows of tents, touching her, letting all look upon their unit's reward.

First they'd tied her wrists and hung her up in the middle of their tent as they'd bickered amongst themselves over who was going to rape her first and where. They'd pinched and poked, leaving bruises wherever they touched her, and laughed at her attempts to twist away from them. They'd reveled in her tears, touching seemingly harmless spots all over her body that caused excruciating pain and made her cry out. However, before they could do any more, they'd been called away – thank the gods. But she soon realised that this too was part of their awful torture.

They'd left her alone to anticipate their inevitable return to defile her in every way – as they had described in great detail. She'd long since stopped shaking in terror at their utterances. This was only the beginning. They would use her until she was dead. She prayed to the gods that she would faint into oblivion long before they were finished with her. But desperate hope clawed to the surface of her dread. If she survived these vile creatures, she was going to find a way to kill them, and then she was going to kill Kane for letting them have her.

Her face was grasped hard without warning and she cried out in alarm. They were back. She'd never heard them come in.

'Did you miss us, whore?'

'I want her cunt and then her arse.' A finger prodded at her rump and she twisted away. 'You can have your turn when I'm finished, Bull. Your giant cock always rips them apart.'

Two of them laughed as the third one complained he never got first dibs. Her lips curled into a snarl as she surveyed them. In truth they weren't much different from Ather, and she would never have given him the satisfaction of the screams she'd given them. The one who held her face smirked at her, and then her temper overcame her fear. She spat in his face.

'You're pathetic. You'd better kill me when you're finished because if you don't, I will hack off your tiny pricks and shove them down each other's throats before I cut out your fucking hearts!'

There was silence as they all stared at her for a moment and then began to laugh at her.

'She's got more spirit than I thought,' one of them chuckled, 'Breaking her will be all the sweeter for it.'

The one furthest away gurgled and fell, blood spurting from a small hole in his neck. Sorin stood behind him, a tiny knife the only weapon in his hand.

Ryon and the other one pulled their swords, but Viktor and Kane were already there. The next one died with his guts spilling out onto the floor. Even a Dark Brother was no match for three of his kind when he'd been caught with his cock out. Ryon was disarmed quickly and pushed to his knees.

He gazed around in fury. 'You can't do this, Kane. I have supporters. This will start a war. She was given to me fairly. You were there!'

'A war?' Kane laughed coldly. 'I have more support than the old fool and you put together.' He grabbed the man's hair and pulled his head back. 'She is ours.'

Ryon's eyes widened in terror. 'She is unclaimed! Our laws–' His words were cut off as his head was jerked and a knife put to his throat.

'Wait!' Lana cried.

Miraculously, Kane did as she said, but he rolled his eyes skyward. 'If he is spared, he is oath-bound to avenge his Brothers. He must die.'

'Cut me down.'

Sorin came forward and cut the ropes that held her, catching her in his arms and letting her down to the floor gently. When he was sure she could stand on her own, he stepped back, and she walked slowly to Kane, hiding the fact that her legs felt as if they would give out at any moment. She reached out tentatively and grasped the knife he held. With an indulgent sigh, Kane let her have it.

Her fingers were cold and tingled after being tied above her for so long, but she held it fast, shaking slightly.

She looked into her torturer's eyes. 'I told you I would kill you.'

She plunged the knife into his chest hard with a cry, cutting through flesh and being deflected by bone in her inexperience, but she buried it to the hilt all the same and he flopped over, moaning on the floor as he died.

She looked at Kane and the others. They were frozen in place in various states of disbelief.

'A cloak,' she said simply.

Viktor gave her his, wrapping it around her shoulders, and only then did her knees give out. He swung her up into his arms and he carried her away. She kept her eyes closed through the camp until they arrived at Kane's tent, and only when they were inside did she open them again.

She pulled away from Viktor and, feeling oddly as if she had come home, poured some warm water from a large jug into a basin. She let Viktor's cloak drop, heedless of the Brothers, who watched her every move in silence, and proceeded to sponge the past hours from her body as best she could. Everywhere they'd touched her had bruised, and she was covered in dark marks.

When she was finished, she didn't even spare them a look as she climbed into the nearest bed and went to sleep.

WHEN SHE WOKE, the first thing she saw was Kane. He was sitting in a chair next to the bed. Without a word, he handed her a wooden cup. Discovering it was water, she drank thirstily.

Kane took it from her and set it on the floor.

Lana regarded him with disgust. 'Betrayer', she whispered.

Kane at least had the decency to flinch.

She pushed the covers away so he could see what they had done. 'I won't thank you for the rescue. Everything they did was because of you. You killed my father and then you did this to me. I don't want to look at you.'

He stood up and she thought he would leave. Instead he began to unbutton his tunic.

'What are you doing?' she asked in alarm.

'Greygor will just take you back and give you away again or put you in one of the pleasure tents to punish us for what we've done if you don't truly belong to us by our laws. Whether you want to look upon me or not, it must be done before he hears that Ryon and the others are dead.'

She sat up with wide eyes. 'What must be done?'

'I should have done it before. I was a fool. If I had, Greygor wouldn't have been able to take you from us.'

'What must be done?' she asked again, pulling the blankets around her as if that would keep her safe from him. Then she noticed Sorin and Viktor standing in the shadows, watching silently.

'A woman who is not part of the Army is treated as spoils until she's allocated a place either in the tents or in domestic labor. In many ways, taken women keep this camp going after they are forced to make their lives here.' Kane kicked off his boots and she shrank back as he loomed over her. 'We've decided not to give you to the Army so you must be bound to us and claimed.'

Her bottom lip trembled and she willed it to be still, hoping he didn't see how afraid she was. After the day's events, she was drained yet on edge. She wanted them all to leave her be, yet she feared being alone.

'So now *you* rape me?' She tried to sound defiant and haughty, but her voice wavered, and inwardly she cringed.

His eyebrow raised. 'Hardly. You'll enjoy it – well, most of it.' He reached for her slowly.

'I don't want it. I don't want you,' she spat as she jumped from the bed and put it between them, neatly evading him.

'Do you want to be given to others? Put in a pleasure tent?' He sounded more like an exasperated lover than a would-be ravisher, she thought, but she couldn't forget what he was.

'No. Of course not.'

He came around the bed and she moved the other way, keeping the distance between them.

'Then it must be done. You'll be one of us after you're claimed and bound. A Fourth, a Brother and a member of this unit. You will be trained and you'll never be a slave again.'

She snorted. 'For a price.'

He rolled his eyes at her. 'A tiny price and the way of things, I think you'll find. How you can be so naïve in this world is beyond me.'

'There must be another way. Please.' She couldn't help the pleading note that entered her voice, though she knew he would have no mercy. He couldn't even understand such a thing.

He stopped moving around the bed. 'There isn't. Now, come here.'

'No.'

'You were more than willing yesterday on the riverbank,' he growled. 'You were practically begging me to fuck you, moaning and gasping for me to fill your tight cunt.'

'Stop it!' she said, covering her ears.

'You will do as I say or I will make you, woman!' His voice was quiet and hard.

'Kane,' came Sorin's voice from the shadows, low in warning.

Kane looked beyond her to the two men who still watched them. 'You both know as well as I this must be done and done quickly.' His eyes focused back on her. 'I know you are untried. I will be as gentle with you as I can be.'

He lunged across the bed and she jumped back, but

Viktor was waiting behind her. His hands closed around her shoulders, trapping her.

'No! Let me go!'

Viktor hushed her and, clasping her hands gently at the small of her back, walked her back to Kane.

'Kane is right. This must be done before Greygor finds out that we've gone against his orders. He will take you back if you're not claimed by our unit. Maybe not today or tomorrow, but at some point, we won't be here to protect you and he'll have you seized. He and as many others as he likes will defile your body however they want. If you survive, he'll kill you just to spite us. We can't let that happen, Lana. You're a part of us whether you want to be or not. This is for your own good as well as ours.'

He held her while she struggled fruitlessly and Kane closed in. His hands skimmed her naked, bruised body, making her shiver even as she twisted this way and that, trying to get away. But Viktor held her firmly and, at Kane's nod, began to kiss her neck, snaking an arm around her waist as the other stayed where it was to keep her arms in place. She made a sound that was meant to be a scream, but to her horror it came out as a breathy moan. She clamped her lips shut and put all her strength into fighting them, but it was no use. She was no match for even one of them, let alone two.

Sorin appeared to her left, walking slowly out of the darkness to stand next to her.

'Please don't let them do this, Sorin.'

He gave her a half smile, caressing her cheek with the backs of his fingers. 'You'll thank us later, I promise.'

He slid his hand through her hair, pulling it, and when she opened her mouth to yell, he claimed it with his own. Hard and unyielding, his tongue probed and explored even as she felt fingers kneading her breasts. Unbidden, her tongue began to mimic his in an odd dance that made him groan and tug on her curls again, angling her mouth up to his as his other hand cupped her jaw.

Kane's lips fastened on her nipple, sucking and biting it softly, making her arch into him with a whimper muffled by Sorin's mouth. Kane's fingers pinched and rolled the other one and she began to quiver.

Kane murmured something and Viktor picked her up, Sorin's mouth disappearing from hers. Viktor sat on the bed with her in front of him and, blessedly, he let go of her hands. But just as quickly, Sorin grasped her arms and held them above her head, keeping her immobile as Viktor took hold of her knees and leant back, taking her with him and spreading her legs wide for Kane. She could feel Viktor's large cock under her through his leathers and wondered what the claiming actually was. Would they all fuck her? The images these thoughts conjured did not revolt her. Instead she heard Viktor swear under his breath at her back and realised she'd been moving her arse against him. She stopped immediately and heard him chuckle.

Kane knelt in front of her. His breeches were still on, but he was bare from the waist up. Though scarred in some places, his stomach, chest and arms were a testament to his warrior life. Her eyes widened as they roamed over him. Like the others, he was a chiseled god.

She swallowed hard as he leaned forward, putting his hands on her thighs to push her legs even further apart.

Kane said nothing, but his expression darkened and Lana suspected he saw yet more bruising between her legs. He put his tongue there, at her base, and her breath hitched. He licked upwards in one smooth stroke up her slit, which made her shudder and her hips move without her meaning them to. She gave a low moan as he pulled her nether lips apart and gave her a slow perusal. One thick finger gently explored, sliding into her, and she gasped, writhing under his touch.

'She's ready.' His eyes met hers with more than a little masculine pride. 'More than ready.'

She knew he spoke the truth. She could feel wetness leaking from her and it seemed to please him. With one final, pleasurable lick, he surged to his knees and unfastened his leather breeches. He too was ready and released his immense cock, which seemed to get even bigger in his hand. She looked up into his eyes, her nostrils flaring as she breathed in and tensed.

'Relax, Lana,' whispered Viktor into her ear. 'He'll do the worst of it quickly.'

Lana willed her taut muscles to loosen with minimal success, but it didn't matter. Kane's cock probed her where his finger had gone before. He moved his hips forward and she watched with a whimper as he positioned himself. He was impossibly thick. Surely it couldn't fit, but he pushed forward until he was just inside.

He locked eyes with the others and their grips on her arms and legs tightened. Then he looked at her and for an instant she saw guilt. She opened her mouth to tell him it was all right, that he was right; as insane as it was, she did want this. But Kane thrust at that very moment in one quick movement, burying himself to the hilt. She cried out, thrashing as she tried to escape the immense fullness and the sting of pain.

Kane didn't move, allowing her tight passage to stretch. The discomfort abated slightly after a few moments, and she opened her eyes to see a sharp dagger in Kane's hand. Before she could make another sound, he'd made a small cut above her left breast.

She watched in confusion as he bent down and licked the drop of crimson that trickled from the tiny wound. Sorin reached down and smeared some on his finger. Her eyes followed his hand up as it went to his lips and he licked the blood from it, and she felt Viktor stretch to do the same.

Then Kane began to move his hips. With every thrust, Lana cried out as his cock filled her painfully and she hoped he would finish quickly. But then, gradually, other sensations began to build, and before she realised it, she was moving her body in time with his, undulating her hips as she strived for even more of him inside her. He pumped into her hard and fast and she moaned loudly.

Somewhere amidst the hard cock thrusting into her, Viktor rubbing himself against her while he bit and kissed her neck, and Sorin reaching down to play with her breasts, Lana saw another man standing in the shadows. She looked up at Kane and found him staring into the darkness himself. He glanced back down at her, his eyes triumphant.

'Spread her wider,' he commanded, and Viktor's fingers tightened on her knees, splaying her legs even more. Kane pistoned into her more vigorously, rubbing against that part of her that they'd touched before. What had been building inside her overflowed. She screamed as ecstasy enveloped her, straining against the hands that held her, and the tight coil of pleasure was abruptly released in a tumult of sensation. After what seemed like forever, she collapsed back into someone's arms and nestled against a large chest as her limbs were freed. She yawned and half-listened to their murmured conversation, her eyes closed in exhaustion.

'It's done.'

'She seemed to enjoy it.'

'You did well. I didn't think she would find release tonight.'

'Open her legs.' That was Kane.

He would show them the other marks that had been left

by Ryon and the others when they'd continually poked at her with their hard fingers.

She made a sound of displeasure as her legs were spread slightly.

'Hush now, girl; no one's going to take you again, not yet.'

There was silence before she heard one of them curse and Sorin spoke in soft tones. 'We should have made them suffer more before we killed them.'

'It's too late now. At least she had some revenge.'

A laugh.

'I couldn't believe it when she stabbed Ryon in the chest. I didn't think she had it in her.'

'If there was ever a sign that she's one of us, that was it, to be sure.'

'I suppose she really is our Fourth.'

'Well if she's not, it's too late now,' came Kane's dry reply.

One of them began to gently wipe Kane's seed from her with a warm cloth, and she sighed in tired contentment, nuzzling into the Brother who held her.

'Let her sleep now. Her training begins tomorrow.'

'Who will tell Greygor?'

Kane chuckled. 'He already knows.'

CHAPTER 21

VIKTOR

Viktor stared down at Lana in his arms, almost not believing that she was truly theirs. He'd been so angry the last time he'd seen her, after she'd stolen from them. He still was if he was honest. Sorin was right. He was still furious at his wife's betrayal, though she was long dead. He might always be, he thought, but it wasn't Lana's fault and she shouldn't have to pay for it.

He'd still have to punish her. After what they'd done, Greygor would definitely demand it. She was part of the Army now. The lesson had to be taught, and it was the rest of the unit's duty to ensure she learned it well. He'd be lying if he said he wasn't anticipating it, but it wouldn't be done out of malice and definitely not until she was healed.

Ryon and his Brothers seemed to only have left bruises though. Thank the gods they'd gotten to Lana in time. Any later and she'd be in a much worse state.

Lana murmured in her sleep and her fingers curled into the hair of his chest. His arms tightened around her and he closed his eyes just for a moment.

When he opened them, she still slept and Sorin was

watching them from a chair. He held up a small ceramic jar of salve and Viktor nodded.

Sorin began to rub the balm lightly into Lana's bruises, covering each one from her head to her feet while Viktor moved her gently this way and that. He opened her legs and watched Sorin's hands massage her inner thighs. Then his fingers began to work between them, up and down her slit, dipping slowly into her channel and the tight pucker of her arse, giving the hurts there the most attention.

She moaned in her sleep, her thighs widening further at Sorin's ministrations, and he smiled. Sorin left one finger in her arse and moved another in and out of her other entrance in a leisurely manner as Viktor found her tight bud and began to rub it gently. Soon, she was squirming in his arms, mewling and gasping. Then her body went taut as a bowstring and she let out a long moan as she found pleasure in her sleep. Still she didn't wake.

They grinned at each other. Her body was made for the things they were going to do with her. She was so responsive and willing even in her reluctance. Once she began to understand the nature of the bond they would soon share, she would stop this incessant need to feel embarrassed about her desires. She would realize that pleasure was infinitely better than shame.

'Take her,' Viktor whispered, handing her over to Sorin, who cradled her like a babe.

'Where are you going?' Sorin asked quietly as he lay on the bed with her.

Viktor pulled on his boots and donned his cloak. 'Her training begins today.'

Sorin looked curious. 'It does.'

Viktor rolled his eyes. 'She needs clothes. She's not going out there with nothing covering her body. We'll likely have to kill the whole fucking camp. And don't leave her alone. It's early after the claiming, and we haven't finished the binding ritual. If she tries to escape, the gods only know what trouble she'll get into.'

Sorin nodded in agreement and Viktor left their tent. The day outside was only just beginning. The sun peeked over the tops of the hills and its light started to spread over the valley below them. He'd slept all night with Lana in his arms, he realised with surprise. Viktor rarely slumbered so deeply these days, and never with a woman. As he picked his way down the muddy walkways between the other tents, he shook his head in wonder. Already he wanted to be back in that bed with her even if he must share it with Sorin as well. He didn't even want to fuck her. Well, he did. Of course he did, but he would be content with simply holding her. What was wrong with him?

He stopped as he came to the main row of their camp. Their army was large and usually on the move. Each unit had their own store of foodstuffs and other supplies, but the camp itself also had the typical useful businesses of a small town such as a tanner, baker and bootmaker, among others. Viktor took care of his business quickly, stopping to retrieve some items he'd ordered a few days before for Lana, glad now that he'd had the foresight. On a whim, he also stopped quickly for some spiced buns. She was probably bored with the meat, fruits and nuts the Brothers lived on. He trudged back to their tent, each step closer to her making his heart feel lighter. He growled at himself in disgust. He was like a lovesick pup. Pathetic. He hadn't even been like this with his wife.

As he neared their tent, he noticed a familiar, mangy wolf sniffing around the entrance. When it saw him, it scrambled away, but not before Viktor gave it a swift kick up the arse. It yelped and darted out of his path as Viktor drew back his foot to strike it again.

'Get the fuck out of here, Uth. She's claimed now. You can't have her.'

The air rippled as Uth transformed into the naked man, holding his arse cheek with a pained expression. 'I don't care if she's claimed. Greygor promised her to us! The debt the bitch owes us will be settled one way or another!'

'What debt, you flea-bitten cunt? She didn't let you and the others beat and rape her. You want to ease your damaged pride is all, because she bested you. I see you or the other two near our tent again and we'll gut you like we did Ryon and the others.'

Uth's lips curled back into an ineffective snarl. Viktor pushed him out of the way and entered their tent without sparing him another glance. He placed the items he'd purchased on the table, stuffed a spiced bun into his mouth whole and looked around. Everything was as it should be. Sorin and Lana were still on the bed. He thought them asleep until he heard a low moan.

Clearly Sorin couldn't wait until later to play with her. Already feeling his cock beginning to harden, Viktor walked around to the bed, but found Sorin asleep on his back. He frowned. Next to him, Lana was dreaming, and it didn't look like a pleasant one the way she was tossing and turning.

'No,' she whimpered, her arms and legs jerking. Tears leaked from her closed eyes. Viktor gripped her shoulder and tried to shake her awake, but she threw off his hand, opened her eyes, and let out a loud scream. She struggled from the bed, pushing him away from her hard enough for him to stumble.

He grabbed her before she could hurt herself. 'Lana. Lana! You're safe. It was a dream.'

She looked around as if wondering where she was and didn't seem to notice him at first. When she did, she covered her eyes with her hands.

'What were you dreaming about?'

She hesitated. 'I … I was back in that tent with those Brothers.' She tried to hold back a sob.

Viktor went to her slowly and drew her into his arms, surprised when she didn't pull away from him. 'They're all dead.'

'I know, but what if there are others? This whole camp is full of them.' She looked into his face. 'Full of you.'

He smoothed back her hair with both hands. 'You're part of our unit now. Word will spread and no one will hurt you again, little bird. I promise you.'

'What about you? What about last night?' she asked plaintively.

He tutted at her. 'Come now. We didn't really hurt you, did we?' It was more of a statement than a question. 'Sorin and I held you so you didn't harm yourself trying to fight Kane when there was no reason to.'

She drew back. 'And Kane?'

'His cock is quite big for your first. He took you as softly as he could. It won't be like that in future.'

'In future?' Lana gulped.

Viktor chuckled, caressing her cheek. He kept forgetting how innocent she was. 'Did you not enjoy it?'

'I did … after the first bit, but what about the knife?' She felt the small cut above her breast, which had already healed shut.

'That was part of the binding. We don't need to do that again. It means you're almost one of us now. You're not a slave anymore. You can come and go as you please. In fact –' He drew the Writ of Ownership Dirk had given him from his pocket and threw it into one of the braziers used to warm the tent. It caught light immediately and was reduced to ash in moments. Lana's mouth hung open.

'I can leave?' she asked in disbelief.

'Not without us,' he amended. 'You have no fighting skills. You need to be trained. Until then, one of us will always be with you. Our world is a dangerous one, as you well know.'

Her brow furrowed in confusion. 'But I thought – now I'm claimed, I'm safe from other Dark Brothers, aren't I?'

Almost unconsciously, he began to stroke up and down her arms. 'Well, you can't be taken from us by another unit and we will protect you. As a Dark Brother, you have the same rights as any one of us, but we have other enemies who would harm us if they could.'

'The fact of it is, my sweet, you're weak.' Another voice joined their conversation. Sorin, now sitting up in the bed, stood and sauntered over. 'We will make you strong, but until then you're a millstone – to all of us.'

CHAPTER 22

LANA

A millstone. Lana frowned at Sorin and Viktor. 'Then why did you buy me from Dirk? Why did Kane bother bringing me here at all after he caught me? I don't understand.' She shook her head in irritation. 'Since I met you, I've been attacked, beaten multiple times. I've lost my father *again*, been hung up like a piece of meat, displayed, taunted and tortured, and now claimed by a murdering sell-sword army. Why? Why me?'

Viktor's expression was hard, but he said nothing; his hands simply moved lightly up and down her arms, trying to soothe her, she supposed.

Sorin walked behind her and she tensed, but all he did was gather her long hair and plait it for her. 'We would have saved you from all of that if we could. If we could have left you in your old life, we would have, but we couldn't.'

'Why not? And,' she felt him tie a leather cord around the end of the braid he'd just finished, 'where did you learn to do that?'

'Because we're drawn to you as you are drawn to us, Lana, and that means something. We couldn't ignore it. As for this,' he tickled her neck with the end of the plait he'd just done, 'like you, I wasn't always a Dark Brother.'

Lana craned her neck to look at him. 'What did you used to be and what does it mean?'

Sorin gave Viktor a pointed look. 'It doesn't matter what I was, but you –'

She never found out what Sorin was going to say, for at that moment Kane strode into the tent.

'Is she ready?' His eyes raked over her naked body in a way that made her want to cover herself even though he'd seen every inch of her last night. 'Clearly not.'

Viktor gave her one last caress and went to pick up a package from the table. 'Clothes.'

Kane snatched it from him immediately and threw it at her. She caught it deftly and glared at him.

'Your reflexes could use work,' he remarked. 'Get dressed, woman. You're not a pleasure slave anymore, and your training starts now. I'll not have a liability in my unit.'

'I was hardly a pleasure slave,' she muttered, eyeing him as he was eyeing her. 'What will we be doing?'

Kane moved so quickly he was a blur and then he was looming over her. She wanted to stand her ground, but her body, conditioned for pain, instinctively cowered.

'Your training is whatever I say it is. Now, get dressed. We have a long day ahead.'

Sorin embraced her, giving her a soft, comforting kiss, and departed. Viktor grabbed her to him and fondled her breasts, making her heart quicken. He kissed her as well, but more roughly, his coarse stubble grazing her skin. They were so different from each other, she mused. Sorin was by far the gentlest, and Viktor was gruffer with her, angrier it seemed, and not just from what she'd done.

Kane was – she glanced over at him – well, she didn't know. He was a mystery; sometimes he seemed as if he cared, other times that he would rather be rid of her. She opened the package, the subject of her thoughts ignoring her in favor of writing at his desk. Inside was a black tunic, shirt, breeches and boots, which all fit as if they had been made for her, impossible as that was. There was no chemise – clearly undergarments hadn't been at the forefront of Viktor's mind – so she tore a length of linen from the bedspread to wrap her breasts.

As she donned the low-cut black vest and buttoned her tunic over it, she realised Kane had abandoned his task and was watching her, his gaze heating though he was trying to hide it.

'Well, you certainly look the part, I'll give Viktor that.'

She looked down at herself. He was right in some ways. The garb was similar to their black attire, but hers was more form-fitting. It wasn't shameless in the least, but the breeches fit snugly over her arse and the tunic nipped in at the waist. But it also left her movements free. 'It's different than yours,' she observed.

His gaze swept over her, lingering on her hips and chest, covered by the tunic but not disguised at all. 'Viktor had them made for you. Ill-fitting clothes are a liability in battle. You could get caught up in them, your movements could be slowed or they could easily be grabbed by your enemy.'

'Oh.'

'Are you …' He cleared his throat and stood. 'Are you in any pain from last night?'

She felt her cheeks heat up and stared at the floor. 'A bit.'

'It won't hurt like that again.'

'I know … It was explained.'

Kane approached her. 'I – The coming weeks will be difficult for you. Training will be rigorous.'

He surprised her by putting a hand on her shoulder almost affectionately. 'We are your unit now. That means we share each other's burdens, but we can't take this for you. It's too important that you are able to take care of yourself.' He stared at her for a moment before continuing. 'It's a good thing you already hate me, because if you didn't before, you definitely will after today.'

'What are you going to do?' she asked, wondering what the coming weeks were going to hold for her.

'What I have to, to ensure you learn to be one of us. But no matter what, you are to stay by my side, do you understand?'

She nodded.

'Come.' He ushered her towards the tent opening.

'Where are we going?'

'The fields. Today is about strength and combat.'

'I'm going to learn to *fight*?' Lana's eyes widened. She'd been filled with trepidation about her new life here, but now excitement flooded her. A month ago, she would never have believed this could happen. If she could learn to defend herself, never again would men like Ryon and Ather be able to bend her to their wills, beat her, hurt her. At last she would have more than some slim hope that the gods would intervene on her behalf. Finally, she would control a piece of her own fate.

'Yes.'

She couldn't help it; she grinned.

He frowned at her. 'It will be grueling. It will take time and I will drive you hard,' he added ominously.

They walked out of the tent and she followed him, still smiling, to where the lines and lines of grey canvas dwellings gave way to grasslands. There were many men training, some with their hands, others with weapons. If anyone noticed her in their midst, they didn't show it or they were too busy to care. Kane showed her how to stand and began to demonstrate how to move. His lithe, quick steps belied his size, and though she tried to match his seemingly basic movements, she found that she couldn't. He made her hold her body in various positions that quickly had her breathing hard and her ears roaring. Sweat trickled down her face and neck as she balanced on her toes and elbows. She felt his boot under her stomach, pushing upwards.

'Keep yourself straight!' he barked.

Her body shook as she tried to do what he asked but began to sink down again almost immediately. Finally, he told her to stop. She got to her feet, realizing that this was only the beginning.

'GET UP!' he snarled at her, making her flinch in spite of herself. 'Do you think your enemy will give you time to get out of the way of his sword?'

Lana rolled onto her front and got to her knees as quickly as she could, every muscle in her body screaming at her to lie back on the ground. She forced herself up with a hard breath only for Kane to catch her unawares and knock her down once again with a well-placed strike, winding her despite the padded leather she now wore for sparring.

'Again!'

Lana gasped, rolling again to her knees and this time keeping an eye on Kane. When he came in for yet another attack, she rolled away and tried to kick his leg out from under him, but he wasn't where she thought, and again she was on her back in the grass. She hit the ground with her fist. He was right, the pompous prick; if she hadn't hated him before, she did now without a shadow of a doubt.

'Keep your focus and get up!'

With a growl and a burst of energy, she surged up and parried his attack, their wooden weapons clonking together so hard, it made her arm hurt, but she didn't care. She had blocked him! Then his leg came around, knocking hers out from under her easily, and she was on her back again.

The morning was spent thus. Then there was a small afternoon meal and more of the same well into the early evening. By the time Kane brought her back to the tent, Lana's body was covered in new bruises and every part of her from her toes to her red plait hurt. She sat heavily at the table and let her head fall forwards into her arms.

'You did well today.'

Lana's eyes narrowed at her tormentor's voice. 'It didn't feel like it,' she muttered.

She heard a chuckle and resisted the urge to throw something at him.

'Come.' Kane pulled her up, but she sank back.

'Where? I can do no more today. I swear it. I doubt my hand can even grip a sword.'

He pulled her up again and she reluctantly allowed him to draw her to where the largest wine cask she'd ever seen had been brought into the tent. She'd noticed it before, but now she realised it had been cut in half, scoured, and filled with hot, steaming water.

'A bath!' she exclaimed.

'Sorin said you had a preference for them. I couldn't get a real bath, not yet, but this will do until then.'

'T-thank you,' she stammered. First the clothes and now this. They were *giving* her things. She wouldn't have believed Kane capable of being so thoughtful, even if Sorin had helped him. 'I don't know what to say.'

To her mortification, tears came to her eyes. It had been a long day. Kane had warned her, but she hadn't really understood. But this ... She couldn't wait to sink into it and relax her aching limbs. She could think of nothing she'd rather do at this moment.

She turned to him and smiled.

His brows drew together. 'Tears?' He sounded confused.

She dashed them away with a laugh. 'I'm just tired is all.'

'I have some business. Sorin or Viktor will be here soon. Have the bath while it's still hot. My men, *our* men, were ages bringing ewers of hot water to fill it.'

She gave him a nod. 'This is lovely. Thank you.'

He said nothing, just left. Lana shook her head. Now she was confused. She would have expected him to make her undress in front of him or join her in the bath; something. The more she thought about it, the more she realised she was disappointed that he hadn't. *He killed your father. He killed your father.* But even that little mantra was no longer keeping her heart hard against him. She climbed into the massive barrel, which was more than big enough for her, and sank down into the hot water, closing her eyes with a sigh of contentment.

'I TOLD you she'd like it.'

Lana started, eyes opening with a gasp to find Sorin and Viktor standing next to her, staring. She sank deeper into the water, uncomfortable with their scrutiny.

Viktor cocked his head slightly. 'You did. I thought she might be over this embarrassment by now, though. We've seen her body countless times.'

Sorin's eyes were fixed on her, making her pulse quicken. 'I like it.'

He began to remove his clothes. Should she get out of the water ... stay? Unsure of what he wanted, she tensed, panicking and futilely seeking escape. He took off everything, and when he was naked, he threw himself over the side of the barrel with a whoop.

Lana leapt out of his way with a shriek, but as he came to the surface laughing, she couldn't help but giggle as well.

Playfully, she splashed him as he cleared his eyes, and he gave a mock growl.

Viktor rolled his eyes. 'Well, there's no way three of us will fit in that thing, as much as I would like to join you, so I'll see you both later.' With that, he vanished from the tent, leaving her with Sorin.

She stared at him bashfully, hiding herself from his eyes.

'I do like it, you know.'

'Like what?' she murmured.

'That you're so shy. It makes me want to fuck you.'

She felt her cheeks heat at his words and hoped the hot water had already reddened them. 'Thank you for the bath. Kane said it was you who told him I'd enjoy this. If any one of you was going to be caring here, I knew it would be you.'

Sorin's eyes narrowed at her words. 'I'm not some virtuous creature, Lana,' he said sharply, making her flinch. 'I've done awful things – even before I joined the Brothers. You do us both a disservice if you believe me to be kind. I'm as selfish as Kane. I'm just a better liar.'

Lana shook her head adamantly. 'I don't believe you.' She held up a hand when his mouth opened to argue. 'I don't doubt that you have, as you say, done awful things, but I don't think you're as self-seeking as you think. In fact, I know you aren't.'

'How would you know?' he scoffed. 'Look at you, innocent little thing.'

She bristled at his condescending tone. 'Well, the bath for starters. You wouldn't have thought of it otherwise, wouldn't even have remembered how much I like them.'

'I would if I knew it would sway you towards me, soften you so I could do what I liked with you without having to tie you beneath me and force your legs open,' he said crassly.

She tilted her head. If he thought his words would scare her or make her turn away from him, he was mistaken. 'You already can; you know you can. I don't understand why, but I would do anything for you and Viktor, even Kane after what he's done. It frightens me, but it's the truth. Even when you say things like that.' She looked away. 'Especially then,' she whispered.

He lunged for her with a growl, taking her mouth hard as his hands gripped her knees and forced her legs wide beneath the water.

'So you like it when I talk about fucking you roughly, eh? Do you want me to force you? What about Kane and Viktor? Shall we all take you whenever we like, wherever we like, just as if you were our little pleasure slave?' He groaned. 'When Kane said that this morning … Oh, the images it put in my head of you … The things I'm going to do …'

She gasped as his thick fingers plunged into her in one swift stroke and whimpered as he eased them out, only to thrust them in again. She clung to him, wrapping her legs around him. And his thick cock forced its way into her passage as his fingers withdrew. He stood, lifting her from the water and half sitting her on the edge of the thick barrel, using it as leverage as he pistoned into her. He caught her lips again, his tongue plunging into her mouth, mimicking his shaft as it moved in her. She came, screaming his name as her legs went to jelly and he shouted, spurting his seed deep into her as she spasmed around him.

They sank back into the water and didn't move for an eternity, their breathing slowly returning to normal. He pulled away from her slightly and she mewled her response. He hushed her with a chuckle and set about washing her thoroughly with the soap she'd noticed on the side. He lathered her hair and body, dousing her clean, and got out of the tub. He used a blanket to towel himself and then helped her out, drying her as well. It was only then that she realised that Viktor and Kane were sitting at the table, eating. The way they were looking at her made her sure they'd been in the tent for most of what had just happened with Sorin. She felt herself flush, and Sorin nuzzled her neck from behind with a grunt.

'How could you not enjoy these constant blushes?' he asked the others, and she lowered her eyes, reddening even more.

He led her to the bed, naked, of course, and tucked her in.

'Get some rest,' he whispered. 'Tomorrow you train with me, my little pleasure slave.'

Her eyes widened and he laughed. 'You'll enjoy it, I think.'

She shook her head at his easy charm and yawned. She knew she was right about him even if he didn't. The last thing she remembered as she drifted into the depths of sleep was something that tasted coppery dripping into her mouth.

CHAPTER 23

KANE

It was for their unit that they lived. His Brothers were his family, as he was theirs. Kane tried to keep those thoughts in the forefront of his mind as Sorin and Viktor stood in front of him, muttering their reproofs in forceful whispers so as not to wake their newest member.

'We watched you with her from the treeline yesterday, Kane. You were treating her as if she's been here for months. It was her first day of training,' Viktor said harshly, his eyes blazing as he stared Kane down.

Kane's lip curled into a snarl. 'We start for the coast tomorrow!' he said in a low voice. 'The invasion of the Islands will begin within weeks and she will have to be with us on the first ships. I'm trying to keep her alive!'

Sorin stepped forward and jabbed Kane in the chest hard. 'You trained with her yesterday. With everything you had her doing, it was up to you to make sure she ate, at least!'

'It wasn't Kane's fault.'

They all turned at the soft voice and watched Lana sit up, her eyes sleepy. She yawned and it took all of Kane's self-control not to pounce. Watching her with Sorin last night had left him rock hard, and things hadn't improved much with the dawn. He forced his eyes away from her delightful body, wishing he could retreat without them all noticing.

'It's early. Go back to sleep,' he ordered.

Ignoring the command, she got out of bed, careful to shield herself from their view completely, he noted in amusement. After wrapping herself carefully in the bedsheet, she walked slowly to where they stood. A free woman she might be now, but she was still theirs and he itched to show her that.

'We didn't mean to wake you,' Sorin began, but she held up her hand.

'Then perhaps you shouldn't have been having an argument while I was trying to sleep,' she admonished to Kane's surprise. She was different this morning, bolder. She sat at the table with a grin. 'I didn't eat last night because I was tired and I wanted the bath more.'

Not saying anything else, she grabbed some food from the table, tearing some bread from the loaf and cutting meat from the joint. She ate slowly, clearly savoring her meal, and disregarded them for the most part.

Meanwhile, Kane mused, the three of them stood there like fools; her court dancing attendance. His eyes narrowed.

'There. You see?' He sneered. 'She's acting the freewoman already.'

Her eyes widened at his tone and dropped to the table. He could see what she was thinking. That she'd spoken out of turn, acted wrongly. He clenched his jaw, silently cursing. She'd spent years as a slave. It would take time for her to remember how to be a freewoman and even longer to learn how to be one of them. She wouldn't be strong if he kept pushing her down and frightening her. In the camp, he might as well paint a target on her back if she couldn't stand up for

BOUGHT TO BREAK

herself. There was a fine line and they all needed to find out where it was.

He closed his eyes and drew a hand through his hair before approaching her. She flinched away very slightly. She was still much more afraid of him than of the others. He didn't blame her.

A part of him wished that it hadn't had to have been him who'd been first, but Greygor would have accepted nothing else. After the things he'd done, it should have been Sorin. At least he could pretend to be gentle. But Kane didn't regret it either. He'd loved every second of it, ploughing deeply into her, making her accept all of him and being the only man to have had her as his Brothers had held her for him. Watching her pain and pleasure had been a heady combination, and he'd never felt its like before … and he could never do it again.

'I'm sorry, Lana,' he said stiffly. 'I didn't intend to mock.'

He didn't miss her response, though she tried to hide it. She was pleased but wasn't sure what to make of his gesture. He ignored the incredulous looks of Viktor and Sorin, who'd probably never heard him apologize to anyone. Instead he sat down next to her, racking his brains for something to say to try and build a bridge between them. Their unit was weak if their bonds with each other were weak. His mind failed him completely, but in the end she spoke first.

'I have questions. I don't know … I haven't been free since I was a child. I don't know what to do – how to be.' The last was said in a whisper.

He lifted her head with two fingers under her chin. 'The transition will be challenging – for all of us. But we will not hurt you, Lana; not unless you need it. You are ours, but we are yours as well. That is how the unit works.'

She perked up and looked up at Kane in consternation. 'What do you mean, that you won't hurt me *unless I need it?*'

Kane looked at the others, not sure how to explain.

Viktor interceded. 'He means that when one of us requires a lesson, the others will see to it. We will brawl and beat each other senseless – until the message is received, I suppose. But we can't do that with you; we won't.'

'So what will you –?'

Kane gripped her jaw and turned her head towards him. 'You'll be thrashed, Lana,' he said matter-of-factly.

She didn't hide her shock, her eyes flitting between them; something she did when she was nervous, Kane realised. 'You'll beat me? What –?' Her throat worked as she swallowed hard. 'What will you use?'

'Our hands, a switch or a cane, perhaps. But only if we think it's necessary.'

Her hands gripped the table. 'Where?'

Not sure of her meaning, Kane decided to answer everything she might be asking. 'You'll be stripped of your clothes, bent over this very table, and held still by two of us while the third lashes your arse and the backs of your thighs.' He hesitated before continuing. 'Perhaps between your legs as well; it depends on which of us is doing it and why.'

Her horrified expression stayed frozen on her face for several moments before she collected herself and it turned thoughtful. 'And what if I think one of you needs to learn a lesson?'

Kane shrugged, surprised yet again.

Sorin gave a short laugh, and even Viktor smiled.

'Well,' he said slowly, 'I suppose it's usually a group affair, so if you have a grievance, one of us could fight on your behalf.'

She wrinkled her nose. 'That doesn't seem fair. You all get to hit each other and,' she swallowed again, 'flog me, but I'll never get to do it to any of you myself.' She shifted in the seat. 'Not that I want to hurt any of you, of course,' she hastened to add. 'I just think if I'm truly one of you ...' She was silent for a bit as she deliberated. 'What if instead of brawling, two of you hold the third and I lash you just as you would me?' she asked finally.

Kane opened his mouth and closed it again. That sort of embarrassment was unthinkable for a Dark Brother to go through, and he said as much.

Her brow furrowed. 'So I can be beaten with a stick but you can't be, because it's humiliating to you? Do you not think it would be the same for me – why, because I was a slave before so I should be used to it?' She looked angry.

He glanced to the others, but they were silent, their eyes averted. So much for Brotherhood.

'The pain would be less for you,' he said finally, 'so there must be more humiliation.'

Her countenance suggested she didn't believe him and there would be more discussion about this later, but she moved on. 'I heard you talking about an invasion.'

Kane stood as one of the others began to explain. He had other business to attend to. Greygor had been avoiding him. He intended to catch the old man early before he could disappear for the day. He grabbed his sword and made for the exit.

'Kane.'

He turned to Lana's piercing gaze.

'Can you not stay for a moment? There was something else.'

He tried to hide his irritation. 'What is it?' he ground out.

'Last night I tasted blood. Was it a dream or did you all do something?'

He nodded at the others and they acceded reluctantly. They'd hoped she wouldn't remember and they wouldn't need to say anything, but they had agreed to tell her if she asked outright. Necessary blood magick in the Brothers wasn't usually discussed, it was just done.

'No. It wasn't a dream. It was the end of the ritual we began the other night when we partook of the essence of your life. You were required to taste ours as well, as we all did when we first became a unit. Each of us gave you a drop of our blood, just as each of us took a drop of yours. You're bound to us now and we to you.'

She leant back in the chair, regarding them not unlike a monarch. The slave of yesterday was rapidly being replaced by a freewoman, and Kane found he liked her newfound fire. 'And you didn't think to consult me?'

'There was nothing to ask. To become our Fourth, to be safe, it had to be done.' He turned to go, thinking about what he would say to Greygor.

He heard her sigh. 'I feel different today. Is that why?'

He turned back and gave her his full attention again. 'How do you feel different?' he asked pointedly.

'I feel … stronger – like I could take on the world. I've never felt like this before.'

'Perhaps that was just my lovemaking,' said Sorin, puffing out his chest.

She smiled and blushed, and Kane found himself wanting to grin. They'd wondered if she'd feel a change. All of them felt an awareness – a subtle and tenuous link between each other that they couldn't really describe. But they had all woken up with a sense of strength this morning and *whole*, as if some piece of them had been missing before.

'Are there other women in the Dark Brothers?' she asked quietly, looking him in the eye.

'There are. They're uncommon, but there are one or two. You'll probably meet Maeve at some point. She's a Fourth, but she grew up in the Camp. It might be useful for you to speak with her about life here.'

Lana nodded. 'But there's something else; something about me that's not usual.' She sat up straighter, watching him imploringly. 'Please, no more secrets. If I'm truly a part of you, keeping things from me will hinder, not help.'

Sorin gave her a sharp look. 'Outside this tent, you are the same as any other member of the Dark Brothers. You never say anything different. Ever. Understand?'

'No.'

Sorin sank heavily into the chair Kane had just vacated. 'It would be dangerous if anyone else thought what we think.'

'You mean what you think,' Viktor piped up from the other side of the tent. He'd abandoned their discussion and was now slowly sharpening his sword.

Sorin threw his hands up in exasperation. 'Whether I'm right or wrong, there are Brothers who believe the stories,' he said in a soft voice. 'Any one of them could be a problem if they suspected what I do.'

'What do you suspect? Tell me.' Lana's voice held fear, making Kane want to wrap an arm around her once more, an impulse that was becoming all too common. Inwardly, he scoffed at himself. As if she would even accept his comfort.

Outwardly, he chuckled and rolled his eyes. 'Stop frightening her with the whisperings of old men, Sorin. My part in this ridiculous discussion is over. I have business to attend.'

With that he turned, slipped out into the dewy morn with palpable relief and began to walk the short distance to Greygor's tent. He frowned. Where were these desires to soothe her and make her happy coming from? He could understand feeling protective. He was the same with Sorin and Viktor to a point, but he didn't give a fuck if one of them was sorrowful or upset unless it affected his Brother in battle.

Kane shook his head. He had to stop being weak with Lana. Their world was a cruel one. Better she found that out sooner rather than later. The invasion would help with that.

By the time the Islands were under their control, she would have seen for herself the brutality of the Brothers; the army of which she was now part. Her innocence of the world would be ripped away very soon. Hardening his heart towards her and pushing away the confusing emotions her presence always elicited, he entered Greygor's tent quietly. Kane wanted the old man to know he could simply appear in his sanctum with no one the wiser. Unfortunately, the bastard was already awake and sitting behind his desk, so his entrance was marked immediately.

Greygor observed Kane silently for a moment, his face a mask of civility Kane knew he didn't really feel now that he – and probably everyone else in the camp – knew his second had gone against his orders. He picked up his goblet, draining it nonchalantly. 'You claimed her, then.'

'As you saw. Bound her as well,' Kane drawled.

Greygor's eyebrow quirked. 'Yes, I watched. Quite a spectacle. It rivalled even the finest brothel shows in the north.' The old bastard shifted in his seat. 'I wouldn't mind a crack at her myself.'

Kane ruthlessly pushed down the sudden surge of intense anger that enveloped him, with only partial success. 'She's ours,' he rumbled.

Greygor waved a hand in dismissal. 'She's a Dark Brother. She can do what she likes with the other Brothers. There are no laws against it. Sorin certainly does whenever he gets the chance.' Greygor smirked. 'With whomever or *whatever* will have him, so I hear.'

'Sorin's bedmates aren't my concern,' Kane said quietly. 'But Lana is one of us now, and she is ours. She wants no one else.' Having said all he came to say, Kane turned to leave, not bothering to make his excuses.

Greygor either didn't notice or chose to ignore him. 'I've heard a story of our newest Brother stealing gold and a horse. Normally, as it transpired before, I wouldn't worry, but considering all that's happened since you brought her here, I want her punishment carried out. Soon.'

'It will be done,' Kane replied.

'We shall see, boy. We shall see. On to other matters. I'm down three of my best men days before one of the most important invasions in a hundred years. I suggest you find a way to make it up to me or perhaps I'll find another second.'

Kane felt his lip curl into a sneer. 'Indeed.'

'You seem different. Is there anything I should know?'

'No.'

Kane left without a backward glance. It was done for now, though he feared it was far from over. At least Greygor couldn't take Lana by force. He could try to seduce her, but he and the other Brothers couldn't do anything else without just cause. And what if Sorin was right? What if Lana was a witch the stories warned of? The alliance that had existed between them and the Army when they were still the sentinels of the realms was long dead. There weren't enough witches now to be a thorn in their side, but that wasn't really the point. If anyone did believe and suspect Lana, all of their lives would be in danger. There was little the Army feared, but the stories of the witches who's magick stole your fight and left you useless as a warrior were told in scared whispers while grown men shivered in terror and blamed the cold.

'There you are, Brother.'

'Quin.' Kane nodded in greeting but didn't stop.

The other man fell into step beside him despite Kane clearly not wanting to talk. 'I just heard something and I wanted to find out the truth.'

So it was starting to make the rounds. Kane stifled a sigh and reminded himself that it was a good thing. The more who knew Lana was untouchable, the safer she was for now. 'It's true. We claimed the girl. She's one of us now.'

Quin looked thoughtful. 'I thought you had no liking for her.'

Kane shrugged and muttered a farewell, veering away between the tents and hoping the man left him alone. He was in no mood to chat. He passed the training grounds and caught sight of Lana and Sorin. He was teaching her how to throw those tiny knives of his, and she wasn't too bad considering it was her first lesson. He watched them for a moment as they chatted easily, laughing freely with each other.

He almost wished he could be like that with her, but he didn't have that easy way about him that Sorin did. Kane frowned. Sorin did seem happier – they all did. Was it just because they'd got what they'd wanted and she was theirs, or was it something more? Was it possible that she was what Sorin said?

CHAPTER 24

LANA

*T*hrowing knives at an unmoving target was infinitely easier than learning swordplay. That much was clear to Lana within a few minutes of beginning her training with Sorin. And though her arms now ached from flinging the little daggers for hours, Sorin's company was markedly more desirable than Kane's. He even showed her how to pick locks, surprised when he told her that Kane was a master of sleight of hand and had taught him everything he knew. She would have thought their unit's indomitable leader too, well, *large* in body to be very stealthy whereas Sorin was a bit more lithe. All three men were so different, and not just physically.

Where Kane was all scowls and severity and Viktor brusque yet quietly caring, Sorin was almost always smiles and jokes. He had her chuckling all day as he told her funny stories and ribald tales. He told her she wasn't too bad with the knives, which she knew was a lie. But at least he made her feel like it was possible to learn these momentous things that all the rest of the Brothers seemed to be able to do so easily.

One day, perhaps, she would be an asset to their unit, or so she hoped. She desired the respect of all three men and knew learning their crafts was the way to get some degree of it. She didn't want her measure to be taken on her back, so to speak. There was more to her than that, and she would show them.

'Come.'

'We're finished already? But Kane said that training lasts until sunset.' She looked around and planted her feet stubbornly. Everyone else was still training. 'What will they think if we just leave in the middle of everything?'

Sorin rolled his eyes and waved a hand flippantly. 'Who the fuck cares, Lana? We're the strongest unit in this army. Anyone who remarks on our absence isn't training hard enough themselves and can suck my giant cock. Now, come.'

He practically dragged her back to their tent and ushered her inside before turning away to stow his knives with his things.

'I care,' she said as she watched him putting his weapons away with meticulous care.

'Hmm?'

He wasn't listening. Lana's brow furrowed. 'You said, "Who the fuck cares?" I care. I want to learn, Sorin. I don't want to be a millstone.'

Sorin twisted around so suddenly, she took a step backward uncertainly. 'Oh, Lana.' He framed his hands around her face and then tugged her plaited hair softly. 'I should have known you'd take that to heart. I'm sorry. Millstone was a poor choice of word. You're not a burden. The training will take time and you'll work hard, but you can't run before you can walk.'

'But Kane said—'

'I don't care what Kane said,' he interrupted. 'Kane can train you his way and I will mine. Understand?'

She nodded.

'Good. Have a meal and a bath. I have some work to do.'

Having been dismissed for the moment, Lana sat at the table and began to fill one of the pewter plates with food. Tonight, she was famished and very glad she'd been given time to eat before she fell over in exhaustion. She hadn't lied about not wanting food the night before, but they had made it a bit difficult had she felt like a meal. Kane's demands during training and Sorin's afterwards had left precious little time for anything else. Her cheeks heated as she remembered the bath she and Sorin had shared. She felt closest to him, without a doubt. He seemed to know what she needed before she did herself.

'And Lana.'

She looked up to where Sorin was now ensconced at the desk, parchments surrounding him.

'After you've bathed, come to the desk and kneel beside it.'

She nodded, wondering what was going to happen tonight. Her nethers clenched pleasurably and she knew that if Sorin were to feel between her legs now, he would find her already wet.

She finished her meal swiftly in anticipation and undressed, feeling Sorin's eyes on her. She didn't cast hers in his direction, however, just got quickly into the hot bath and sighed in contentment. She stayed in just long enough for her fingertips to wrinkle before she made herself clamber out gracelessly and wrapped herself in a blanket to dry.

'Remember what I said,' called Sorin, not looking up from his papers.

She breathed in deeply and let the blanket drop, wondering if she'd ever not feel embarrassed by her nakedness. She began to sink to the floor beside the desk as Sorin had bid her, but he stopped her with a gesture.

'Bend over the desk.'

'Why?'

He gave her a look. She hesitated a moment, but then did as he ordered, bending at the waist and laying her arms carefully on top of the piles of parchments so as not to disturb anything.

She felt Sorin behind her and started as his hand slid down her spine, over one globe of her arse and down between her legs. He pulled them apart and she gasped as he lightly caressed her slit before parting her and slipping his hand between. He made a contented sound when he found her wetness and his fingers delved into her slowly. Her breath hitched as he found that part of her inside that felt so pleasurable, but then his touch left her. She whimpered, straining back to find his hand, and he chuckled.

'Such a needy little thing now.'

He opened her again, but this time a digit pushed at her back passage. She pulled away, pushing into the table with a hiss as she tried to escape his persistent finger. He gave her arse cheek two quick smacks, making her rear up in surprise rather than pain as she cried out.

'Do as you're told or you won't like the consequences. Hold still.'

The command in his voice brooked no disobedience and she froze at once. She shook in distress, her previous ardor having fled completely.

He eased his finger past the tight outer ring and then eased it out again. In. Out. In. Out. Then something new prodded at her entrance. It was smooth and slippery and cold. She whimpered as he pushed it relentlessly, a thick round bulb that suddenly popped into her. She lay on the desk, unmoving as she tried to grow accustomed to the object embedded in her, but no amount of time seemed to help. She recalled the apothecary doing something similar to her, but his instrument had felt much smaller than this.

'Up you get.'

She stood, a hand immediately fluttering to investigate, but he slapped it away.

'You're to leave it there.'

'What is it?'

He smirked. 'Training.'

'Training?' she echoed.

'Of a sort.'

'I don't like it.'

'Some don't at first.' He tapped it with his finger and she jumped. 'But you will. Now, I'm afraid that your ordeal isn't over just yet.' Sorin looked behind her.

Viktor seemed to come out of nowhere. His face was hard and unyielding.

'What's going on?'

'It's time for a reckoning, little bird.'

'What do you mean?' But she was afraid she already knew. The punishment that had been alluded to.

'The penalty for taking my horse, knife and gold. The lesson must be learned. It has to be done. 'Sorin, lay her over the table. Twenty should do it.'

In his hand was a crop, and her mouth went dry. She saw Ather, his nasty grin, and broke out in a cold sweat.

'No! Sorin, please. I'm sorry. Viktor, don't.' The pitch of her voice began to rise. 'Don't do this. Please, I beg you! I'll never do it again, I promise!'

'Quiet her or gag her,' was Viktor's only response.

Her heart thudded in her chest and she gasped. Her breathing was shallow and quick. She felt like she was suffocating. She gripped Sorin's arm, her fingers digging into his flesh, and finally, finally he looked down at her.

His eyes widened. 'Viktor, wait. Lana? Lana! Breathe.' He

cradled her and sat down, stroking her wet hair while she tried to calm down.

'What's wrong with her?' Viktor asked, concern in his voice.

She didn't hear Sorin's reply, but when she lifted her head sometime later, the crop was nowhere to be seen.

'What happened, Lana?'

She looked away. 'It's foolish,' she muttered.

'Tell me,' Sorin insisted.

Her lip trembled. 'It was the crop. All I could see was Ather. It was as if I was back in that stable, bent over the saddle. I don't understand. He beat me lots of times and I was scared, but I never felt like this.'

Sorin sighed, hugging her close. 'It's not foolish, Lana. If you're this afraid, Viktor will use his hand, but the punishment will still need to be carried out. I'm sorry, love. If we don't do it, Greygor will have someone else carry it out publicly, and it will be much worse,' he whispered.

He stood up and set her on her feet. 'Come on.'

Tears came to her eyes as Sorin led her across the tent. She didn't struggle. It just delayed what was going to happen anyway. He bent her yet again, this time over the larger meal table. He easily held her immobile, clasping her wrists with one hand and his other arm across the middle of her back, anchoring her to the table.

'Kane?' Viktor asked from behind her, and Lana craned her neck to find out what was happening, but she could see nothing.

'I couldn't find him.'

'No matter. He isn't needed. Our word should be proof enough.'

She looked beseechingly at Sorin as he nodded at Viktor, ignoring her again now. 'Begin. She's not going anywhere.'

She froze as Viktor's hand caressed her arse, fluttering

over the thing Sorin had put inside her. His touch disappeared and was gone for so long she wondered if he was even still there. Then it came: a hard, painful smack of his palm that propelled her forwards, scoring her nipples on the hard grain of the tabletop. Another followed almost immediately, tearing the breath from her lungs. She gasped and bit her lip. Two more followed and another two, alternating sides. The flogging itself was being done quickly, but she wasn't sure if that was a good thing. The agony was so very severe, she lost count after eight. Tears flowed freely down her cheeks, but she didn't make a sound bar the occasional hard breath out. Strike after strike; her hips dug into the table's edge as she sobbed mutely, wishing her torment would end.

The final two were by far the hardest blows of all and made her open her mouth in a silent scream before Sorin let her go. As soon as he did, her legs buckled and she slid to the floor, her arse on fire and her nipples sore from being abraded on the rough wood. More tears fell as Viktor picked her up gently and settled her on her front on the bed.

'There now,' he cooed. 'You took your punishment well. Nary a sound. It's all over now.'

She buried her head into the pillow and sobbed as Viktor smoothed her hair and, a moment later, she felt the cold salve they used. He rubbed it into her skin hard, making her writhe, the pain of it almost as bad as the thrashing itself. She cried anew and he picked her up and cradled her against him.

'Hush now. It's done.'

But the tears wouldn't stop. 'I'm sorry, Viktor. I'm sorry for stealing from you. I didn't want to,' she hiccupped.

He hugged her hard into his chest. 'Hush. It's finished now. You'll feel better soon, I promise.'

To her surprise, she found that she did. She hadn't

realised the guilt she'd been carrying for abusing Sorin and Viktor's trust; for stealing Viktor's horse especially. She knew how much Viktor cared about his mount and hated that she'd done it even though she'd seen no other way. Now she felt cleansed of it, renewed, and the shame she hadn't known she was carrying seemed to have evaporated under the strikes she'd endured. Her tears dried and she shifted, trying to find a position that didn't make her wince, until Viktor took pity on her and finally deposited her back onto her tummy on the bed.

His hands began to skim over her cheeks reverently. 'You can't see it, but take my word for it when I say that your arse is a most beautiful shade of red.'

His hands continued to touch her lightly. It wasn't painful exactly, but the skin was so sensitive now that she squirmed under even the subtlest stroke. 'I do love a good flogging,' he murmured as his hand dipped between her legs. He gave a low whistle. 'So do you, it seems.'

She flushed. 'I don't understand.'

She looked up to see Sorin standing over them. He caressed her thigh, then travelled upwards, feeling her as well. His eyes shone in the low light. 'So she does. Positively dripping, you naughty girl.'

'But I didn't enjoy –' Her words died in her throat as two of Sorin's fingers easily slid into her. She moaned loudly and widened her knees as she angled her hips up to give him better access.

'You like submitting to us,' Viktor whispered in her ear. Lana scowled and he smiled. 'You hate that it excites you. But it does, Lana.' Viktor's hand delved beneath her and found her slit. Sorin was still plunging his fingers into her, and Viktor began to rub his thumb over her tight bud in little circles that made her mewl. 'It makes you so ready for us.'

She knew he was right, but she did hate it. She was a freewoman now. She shouldn't want to be told what to do or ordered about, and she definitely didn't understand why a painful spanking should excite her so. It never had when Ather had beaten her, so why did it now?

All rational thought fled as Sorin pressed the object in her arse in time with his other thrusts, and she gasped and panted under his ministrations. 'Please. More. I need …'

She whimpered in frustration as Sorin's fingers slowed and softened in their actions, as did Viktor's. Didn't they know what she wanted? She pushed her hips back further, silently begging them to continue. Then she growled as understanding dawned. They were denying her on purpose. She twisted her head around to look at them.

'This is part of my punishment.' She couldn't keep the hurt from her voice and Viktor leaned forward to put his lips on hers, his tongue exploring in gentle movements.

'No, this isn't penance, Lana. This is where you learn that patience has its rewards,' Sorin murmured.

His fingers began to move again, as did Viktor's. Her front sank down onto the bed as she moaned and the pleasure began to build, but just as she was reaching the crest, they stopped again. She snarled, but they ignored her and, once the pleasure had ebbed, they began again. Over and over they did the same. She lost count how many times until she felt the pleasure coming and, instead of ceasing, Viktor and Sorin switched places. But it wasn't Viktor's fingers he pushed into her tight channel; it was his cock, hard and fast and deep.

She screamed in sudden release, her hips bucking and her body convulsing wildly as every piece of her exploded in pleasure. She vaguely realised she'd sunk onto the bed, her arms and legs unable to support her weight as the waves of pure ecstasy crashed over her again and again. She heard Viktor cry out and felt his seed surge into her but was powerless to do anything but lie on the bed, her body sated beyond anything she'd felt before. They lay beside her, one on each side, and she closed her eyes in contentment. A sense of peace washed over her, broken only by a wayward thought that Kane wasn't there with them.

CHAPTER 25

SORIN

'You said I would grow to like this. I don't.'

Sorin sighed as he and Lana pored over books he'd had brought from their stores. The texts were new and old, but all were about war, battle and the history of the Brothers. There were also one or two on herb lore and basic medicine. Tending injuries was a daily task, especially on a campaign, which of course they'd soon be in the middle of. They'd arrived at the coast yesterday and would set sail tomorrow morning with the tide.

But back to Lana's problem. He knew what she was talking about. 'What is it about the object that you don't enjoy?'

Lana looked up at him and huffed. 'Yesterday I was training with Kane and I ... well, the movements we were practicing made me ...'

'Made you what?' Knowing at once what she meant, Sorin tried his best not to smile and was sure he'd succeeded until he saw her countenance darken.

'Made me ... Oh, I don't know what it's called! That thing that happens when you're touching me ... *there*.' She blushed.

'Did you come?' This time he didn't hide the unrepentant grin spread over his face.

'It's not funny! There were others training nearby and I'm sure they knew – and even if they didn't, Kane heard me! Smug bastard.' The last was muttered under her breath.

Sorin went back to reading his book, turning the page slowly. 'So, you don't like receiving pleasure.'

Lana's lip curled and her eyes narrowed. 'That's not what I mean and you know it. I want to learn. I want to train. How can I focus when that's happening?'

Sorin closed the book he was reading gently and regarded her. 'Do you believe that when you're in battle your enemies will let you focus on trying to kill them?'

'No, but–'

'Then perhaps this too is part of your training as a Brother. Have you considered that?'

Lana rolled her eyes. 'Sorin, if you're trying to make me believe that this *thing* up my backside is making me a better warrior, fuck you.'

Sorin laughed outright. He hadn't meant to, but Lana always did that to him; made him forget the serious Dark Brother and remember who he'd been before; a light-hearted lad who'd loved a good joke.

'I'd like nothing more than for you to fuck me, love, but there's no time just now.'

She looked taken aback and he regretted the endearment instantly. He didn't mean to keep saying it, but it fit. Of course it did. He just didn't want her to know the power she had over him. It was too soon. They'd only known each other a matter of weeks. And what if she didn't feel the same?

He tried to make light of what he'd said by feigning ignorance. 'What is it?'

'You called me "love". You've said it before, too.' She hesitated, looking shy. 'Do you?'

He should have known she wouldn't leave it. She was the type to unravel an entire horse blanket from one loose thread on a journey just because she was bored. 'Yes,' he said simply, shrugging unapologetically.

She grinned at him, shaking her head. 'I am a freewoman – I'm going to take it out.'

'As you will.' He looked at her deviously. 'But it does give you pleasure.'

Lana closed the book she'd been reading with a snap. 'You try going about your everyday business with a thing like this up your arse.'

'I did.' He flinched. He hadn't meant to say that out loud, either.

'What do you mean?' Her gaze bore into him.

Too late to take it back. Lana was exceedingly tenacious when it came to information. He'd found that out after he'd had the books brought. Expecting her to be a reluctant pupil, or at the very least to have to help her to relearn to read after years of not practicing, he was astounded when her eyes had lit with excitement and she'd fallen on them like a starving beast on a piece of meat. Not only did she remember how to read and write, but she was faster at it than he was.

'I ... before I was a Dark Brother, I was a pleasure slave.'

Her mouth opened and closed several times before she spoke. 'You. A pleasure slave? I don't –'

'I was young,' he cut in. 'A boy. I was born a slave into a wealthy house. I worked in the stables. They fell on hard times, so I was sold. I became a body slave. My master taught me pleasure when it suited him. He also taught me fear and pain and hate.' Even now, to think of those years made his fists clench so hard that his nails dug into his palms, making them bleed. Why had he told her these things? Viktor and Kane knew, but they had had to. If not for them, he would not one day have revenge.

'So you wore one of these as a slave?'

'Yes.' Sorin looked up, daring her to pity him, and swore to himself that if he saw it in her eyes, he would thrust his cock into her arse right now on this table and make sure he hurt her. But when he looked at her face, he found only an innocent curiosity. Sometimes he forgot how little she'd seen of the world.

'What was the worst thing he ever did to you?'

The question caught him unawares, but he knew the answer instantly, though he made a show of thinking. He tried to ease his uneven breathing as the old uncontrollable panic threatened to return. This was what happened when he talked about those dark days, the same surge of fear Lana had endured some days before, but Lana had asked and she was one of them. She had a right to know, even though Kane had cautioned them not to tell her too much.

He was hot, his palms sweating, but he continued. 'When I was sold, my mother wasn't. She stayed with the family. She was ... I loved her and she me. My master decided that though he had put many, many hours into breaking my body, my will was not tamed enough for his liking.' Sorin swallowed hard, not looking at Lana at all. 'The bastard bought her and he and some of his friends raped her in front of me. They spent hours at it, hurting her over and over. I couldn't help her. When they were bored with her and she'd long since stopped screaming, he told me to slit her throat or they'd do all of what they'd done to her, to me.'

He realised that she had come to him and knelt in front of him. She took his hands in hers and squeezed them gently. A part of him wanted to push her away and leave, but, for some reason, he didn't.

'How did you become a Dark Brother?' she asked quietly.

'One night someone came to kill my master. He almost succeeded, but my master was too slippery and escaped. He found me instead. I was a shadow; a pathetic little sex slave that he used and passed around to anyone he owed anything to – but my will was not entirely extinguished. Loathing still burned through my veins. The assassin saw that my hatred was as deep as his own, so he freed me and brought me to the Dark Brothers so that we could have our revenge together.'

'We?' Her brow furrowed. 'Who was the Brother who found you?'

'Kane.'

CHAPTER 26

LANA

Kane. That surprised her. She hadn't really thought about how the Brothers had come to be in the same unit. She'd assumed almost abstractly that there was some sort of system to choose – straws, perhaps. She'd also got the impression that Kane had been a Brother for longer than Viktor and Sorin, as he was second in command only to Greygor.

Lana kept Sorin's hands clasped in her own. She didn't feel pity, never that, but she wished she could take the pain she saw in his eyes away and replace it with something better. 'But didn't Kane already have a unit?'

Moments ago, she had been afraid she'd pried too much. His countenance had taken on a darkness that she had been sure meant he was going to hurt her, but he hadn't. Instead he had answered her questions as if confessing his past to her would lighten his burdens. Perhaps they would.

'He had the beginnings of one. He and Viktor were waiting for their third.'

Sorin's hands began to caress hers, fingers sliding to her wrists and dancing over the sensitive skin of her palms. Lana felt her body responding to his touch almost immediately. Her clothes felt too heavy against her and she could feel her nipples hardening through her tunic.

'Who was first? Who found the second?' She asked the questions quickly, as he had a tendency to rob her of her faculties. She already sounded breathless even to her own ears, and focusing on his words was becoming difficult.

'Kane found Viktor.'

'After his family was killed,' she murmured, talking more to herself than to Sorin, but he looked surprised.

'He told you about it?'

Lana hoped she hadn't spoken out of turn. 'Yes. He said they were killed in a fire.'

'That's all he said?'

'He told me that his wife and children died in a fire. He said he killed the men responsible and then he joined the Dark Brothers.'

Sorin's hands had stilled when she'd mentioned Viktor's past. Now he pulled them gently from hers.

'I think it's time you knew the rest. Do you want me to tell you?'

Lana hesitated, then nodded. She knew it wasn't Sorin's story, but she didn't think Viktor was likely to tell her more.

'Viktor and his wife married when they were quite young, as they ofttimes do in the remote villages of the north. His wife, Greta, was dissatisfied with her lot. She had married a farmer with few prospects, had two children, but she was still very much a beauty, as Viktor tells it. She was not faithful to her husband and she had a particular weakness for sell-swords. Viktor says he didn't know, but he must have suspected.'

Sorin shrugged. 'Anyway, one night a party of them rode into their village led by a man who was ... different; powerful and refined. She was drawn to him and ended up in his bed.

When it came time for them to leave and Greta found she would not be going with them as he had promised her, she was enraged. When she confronted him, this man had her beaten and taken to the house she shared with her family. He had the two young children secured in their beds and then he burned it to the ground. Viktor found them. Afterwards, he hunted most of them down and killed them, but one escaped.'

Lana shook her head. Poor Viktor; his poor children and even his wife hadn't deserved such a thing. 'I don't understand. Why would the man have done such a thing?'

Sorin smiled coldly. 'Because he could. My master likes to make sure everyone knows his control over them, and he enjoys making examples out of people.'

Lana's mouth fell open. 'Your master?'

'Yes.'

'The same man that made you his slave killed Viktor's family? But how did you find each other? Both of you hunting the same man is quite a coincidence.'

'Three. Kane also.'

Lana breathed out hard. 'What did he do to Kane?'

Sorin stood slowly and she rose as well, sensing this conversation would soon be at an end. He tucked a tendril of her hair that had come loose behind her ear.

'He's never confided the whole story. It was when he was a boy. That's all I know. Perhaps he will tell you one day.'

'Doubtful,' Lana scoffed. Kane had barely looked at her since the night she'd been bound to them. Even while training her he was cold and detached, only speaking to reprimand her or explain something, making it clear that even a child would know better than she, whatever it was. He seemed to exist only to humiliate her and find her wanting in every single way.

'Whatever he did,' Sorin continued, bringing her thoughts

back to the present, 'it was enough for him to devote his life to finding this man. Since we were barely men, all of us have spent our years looking for him so that we can have our revenge.' Sorin eyes lit with excitement. 'We've searched so many places and found only traces of him, but he is close. In just days we invade the capital city of the Islands. He had ties there, we're sure. We are going to find him, Lana, and finally we are going to do all the things to him that we've been dreaming about for years.'

'What does he look like, this man? What else do you know about him?'

'His name is Vineri. He's thin, tall and his lip is always curved into a sneer, as if he thinks himself better than all those around him. He likes boys, but women too. No one is safe from his attentions. He lives to break people any way he can. He dresses in the finest silks, owns fine houses. He's a collector.'

'What does he collect?'

'Objects that are interesting or unique. He likes to have things that no one else does, and he will pay, steal and kill for his prizes.'

Without thinking about what she was doing, Lana's hand fluttered up to cup Sorin's cheek, caressing the stubble starting to grow, though he shaved his face religiously every morning. Surprising herself, she eased her fingers into his hair and tentatively ran them through the coarse dark strands. Then she clasped the back of his neck gently and pulled his head down towards hers. He looked as shocked as she felt by her actions, but something else as well. *Hungry.*

'Do you want me to leave you to your demons?' she asked quietly.

'No.'

His voice was hoarse and strained. He sank back onto the chair behind him and pulled her onto his lap, stroking her back and shoulders slowly through her clothes with an almost reverent fervor. She could feel his cock hardening and she loved that she could do this to him. It was a funny sort of power, but power it was, and it was hers. For this, she didn't need to learn the skills of the Brothers to succeed.

She put her lips to Sorin's cautiously; a bird ready to take flight if startled. He didn't move under her ministrations, however, and she realised that he was letting her keep control. She moaned into his mouth, deepening the kiss and flicking her tongue against his lips to gain entrance. She heard him growl as he pulled away just enough to speak. 'We don't have the time for this. Gods, I wish we did, but the others will be here soon.'

'Then I'd better be quick,' she murmured with a wildness she didn't feel. Her heart raced as she clumsily pulled his hard cock from his breeches. Her gaze fluttered up to him, looking for reassurance, but his head was thrown back and his eyes closed. She caught the rounded tip of him in her mouth and sucked lightly. He made a guttural sound that vibrated the length of his body, and she smiled in spite of her uncertainty. She did it again, pulling more of him into her as she laved the end with her tongue and moved down the length of him. His hips jerked beneath her as she moved her mouth up and down, using her hand at the base of him, gently sucking until she felt him becoming restless beneath her. Then she pulled harder, pumping him with her hand faster as she took as much of him into her mouth as she could. He gave a hoarse cry, bucking beneath her and anchoring her head with a fist in her hair as his seed spurted to the back of her throat. She swallowed instinctively and, when he was finished, she cautiously looked up. He didn't say anything, just watched her from beneath hooded eyes until she was finally forced to speak, her color heightening. 'Was that ... all right?'

His lips crashed down onto hers hard as his arms twined around her, pulling her back up and onto his knee. 'It was more than all right. It was perfect, Lana. You're perfect,' he whispered before kissing her savagely once more.

Feeling self-conscious and uncomfortable, Lana broke away from him, though his words thrilled her.

Viktor and Kane appeared in the tent. Lana began to scramble from Sorin's lap, but he held her fast, tutting. 'I'm not quite finished with you yet.'

Still, she tried to pull away from him, and he chuckled. 'Still so easily embarrassed,' he murmured. He craned his head back at the others. 'We still have a few moments, yes?'

'A few, but not many,' came Viktor's response. Kane said nothing, his gaze cold and impassable as usual. Lana looked away from them. She realised that the control Sorin had relinquished just moments ago had been taken back completely as he stood with her, turned and pushed her, front down, onto the table.

He eased her breeches down to her knees and thrust his fingers into her, keeping her in place with a hand on her back. She cried out in surprise even as her walls clenched around him.

'So wet,' he whispered. He eased his fingers from her slowly and then pushed them in again – hard, and she gripped the table with a whimper. Then he added another finger. The intrusion was almost punishing, but so pleasurable! The friction his movements created made her writhe and moan as he pumped his fingers into her. His hand on her back disappeared and she felt him moving the *other thing*. In and out, in and out in time with his fingers. The sensation was so utterly sublime that she forgot she was being watched, forgot that there was anyone else there at all. She moaned loudly, and her body spasmed and she screamed, clamping down on his fingers so hard they were pushed out of her even as he tried to thrust them inside again.

She was breathing hard as he leaned down and kissed her, at the same time easing the other object from her.

Completely sated, she stayed as she was. She felt him set her clothes to rights and he pulled her gently to standing, holding her as she swayed slightly.

'You took it out,' she said, the surprise entering her voice.

He grasped her chin softly. 'You'll have little privacy during the crossing to the Islands and I don't want you worrying about it during the invasion. You're still a novice, after all. But,' the hungry look entered his eyes again, 'I will be putting it back in. And I think you'll beg me to.'

Her eyes widened slightly at his words. Then she remembered that the others had been in the tent, but when she turned, only a blatantly aroused Viktor was there. Kane was gone.

'Would that we had the time, little bird,' Viktor ground out. 'But we need to go.'

CHAPTER 27

VIKTOR

It had been two days of smooth sailing since they'd departed the mainland. Everything seemed to be going according to their plans. They'd left on time with the tide – no mean feat, as they were a fleet twenty ships strong. The winds were in their favor. Even the weather was cooperating and staying fair. So why couldn't Viktor shake the niggling feeling that something was amiss?

Viktor stood at the prow of their flagship, the first vessel that would breach the guard towers of the largest island in the archipelago and, consequently, where the capital city of the Islands stood. The plan was simple, as the best were: take the capital city. After that, the other, smaller islands would fall into line quickly. Getting past the guard towers and subduing the Islands' militia would be the most difficult part, but they had men on the inside. Viktor wasn't worried.

As he stared out to sea, he realised he wasn't much of anything. Since becoming a Brother, he had always felt at his most alive just before battle. He would be restless, eager to fight, to pit himself against the enemy and find out who was stronger. This he had done over and over for years, but today he felt ... impatient, anxious for the battle to be over. His brow furrowed with the awareness that this life was no longer enjoyable to him.

He pushed himself away from the rail with a silent curse. Nothing was simple anymore. For so long his days had been filled with the bare requirements needed to keep him alive, violence, the camaraderie of his unit and their plans for revenge. He'd needed nothing else. Until Lana. She was the only thing that had changed. She had appeared and his days and nights had become complicated. And he wasn't even sorry. The others weren't either. Well, Kane, perhaps. Viktor could see he was trying to fight it, trying to keep control over what she was doing to them without even realizing it. Perhaps there was truth to what Sorin had said, though he hoped not. If she was a witch, she would be in very grave danger from the entire army of Dark Brothers. If they even suspected, the old laws would be invoked. There wouldn't even be a trial. They'd simply torture and kill her.

He found himself in the hold without even realizing he'd made his way down to the bowels of the ship. Shaking himself out of his thoughts, he turned to take the ladder back up to the small cabin he was sharing with the others when he heard a sound. He turned back and saw the soft glow of a lantern.

'Is someone there?' he called.

'Viktor?' Lana's head appeared over some of the larger crates to his left. 'What are you doing down here?'

He made his way over to her. 'I was going to ask you the same.'

She shrugged. 'Sorin was busy and asked me if I'd check the inventory; make sure we didn't forget anything.'

Knowing Sorin, giving Lana a task down here was probably less to do with inventory and more about keeping her away from the other Brothers without confining her to quarters. As the only woman on the ship, two-hundred bored Brothers and mercenaries had found her to be the most interesting of diversions. She wasn't in any danger, but it was more than a little annoying that almost every man was making calf eyes at her all the time.

'A bit fucking late for inventory now we've left port,' he said with a chuckle, and she smiled wanly.

He looked more closely at her. She looked pale, and the faint smudges under her eyes spoke of tiredness or illness. 'What's the matter, little bird?'

'Nothing,' she said too quickly.

'Are you seasick?'

She chuckled. 'No. I thought I might be. I've never been on a ship before, but no. I'm fine. Really I am.'

He tutted at her as he took the ledger she'd been writing in from her and put it on the crate next to them. Then he put his hands on her shoulders and turned her. 'It's Kane.'

She said nothing, but he saw from the look she tried to hide that he'd hit on the truth. 'What has he done? Or said?'

'Nothing.'

His hands left her. 'I know when you're lying. I always know, so there's really no point in doing it,' he said coldly and made to leave.

His harsh words brought her eyes to his, and the tears he saw pooling in them were like a punch to his gut.

She gave a hiccupping sob. 'Please, Viktor, not you as well. I can bear Kane to be cruel. He almost always is, but please not you as well.'

He cursed and drew her to him, tucking her body as close to his as he could. 'What has he done?'

'Nothing. He's no different than usual. But,' she sniffed and nestled in closer to him, 'he never speaks to me except to reprimand. Everything I do in training is wrong, and when we aren't training, he just ignores me. If he does notice me, it's usually to give me a cutting remark. And he never touches me, not ever. We're bound together, but he hates me, Viktor, and I don't know why.'

Viktor was silent, trying to find the words to comfort her. It had been a long time since he'd had to deal with *this*, and he was finding it very difficult.

'He doesn't hate you,' he finally said. 'Kane can be a fucking prick at times, but I promise you he doesn't hate you.'

'How do you know?' she sniffed, pulling away slightly to look up at him.

'Because none of us could hate you. You're a part of our unit. We share a bond that can only be broken in death. Perhaps not even then. Come.'

He took her hand and led her up the ladder and down the corridors to their cabin. He opened the door and saw Sorin writing at the small, corner desk. He looked up from his work in disapproval.

'Kane,' was all Viktor said, and Sorin's countenance darkened.

'What has he done?'

Viktor waved a hand. 'Just Kane being Kane.'

He sat Lana on one of the two narrow bunks and began to unclasp her tunic, ignoring her half-hearted protests. She was clearly upset, and in his book there was no better way to make her feel better than to fuck her into oblivion.

'But it's the middle of the day,' she admonished, and he grinned.

Behind him he heard Sorin rustling about at the desk and beckoned him without turning around. Whereas Kane had only rarely shared women with them in the past, he and Sorin had no qualms about it. The sight of Lana writhing beneath Sorin – or taking his cock in her mouth, which Viktor was practically still hard from after watching it the other morning – was pleasing, and he knew Sorin felt the same.

Having bared her delectable tits to them, he wasted no time in capturing one pearly nipple in his mouth, making her gasp. Sorin stood her up and divested her of the rest of her clothes before letting her sink back onto the cot, which she did with a contented sigh.

Viktor loved it when she was completely stripped while he and Sorin were still clothed. He would not have her as a slave now, but that vulnerability awakened the predator in him. He wanted to fall on her at that moment and thrust himself into her tight, wet channel, but he held back. He wanted to show her what she meant to them by making it as pleasurable as possible.

Sorin's fingers drew up and down her slit as he widened her legs, and she moaned while Viktor attended to her other breast, licking and sucking and biting as she squirmed, wiggling her hips wantonly. He almost laughed. If she could see herself now, she'd turn the veriest shade of crimson, he knew, but to them she looked even more beautiful like this, untamed and wild.

He pulled her up gently and eased her to her knees on the floor as he freed himself from his breeches. She needed no prompting and her mouth descended on him. He groaned. She licked and suckled as he thrust past her lips, quickly dissolving into only thoughts of her and her satisfying little mouth.

CHAPTER 28

LANA

Try as she might, Lana couldn't keep herself quiet. She moaned loudly as she felt Sorin thrust into her from behind as Viktor fucked her mouth. Sorin eased out slowly and then pushed back in harder, making her cry out again. He leant forward languidly and kissed her neck, then picked up the pace, pistoning into her hard and deeply as she whimpered and panted. Then she gasped as she felt a finger enter the *other* place and she was completely undone. Unable to contain the cries that were being ripped from her throat, muffled though they were by Viktor as she sucked him, she found her release just as the other two found theirs and screamed in pleasure as they both roared loudly, spilling their seeds into her.

She vaguely noticed the door opening as Viktor pulled his softening cock from her mouth and she felt Sorin do the same behind her.

'What the fuck do you think you're doing?' came a menacing voice that chilled her.

She looked up in alarm. Kane stood in front of her and looked angrier than she'd ever seen him. He closed the door and she scrambled up, putting herself safely behind Viktor and Sorin as she pulled a blanket from the bed to cover herself.

He stalked towards them, his presence making the room seem even smaller. 'The other Brothers, the soldiers, everyone can hear you,' he said quietly, the tension in the room thickening with every word.

Sorin was the first to say something as he tucked his cock away nonchalantly. 'Who the fuck cares what they can hear?'

Kane's eyes narrowed and he became even more intimidating. 'She's naught but holes to fuck, no better than a whore on the street. That's what they think.'

Lana's breath caught at his crude words and, before she could think better of it, she stepped out from behind Viktor as she wrapped the blanket more tightly around herself. 'Or is that just what *you* think, Kane?'

His jaw set as he gestured towards Sorin and Viktor. 'When I and everyone else can hear you through the ship moaning and screaming and I see with my eyes what you're doing, is there any reason for me not to? Shall I take my fill of you now as well? Shall the rest of the men on the ship?' he growled.

She flinched and, unbidden, her bottom lip trembled, and she bit it to keep from making a sound. The tears, though, she could do nothing about but dash them from her cheeks. How could he be so cruel? How could he hate her so? What had she done? Suddenly she was ashamed of herself, not for what she had done with Viktor and Sorin, but for letting Kane make her feel that she should be sorry.

She raised her head and looked him full in the face, defiant in her anger. She didn't take her eyes off him as she addressed the others. 'Sorin, Viktor, please could you leave us?'

Viktor pulled open the door angrily and left without a

word. Sorin, however, put an arm around her and whispered in her ear that he would be close if she needed him. She gave him a small smile and watched as he too left the cabin. Kane closed the door with a slam and locked it.

Taking a small breath, she let the blanket covering her nakedness slip to the floor. 'There. Take your fill of me then, Kane,' she sneered.

His eyes dragged down the length of her, lingering on her breasts and mound before coming to rest on her face. And then he was not a step away, pushing her into the wall roughly and kicking her legs apart.

She quivered slightly, but her eyes didn't leave his. 'Am I a slave or am I one of you? I wish you would make up your fucking mind!' she growled. 'You tell me I'm a Dark Brother now, but you don't act like it. There should be a bond between us, but there's nothing but coldness and anger. I might as well fuck every man on this ship. Why should it make any odds to you?' Her voice raised, though she tried to keep it low. 'And that you would make me feel shame for taking pleasure with Sorin and Viktor, who I care about and trust while all you give me are hurtful barbs and cruelty, disgusts me.'

He was silent, and still there was nothing in his expression but impassive boredom, which, if anything, made her angrier. 'Why don't you put less energy into making me miserable and more into finding the man who destroyed your life? Perhaps then you'd actually find him.'

His jaw clenched and his eyes burned into her, and she realised she'd pushed him too far. She made to duck away under his arm, but his hands grabbed her roughly and spun her around, pressing her into the ship's bulkhead.

'It doesn't matter what you make me do,' she shouted. 'Make me hurl myself into the sea. I don't care. I hate you! Do your worst!'

Still he said nothing, but now it was a pregnant silence, one that made her feel dread. One hand left her and she heard him pull open one of the drawers that were built into the wall next to him. He pulled something out and she twisted her neck to catch a glimpse of it. What she saw made her stomach turn to lead. *No.*

'No. No!' She turned in his grasp so that she was facing him again, and she could see she wasn't mistaken. He held a dark, leather crop.

She found herself back in Dirk's stable, bent over a saddle while Ather lashed her again and again with his favored black one. She could see the gleam in his eye as he hurt her. She could even smell the horses.

Her breath came in fits and starts. Her knees felt weak and tears leaked from her eyes. Her gaze found Kane's, but all she saw in it was fury. This wouldn't be like the spanking that Viktor had given her, where he'd comforted her afterwards and taken the pain away. This would be a vicious beating to ease Kane's anger; one that she might not survive.

She was shaking as she took a deep breath, a muffled sob escaping as she turned back to the wall away from him, closed her eyes and waited for him to begin. There was nothing else to do, nowhere to run.

The room was deathly silent save for her uneven breaths and stifled sobs. She wondered where Sorin was. He had said he'd come back if she needed him, but how would he know to? She was too breathless to scream. What if Kane beat her even harder? What if Sorin came back but let Kane do it anyway? What if, like Kane, Sorin didn't really care for her at all? What if all of this was some elaborate game they were playing with her? That would flay her worse than a flogging ever could. Her legs shook, and she was sure they'd give way by the time Kane began.

He was making her wait. Ather had done this as well. It

prolonged her suffering if she didn't know when the first blow would come. How did her tormentors instinctively know how to do these things? Ather had sometimes paused in the middle of a beating, waiting for her to believe he was finished before starting up again without warning. Cruelty came to these men as easily as breathing.

Lana pushed her palms into the rough planks of the wall, trying to hold herself up, tears blinding her as she cowered like a dog. She hated herself in that moment. She was no freewoman. She was a fraud. She might as well go back to Dirk and muck out stables for the rest of her days, dodging Ather as best she could. *Pathetic.*

Something thudded down next to her and her body instinctively recoiled, quaking legs making her lose her balance. She fell to the hard floor and immediately curled into a tight ball. A moment later the door opened and slammed shut. For a long time, she couldn't make herself look. Would Sorin be there? Were they just waiting for her to let her guard down so they could continue their twisted diversions?

Finally, hearing nothing, she peeked through her arms. The cabin was empty. She sat up gingerly and pulled herself up onto one of the bunks. Not bothering to get dressed, she lay down, curled up and covered herself with a blanket completely. After a time, her breathing returned to normal, but as the terror ebbed, something else took its place: a sadness so deep she was racked with sobs that wouldn't abate.

CHAPTER 29

VIKTOR

Sometime after his retreat from the cabin, Viktor leant with his back against the rail on the main deck, watching the sun begin its descent beneath the waves. He'd left because Lana had asked it of him and Sorin, though it had been against his better judgement to leave her alone when Kane was in such a mood.

He ignored yet another knowing look from one of the soldiers as he walked by and muttered a curse. Perhaps Kane was right. Lana wasn't their slave or their whore, but maybe from the outside it would seem to others that she was. While no one could harm her, a lack of respect for one member of their unit would in turn affect the whole.

Kane appeared on deck, stomping up the stairs from the belly of the ship. Without even a glance Viktor's way, he made for the prow, where the captain stood conferring with the navigator. At the same time, Sorin came up from the galley.

'I thought you were staying close to the cabin,' Viktor called.

Sorin approached. 'There was a problem in the hold. I

was called away.' He looked over at Kane, who was walking slowly away from them. 'I've had enough. He treats her like she's nothing. It's a mockery of our unit's bond.'

Viktor sighed. 'Do you not think he has a point?'

'No,' Sorin said darkly. 'I meant what I said before. What the rest of them think matters little.' With that, he strode forward to intercept Kane.

Viktor followed.

'Kane!'

Kane's footsteps faltered as they advanced, his body stiffening.

'What did you say to Lana just now?' Sorin ground out.

Kane was silent and didn't face them.

'Come now, Brother, no banter? No witty retort?'

Kane turned slowly, and where Viktor had expected to see his usual expression of bored disdain, instead he saw two things he'd never seen on his Brother's face before. Fear and ... guilt?

Sorin's face drained of color, and Viktor, his stomach leaden, suspected he looked the same.

'What have you done to her?' Sorin all but whispered.

Kane's mouth opened, but nothing came out. He shook his head and tried again. 'I–'

Viktor didn't wait. He ran for the stairs, leapt down them in one and raced along the corridor. He stopped when he reached the closed door, Sorin on his heels, breathing hard, and slowly opened it, terrified at what scene might await them. At first, he didn't see her, but then he noticed a bundled form on one of the cots.

'Gods,' Sorin breathed. Viktor followed his gaze and saw a crop lying on the floor.

'Do you think he ...?'

'Lana?'

She didn't respond, but he could see the even rise and fall

of the blanket. She seemed to be asleep. Viktor crept forward and raised the sheet, hoping against hope that he wouldn't find her bruised and bleeding beneath it.

The skin of her back, arse and thighs was unmarred, and Viktor sighed in relief. 'He didn't beat her.'

'It doesn't matter whether or not he did, you fool, the fear is enough.' Sorin picked up the crop quickly, strode to the porthole, thrust it open and cast the offending object into the sea. 'We agreed after her first punishment that we'd only ever use our hands because of what she suffered in that village. No canes, no crops nor switches – nothing. Where did that thing even come from?'

Viktor clenched his fists. 'Kane must have brought it. But why?'

Sorin sat down heavily at the desk in the corner. 'I owe Kane my life, same as you, Brother, but we owe Lana more. If we must make a choice between the unit – between revenge – and her, I know what I will choose.'

Viktor nodded. He was in complete agreement, he realised without surprise. A few weeks ago, he could not have fathomed leaving the Dark Brothers – not for anything. They had saved him and provided a path to avenge Greta, little Hari, and baby Gilly's deaths. But while he would always remember his wife and children, they were from a different life. He had been another man then. It was time to make a new start and perhaps find some measure of happiness. He saw now that he had chosen Lana the moment he'd seen her in that stable.

But what about Kane? Viktor had known that Kane would strike out at Lana. He had spent longer alone and, as far as Viktor knew, had never known the bonds of love outside the Dark Brothers like he and Sorin had – but enough was enough. They couldn't wait for Kane to understand whatever his feelings were. They couldn't stand by while he hurt Lana.

'We'll sort out what to do after we take the Islands,' Viktor decided. 'Until then, she shouldn't be alone with Kane. He can't be trusted.' Viktor hated to say the words aloud, but it was true. Kane was a threat to her.

'Agreed.' Sorin turned to leave.

'Where are you going?'

'Kane needs a lesson and I'm going to make sure he learns it well. Stay with her.'

He nodded once and Sorin left quietly.

Viktor took in the visage of the exhausted girl in front of him. She rolled over slightly, and he could see her face still wet with tears from crying herself to sleep. Sorin wasn't usually the one to mete out punishments where Kane was concerned, preferring to leave it to Viktor, but on the rare occasions Sorin used his fists against his Brother, Kane's face in particular was always the worse for it. As he stared down at Lana's sorrowful appearance, Viktor hoped Sorin didn't hold back one whit. For once not fighting the impulse to console her, he lay down carefully on the cot, trying not to wake her, and drew her to him.

She didn't stir for a few moments, but Viktor knew when she woke. She shifted next to him slightly, and he could feel tiny tremors shaking her body. Gods, she was crying. Her silent misery speared him through his chest painfully and he gathered her up.

'Hush,' he whispered as he tried to kiss away her tears – but more just took their place, wetting his clothes. 'Lana, don't cry. Sorin and I will keep you safe. I promise.'

'What about Kane,' she hiccupped.

'Kane is being a fool and, if he doesn't soon realize it, he won't be a problem anymore,' he said ominously.

She buried her face in his chest and heaved a breath. 'He

wanted to hurt me, Viktor. I could feel it. He was going to whip me worse than Ather ever did.' She stifled a sob.

Viktor closed his eyes and hugged her more tightly. 'But he didn't, and he won't get another chance. I swear to you we will fix this. Come, let me make you feel better.'

Her tear-filled eyes found his and she nodded. That was all the encouragement Viktor needed as he gently pulled the blanket down to expose the creamy mounds of her breasts, the pink nipples tightening deliciously in the cool air.

He bent his head and pulled one beaded nub into his mouth, sucking it gently. She moaned and arched into him, her fingers threading through his hair and pulling him closer to her. He moved to the other breast, giving it the same treatment and reveling in the soft whimpers he was eliciting.

He shed his tunic and shirt, baring himself from the waist up, and she immediately began to caress him, following the contours of his body with a reverence he'd never experienced from a woman before. Her touch lingered over his chest and she pinched one of his nipples hard enough for him to gasp like a maid. She grinned at him impishly and he smiled back just before pulling her sheet away completely, leaving her entirely naked to his eyes.

'You're going to pay for that, little bird,' he growled, glad her tears had dried and loving this other playful side of her as she scrambled back on the cot, against the wall and out of his grasp. He divested himself of the rest of his clothes quickly and grabbed for her, catching her legs and pulling her back to him. She giggled and struggled away, twisting and turning to escape him, but he didn't let her go, instead forcing her knees apart. Opened to him, he looked his fill, pulling her nether lips wide to examine her at his leisure.

'Remember the apothecary,' he murmured. 'I still dream about you spread on that table. I could see every inch of you on display. I'm going to tie you up like that in our tent and leave you there all day so I can see you and touch you and play with you whenever I like,' he promised darkly.

She wriggled under his gaze, her cheeks coloring, and he chuckled at her embarrassment.

He began to touch her lightly, up and down her slit, delving into her channel with a finger just a bit and her arse as well, giving attention to every fold and crevice except that place he knew she longed for him to touch. She whimpered and squirmed, the little minx trying to force his hand to rub against that vital area by accident, but he didn't let her have her way.

He pushed her thighs open and dipped his head down, the smell of her arousal and the wetness glistening there almost enough to finish him right then. He groaned as he tasted her, licking and sucking gently as he thrust two fingers deeply into her. She cried out her release instantly, bucking wildly as she came hard, writhing under him and calling out his name. Giving her a final lick, he grinned as he moved up her body, kissing her, knowing she could taste herself on his lips. He pushed into her hot, tight entrance, still pulsing from her pleasure, and began to move within her. He'd wanted to take her slowly, gently, but found he couldn't.

Viktor pulled out and slammed back in hard, and she gasped as her body tried to adjust to his size. He searched her eyes, afraid he had hurt her.

'Don't stop,' she gasped.

With a feral snarl, he flipped her easily onto her front, holding onto her hair with one fist. She arched her back and raised her hips in invitation and he pushed his cock into her depths. She moaned as he set a punishing pace from the outset, pounding into her hard and deep, making her take every inch of him. The noises of pleasure she made spurred him on as he let go of her hair and reached down to rub the little bud between her legs. He pinched it and she screamed, her walls clenching and spasming around him as he shot his seed into her with a yell of his own.

Sated, he collapsed next to her and gathered her to him. She let him, breathing hard.

'Did that help?' He kissed her forehead.

She snuggled closer. 'I feel better, thank you, but, Viktor …' She was silent for a moment before she spoke again. 'There's a … a void inside me, a grief. It's difficult to explain, but I feel so sad. There's something missing.'

He sighed, wishing he had more of a solution for her than fucking her into oblivion. 'I will help, I promise. Sleep now. Tomorrow is a big day.' He heard her murmur contentedly even as he frowned in the now-dark cabin, wondering how he was going to fulfil such a vow.

CHAPTER 30

LANA

Lana had been listening for the sounds of battle from the cabin since before sunrise. She looked out of the porthole and, seeing nothing for the thousandth time, cursed. It must be mid-morning. How long did a battle usually last? And how did one know when it was over?

Viktor and Sorin had woken her in the dark, but when she'd thrown back the covers to get dressed and join them, they'd stopped her. She was still too new to the Brothers, they'd said, and it was best she stayed on the ship and waited for one of them to come for her or she would be in danger. She had wanted to argue, but she knew they were right. What they hadn't said was that the units that were fighting were whole, their bonds strong, and theirs was not. That too was truth.

So they had both kissed her chastely – which she had found odd, especially given Viktor's possession of her body a few more times during the night while they'd shared the cot – and left her in the cabin, going off to fight with the rest of the Dark Brothers. Practically by herself on the ship, Lana had never felt so alone nor such an outsider. It wasn't that she aimed to hurt or kill anyone, but she didn't want any of them to be in danger while she twiddled her thumbs in this *bower*, not even Kane.

She hadn't seen him since yesterday evening. She tried not to think about what had happened only hours before, not wanting to start crying anew when they were out there in the mêlée. She paced, not able to stay calm as the hours crawled by, even though she didn't feel well at all and longed to lie down and sleep. She hadn't mentioned her malady to the Brothers, though she thought now it had been coming on gradually for days. She didn't want whatever ailed her to be a distraction that might get Sorin and Viktor hurt or worse. She snorted in spite of herself. She doubted Kane would care.

She sat on one of the cots as the headache she'd been trying to suppress for hours finally took hold. Pain in her temples and eyes came in waves, forcing her to rummage in Sorin's healing bag for something to relieve her symptoms. She found the powder he'd showed her during one of their lessons and poured it into her mouth, grimacing at the bitterness. But soon the medicine did its work and the light of day became tolerable again, though there was still a lingering ache and fatigue.

She stayed where she was with the door bolted, as she'd promised Sorin and Viktor faithfully that she would. More hours passed until the sun was at its highest. Even then, no one came for her.

She waited until finally she could bear the worrying no longer and, donning her cloak, ventured into the abandoned corridor and up onto the deck slowly. There was one sailor who seemed to be on guard, but he didn't try to stop her as she made her way along the narrow gangplank and onto the long, wooden dock that led into the city.

She wandered sluggishly towards the citadel that was nestled into the hillside, knowing that Greygor and the others in command would be there – assuming the campaign had been successful. *And if it hasn't been?* She shuddered. If the Brothers were all dead, then she supposed she would soon be as well. She doubted she could raise a sword at the moment even if she was proficient in its use. Oddly, thoughts of her own demise didn't terrify her as much as the idea that any of her unit were gone.

She walked uphill, little by little, not seeing or hearing anyone, though once in a while she caught the twitching of a curtain or the slightest movement of a door, as if she was being watched by the Islanders huddled in their homes. But if that was the case, no one confronted her, and finally she made it to the great open drawbridge of the keep unmolested.

She looked back the way she'd come with a slight frown on her face. She'd never been in a battle before nor seen the remnants of one, but she would have thought there'd be more … bodies, blood, signs of battle, perhaps? Instead there were just deserted streets. The Brothers weren't known for their restraint. In fact, the opposite was true. Stories of their bloodlust and desecration of, well, everything, were told in shocked tones and lowered voices in the taverns all over the land. Even the mention of Dark Brothers merely passing through sent some scurrying into the forests and hills to hide.

Lana entered through the raised portcullis, finding two bored-looking soldiers on the other side. They stood to attention when they heard her footsteps but quickly relaxed when they took in her attire, the color and cut of her clothes identifying her as one of the Brothers at once.

'Where is my unit?' she asked without preamble.

The bearded one smirked at the other and looked her up and down in a way that made her skin crawl. 'We've heard about you. Can't go even a few hours without one of their cocks in you, eh?'

A significant part of her wanted to turn away from their lewd words and escape, but instead she drew herself up and adopted the bored expression she always saw on Kane's face. It seemed to work well for him and, regardless of how that bastard treated her, she *was* a freewoman. 'Are you going to answer me or shall I stuff yours down your fucking throat?'

The other one chuckled. 'He don't mean nothing by it. Just jealous of the cunts.' He pointed towards the other side of the square. 'They're in the main hall with Greygor.'

Her unit was all right. Of course they were! Instantly she felt relief, but she needed to see them for herself just to be certain. Without another word to the two soldiers, she strode to where the guard had pointed, pretending a strength she did not feel. As soon as she had slipped through the bulky wooden door – which, thankfully, was ajar – and she could no longer be seen, her shoulders slumped and she had to lean on the wall to catch her breath. What was wrong with her? She'd never felt so depleted of energy.

Once she had recovered enough to continue, she looked around, staying in the shadows until she was ready to make her presence known. Truth be told, she might just turn around and go back to the ship once she knew without a doubt that they were all right. They need not even know she'd come.

The main hall was a leviathan of a room. Tapestries depicted scenes of the island and surrounding seas, and chandeliers hung from an impressive, domed ceiling. There was a large table off to one side where a few men were gathered, her unit and Greygor included. They spoke in hushed voices and Lana suppressed a shiver as she watched the Commander – the man who had so readily given her to Ryon and his Brothers to be their *entertainment*. He didn't look at all as impressive to her now that she wasn't scared shitless. He looked strong and he was obviously ruthless, but his years showed.

She edged closer to listen as a Brother she didn't know gave a report.

'... deploy to the other main islands. I recommend we don't bother with the outer banks. There are hundreds, and their populations are too sparse to be much more than an annoyance to us.'

'Agreed. The inner isles will have heard by now. Send a contingent of three hundred men to each of the five until we've found it. We shouldn't have a problem with them. They're mostly scholars and priests. Minimal threat once the citadels are under our control.'

Found what? Lana's brow furrowed. This entire invasion was to find something?

'Do we know where it is?'

'They're bringing the High Priest of the Mount here as we speak. He should arrive imminently. He'll know the location.'

'Excellent. Now, casualties. How many men have we lost?'

'Five.'

The room fell silent, astonishment and incredulity written on each of the faces Lana could see.

'Five?' one man finally murmured before a chorus of voices sounded through the room.

'Five hundred?'

'No. Five.'

'Are you sure?'

'Have all the units checked in?'

Greygor held up a hand and all were silent. 'Islanders?'

'Seven.'

Again, the hush was complete.

'There's something else. The five men were soldiers. They

were killed when a staircase collapsed. The seven islanders were killed in the same accident.'

'So no one was killed in battle. Any injured?'

'A few, but not many. Flesh wounds, mostly.'

'What does this mean?'

Greygor smiled coldly. 'It means the gods were smiling upon us. We must find the artefact and deliver it to its rightful place or their wrath will, doubtlessly, be swift.'

Nods of assent were mirrored in the expressions of many of the men. Some, her unit included, were giving each other pointed looks instead.

'Kane, take your unit to the east gate and ensure all is well. There have been reports of a skirmish.'

Kane, Viktor and Sorin didn't look happy, but they left quickly without grumbling through a smaller door on the other side of the room. The Commander was getting on in years, but Lana could see that his power over the Brothers was still absolute where most things were concerned. She got the impression that her unit butting heads with him as they had over her was an exceedingly rare occurrence. But why, then, did Kane treat her so cruelly when he had clearly risked so much to champion her? The man didn't make sense; none of this did, really. What was the army even doing here if not to pillage, rape, kill and do whatever else the Brothers did?

Lana shook her head and focused on what was in front of her. She hadn't meant to eavesdrop. She'd assumed someone would notice her and she could slip into the crowd without ceremony, but now that the others were gone, she was left in a vague sort of panic. She shouldn't be here. Escaping the confines of the room was her first priority, and then she could either find the others or go back to the ship and wait for them there.

She backed towards the far wall slowly, intending to go back the way she'd come, but just before she reached the door, she heard someone on the other side of it. She retreated quickly, further into the dark periphery of the hall, glad of the missing wall sconces here and her dark clothes as she pulled up the hood of her cloak to conceal herself more thoroughly.

The door opened and three Brothers came through, a smallish, thin man in black robes with tied hands in the center of them. The Brothers passed without seeing her, but their prisoner looked up as they went by and seemed to stare directly at her. She darted even further back silently and turned her face away. But when she peered at him a moment later, he was no longer looking in her direction, and she let out a slow breath. He must not have noticed her after all. Greygor ignored them as he spoke with another of his men, and the three Brothers, along with their quarry, stood in silence as they awaited his address.

'Sir, there's talk among the men.'

Greygor rolled his eyes. 'Let me guess, Gorran. Whispers of witches and other irrational nonsense.' He gave a hard laugh. 'Next you'll be telling me they won't return to the mainland for fear of sea dragons!'

'Sir, I–'

'I have real work to do here that will make us wealthy beyond our dreams. I'm not playing nursemaid to an army of men scared of their own fucking shadows. Gods, we are Dark Brothers! Quash this nonsense and let it be known that any talk of witches will earn a man fifty lashes. Now, fuck off.'

'Yes, sir.'

Gorran practically ran for one of the other doors and was gone before another word could be uttered.

Greygor glanced at the unit who'd arrived with, Lana assumed, the priest they'd spoken of before. 'Well?'

The prisoner was pushed forward. Lana could see that

he'd been beaten already. His face was bruised and bleeding and he favored his right side even as he held his left arm close to him with his other hand.

Greygor looked at him only to give the vaguest sneer. 'You know why we're here, priest. We can search the citadel and the others in the Islands. We will find it eventually, but until we do, we will occupy your shores. We will plunder. We will reside in your houses and walk your streets. We will slake our thirst in your famed wine cellars and fill our bellies with your people's fayre. Your women and girls will be raped in the streets and taken for our pleasure tents. And …' He picked up a large book that had been resting on the table and weighed it in his hand. He finally looked the priest in the eyes as he casually threw it into the fire that burned in the center of the hall. 'You can be sure our search will take its toll on your many irreplaceable pieces.'

The priest gaped at him and then at the fire, where the book was quickly being consumed, his mouth opening and closing like a landed herring. Lana saw the instant that his anger and disbelief won out over fear.

'That tome was over six thousand years old and the only one in existence!' he cried, his face turning the veriest shade of purple.

Greygor shrugged. 'Now it's ash. And I speak from experience when I say that the older they are, the faster they burn. Tell me where the Vessel is and we leave with the tide.' He shrugged. 'Or don't and we destroy the citadels and the histories one piece at a time. The choice is yours.'

It wasn't a bluff. The Commander really didn't care one way or the other. He would win in the end no matter what the priest did, and he knew it – everyone did.

He bowed his head in defeat. 'I know who paid you to come here.'

'Then you know he always gets what he wants no matter the cost. Where is it?'

The priest let out a slow breath and closed his eyes, his shoulders hunching with the weight of what he was about to do. 'In the cellar behind the very last door at the back is a wall under the east wing. Knock through it and you will find it,' he whispered.

Greygor nodded to the men. 'Chain him and take two units to the cellars. Find it and bring it to me.'

They nodded and did as their Commander bid. The priest didn't struggle as a manacle was fitted around his ankle with a short, thick chain attached to the stone wall.

And then she was alone with the priest. She didn't move, unsure if she should try to assist him. The stable girl in her was shocked that she was even contemplating not helping, but she was a Dark Brother now, after all. If she set him free, wouldn't it be treason against the Army? She cast her eyes back to the shackled man. She couldn't leave him. Once they found this Vessel, Greygor would kill him as soon as look at him. But if the man had disappeared by then, surely they wouldn't think much of it, nor waste time trying to find him.

She stood still as she deliberated, finally deciding to try to help him escape. She hadn't yet moved when he turned his head and stared at her as if he could see into her very soul.

'I know you're there. I felt you as soon as you set foot on our shores.'

She jumped and looked around for someone else, sure he couldn't be directing his words at her.

The priest sat down carefully, nursing his wounds. 'You. In the shadows. I can't see you, but I sense you're very near, and that's the only place you could be so well concealed.' He coughed, his palm coming away splattered with bloody spittle. 'You chose a terrible time to visit our beautiful isles. This Dark Army will destroy you. You must run into the hills and hide until they're gone. I only told them what they wanted to know so they'll leave and you'll be safe.'

In the dark, Lana's brow furrowed. Perhaps they'd hurt his head as well. But she found herself drawing nearer to him until she saw his eyes focus on hers.

'There you are.' He smiled genuinely. 'I never thought I'd actually see one of you. So rare.'

She shook her head and edged nearer. 'I don't know what you mean.'

His eyes widened as he took in her clothes. 'You're one of them? But – I don't understand …' Something changed in his expression, as if he'd found the answer to some mystery. 'That's why they haven't killed us all. Of course. You're with them.' He cocked his head to the side. 'Except you aren't, or you haven't been for very long. Days? Weeks?'

Lana nodded. 'How do you know these things?'

'I am a priest of the Mount. It's my job to recognize the gods.'

Oh no, not one of these fanatics. She rolled her eyes. 'I'm no god.'

'But you are distant kin. There used to be many of you – a long time ago, but now there are few – very, very few. Most of you don't even know what you are.'

'A witch?'

The priest's lip curled into a sneer. 'They'd call any woman with power a witch. Because you curtail their natures, stop them from reveling in the violence and destruction they crave without you near. To us, you are a being of light, a child of the gods themselves. I can see the brightness inside you. It's blinding.'

Lana's brow raised skeptically. She'd never met a priest, but she'd imagined they were like this; quoting scriptures and believing this drivel – see her blinding brightness indeed! 'If I'm a child of the gods, then why did none of them ever help me? Why was I left to pain and suffering if I am one of these beings of light?' She chuckled. 'I will help you, priest, but no more silly tales, I beg you. We have to be quick. If I'm found freeing you, I'm in a world of trouble.'

As soon as she clasped the manacle around his foot, he reached out and grabbed her wrist. She tried to pull away. 'Let me go. I'm trying to save you, you fool.'

He looked at her imploringly. 'You must leave me. The Dark Army isn't even of this realm anymore. It's ties are to much darker ones than this. They were once caretakers and peacekeepers, did you know that? Sentinels and protectors of all the realms. Now they are simply mercenaries and the darkness beyond the breaches grows ever closer to us with no one to keep it at bay. Please. Save yourself. After what happened – or rather, didn't happen – today, they'll realize what you are and they will kill you – horribly. I couldn't bear seeing you so defiled.' The priest slapped her hand away. 'Leave me! Someone's coming!'

'Someone's already here,' came a soft voice behind her from the very shadows where she herself had hid.

Lana turned with a gasp to find a Dark Brother she recognized. Kane had spoken with him the day she'd tried to drown herself in the river and she'd seen him since, hovering near her unit sometimes while they trained. Quin.

He came forward out of the shadows slowly, tutting at her. 'So not only are you a witch, which some of the men already suspect, but you're also about to betray the Brothers by setting this man free.'

Lana swallowed hard. 'No, I wasn't ... I mean, I'm not. I ...' Words failed her as she scanned the room for avenues of escape. The closest door was now behind her, she remembered. The one Gorran had taken.

'Run, girl!', the priest urged, and Lana spun on her heel. But she was too slow by half, and Quin's fingers tangled painfully in her hair before she could leap away from his grasp.

A cloth clamped over her mouth and nose, cutting off her scream, and the priest got to his feet, yelling at him to let her go. Quin quickly silenced him with a well-placed blow to the jaw. He fell to the floor, unmoving, as Quin dragged her back, the darkness enveloping them. She struggled against him, but it was no use; whatever affected her made her efforts feeble and completely ineffective.

There was a cloying smell to the rag over her face. It permeated her mouth and nostrils and made her see spots. She pulled at his arm weakly, but her legs crumpled and some force compelled her eyes to close. She fought to keep them open and looked up at him, pleading. They were still moving through the dark, but he now held her in his arms like a babe.

He was speaking to her, but his words sounded muffled, as if he was very far away. '... a witch, I know. It will all be over soon, Lana.'

CHAPTER 31

SORIN

There was no skirmish. That much was clear when he, Viktor and Kane made it to the east gate to find naught there but a bored-looking contingent of twenty or so soldiers lamenting that they had not yet killed anyone and that this was the dullest campaign they'd ever been part of.

Frowning absently, Sorin rubbed his sore knuckles. His lip curled into the ghost of a smile when he looked over at Kane's bruised face. It wasn't the only place his fists had landed the day before, but it was where he'd concentrated the bulk of his blows. Nothing was broken, but Kane would feel the pain of the beating Sorin had given him for weeks.

'Perhaps Greygor's information was wrong,' said Viktor from behind him, but his voice lacked conviction.

'Perhaps,' Sorin agreed. 'Or perhaps we have a big problem.'

Kane's eyes darted around as if he expected an attack. 'Where is she?'

As if you fucking care after what you did to her. But Sorin didn't give voice to his thoughts. The matter had been dealt with. This was how disputes were settled in the Brothers, and even though he wanted to beat Kane anew every time he thought about it, he resisted.

'On the ship,' he said tersely.

None of them said anything more as they headed back down the hill towards the port, but Sorin had a bad feeling that Lana would not be where they'd left her.

Viktor reached their vessel first and practically ran up the gangplank.

'If you're looking for your woman, she went into the town,' someone called from above them.

Sorin looked up to see one of the soldiers peering down from the crow's nest. 'When?'

The man shrugged and looked up into the sky. 'Bit after midday, maybe.'

'Fuck!' Viktor exclaimed. 'She could be anywhere by now. She promised us she'd stay on the ship.'

Sorin heard a derisive snort from behind him and it took all of his restraint to keep from launching himself at Kane. 'Just because you don't give a shit about her, doesn't mean we're going to leave her to Greygor's justice, leader or not,' he snarled.

Kane's face was suddenly a hair's breadth from his own, his features contorted in rage, and it took every ounce of gall for Sorin to stay exactly where he was. He wouldn't give Kane the satisfaction of retreating. His Brother said nothing for a moment, as if trying to calm himself. Then he pulled back with a slow breath.

'Where could she have gone?' he finally asked.

Viktor ran a hand through his hair and looked up. 'You know she can't stay still for any length of time, and she was waiting alone since before the dawn.'

'She would have gone in search of us.' Sorin looked in the same direction as Viktor.

'The citadel is the highest point in the town,' Kane surprised Sorin by saying. 'She'll be there. With Greygor.'

Wordlessly, all three began to race up the cobbled roads towards the hillside. Sorin's heart pounded with fear. When they'd left the ship this morning, the battle – if one could even call it that – had been swift and subdued, with most of the Brothers merely milling about while the Islanders stayed in their homes. The citadel, initially barricaded by the priests, had been breached quickly by their men on the inside, and its portcullis had opened by midmorning. The priests hadn't even been slain, just herded into one of their dormitories and locked in.

Sorin hadn't really thought anything was amiss at the time. It was strange but not completely unheard of for the battles to be small and waged in backstreets out of sight or for most of the population to have fled before the Brothers arrived, and hence there were few to actually resist. But it wasn't until Sorin had heard the ridiculously low number of casualties in the hall that he'd realised just how odd the morning's events were and also the army's strange and muted reaction to them. Hundreds of men ready, primed for a fight, only for it not to take place ... At the very least they should all be at each other's throats or hauling Islanders out of their homes for sport. But there was nothing, only a calm that had settled over all of them – a relief of sorts.

Sorin's brow furrowed. Could he really have been right about Lana? Was she a witch powerful enough to be affecting the whole Army? If it was true, how long before the other units realised? How long before Greygor did? He was already suspicious of her. Sorin picked up his speed. They would accuse Lana soon, if they hadn't already. She wasn't safe even as one of them anymore.

They reached the main hall as quickly as they were able, only to find it deserted save one groaning priest, sitting with his head in his hands.

Kane immediately hauled him to his feet by his robes before Sorin could utter a word. 'Where is she, priest?' he spat.

The man moaned in pain as Kane shook him, his body flapping about bonelessly. 'I've already told you where it is. By the gods, leave me be.'

Sorin pulled the man's head up by his scraggly mop of hair to look into his face. 'We're looking for a woman. One of us. Have you seen her? Tell us and we'll free you.'

'It's in the cellar,' he mumbled deliriously. 'I told you. Give it to your precious Collector and leave our shores.' His eyes began to roll back.

Sorin's stomach turned to lead in an instant. *Collector? It couldn't be.* He slapped the priest's cheeks to wake him. 'What collector? What is it? What are we here for?'

'She's so precious. Must be protected,' the man whispered to himself. Then he went limp.

'Fuck!' muttered Kane. 'We won't get anything else out of him now.' He dropped the priest, letting him fall back to the stone floor with a thud.

Sorin eyed the priest's crumpled form, the wheels in his head turning quickly. 'She must have been here. We need to find Greygor. He might already have her.' He cast a look at Kane. 'There's only one man who would be able to fund the Dark Brothers on a campaign like this, looking for one artefact. I thought we were here to raid, but that's not the true reason, is it?'

Kane stared stonily back, not giving anything away.

'You're second in command, Brother. You must know more than you're saying. What if it's Vineri?'

Viktor shook his head and began walking away, not bothering to wait for them. 'I don't care if it is. Lana is what's important right now. I'm going to find Greygor.'

Sorin nodded, his eyes narrowing as they met Kane's. 'We aren't finished.'

Kane didn't spare him a look, and they both followed Viktor without another word.

CHAPTER 32

LANA

Whispers and low conversation. That was all she was aware of when she began to wake. She didn't try to move or open her eyes at first, not sure what to make of her swimming head and tingling limbs. She remembered a sickening smell around her nose and mouth and then nothing.

She had been taken. *Yes.* By Quin, one of the other Brothers. Images of Uth and Ryon rushed into her mind and she suppressed a shudder, not wanting whoever was there to know she was awake. If she could delay whatever plans they had for her, she might be able to escape them. She turned her attention to the two hushed voices not far away.

'Well, at least we're risking our lives for a pretty girl. Maybe she can make it worth our while later.' She felt fingers trace her collarbone and stayed completely still, hoping against hope that she had enough luck left in her coffers to get away unscathed this time.

'Leave her, Payn.'

The touch disappeared and she was sure her savior's voice belonged to Quin.

'We never have any fun anymore,' Payn whined in jest. 'Are you going to let them know where she is?'

'I haven't decided yet.' *Quin.*

'Well, you'll need to tell either them or Greygor. She can't stay here forever. Greygor has sent some soldiers to look for her. Isn't she one of us now? What has she done?'

'Gods, Brother. Shut your mouth. Did you dump her clothes into the sea?' Quin changed the subject.

'Aye,' Payn answered. 'I ripped her tunic and that little white chemise that was under it, stained them well with blood and threw them in by the port just like you said. They'll wash up with the tide. Are you going to explain to us what's going on?'

'We want everyone to think she's dead. Just make sure no one knows she's here. Not yet.' *Quin.*

Lana stifled a gasp. What did they mean to do with her?

'But it's not as if –'

'Hush. She's listening to us. Aren't you, girl?'

Dropping her pretense, she opened her eyes to find Quin sitting not far away on the ground. The other two members of his unit were there as well, though only one of them had been talking to Quin. She lay on the dirt-covered floor on a blanket in what looked to be a small cave.

She also saw that her top half was clad in just the linen that was wrapped around her breasts. Had one of them just said he'd thrown her clothes into the sea?

She didn't say anything to him as she attempted to sit up, belatedly realizing that her arms and legs were bound. She began to struggle while they all simply watched her impassively.

Quin stood. 'No one can hear you up here, but if you do scream, I'll simply drug you again. Understand?'

Lana nodded, not trusting her voice.

He gestured to Payn and the other one to leave them. They did so without a word, and she and Quin were alone.

He stepped closer and she shrank away, kicking and twisting her body until she felt the damp wall of the cave at her back. She was panting hard by then.

'What do you want with me?' she gasped between breaths, finally finding her voice. 'What did you do to me?'

Quin crouched down in front of her but made no move to touch her. She noticed a tattoo on his neck and stared at it, trying to keep herself calm by concentrating on the intricate swirls of the design.

'I mean you no harm, Lana. I didn't want to have to do it that way, but, with such limited time, it was the only option. The drug will wear off and your head will clear soon, provided you don't make me dose you again.'

'My unit will find me,' she muttered.

'They will,' he agreed, 'but it would have been too late if I'd left you in the hall unprotected. Greygor wants you dead. After the shambles of this morning, he and most of the Army suspect you for what you are.' He stood up again, towering over her and forcing her to crane her neck to look at him.

She didn't speak, fearing she already knew what he was going to say.

'They know you're a witch. So do I. I've known since the day Kane pulled you from the river.'

'How?' was all she could think to ask as her heart began to pound hard in her chest. What was she going to do? Sorin had told her how dangerous it would be for anyone to suspect, even if it couldn't be true.

He gave her a small smile. 'My mother was a … well, let's just say she was a wise woman. Told me that if I was ever to meet one of your kind, I must make sure she was safe.' He stepped back and subjected Lana to a slow perusal that made her wonder how secure she really was with him.

'Would you like some water?' he asked finally, and she nodded.

He grabbed a waterskin and gave it to her, watching as she drank thirstily.

She handed it back. 'Please,' she implored him, 'my hands and feet are numb. The ropes...'

Still observing her closely as if she were some rare beast in a traveler's caravan, he took a small knife from his boot and slashed the cords that bound her. They fell away and she immediately began to rub her wrists and ankles, willing the circulation to return quickly as she waited for him to turn his back on her.

'They were tied too tightly. That was Malkom's doing. Doesn't know his own strength. My apologies. I have some salve in my bag.'

His eyes left her and he turned. Without a second thought, she was on her feet and running. She cleared the cave and found herself in the bright sun. She sprinted along a path as her eyes adjusted to the light and she realised she was high up on the hillside. Over the cliffs at the side of her route was the sea, far below. Quin was right. No one would hear her all the way up here.

Already breathing hard from the minor exertion, she slowed her pace and wondered again what was wrong with her and if she even had the strength to make it back down to the town. But as she rounded a corner, she slammed into a solid wall of muscle. She fell back with a cry and looked up to find Quin standing over her.

She gasped. 'How did you get in front of me?'

He grabbed her wrist, jerked her to her feet without a word and began to lead her back the way she'd come as if she were an errant child. She fought him, pulling and kicking, scratching at his hand and trying to make him let go of her, but he ignored her efforts completely. He dragged her into the cave and threw her onto the blanket still laid out on the ground, pinning her down with his body. Fearing the worst, she struggled and bucked, but all he did was deftly tie her up again with a cold and detached expression.

'What do you want of me?'

He got to his feet again and viewed his handiwork as she tried to catch her breath.

'Did you not hear me?' he snapped. 'Greygor knows what you are.' He shook his head. 'You little fool. You have no idea what will happen if they find you now, do you?'

He leaned down. 'They will do terrible things to you that will make your time in Ryon's tent seem like a stroll in the sun. You will pray for death long before they kill you. And even if you somehow escape, Greygor will ensure you're hunted. You could flee to the darkest realm you could find and he would still discover you.'

Lana blinked back tears of anger and frustration at her helplessness. 'What are *you* going to do to me?'

'When your bloodied tunic washes up, they'll believe you're dead and no one will look for you.'

'And where will I be?' she asked faintly, wondering if he would try to make her a slave to yet another unit.

'You can stay here with the priests or you can travel back to the mainland after the Army has gone.'

'You won't make me stay with you?'

'No, Lana.' He regarded her gravely. 'We are Dark Brothers still; we are a danger to you and you to us. We will be leaving with the rest once we're finished here.' He reached down to cup her cheek. She didn't move. 'Make no mistake,' he said gently, 'if I had made my pledge to anyone else, I would break it. I'd give you over to Greygor and I'd be first in line to help him destroy you.'

Unsure of how to reply, she was silent for a moment as he continued to caress her cheek in a way that reminded her of just how dangerous he was, how dangerous they all were to her regardless of the fact that she'd been living in their midst for weeks.

'You must have loved your mother very much,' she said at last.

She almost sighed with relief as his hand finally dropped away.

'I did,' he said, 'but don't try to escape again or I *will* give you to the Commander, promise or no.'

She worried her lip with her teeth, stopping immediately when she saw his sudden interest in what she was doing. He wanted her, she very belatedly realised, but he was controlling himself. He was handsome, but she felt nothing when she looked at him. He was not one of the men she loved.

'What about Kane, Viktor and Sorin?' she asked, trying to change the subject to remind him that there were Brothers who would protect her – she hoped.

'What about them?'

'Are you going to make them believe I'm dead too?'

'That's up to you.'

'Please tell them I'm not,' she said after a moment.

Not replying, he took her wrists and raised them over her head.

'What are you doing?' she asked, trying not to reveal her rising panic.

'I need to be seen back at the citadel, and I don't trust you to know what's good for you. Can't have you getting away again.' He looped the rope through a convenient iron ring affixed to the cave wall and pulled it tight, putting an arm around her middle and sliding her along the ground backwards until her back scraped stone. He tied it off, but his arm around her lingered. His breathing quickened. She held hers, expecting at any moment for his control to snap and for him to ravish her against the cave wall. Thankfully, he let go and turned away from her as if he could no longer stand to look. He took a shuddering breath and swore under his breath.

'I don't know how Kane does it,' he said softly to himself and, taking the only oil lamp with him, left the cave without a backward glance.

Lana pulled at the restraints, but they didn't give even a bit. So she sat in the shadows and waited, the only light coming from the entrance, and soon even that began to wane with the approaching darkness.

Her arms began to ache, raised as they were, and as the hours passed, they became more and more painful. She let the tears come in the pitch black and fell into a fitful sleep sometime in the night.

A NOISE SOUNDED OUTSIDE and her slumber was banished immediately. She sat upright, her arms numb and her body freezing from the damp stone. It was still dark, but she could hear footsteps in the gravel on the path, getting closer.

Torchlight flooded the cave, blinding her.

'By the gods. You were right.'

'You see? I told you what I heard them say. The bitch Greygor is looking for *is* here.'

She squinted in the light, making out two men – soldiers. They were both quite young, probably not much older than she, but dark haired and typically rough-looking, with battle scars marring their faces and tattered clothes. Each held a torch, which they placed in the brackets set into the stone by the cave's entrance, illuminating every nook and cranny.

'Free me,' she ordered hoarsely.

They ignored her command, so she tried a different tack.

'Please, I beg you. Cut the rope and let me go. There's been a mistake.'

'Greygor will make us Dark Brothers for this,' one of

them said to the other, practically rubbing his hands together.

'What does a witch do anyway?'

'Fucked if I know. Whore herself– if the tales are true.'

'She looks unwell.'

They both really stared at her, taking in her half-naked, bound body and her utter helplessness. They approached her, one of them reaching for her.

'I'm a Dark Broth–' she gasped, pulling away as he back-handed her casually across the cheek. Her head struck the rock behind her with a resounding thud and she cried out, at the same time kicking out with her legs. She connected with one of them and heard an 'oomph', but her legs were quickly grabbed and one of the men straddled her, his fetid breath turning her stomach.

'You're making a mistake,' she ground out as his hands slid up her body. The mercenary brandished a knife that he had pulled from somewhere on his person, grazing it down her face and nicking her cheek with a grin. She clenched her teeth as she felt a trickle of blood and stared him down. The knife skittered over the flesh of her neck to her chest, cutting her again before beginning to saw at the bindings that shielded her breasts from them. She spat on him and he chuckled, continuing to slash at the linen until it fell away.

She willed herself to look past them, focusing on the flames of one of the torches as she felt him pawing at her roughly. A whimper burst from her lips.

'Stop wasting time,' the other complained. 'I want my turn.'

'Get her breeches down then,' the first one replied distractedly.

Her boots were ripped off and thrown unceremoniously across the cave and the other soldier began to tug the legs of her snug trousers hard, pulling her body with them, her arms taking the brunt of the pressure. She heard something pop in her shoulder and was glad everything was still numb.

Then she heard a sound – the tell-tale crunch of a boot on the path. She screamed, praying that they would help her. She looked back at the two men, their desperation for her body making them stupid. The other one continued to pull at her breeches and she saw a shadow at the cave entrance. Then Kane appeared behind them. He froze for a moment when he saw the scene before him and let out a murderous roar that at any other time would have terrified her, but not then. Right at that moment it was the best sound she'd ever heard. He pulled the one still trying to get her trousers off up by his hair and slit his throat with such force it practically severed the man's head, throwing his body aside before pulling the other one off her and flinging him away. The mercenary turned, drawing his sword.

'Wait your fucking turn,' he snarled, attacking Kane head-on. Kane parried easily, feigned left and had his dagger embedded in the man's abdomen before he could make another move.

The mercenary stared down at himself in disbelief, his cock still hard in his breeches. Kane looked him in the eye and pulled the blade upwards, gutting him like an animal. His innards spilled out onto the floor and he fell to his knees with a moan before falling to one side.

Kane ignored the dying man and advanced on her. She just stared at him, wondering if this was real or just her mind unwilling to comprehend that she was being defiled in this cave.

CHAPTER 33

KANE

She was looking at him, but it was as if she wasn't really there. Kane called her name and her brow furrowed. Still she said nothing, didn't move as he knelt beside her.

She was naked to her knees, her breeches halfway down her legs. Blood ran freely down her face and chest and was smeared across her skin by their hands. He cursed Quin as he pulled what was left of her clothes up as far as he could and then cut the ropes from her wrists. Her arms fell and she left them where they landed, staring at a place on the wall behind him. Her left shoulder looked lower than the other. It was out of its socket. Putting it back into joint would have to wait for Sorin's skill. Kane growled, wishing he could kill the two cunts again and make it more painful for them.

'Lana?'

Nothing.

He pulled her to her feet and fumbled with his tunic, intending to take it off to wrap her in. Her legs buckled and he caught her with a curse, holding her against him as he pulled up her trousers with his other hand. He lowered her back to the ground gently and put her boots on. Then he removed his tunic and covered her.

With a final look around the cave, he lifted her into his arms and left, moving quickly down the hill in the moonlight towards the port, where Sorin and Viktor were finding a ship to take them back to the mainland.

After searching practically the whole island for Lana that afternoon, he, Sorin and Viktor had returned to the docks to learn that her clothes had been found in the sea.

Even now, after discovering her alive, Kane was still reeling from seeing those bloodied scraps that afternoon and believing that she was dead for hours. Something had broken in him and the others. They'd milled around, all three in a daze as 'the witch's clothes' were passed around and the men raised horns of ale to her death.

It wasn't until the moon was high that Quin approached, whispering to them that she was alive and in that fucking cave. He still wasn't clear about the man's reasons for taking her in the first place, but Quin had assured him that she was not dead.

So he'd ordered Sorin and Viktor to procure a ship and supplies so that they could leave the Army of the Dark Brothers. For her. Neither of them had liked the fact that he was going to find her alone. They'd both wanted to see for themselves if she really was there – and they no longer trusted him with her, he'd realised. It was a blow, though he wasn't surprised. He didn't trust himself either, truth be told. The things she made him feel, he didn't recognize, for if he had ever felt them, he didn't remember. He was so protective of her that he was terrified of her coming to any harm. He saw that now. He was afeared and it made him angry. How could this girl have burrowed past his inner darkness and made him so vulnerable to her?

He looked down at her stiff form in his arms. He could

just see her eyes, still open, staring unseeing into the darkness, and found that he didn't feel even the smallest amount of resentment that they were having to leave. The Brothers meant nothing compared to her. He didn't even care that they had no plan save getting to the mainland. None of it mattered now. Not even Vineri, the Collector, the man who had haunted his nightmares since he was a boy. Kane had lived on thoughts of revenge in the Dark Brothers for so long, he wasn't sure what else there was, but there *was* more. Lana was proof of that.

As he reached the buildings by the docks, she began to shiver, and he wrapped his arms more tightly around her, carefully so as not to cause her pain. Had it really been only the day before yesterday that he'd been so close to whipping her? He shook his head, promising himself that his temper would never get the better of him again where she was concerned. Sorin had been right to beat him so severely. He'd deserved it.

Kane could see the dwindling fires on the nearby beach as he approached the water. The men had been drinking heavily in celebration of the successful invasion and Lana's death. Most would be in drunken stupors by now. He passed one or two still making merry and kept to the shadows as he made his way over the wooden planks to the smaller fishing vessels where the others should be waiting.

He saw movement, which was immediately followed by three soft taps of a boot against the wood. He relaxed, returning the signal with his own.

'Do you have her?' came Viktor's whisper, cutting through the dark.

'Yes,' he replied, 'but she's hurt.'

'Bring her.'

He followed Viktor through the short but complicated maze of docks and boats until they reached the one that would carry them back to the mainland. It looked like a smaller version of the ones they'd made the crossing on, which was fortunate, as it would have at least one cabin where they could keep Lana out of sight.

He boarded and found Sorin waiting for him.

'Take her below,' he said in a low voice. 'We sail soon. Viktor's standing watch, but the captain and crew are being well paid. I doubt there will be trouble.'

Kane nodded, maneuvering himself and Lana into the depths of the merchant ship. He followed Sorin down the corridor to a small cabin with four bunks. He lay Lana down on one, wincing as her face showed the pain she was in.

'Lana, thank the gods you're alive,' Sorin breathed. He turned to Kane. 'Why is she not speaking? What's wrong with her?'

'I don't know. One of her shoulders is out of joint, though. Other than that, some cuts, and she's shivering, though she feels warm. She hasn't spoken since I found her.'

Sorin knelt by the cot and tugged Kane's tunic away. 'Did you do this?' he asked, his voice sharp.

Kane's eyes narrowed. 'Of course not. When I got to the cave, she was bound to the wall and two soldiers were attacking her.'

'Attacking her?'

'Trying to rape her,' Kane clarified.

'Gods,' Sorin growled. 'And she's been like this since you found her?'

Kane shifted on his feet, wishing Sorin would hurry up and do something to help her. 'Yes.'

'Prop her legs up higher than her head and get me salve. We won't be able to put the shoulder back in until we're at sea – she'll make too much noise – but we can sponge the blood away, see to the bruises and close the cuts.' He paused as he surveyed her swollen eye, the blood crusted over her skin and the bruises over her breasts. 'The ones who did this are dead?'

'Of course. Too quickly, though.'

'We should have found her sooner. Quin, Mal and Payn will pay for this.'

'Yes,' Kane agreed, 'but not tonight.'

'Find some extra blankets. She needs to be kept warm.'

Kane grabbed a blanket from one of the other bunks and gestured to the small bed she occupied. 'Should I …?'

'If you can keep from beating her or fucking her then yes, the heat from your body would be beneficial,' Sorin said wryly, mixing some herbs from the medicine pack and rising. 'I need hot water. I'll be back. Try not to move her overmuch.'

Sorin left, closing the door securely behind him, and Kane climbed carefully over Lana's slight form to settle into the small bed next to her, drawing the thick cover over them both. He watched her for a long time and when her eyelids finally began to close, only then did he allow himself to sleep as well.

For the first time in weeks, he dreamed of her.

CHAPTER 34

LANA

His hands slid up her arms, caressing her skin, moving to trace the cords of her neck before drifting down to knead her breasts. He plucked at the nipples and she sighed contentedly. Her clothes were gone, but she didn't mind. Her fingers smoothed the coarse hair of his broad chest, feeling the taut muscles beneath. He was as bare as she was. He kissed his way down her body from her navel and gripped her thighs, spreading them wide.

She gasped as his head delved between her legs. He laved her with his tongue, up and down, leaving nowhere untouched, and she gave a moan, opening herself wider for him. He thrust it into her, making her squirm beneath his unyielding hold before moving up and fastening his lips over that part of her that craved it the most. Her hips rolled as she felt him enter her slowly. He moved within her and she screamed as pleasure flooded her.

She groaned, becoming aware of creaking sounds that seemed quite rhythmic and then a rocking motion to match.

Her body ached and felt so heavy she could barely move her arms. She was on her back. Her head was pounding. She shifted slightly, intending to roll onto her side, and gasped as pain shot through her shoulder and arm, making her want to cast up the contents of her stomach. She grunted, clenching her jaw and shutting her eyes even as she froze, easing back onto the blanket she lay on, trying to breathe through it. Someone was next to her. She turned her head slowly and opened her eyes to look. *Kane.*

The sight of him filled her with elation, yet despair. She wondered how she could feel such opposites at the same time as she watched him. How could his presence be such a comfort to her after everything he'd done?

He was fully clothed. His eyes were closed and one of his hands was under the blanket – on her, she realised as his wrist twitched. His fingers, which had been still, twisted inside her, and she whimpered at the pleasing sensation that coursed through her.

His blue eyes met hers and for a moment he looked endearingly confused. She studied his face, realizing for the first time that, beneath the short dark beard, he looked younger than both Sorin and Viktor. When he was properly awake and ordering everyone around, he wore his command over himself like an impenetrable fortress. She'd never seen him like this. Open. He'd been beaten recently. She wondered who had done it and for what. Kane wasn't the type to take a thrashing lying down, so it must have been someone with as much fighting skill as him to inflict so much damage. One of his eyes was still almost shut and his jaw was swollen. Cuts marred his lips and a shallow one ran down the side of his face; the side that wasn't already scarred. She wanted to reach out and touch him – as if that would make him feel better somehow – as if he would welcome it.

Abruptly feeling like bursting into tears, she was glad when she heard the sound of a door. She turned her head towards it slowly with a grimace as her shoulder twinged at the tiny movement.

'You're awake,' Sorin said as he shut it with a quiet click.

Kane shifted away from her on the narrow cot they'd shared, and she couldn't help the small sound that escaped her lips as his fingers slipped out of her.

Sorin's eyes darted to him suspiciously, but he said nothing.

'Where are we?' she asked, finding her voice a hoarse whisper.

'On a ship bound for the mainland.' He put a small wooden cup to her lips and she drank thirstily.

Her brow furrowed. She couldn't shake the feeling that there was something important she ought to remember. 'Why?'

Sorin shared a look with Kane and brushed his knuckles across her forehead gently. 'We can talk about that later. How do you feel?'

'Half-dead. What happened?'

Another look between them.

Lana frowned. 'What is it?' she asked, starting to get annoyed with them.

'What's the last thing you remember?'

Lana thought hard through the fog, trying to piece together the events that had transpired to set them back on a boat so soon.

'I left the ship to look for you. I walked up a hill … I was so tired.' She closed her eyes as she saw the road she'd taken and the citadel looming before her. 'I snuck into the hall while you were all meeting with Greygor. Then you were sent away and they brought a priest. He told them where to find something. Greygor and the others left. The priest knew I was there. I – I'm sorry.'

She felt Kane's eyes on her, but he said nothing. She couldn't look at him.

'What for?' asked Sorin gently.

'I tried to save him. I couldn't leave him like that. I know I'm a Dark Brother and I shouldn't have helped him, but I had to.' She opened her eyes expecting Sorin's censure and was surprised when she saw none in his gaze.

'But then Quin came,' she continued. *Quin* ... 'He put something over my mouth. I couldn't breathe. When I woke up, I was in a cave.'

Gods. The cave. She swallowed hard as a rush of images came back to her.

'What happened in the cave? Lana, did Quin or one of the others hurt you?'

She suppressed a shudder. 'No. Not them. Not really. But I tried to escape, so Quin left me tied up there – for hours. Two men came much later. I tried to fight them, but I ... I couldn't.'

Kane had come for her. She remembered how he'd burst in like a shining knight saving a princess and almost laughed at the absurdity. He was about as far from a chivalrous savior in a childish story as she was royalty. She turned her head slowly to look back at him.

'I thought I was imagining you when you found me,' she said softly. 'Thank you for stopping them. I owe you my life.'

'You owe me nothing,' was all he said, his face somehow more expressionless than usual.

Sorin knelt by the side of the cot and probed her shoulder gently. 'Did the soldiers do it?'

She winced and nodded.

'It needs to be put back into place. We're far enough out to sea now to do it.'

'What do you mean?' Lana asked, a cold fear settling over her.

'It's going to hurt, I'm afraid,' Sorin warned her darkly, 'but the quicker we see to it, the better.' He pulled the blanket down, his eyes surveying her body swiftly as if looking for more injuries. 'Can you stand?'

Unable to summon even a modicum of her usual embarrassment at that moment, she merely grimaced as she took the hand he offered and he pulled her into a sitting position. Swinging her legs over the side of the bunk, she tried to rise, only to fall back with a groan. 'I don't have the strength. I don't know what's wrong with me. I'm sorry.'

Sorin's hand cupped her cheek and smiled at her. 'There's nothing to be sorry for. Stop apologizing.' He held another cup out to her. 'Drink this.'

'What is it?'

'It will help with the pain and send you to sleep.'

She took it, poured the contents down her throat without tasting it and handed the empty vessel back to him without a word.

'Kane, hold her still if you can do so without mauling her.'

Kane moved around her and smoothly extricated himself from the tiny bed. He put his arms around her and pulled her gently into him so that her good shoulder pressed into his body while Sorin picked up her other arm and raised it. She grabbed onto Kane's arm, holding it tightly as she buried her head into his chest. She braced herself for the pain Sorin had described while stupidly reveling in Kane's touch, innocuous though it was.

CHAPTER 35

KANE

Lana's scream echoed through the ship as Sorin pushed the joint back into its place with a pop. She struggled against Kane, but he held her fast, not letting her move as her tears of pain wet his shirt.

When it was done, she sagged against him, her eyes closed, and he put her gently back into the bed. When Sorin pulled the blanket over her, hiding her from his sight once more, he wanted to tear it off her simply to see her again. She wasn't even awake. Whatever Sorin had given her had worked quickly. She had sunk into oblivion. But that didn't stop him from wanting to cover her body with his at that very moment.

Disgusted with himself, he turned away from her to watch Sorin clearing away his tinctures and powders. 'What *is* wrong with her?'

'I gave her a sleeping draught. She'll be out for a few hours. Here.' Sorin tossed him a jar of ointment. 'Rub that on her injuries while she can't feel the pain. Put it around the shoulder, too.'

Kane caught it deftly and flung it on one of the other beds with a scowl. 'You fucking do it.'

Sorin shook his head with a chuckle. 'I'd give a large portion of gold to be there when she finally breaks you.'

Kane ignored him. 'I meant why does she seem so weak?' He looked back at her, taking in her wan complexion and the dark circles under her eyes.

Sorin shrugged. 'She's tired. She's been through an ordeal – a few, actually – in a very short time. She's not used to this life.'

'Well, she'd better get used to it or she won't last long,' he forced himself to growl even as every fiber of his being cried out at the idea that she might not survive the path they were leading her down.

Sorin didn't reply, just methodically covered Lana's cuts and bruises himself and then put the salve away. 'I have some things to attend to. Stay with her. If she seems afraid, soothe her. If she wakes, have her drink some water.' He left without waiting for a response, leaving Kane standing awkwardly in the berth. He supposed he should lie on one of the other beds, get some sleep, but instead he climbed over her limp form and settled next to her, ensuring the blanket was pulled up to her chin and that she was warm.

As he made her more comfortable, all the times he'd performed a similar ritual came to mind. He'd been no more than a boy then. For the first time in a long time, he allowed himself to briefly remember the events that had led him to join the Dark Brothers. He thought about Lily and Toman, but it was too painful even for a moment, so he shut them away in his mind once again. There were more important things to think about now.

What would they do when they reached the mainland? How were they going to survive now that they were traitors for deserting the Dark Army? Killing was his only skill, but

Viktor had been a farmer before, and Sorin could make a passable alchemist and healer. They'd have to move around, though. Not for the first time since they'd departed did Kane find himself wishing he'd gone back and slit Greygor's throat before they sailed.

While first and foremost getting rid of an enemy that may well follow them, the ensuing power struggle, with him gone as well, would have delayed the army in the Islands for weeks. Too late now, though. He'd stayed with Lana instead. He would just have to trust that Greygor would be more interested in getting his payment for that relic they'd been looking for than in hunting them.

Kane's eyes widened and he sat bolt upright in the cot. If Sorin was right and it was the Collector who had hired them to invade the Islands, they could use all of this to find him once and for all.

By his side, Lana stirred in her deep sleep and cuddled closer. He settled next to her again, not wanting to disturb her, but in his mind, the cogs were turning quickly. If they bided their time, all three of them could still have their revenge.

A WHILE LATER, Sorin and Viktor came back to the cabin, and Kane carefully extricated himself from the bed once more.

'Glad to see you can be trusted not to fuck her while she sleeps, at least,' Sorin remarked, and Kane's lip curled as the comment hit too close to the mark.

'Why are you still harping on? You avenged her, didn't you? After going for my face like a crazed whore. I still can't open my fucking eye.'

'You deserved everything I gave you and more.'

'That isn't our way. You used your fists, the mistake was

punished, and you got your satisfaction. It's done. Keep bringing it up and I'll rip your pretty face to pieces as well.'

'As if I ripped your face to pieces,' Sorin scoffed. 'I could have done much worse to you. I would have, too, but I know she wouldn't like it because even though you're always a fucking bastard to her, she still cares about you.'

Kane didn't reply. He *had* been a bastard to her. He wanted to make amends; he just didn't know how. As for her caring about him, he doubted it. He hadn't been kind to her in all the weeks since they'd met. He had been cold and harsh. He'd pushed her harder than he should have in their training sessions to make her suffer – as he was suffering, he supposed. He hadn't said one nice word to her and in fact had gone out of his way to be cruel. He'd told himself it was to make sure she didn't get arrogant, but each time he'd seen the tears in her eyes that she'd tried to hide, it had given him a petty satisfaction. Every time she'd walked away with a new bruise from their sparring, he had been a tiny bit delighted that she was paying for making him want her so completely.

Now, things were changing. What pleased him was the strength he could see in her eyes as she adjusted to being a freewoman, the happiness she exuded when she learned a new skill, the noises of contentment she made at his simplest touch.

In his breeches, his cock throbbed painfully. He rubbed his hands over his face. Being in here with her and not able to have her was torture.

'Did she wake?' Viktor asked.

'No. She's just slept since Sorin left.' Kane sat heavily on one of the other beds and tried to focus on his plan. 'There's something I've been thinking on.'

CHAPTER 36

LANA

As she lay unmoving with her eyes firmly shut, listening to the Brothers' low voices, Lana felt she should really stop waking up to eavesdrop on conversations. But what Kane, Viktor and Sorin were discussing now was seated firmly in the sphere of subjects they never spoke of in front of her, though she was purportedly one of them. She knew she shouldn't really expect to be told everything, but she did wish they would trust her a bit more. It was the wrong way to go about it, but she needed to know what was going on.

'This may well be our only chance. That is, if you truly believe it is he who paid the Brothers to invade the Islands, Sorin.'

'I do. Who else would have the wealth? Who else would bother sending an army to collect some rare trinket? It's him and you're right; this might be our last chance at revenge.'

Viktor's voice joined the others. 'It's simple, then. We know where they'll make landfall. We just need to wait for them and follow them to wherever they're making the exchange. We follow his agent and hope we are led to the bastard.'

'What about Lana?'

'What about her? She comes with us.'

'It's too dangerous. He collects anything that is rare or valuable. Can you imagine what he would do with her if he found out what she is? And, remember, the further north she goes, the more dangerous it becomes for her.'

'The captain says the wind has been favorable and we'll dock earlier than expected. His first port is a small town up the coast from where the army will land. We could leave her there while we–'

'No,' Kane's voice snarled. 'She is one of us. We're not leaving her with a keeper. Where we go, she goes.'

To say she was surprised was an inadequate description. Kane *wanted* her with them? What was going on? She made a show of stretching and their voices hushed. A cup was put to her lips. She drank every drop.

She opened her eyes to find all three Brothers sitting on the beds around her, making the already small cabin seem positively tiny.

'Are you hungry?'

She nodded and a plate of meat and bread was placed in her hands. 'When do we reach the mainland?' she asked between mouthfuls.

'Soon.'

She just about stopped herself from rolling her eyes at them. 'Will you give me more than one-word answers or must I wring them from you like water from a strap? Am I not still one of you?'

'Yes, of course you are, but–'

'But nothing,' she interrupted Viktor. 'Tell me what is happening. Please. Have you – have we – left the Brothers?

Are they coming for us? For me? What is our plan? I'm not a child that must be coddled! Tell me the truth.'

She tried to keep her eyes open during her little speech, she really did, but they began to drift closed of their own accord towards the end, which, she suspected, somewhat damaged what she was trying to convey. She vaguely heard the plate fall from her hand and clatter to the floor and she was glad she had eaten most of it.

'You see? I told you there's something wrong with her.'

The next time she opened her eyes, she was on a horse in Viktor's arms. Her brow furrowed. 'Where…?'

'Hush, little bird. You aren't well. We're on the mainland and we're taking you to a hedge witch.'

'A witch?' she mumbled puzzledly.

'A wise woman,' he amended.

'Which is it?'

Viktor made a noncommittal sound. 'All these old hags are basically the same. Regardless of what they call themselves, they aren't actual witches.'

She turned her head to see where they were going and spied a tiny cottage in the forest, its thatched roof and wooden structure making it blend in well with its surroundings. As they cantered up, the door opened a crack.

'Woman. We have need of your services.'

A hunched mass of rags hobbled out slowly, leaning heavily on a stick. 'What do three Dark Brothers want with the likes of me?' rasped the voice of a crone.

'Our friend is ill. They said in the town that you might be able to help.' Sorin paused. 'We can pay.'

The woman eyed them all long enough for them to start shifting impatiently.

'Can you help or not?' Kane barked.

She simply watched him as if debating something. Then, making her decision, she let go of the stick and stood up straight.

'Bring her in, then,' said the voice of a much younger woman.

Viktor carried her into the house. Dried plants and bundles of leaves hung from nails protruding from the thick oaken beams overhead. There were books and scrolls piled on a table and the bottles and jars of an apothecary were crowded untidily on haphazard shelves.

'Lay her on the table.'

Viktor did as he was ordered and stepped back. 'What's wrong with her?'

The crone took off the ragged cloak she wore and hung it on a peg. Under it was a serviceable woolen dress and, surprisingly, the face of a middle-aged woman with mousy brown and slightly greying hair. She waved Viktor away. 'What are her symptoms?'

They all looked at each other.

'Well,' Sorin said finally, 'she's tired. Drained. She can't walk. She can hardly keep her eyes open for more than a few moments.'

The woman peered down at her. 'Do you feel any pain?'

Lana shook her head feebly as the blanket Viktor had brought her in was drawn away.

The woman proceeded to poke and prod for a few minutes before addressing the Brothers once more, though she didn't spare them a look. 'You bound her to you with blood magick,' she stated.

'A Brother's initiation ritual,' Sorin clarified, staring at the wise woman icily.

She muttered something they couldn't hear before she cleared her throat and spoke clearly as she continued her examination. 'So she is tied to all three of you and you to her.'

She shook her head slightly and didn't bother to lower her voice. 'Fools.'

'We are Dark Brothers, woman! You will speak to us with respect,' came Kane's answering snarl.

The woman gave the men a quick, lopsided grin, clearly unimpressed. 'Do not play me false. Perhaps you were part of the Dark Army yesterday, but you're as much Brothers today as I am the old hag who met you at the door.'

'How do you know we–'

She waved a hand. 'Do not insult my talents in my own home. You've quit the Army, you're looking for revenge, blah blah blah. What I cannot fathom, however,' she finally looked up from Lana, staring all three of them down suspiciously, 'is why the fuck three Dark Brothers would bind themselves to a witch.'

'We didn't know.'

The woman cast her eyes broadly over Lana. 'To me, she veritably shines, dull though she is,' she muttered to herself.

'Dull?' Lana croaked.

'You're dying, girl.' She put her hand to Lana's brow.

'Dying?'

The woman sighed.

'Anyone suspected of conjuring is usually killed these days in the north. Did you know that? It's getting that way in the south too. They say that witches are descended from the gods, yet they are marked for death. Odd, no? Find any priest of the Mount and they'll talk your ear off about it. There are entire tomes written about them and their connection to the God Realm in the Great Library in the capital.'

'So we've heard,' came Kane's sardonic voice, which Lana was beginning to realize was what he sounded like when he was upset. 'What of it?'

'It's not true. Once, witches were part of the Dark Army. Long, long ago when it still existed for good. They kept the

Brothers true and, when the Army cast off its mantle of protection to become mercenaries for coin, they killed their witches. Only a few escaped the massacres.'

'Yes, but what does that have to do with what has caused this?' Sorin asked. 'She was fine until recently.' He looked disturbed. 'Was it the blood magick?'

The woman gave him a level stare. 'I doubt it,' she conceded. 'She likely passed near to a breaching portal. The protective wards are failing so, if she had latent Dark Realm blood, as some do, it may have been awakened. Such things are happening with more frequency if the rumors are anything to go by.'

The men nodded and Lana frowned, resolving to ask about these wards later.

'She wasn't born this way. Her mortal body cannot contain the power it holds. She will worsen until she can no longer draw breath,' the woman continued. 'I can see it trickling out of her like a thousand invisible cracks.' Her fingers moved as if feeling something in the air that they couldn't see.

'What can we do?'

'Nothing. What's done is done.'

'No!'

Sorin stepped forward and took Lana's hand. 'There must be something.'

Viktor came to stand next to him, squeezing her knee gently. 'We will not allow you to die, Lana.'

'Wait,' she said, her eyes fixed on her patient. 'You.' She pointed at Kane. 'Touch her flesh to yours.'

Looking mildly perplexed, Kane did as he was told for once.

'Do you feel better?'

It was a moment before Lana realised that the woman was speaking to her.

'Yes,' she said, taking a breath. 'Better than I've felt in days.' Her head began to clear and her body felt a bit stronger.

The woman stared at her face a moment longer. 'There may be a way. I doubt you will like it at first, but it might save you.'

'So you can help,' Sorin summarized.

'I can try,' she said slowly, as if speaking to a child, 'if it isn't too late, but you can do nothing to assist her at the moment.'

'What will you do?' Lana asked her, trying to sit up.

'There are rituals that can be performed; tinctures and potions you can drink. But,' the woman said the last with finality, 'you need to rest here for two or three days.' Her eyes landed on the Brothers. 'Without them.'

'We aren't leaving her here.'

'She goes where we go.'

'Anything that has to be done can be done with us here.'

Lana almost smiled as they all spoke at once, but she thought the woman was right. She needed time to recover some strength with someone who knew how to heal her.

She drew the blanket around herself, shaking off the hands that held her. 'I will stay. You three can follow the Brothers as they make that exchange and see if you can get your revenge,' she said sweetly.

Sorin put a hand on her shoulder. 'We can find someone else to help.' He lowered his voice. 'I don't trust her.'

She put her hand over his, savoring his strength. 'I can already feel myself weakening again. If she can help me, then I want her to try. If she's lying, well, I won't last very long anyway.'

The woman grinned. 'My name is Vie. I'm not lying. I'll do what I can, but the ritual is not for the fainthearted.'

Lana nodded. 'I understand. What do you want for it?'

'Thirty gold pieces.'

'Half now. Half when they return, if I'm still alive.'

'Done.'

Lana lay back on the table, breathing out slowly. She grinned at the Brothers for appearance's sake. Inside, she was terrified.

'Go on then,' she said to Kane. 'Pay the woman.'

She watched as Kane gritted his teeth. No doubt he believed she was little worth all this trouble and coin. She half-closed her eyes with a sigh.

'Take her to the bed. I need to begin immediately. Leave and return in not less than three days.'

Lana vaguely felt herself being lifted and deposited on top of what felt like a mountain of furs. She heard them murmur comforting platitudes and felt them hold her hands, and then they were gone and she slipped back into the haze.

THE NEXT THING SHE KNEW, her hair was being pulled. 'Ow,' she mumbled, trying to go back to sleep, but the pain persisted until she opened her eyes.

'There you are,' said the woman – *Vie*. 'I'm ready to begin. You need to drink this.' The contents of a cup were poured down her throat. 'That should give you strength enough to begin.'

Lana coughed and spluttered but swallowed. 'Begin what?' she asked groggily, trying desperately to remember what was going on.

'The ritual, of course,' said Vie, holding something up. 'I should tell you now that I'm a witch. I was born though, so different than you, but a witch just the same. You have to keep it to yourself though. As far as my neighbors are concerned, I'm a simple wise woman with herb skill.'

'Why are you telling me?' Lana tried to focus on the

blurry object the woman held and, seeking to rub her eyes to clear them, tried to move her arm. But she couldn't. She couldn't move anything; not her arms or her legs – only her head.

'So you understand that I know what I'm doing,' the witch replied.

She began to breathe quickly and shallowly, unable to draw a full breath. 'Why can't I–'

'Calm down, Lana. It's just part of the ritual. You won't be able to move this body until it's done, but don't worry; you won't need to once it begins. Look at me.'

Lana did as she was told. Her eyes had cleared and she was finally wide awake. She also saw the strange item Vie held with clarity. It was a thick cylinder with a rounded bulb on one end and what appeared to be a handle on the other. 'What is that?'

'This,' she said, bringing the long, stone thing closer to her, 'is a phallus that once adorned a statue in the first gods' temple on the Mount. It will get you to the ones who can help you.'

'How?' Lana swallowed. 'What are you going to do with it?' she asked, fearing the answer.

'Exactly what you're thinking, I'm afraid. The Gods have odd senses of humor,' she said simply, giving Lana a sympathetic look. 'Sorry.'

Lana tried to struggle, but it was useless. There weren't any bonds to strain against. In fact, she wasn't even on the bed, but hovering in the air quite far over it, she realised.

'No!' she shrieked. 'Why are you doing this? I thought you were going to help me!'

The witch grimaced. 'I'm sorry, Lana. God magick is generally a carnal thing, and it's the only way to get you to where you need to go so you don't die. I'm not some pervert gaining pleasure from this, I assure you. If there was another way, I'd do it.'

Lana gasped as her legs were wrenched wide by some unseen force. Vie parted her inner lips gently.

'I beg you. Please don't.'

'Hush. I'm being paid well to save you, and this is the only way I know. I will go as gentle as I can,' she said, sounding distracted, and Lana felt the head of the very cold instrument probe her opening. 'Try to relax. I've used oil so it will move easily within you. And, Lana,' she hesitated and gave her a look of warning, 'just do what they say, all right?'

Lana cried out as the phallus entered her, the stone forcing her channel to widen. It was pulled out and thrust back in, this time going further and forcing her to bite back a moan. Vie did this a few more times as Lana twisted and whimpered. It didn't hurt; it felt good and that was perhaps the worst part. She should not be enjoying this, she thought, as she began to welcome the feeling of it filling her, pleasure mounting quickly. But, then, the energy the potion had given her left her and she spiraled down into darkness, thinking that at best the ritual hadn't worked and at worst Vie was depraved and evil and there was no ritual at all.

'WELL, well, it's been a while since one of you found your way here, mortal.'

Lana was standing in a white stone hall. Majestic columns surrounded an enormous room. Fountains nearby trickled and babbled, their sound unnaturally pleasing to the ear. A stream meandered through as well, its path in the marble of the floor worn completely smooth.

She looked down at herself and saw a flowing white dress that was held at the shoulders by two rows of delicate gold clasps.

'Are you simple?'

She looked around, trying to locate the speaker, and finally spied an impossibly beautiful man lounging on a bed. He was dressed in white as well. She approached him cautiously.

'No, I'm not simple. Am I dead?'

The man chuckled. 'No, my sweet girl. You aren't dead. Not yet, but your aura suggests you will be soon.'

He sat up slowly, surveying her. 'What do you think, Magnus?' His question was directed at someone behind her, and she quickly turned to find another man, just as handsome as the first. His garb was similar, but his hair was blond where the other's was a light brown.

'I think you're right, Bastian. It's been a long time since a mortal girl came looking for us.'

His eyes danced with mischief – at her expense, she realised. Anger rose in her. Where was Vie? Who were these men? They were pleasing to look at, to be sure, but the last she remembered, the witch had been defiling her with a white marble phallus.

'How did you get here, girl?' Magnus asked.

Lana blushed crimson and her anger was replaced entirely with mortification. 'A – a ritual,' she stammered. 'A woman…a witch …'

Bastian chuckled again. 'I don't suppose it had something to do with a big, stone cock?'

If it was possible, Lana's face became redder. 'Well … she didn't tell me–'

'I'll bet she didn't!' Magnus guffawed loudly, making her jump.

Bastian slowly got up from the bed and came towards her. 'Whatever shall we do with you?' he asked, his voice low and honeyed.

'Gaila will want –' started Magnus.

'She'll get her turn,' Bastian said mildly. 'For now, we found her first.'

Lana looked around her again and a suspicion dawned. The more she noticed of her surroundings, the more she feared her theory was right. 'You'll do whatever you want with me, I suppose,' she answered him. 'I know where I am.'

He looked mildly surprised but schooled his features quickly. He reached out and, with a flick of his fingers, undid the clasps holding her dress together. It floated gently to the floor.

She didn't take her eyes off his face even as his eyes travelled the length of her.

'Say it,' he whispered in her ear. 'Aloud.'

'I'm on the Mount.' She breathed out slowly, trying to keep calm, though her knees felt as if they might buckle. 'You're gods.'

She felt his smile against her cheek.

'And it's been a very, very long time since a mortal was tricked into coming to our realm.'

She stepped away from Bastian, frowning. 'I wasn't tricked.'

'Weren't you?'

Lana's eyes narrowed. She was scared, but she really didn't have anything to lose. 'I'm dying,' she said simply. 'You said so yourself. Now, if you aren't powerful enough to help me, I'll find one of you who is.'

Both gods looked equal parts scandalized and fascinated.

'Listen to how she speaks to us!' Magnus exclaimed. 'They certainly have changed since the early days, haven't they? Do you hear that fire? I love it!'

The other nodded. 'Refreshing,' he agreed. He turned to her. 'Whether or not we can help you depends on you.'

'What do you mean?'

'You must complete three challenges,' the blond interjected as the other opened his mouth to speak. 'Show valor, loyalty and strength. But be warned – no one has ever prevailed.'

Lana's lip quivered and she bit it, standing up straighter. 'Where do I begin?'

'Go over to that fountain.'

She looked where he pointed. A beautifully ornate marble statue of a woman bathing, water flowing from a pot she held, stood in the middle of the stream.

'To begin the first challenge, you must open the passage.'

Lana looked back at the two gods watching her from across the room. 'How?'

'Use the tits,' Magnus called.

She gave the statue's breasts a push.

'Harder.'

'Twist the nipples a bit.' Bastian said helpfully.

Lana gave the statue a shove with all her might and tried to turn said nipples, but they wouldn't budge.

Both Gods burst out laughing, and Lana turned on them with a scowl.

'I don't understand what's so amusing.'

They laughed harder. Bastian took a swig of wine from a skin. Before she knew what she was doing, Lana had marched over to them and snatched the skin from his hand.

She threw it down in disgust. 'Look at you. You're not gods. Two drunken fools wasting all the time in the realms on *nothing*. I am weak and dying, but still not as pitiful as you!' With a growl, she turned away from the men, who now looked genuinely shocked at her outburst. 'You cannot help me,' she muttered, sure that at any moment she would be reduced to a pile of ash.

A tinkling laugh cut through the babbling of the water. A woman stood not far from them in the same sort of flowing dress that Lana had been divested of earlier.

'Well, she told you two wastrels well enough. Don't listen to them, girl. What is your name?

'Lana.'

'You are right, Lana. They cannot help you. They wouldn't have the first idea of how.' The woman raised an eyebrow. 'But I can.'

'Who are you?' Lana asked suspiciously.

'Gaila. The first.'

'The first?'

'I was there at the first dawn,' Gaila said airily and rolled her eyes at the other two gods. 'These fools and others like them just appeared one day and I haven't been able to get rid of them. Ignore them and come with me, child.' She held out her hand and Lana took it. The goddess she'd never heard of led Lana up some worn stone steps she hadn't noticed before.

'Perhaps we can help each other, my dear.'

Lana was taken through a door and found herself in a room with three stone walls. The fourth side had no wall at all and looked out over a sunny valley as if the room was built into a hillside. The furniture and the walls reminded Lana of her father's house in that every piece of decoration looked expensive.

Gaila flopped down onto a plush settee with a sigh. 'The Mount. Such a taxing place,' she said, closing her eyes for a moment.

'We aren't on the Mount any longer?' Lana asked.

'Oh no; this is my private realm away from the others' petty squabbles. Do sit, Lana. Would you like wine? Food? No? Well, if you do change your mind …'

Lana sank down on one of the other chairs, all facing the outside. A few moments passed quietly and Lana, for once uncomfortable with the silence, grasped for something to fill it. 'It's beautiful,' she murmured, gesturing to the tree-covered hills and the sky.

'Yes, it is, isn't it?' The goddess smiled somewhat sadly. 'That's my window into your realm. I can see whatever I like from here, but I cannot set foot there.' At Lana's expression of curiosity, she waved a hand. 'A bargain I made long ago. It doesn't matter now. Only the highest priests remember me there anymore. My devotees are all Dark Realm these days. I intend to hold up my end of the deal I made, but, you see, that's why I need you.'

Gaila sat up and stared intently into Lana's eyes, reminding her of a feline about to pounce. 'Something's been stolen from me and I need it back.' She grasped Lana's hands in her own. 'You arriving just at this time was fortuitous for both of us, so this is what we will do. You will find what was taken from me and restore it to my caretakers and, in return, I will help you with your little problem.'

Lana had begun to nod before the goddess had even stopped speaking. There was nothing to consider. 'If you can truly save me, then whatever you ask of me is yours. You have my word.'

Gaila nodded. 'An object of mine was recently taken from its hiding place under a temple in the Islands.'

'The Vessel,' Lana breathed, remembering what Greygor had wanted.

'Yes. At the moment it's in the hands of this man.' The view of the hills changed to one where Greygor sat writing inside his tent, a black, rotund urn with a handle sat on the desk in front of him. The Vessel. 'But soon he will sell it to another.' The pictured shifted to a thin figure standing in shadow. 'I cannot see his face, nor where he is. Almost everything about him is hidden from my sight. This man is the real threat. He has accumulated many, many potent artefacts from your realm as well as others. He has become very powerful and he's starting to realize it. Soon even the gods won't be able to stop him.'

'Stop him from doing what?' Lana stared at the shadow. This was the Collector, she was sure. This man had tortured Sorin, made him a body slave and made him kill his mother. He had burned Viktor's children in their beds. He had done something so awful to Kane that his entire life had become simply an avenue for revenge. How many countless others had been hurt or killed because of him?

'Amassing power – as much as he can. If he gets strong enough, he could take the Mount itself. He would become a god, stronger even than I, and many more would die than have already been killed by him.'

'You only want me to take the Vessel from him?' Lana asked.

'You won't be able to do much more. He has protection. The only thing holding him back is his own ignorance. That is why the Vessel is so important. It is knowledge. With it, he could destroy the portals, the realms, meld them together, kill anyone – everyone.'

Lana looked back at the goddess. 'The Brothers – *my* Brothers want to kill him.'

Gaila stood. 'I hope they'll succeed, but it will be without my aid. I am forbidden to act directly.'

'What about me?'

The goddess looked devious. 'You have Dark Realm blood; very diluted, but it's enough. A delicious little loophole. I can help you – just a bit.'

Gaila drew Lana to her feet and took her face in her hands. 'Your life drains from you even now. The bond you have with the three Brothers has given you more time but its barely sustaining you.' She looked down her nose at Lana. 'Luckily for you, I have an abundance of such power. Though your realm has forgotten me, many others have not. I can lend you my strength and give you time. It will be difficult, though.'

She tutted, and when she spoke again, her voice was soft. 'The witches of the old days were much stronger than you. They knew their worth and their power came from belief in themselves and each other as well as the bond they had with the Dark Army. They were like Gods in that way. But you,' Gaila cocked a brow, 'you doubt yourself. Though perhaps it's because your blood was awakened by happenstance, not born.' She let out a long sigh. 'So few are born now.'

Lana looked down at the floor, not wanting the goddess to see the tears she blinked back, how her words rang with truth. She was just a slave girl from a village in the middle of nowhere with a mother who had sickened and died, not even willed herself to live for her child – just died. And Lana was angry, she realised, even all these years later. Why had her mama not fought for life? Why had her father not been much better? Leaving, taking the word of a stable boy that his only daughter was dead, and then all the rest that had happened just a few short weeks ago. Why had she been worth so little to them both? She shook herself out of her unhelpful, dark thoughts.

'Are you sure you can help me?'

'You doubt me?' The goddess' voice brimmed with power and the room shook, the goblets on the table falling over with a clatter.

Lana put up her hands to placate her as she tried to keep her balance. 'No, of course not.' Her voice trembled.

The room stilled. 'You're like a sealed vase leaking through tiny cracks. I must force strength into you. It will not be comfortable.'

Lana wrapped her arms around herself. 'How many days will I have once I leave here?' she asked, changing the subject.

'After I give you my essence?' Gaila's head bobbed from

side to side slightly as she considered. She looked so *human* now, all hints of her tremendous power hidden once again. 'If you stay well rested and take care of yourself, you'll last until midwinter. If you exert your body, less.'

'So if I get you the Vessel, you'll lend me your power for the rest of my life?'

'We'll see. Get me the Vessel first.'

Lana took a deep breath. 'How will you do it?' she asked, fearing something like the last ritual she'd suffered through to get to the Mount in the first place.

Gaila smiled knowingly. 'Don't worry. It's not quite so taxing as getting here was.'

The goddess leant forward, put her hands on either side of Lana's face again and kissed her gently, her lips silky on Lana's own. She opened her mouth and coaxed Lana to do the same, her tongue delving into her boldly but delicately, softly. It was completely unlike anything Lana had felt before, insistent and yet yielding at the same time.

A blinding light emanated from the goddess's ethereal body. It seeped into her and she closed her eyes with a moan, muffled by Gaila's lips, as it warmed her. She arched her back with a cry as her knees buckled, ecstasy flooding every part of her out of nowhere. The kiss ended, but, as if she had been caught unawares by a wave in the sea, Lana was pulled under, turned this way and that. She couldn't breathe, but the pleasure was so intense she didn't want to, afraid that any movement of her own would cause it to cease. It pulsed within her, filling her with strength she had never before felt the like of. The Goddess' Realm faded out of her vision, but she hardly noticed.

SHE WOKE WITH A GASP, sitting up straight and opening her eyes all at once.

'You made it. How do you feel?'

Lana took a deep breath. The joy her body had felt was ebbing. It had seemed to go on for hours and sated her in ways she had never felt before, as if she had gorged on the very food of gods. But instead of feeling tired, she was the opposite. Her body hummed with vitality. She hadn't felt so strong in a very long time, perhaps not ever.

Looking around, she realised she was back in Vie's cottage and she was, thankfully, wearing clothes – a dress of dark homespun wool, to be exact. The witch herself was standing not too far away, warily as if she was afraid to get too close. Lana's eyes narrowed as she threw a pillow at her. It bounced off her harmlessly, of course, and fell to the floor.

'You could have fucking warned me!' she snarled.

Vie had the decency at least to cringe. 'I couldn't. I'm sorry. The ritual wouldn't have worked if I'd told you everything. I swear it. And that was the only way to get your spirit to the God Realm.'

Lana ignored her, stood up and stretched, the movements eliciting a groan as her muscles and joints awakened. The witch stepped back without another word and Lana rolled her eyes. 'After what just happened, I believe you.'

Vie seemed to relax. 'It worked, though. You look … better. *Brighter.*'

'I have until midwinter,' she said.

Vivienne's brow furrowed. 'Who said?'

'The goddess.'

'Goddess?' The witch looked confused. 'The gods, you mean. The ones you pleasured?'

'No.' Lana shook her head. 'No. I pleasured no one.' She grinned in spite of herself as she remembered what Gaila had done to her. 'The opposite, in fact.'

'But the ritual was meant to transport your spirit to the Mount. There, the mortal visitor must pleasure the gods found there however they see fit. They are then granted a reward. Is that not what happened?'

'I did meet two gods. They were fools. A goddess appeared not long after I arrived and she took me to another place. We talked. She told me what I must do, then she kissed me …' Lana closed her eyes, remembering the taste of Gaila and the passion of said kiss, the sensations of pure euphoria that she'd felt. She shuddered as her nethers clenched, and the witch cleared her throat.

'Well, clearly *something* happened.'

'The goddess gave me some of her essence. Thank you for your help, but time is not on my side. I can't wait three days for the Brothers to return. I have to go and find them now.'

'But there is no need. They will be back here by the time the sun is at its highest.'

'But how? You told them not to come back.'

'Lana, you were with the gods for almost three days. Today, as agreed, the men return for you.'

Lana sank down onto the bed. 'But how can that be? It felt like I was gone for less than half a day.'

Vie shrugged. 'Gods,' was all she said by way of explanation.

There was a hard knock at the door. 'Woman! I have need of a poultice,' came a hard, manly voice from outside the cottage.

She grabbed her ragged cloak from a peg on the wall and a cane. 'Stay here and stay quiet,' she ordered in a low voice and all but ran to the thick wooden door.

'Just a minute, dearie,' croaked Vie in her crone's voice. 'Me old legs aren't what they used to be.'

The door creaked open and she hobbled out slowly. A quiet conversation ensued before she limped back in. Pushing the door to behind her, she spun the cloak off with a flourish and hung it back in its place.

'Why do you pretend to be an old woman?'

Vie shrugged and went to one of her shelves, grabbed a couple of bottles and set them on her worktable. 'I have three faces, actually. The old woman, this one, and my true self.'

'Why?'

The witch grimaced. 'Lots of reasons. Partly it's for business. People expect a wise woman to look the part. It makes them believe I can do what I say I can. Also, folks in town know this face as a widow who lives on the other side of the hill from here, so I can move about freely and buy supplies. And, well, times change, I suppose. It's dangerous for those who are different at the moment, witch or no, and it's getting worse. Storms destroy settlements on the coast. Terrible sicknesses kill babes. Raiders plunder and kill. When those sorts of problems descend, people go looking for someone to blame and who do you think their gazes swing to first?' She pointed a thumb at her own chest. 'If they ever come for the strange, wise woman, I can get to my tiny house over the hill in minutes with no one the wiser. After that, I can move on in my own time if I choose without a mob of villagers dogging my every step.'

'Sounds sensible,' Lana agreed. 'And your true face? Why do you hide that?'

Vie hesitated before she spoke. 'I come from a place that I was never meant to leave. If they knew where I was, they'd drag me back.'

'Can I see what you really look like?'

The witch looked up at her, clearly at war with herself. 'I haven't shown anyone my face in a long time,' she admitted, biting her lip.

She seemed to make up her mind. Her face changed; the greying hair becoming a dark brown and her face younger until she looked only a few years older than Lana herself.

Lana's mouth dropped open. 'You're beautiful,' she stammered, not sure what else to say.

'Thank you,' she said stiffly, and her face changed back to that of the middle-aged woman. She looked uncertain, as if she was afraid she'd made a mistake.

'I won't tell anyone, I promise.'

The witch nodded once and went back to her task.

'Can I help you?' Lana asked, pointing at what she was doing.

'Do you know anything about herbs?'

Lana shook her head. 'Only a few things I've learned from the Brothers.'

'Best get yourself some food. There's bread and cheese over there, or I've always got some stew over the fire.'

Lana *was* hungry, she realised. She helped herself to the stew as the witch had suggested, discounting the sudden thought as she ladled it into the bowl that the witch was trying to poison her. If Vie had wanted her dead, she would have had ample time to do her in over the past three days.

Lana sat at a small table, the only surface of the house not covered in vials, herbs and unrecognizable objects. The stew was rich and thick – just the fayre her body craved, and she tucked into it with vigor, using the bread to soak up every bit of it. When she was finished, she leant back and found Vie regarding her thoughtfully.

'What is it?' she asked.

'I was just wondering.'

'What?'

'Well.' Vie went back to filling a small vial with a brownish liquid. When it was full, she put a stopper in the top and turned back to Lana. 'Why did you attach yourself to all three of them? I know Brothers come in threes, but one man's bad enough. Why all of them?'

'I didn't really have a choice at the time,' Lana explained. 'But I care about all of them. I wouldn't change it.'

The witch turned back to her task and didn't say anything more.

'Can I ask you something?' Lana said.

Vie nodded.

'You said you're a witch. Why hasn't what happened to me happened to you?'

Vie gave her a small smile. 'You weren't born with the power, it flowed into you from the breech because your latent blood made you receptive and the protective wards are weakening.'

'And you were born with it?'

'Yes.'

'And why are the wards failing? How do you know?'

Vie looked away, her expression closed. 'There are rumors, more every day, of strange occurrences in the deep forests, of people changing, disappearing, of creatures arriving in our realm that no one has seen except in drawings in the oldest tomes about the Dark Realms. I know the wards are failing because they're no longer doing what they were meant to do.'

'But why?'

'I don't know.' Vie said.

Lana frowned. She was sure the witch was lying.

CHAPTER 37

KANE

Kane's eyes never moved from their target as he, Viktor and Sorin watched the group gathered for the exchange. Greygor had come himself with his own men and brought Quin's unit as well. Kane was surprised the Commander was there. In the past he would have sent Kane.

At first Kane had thought that perhaps Greygor had not chosen a new second yet, but it soon became apparent that Quin had moved up in the world. Kane would be glad for the man, or at the very least indifferent, if he hadn't put Lana in a position to be hurt while they were in the Islands. His motivations for 'saving' Lana and making the Army think the witch dead were still unclear. Why take her out of Greygor's reach only to put her in harm's way by leaving her defenseless in an area teeming with soldiers? Now was not the time, but Kane vowed that when next he saw Quin, he would get some answers out of him.

Beside him, Viktor swore softly. 'We need to make that cunt pay,' he murmured, echoing Kane's own sentiments.

Vineri's agent had arrived by midmorning and, after

some murmured haggling, the deal looked set to be done. But after the coin and a small box switched hands, Quin, Malkom and Payn brandished their weapons, shouting about betrayal. Arrows shot through the trees, killing several soldiers as well as Payn outright. A short battle of evenly matched forces ensued. By the end, bodies from both sides littered the forest floor and the survivors limped away with their prizes.

Kane and the others simply watched and waited. It was no longer their fight, after all, and these sorts of things frequently ended in such a way. The battle had served only to delay their pursuit. He was bored with waiting. On his other side, Sorin yawned and shook his head, murmuring something about not missing being a Brother. Before they knew it, they were all silently following the handful of remaining men through the trees on foot back to their camp while their horses meandered after them a fair distance away. Kane hoped the Collector was close. In an ideal scenario, he would be at the camp nearby, but it wasn't likely. These days, Vineri rarely seemed to venture outside whatever hole he resided in, so they would follow his men, however long it took to be led to their quarry.

Kane ran a hand over the stubble along his jaw absently. He and the others hadn't wanted to leave Lana with the woman in the first place. That they'd been ordered away from her for days was like a festering wound. They needed to return for her as soon as they could, and if the enemy was further away than they had assumed, one of them would have to go back while the other two continued on. They couldn't lose him, not now that they were so close. Revenge had been too big a part of their lives for too long. But they couldn't lose her either. Even Kane could see that now.

They tracked Vineri's men from a good distance, splitting up and circling the camp when they came upon it. It was at the edge of the forest, looking out over the rolling and rocky terrain that led to the mountains. From Kane's vantage point, there were thirty men at least. Well trained. Kane's eyes narrowed. In fact, they looked much like Dark Brothers, which was impossible. The Army's secrets were closely guarded. Even those few who left the Brotherhood remained loyal and would never betray them. Who were these men?

A cry went up and, moments later, Sorin was dumped in the center of the camp. He groaned as he hit the ground but lay unmoving. Kane's jaw clenched. There were too many. There was nothing he could do. Viktor appeared at his side.

'Fuck,' he breathed.

They watched as a sword was pointed at Sorin's chest and the agent appeared from a tent. He glanced down and, even from their position, they could see his expression change as he looked closer. He barked some orders. Sorin's arms and legs were bound immediately and he was thrown unceremoniously into a wagon, which began to move instantly with the agent and many of the men in tow. The few remaining soldiers began to break camp.

'What happened?' Viktor asked.

'I don't know. But Sorin was Vineri's favorite. I think the agent recognized him. He's safe enough for now. The Collector won't kill him outright. He'll want to make an example of him first. Follow. I'll get Lana and track you.'

Viktor scanned the horizon, watching the procession quickly fading from their view. 'You won't need to. They're heading north to the Forge. It's not more than a week's ride at the edge of the mountains. The only town past that is Westport, but they'll only go there for a ship north. There's nothing further on that road until the spring thaw.'

'I'll meet you there with Lana.'

'If they go through to Westport, I'll leave word and follow them.'

Kane clasped his shoulder. 'Be careful.'

Viktor looked surprised. 'Of course, Brother, and you.'

Kane found his horse close by, just inside the treeline, and rode as fast as he could back to the witch's house. He banged on the door as soon as he arrived.

'Woman!'

'Just a minute, dear, give an old woman time to –'

Kane shoved the door hard, and it opened with a crunch. He all but fell into the cottage.

The woman was stirring a pot on the hearth. 'My door!' she exclaimed.

'I'll pay for it to be fixed. Where is Lana?'

'Kane?' Lana sat at a table, having just finished a meal. He stopped short. She looked *well*. Better than he'd seen her.

'Gods, it's not as if I can have someone from the village just come and fix it for me, is it?' she muttered indignantly from across the room.

He ignored her. 'It worked.'

Lana grinned. 'Yes. I'm healed.'

While willing himself not to smile stupidly at Lana, he missed the look the woman gave her that she pointedly disregarded.

'Good. We need to go. Now.' He threw a bag of coins on the table. 'It's all there.' He spared the older woman a glance. 'My thanks.'

Lana was looking past him, towards the door. 'Where are Viktor and Sorin?'

He flinched. She wasn't going to be happy when she found out what had happened. 'Not here,' he said shortly, hoping that would be enough to hold further questions for now.

He watched as Lana said goodbye, surprised when the older woman embraced her and whispered something. Lana nodded and he led her from the house.

He mounted his horse and lifted her up in front of him,

resisting the urge to hold her in his arms. She was back in a dress, so he left both legs on one side to preserve her modesty, surprised that he would even think to do such a thing.

'Where are Sorin and Viktor?' she asked him again.

He said nothing until she turned her face towards his, panic plainly rising. 'Kane. Where are Sorin and Viktor?'

Gods, she was tenacious. He sighed in resignation. 'Sorin was captured. Viktor has followed them. We follow him.'

Lana took in a shuddering breath. 'Captured? By whom?'

He opened his mouth to tell her.

'You were going to go to the exchange to be led to the Collector,' she gasped. She gripped his arm, tears pooling in her eyes. 'Please, Kane, please tell me Sorin hasn't been taken by him; not him.'

'Not the Collector, not yet, but the agent has him. He's safe for now.'

'Safe?' she all but screamed.

'Lower your voice, Lana!' he snapped.

'Safe?' she asked in a lower voice. 'The Collector did awful things to him. Awful things. He is not "safe". We have to get him back!'

Kane let the reins go for a moment and grasped Lana by the shoulders gently. 'He is safe for the moment. It will take time for them to reach their destination. Sorin will not be harmed – not yet.' His eyes narrowed. 'How do you know all this? Have you been spying?'

She looked uncomfortable. 'I ... heard your plan on the ship. You thought I was asleep. The rest Sorin told me.'

'Sorin told you?' he asked incredulously, taking up the reins again. 'He never speaks of that time. And Viktor? Do you know his sorry tale as well?'

Lana hesitated and then nodded. 'He told me about his wife and his children.' She looked back at him. 'Yours is the only story I don't know,' she said softly, and he ached to tell her, speak to her about things he'd never said aloud to anyone. But he resisted.

'You'll ride with me to the Forge,' he said gruffly. 'I didn't think to bring your horse. He will have gone with Viktor's and Sorin's by now.'

Her back straight, she nodded and turned her face back to the road in front of them. They rode well into the night, Kane estimating that if they did so every day, they'd catch up with Viktor by the fifth afternoon.

They dismounted and Lana immediately gathered some sticks and twigs for a fire while he unpacked their bedrolls and made them a simple dinner. They ate in silence, Kane glancing at her frequently while she stared into the flames.

'What else did you hear on the ship?' he finally asked.

'Nothing else.'

'Didn't your parents teach you not to eavesdrop?'

'Well, my mother died when I was a child, so if she did, I don't remember. As for my father, well, we can't really ask him, can we?' she parried.

Of course, her mother died of an illness; Viktor had mentioned it. And he had killed her father, though the bastard had deserved it as far as he could tell. He changed the subject

. 'What happened at the cottage?'

'Nothing.'

'She didn't do the ritual?'

'Oh. The ritual. Yes. She did that and cured me, of course.' She seemed flustered and didn't look at him.

He leant forward and turned her face towards him. She looked down. 'What aren't you telling me?'

'Nothing,' she said too quickly, pulling out of his grasp. 'Though I suppose you could just make me tell you if you really thought I was hiding something.'

Kane took in the sight of her for a moment, from her plaited red hair to the durable hobnail shoes she wore – courtesy of the woman, he guessed – and felt his heart begin to pound in his chest. 'Is that what you want?' he asked softly. 'Do you want me to tell you what to do? To command you? To give you no choice?' He shifted closer. 'What would you like me to make you do, I wonder,' he murmured in her ear.

She retreated from him slightly, and he could tell that it excited as well as terrified her.

'Nothing, Kane. I don't want you to make me do anything.'

He let out a snort. 'I should probably tell you that my gift doesn't work on you. I should have before. Now that we are unit-bound it wouldn't anyway, but even before that you fought me harder than anyone I've never met.'

'Why didn't you tell me?' she asked softly.

'Because I didn't like the power you had over me.'

She sat back and looked at him and it was if she was really seeing him for the first time.

'Will you answer me something?'

'Ask.'

'On the ship. When you …' She swallowed visibly. 'When you were going to beat me, why didn't you?'

'Do you remember what you said?'

She stared at him for a moment, clearly wondering if he was going to turn on her.

'Yes,' she said finally.

'It made me angry – at myself because I realised that I had failed them.'

'Who did you fail?'

'My brother and sister,' he said finally. He hadn't meant to, but the words just began to tumble out.

'We lived on the streets in a large city in the north; me, Toman and Lily. We played together, ate together, stole together. We cuddled each other at night to keep warm. We survived.' He chuckled mirthlessly. 'We were good at it, too.'

'You had a family?'

'They weren't blood kin,' he confessed. 'But we might as well have been. I was the oldest – well, the biggest at least.' It had been up to him to keep them safe. He flinched. He remembered the last day he'd seen them vividly. It had been a sunny afternoon. There were colorful decorations littering the streets for some festival.

'Toman was the smallest. He was always frail, and he fell ill. Lily was blaming herself, though she couldn't have been more than ten winters, and I had to leave them for something. I don't remember why – food or medicine, perhaps – I don't know.'

He paused and her hand found his. 'What happened?'

'When I returned, they were gone. I searched for them, but they'd disappeared. I scoured the city. I found out they'd been snapped up and sold to the games arena, but it was too late.' He closed his eyes as he remembered. 'I snuck in, high in the stands, but it had already begun.'

They'd looked like insects, he was so far from them, as they'd scurried around trying to escape from the beasts that were let in to sacrifice them. He covered his face with his hand.

'There was a group of children; Lily and Toman among them. I watched them all torn to pieces. I couldn't even hear their screams over the crowd.'

'Oh, Kane,' she said softly. 'That's awful. I'm so sorry.' He stroked her fingers with his thumb and she squeezed his in return. 'What does this have to do with the Collector?'

'After, I wandered the streets in a daze. I happened upon a group of mercenaries bragging about the coins they'd earned for selling flesh to the ring. Their leader didn't look like the others, but his face … I'll never forget it. I was terrified but filled with hatred. This man had killed my friends as surely as if he'd torn them apart himself. I knew who he was; everyone did, and everyone stayed out of his way. I wanted to avenge them, but I couldn't. He was too powerful, even then. Gods, I felt so helpless.' He shook his head.

'Go on.'

'I vowed I'd find a way to destroy him. I joined the Army at the bottom as a soldier.' Kane sighed. 'Except that by the time I was a Brother and strong enough to destroy him, Vineri had become a very powerful man. He's impossible to get close to. I stumbled upon him once by accident and he slipped through my fingers.'

CHAPTER 38

LANA

After Kane stopped speaking, he stared at the fire in silence.

Lana didn't say anything. Now she knew each of the Brothers' stories, and she was filled with anger. The Collector was a plague and, regardless of what Gaila had said, she knew she had to try to kill him somehow after she had taken the Vessel from him.

She glanced at Kane's profile, the light of the fire dancing on his features, and wondered if she should tell him about the goddess. He might believe her, but she doubted it. She wasn't sure she would herself if she didn't feel so much better than before. In truth, she felt a bit guilty for telling him she was cured when of course it might only be temporary. She didn't like to lie so brazenly, but she just didn't know what to say to him about it. She would just have to make sure she didn't renege on the deal she'd made with Gaila, that was all.

He was sitting so still, lost in his memories of Toman and Lily, she supposed. She imagined him as a boy, trying to save his family, and her heart ached for him – for all of them. Without really thinking, she put her hand on his arm. She felt it tighten beneath her fingers, but he didn't move. She inched closer and put her hand in his as she had during his story. This time, though, he didn't respond in kind.

'I don't want your pity, woman,' he snarled so vehemently that she would have stumbled back if he hadn't also closed his hand over hers, effectively trapping her.

He turned his head towards her. His face in shadow now; she could only guess at his intentions and hope against hope that he wasn't going to finish what he had started on the boat.

'I would never give that to you,' she said softly, wondering if he could see fear in her eyes.

He surged to his knees, pulling her up with him, and before she knew what was happening, his lips were on hers. He pushed her arms into the small of her back, urging her closer so that her body was flush against his. She could feel him in front of her, already hard, and she moaned. He had hardly touched her since the night she'd been claimed, and she had wanted him to so many times since; every time they sparred and fought, whenever she'd seen him watching her with the others, even on the boat when he was going to whip her. She had hidden it, fearing his scorn when he found out she desired him so badly when he clearly didn't want her. But he did – at least at the moment. And she would take it.

She kissed him back, employing some of the devices the goddess had used on her, and heard him groan.

'You've learned a few things since last time, I see,' he breathed, and she smiled against his lips.

He raised her arms over her head. 'Leave them there,' he ordered, and she did as she was told, holding her breath as he loosened the laces of her dress under her cloak and bared her breasts to the warmth of the fire.

She realised he didn't need his gift to have command over her. It didn't frighten her, it made her crave him. Her nipples puckered and she shivered as he played with them, pinching and rolling them in his fingers until she could bear it no longer. She lowered her arms and delved into his breeches until she felt his cock. Taking it in her hand, she moved along it, feeling it grow harder and harder, straining against the cloth.

He muttered a curse and she felt his hand caress her leg, moving up. He grabbed her mound hard, eliciting a whimper from her lips as she parted her thighs for him. Fingers found her aching bud and began to tease it, pinching and touching in gentle circles that made her legs go weak.

'Please,' she begged, tightening her hand around him as he paused his ministrations.

'Put your arms back over your head or I'll bind them there,' he growled.

Knowing he would make good on his threat, she immediately did as he said even as her nethers clenched at his order. He made a sound of approval as he got to his feet, taking her with him. He stood in front of her and lifted her dress slowly, staring at her as more and more of her flesh was uncovered for him.

'Are you cold?' he asked as her teeth chattered, but she shook her head.

She was not cold, not at all.

'Good.' He bunched the skirt up to her waist and told her to hold it as he kicked her legs apart. Then he stepped back and looked his fill. She could only imagine the sight of herself, half undressed and on display for him, and felt herself clench in anticipation.

He looked like he was enjoying the sight of her, she thought, his eyes sharpening on her breasts and mound as he stroked himself through his breeches while he stared.

He stalked back towards her with a predatory gleam in his eye that made her want to flee, yet she held her ground as he took her arms and wound them around his neck. She gasped as he picked her up with ease and settled her against him, his jutting cock rubbing against her, drawing such a pleasurable sensation from her body that she moaned and ground against it, almost not understanding what her body was doing. But he did and grinned at her response as she wrapped her legs around his hips, needing more.

And then there was more; his staff thrust into her as he pushed her back against a thick tree trunk. She panted and scratched at his cloak, pulling at his hair as she wriggled around, moaning with his sudden intrusion. He stilled, letting her tight channel conform to him. Then he began to move, gently. He eased into her, making her cry out in pleasure with every thrust. Then he went harder, lifting her up only to let her fall over and over, his cock driving into her so deeply it hurt. But with it was a feeling she now knew well – that coiling in her belly, the places he stroked again and again inside of her while his thumb brushed over the sensitive bud. His hand clamped over her mouth as she screamed her release, cutting the sound short. He buried his face in her neck and cried out with her, surging deep.

They didn't move for a few moments, then he pulled out of her and lowered her to her feet. Her knees wobbled and she grabbed him to keep from falling.

She thought she saw the ghost of a smile, but then it was gone. Without a word, he picked her up again, cradling her like a babe, and brought her back to the fire. As she began to doze in his arms, she felt him put her dress to rights and wipe his seed from her and sighed contentedly.

Well, he didn't hate her, of that she was certain. Eyes closed and a small smile on her face, she nestled against Kane, for now, his warmth banishing the cold.

CHAPTER 39

SORIN

Sorin woke to sounds he already knew well. The drip, drip, drip of rancid water on stone, following grooves made over countless years. The clanking of far-off chains. The rustling of men or beasts in the black, moldy reeds covering the floors. As far as he could tell, the cleaning of the cells consisted of two men, who looked as bad as the prisoners, throwing fresh straw on top of the old and that was it. Consequently, a musty, dank smell permeated the air, beneath which was the usual for places like these: shit and rot.

He looked at the three marks he'd scratched into the wall. Three days and nights and still he had not yet seen his enemy. It wasn't surprising. If he knew Vineri, he would be made to wait upon his former master's pleasure, contemplating the awful fate that awaited him, the fate of an escaped slave. But Sorin was no longer the cowardly boy who had run away that night years before. He no longer let fear rule him, and he vowed that the cunt would get no satisfaction from his torture and death. None.

The thick, heavy door to this, the lowest dungeon, opened with a creak and someone with an almost indiscernible limp moved towards his cell. The man himself. Sorin smiled darkly. The injury to his leg that Sorin's mother had inflicted before they'd killed her still caused him pain.

The figure came and stood in front of him. Sorin didn't look down. Instead he did what he had never dared to do as a slave: he stared straight into Vineri's face, one well weathered by the passage of time. His jowls hung down, in contrast to his other sharp features, and the flesh of his neck was creased and loose. He was still much the same man bodily; his shoulders had always lacked broadness even in his younger days. Now, though, his finely tailored clothes seemed to swallow him just a bit. But then, not much strength was needed when you had men to crack the whip for you, and the man still had a presence. Much as Sorin hated to admit it, the sight of his former master made him break out in a cold sweat.

'You are much changed, boy,' Vineri finally said, though his tone held no inflection.

'Come closer and see how much changed, you old fool,' Sorin goaded, hoping the man couldn't see his discomfort. And wishing he'd be stupid enough to get within arm's reach.

Vineri flashed his white teeth so quickly that Sorin wasn't sure if it was a smile or a grimace. He didn't move.

'You disappeared so suddenly that night and I had such plans for you.' Vineri's tongue darted out to moisten his thin lips as he leered, making Sorin want to retch.

The bastard squatted down in front of Sorin. He was more agile than first appearances suggested. 'You are *bigger* than my tastes currently run, but after seeing you perhaps I'll make an exception. The others will be here soon as well. I'm sure you remember them. It'll be quite the reunion.'

Sorin didn't try to reply. He wasn't sure he could. He pressed his hands into his thighs to keep Vineri from seeing them shake as he outwardly tried to keep himself composed. He had been trained to be part of the most formidable army in the realms. Men feared him. He would not cower like a beast. Not ever again.

CHAPTER 40

LANA

It had been days. Days since Sorin had been taken, and Lana was at her wit's end. Kane and Viktor talked in hushed tones on the other side of their room by the fire, so calm that she wanted to shake them, yell in their faces and demand that they do something to help him. Now!

They'd found Viktor at an inn in the Forge, a large town at the foot of the mountains. He had tracked the men who had taken Sorin to the town itself, but then they'd disappeared. They had no idea where he was exactly – only that he was close by. They would know soon, though, or at least she would.

She had told Kane of her plan first while they travelled, hoping to make him see that it was the best option before she was outnumbered by Viktor. Over the days, he had been steadfastly against it. They had bickered heatedly while they rode, but then at night there had been a very different sort of heat. Lana's face colored as she remembered. She'd been afraid that that first night together might have been a one-time occurrence, but on the second night Kane had pulled her to him as soon as they'd made camp and proceeded to show her that that wasn't the case. He did the same on the third and fourth nights. Very thoroughly. She shivered in spite of the warmth as she thought of those nights they had spent together.

'You'll wear out the floorboards pacing like that, woman. Sit down,' Kane said, and she realised their chatter had gone silent.

'I can't. I can't sit. I can't rest. I don't even want to eat. Why has the agent not sent us a message? Do you think he sensed a trap? I told you my bindings were not tight enough!' She knew she was being unfair to them, but she couldn't help it.

'It's not been long enough. Once he speaks to the Collector, then he will send word of a location.' Viktor sighed. 'Come, little bird.'

She padded over to where he sat in a chair by the hearth and he pulled her onto his knee.

'I'm afraid,' she said softly into his shoulder as she inhaled the scent of him.

'I know you are, but he is one of us. He's been through worse than this since joining the Army.'

Lana nodded, though in her heart she didn't believe him. Sorin was in the hands of the man – nay, monster – who had broken him. What if they were too late? What if she couldn't save Sorin? What if she couldn't get the Vessel away from Vineri? If he was too powerful ... if she failed the goddess, would she take her power back or would she simply kill her? Could she really do this by herself? Even if the Brothers helped her, the odds were against them.

'I don't understand something, Kane.' He didn't answer but stopped polishing the knife in his hands, so she continued. 'Why don't you just make Vineri and his men do what you want the way you did with my – my father's men in the forest?'

BOUGHT TO BREAK

He and Viktor shared another look and she put her hands on her hips, daring him not to answer her.

'I can't,' he answered finally, his voice and face cleared of all feeling. 'I tried the night I found Sorin.' He shook his head. 'I don't know why, but it doesn't work on him nor on any of his men.'

The goddess had said that the Collector had amassed many artefacts of power. Perhaps that was why. The more Lana learned, the more she was certain that she had to do more than save Sorin and take the Vessel. She had to find a way to destroy their enemy completely.

'Are you sure you want to do this?' Kane asked her for the hundredth time.

'Yes!' she said, exasperated. 'How else are we going to find him?'

'There are other ways.'

She rolled her eyes at him. 'We've already talked about this. My plan is the quickest way to save him. The longer it takes, the more chance he –' Her voice broke and she turned her face into Viktor's shoulder.

'I know you think –' Viktor began, but Kane raised a hand and looked towards the door.

Footsteps. Their door rattled as someone pounded on it noisily.

'I have a message,' called the innkeeper.

Lana sprang from Viktor's lap like a startled doe. They'd made a show of parading her around with her arms bound behind her. Her head turned this way and that as she searched the room wildly. No one could see her free like this, but there was no time.

An idea coming to her; she sprinted lightly to the corner and slid to the floor with her hands behind her back. She stared at the floor, trying to look despondent.

Kane tore open the door with a scowl. 'Can't you fucking wait?'

The innkeeper stepped into their room unapologetically, looking straight at the bed and then seeking her out immediately. 'I thought you might be enjoying your prisoner's company.' His gaze wandered over her and she tried not to let the disgust she felt show on her face.

Kane's frown deepened. 'The message.'

The man didn't even look at Kane or Viktor; his beady black eyes were riveted on her. 'He says to meet him by the river. Under the second bridge at sundown,' he mumbled distractedly. Finally, he glanced at the Brothers. 'If you two need to leave your prisoner here, I'd be glad to watch her for you.'

Viktor stood, blocking the man's view of her. 'Get the fuck out.'

Kane slammed the door and pulled the bolt.

Lana sighed, getting to her feet. 'So the agent wants to see you. What does that mean?'

The men regarded each other in silence. Again. 'No, don't have secret conversations with each other. Tell me.'

'It's not us he wants to see; it's you, Lana. He's only glimpsed you from afar. Now they'll want to examine the goods. If they like what they find, the exchange will happen then and there.'

Her gut twisting at the reality of what she was going to do, she sat down hard on the bed.

'Oh,' she said faintly.

'You can still–'

'No,' she said, setting her jaw determinedly. 'How long do we have?'

'Enough time to enjoy our prisoner's company,' answered Kane.

Viktor gave Kane a sideways glance, looking surprised.

Obviously Kane hadn't apprised him of the past few nights he'd been alone with her.

Lana took a small step back. 'No, I don't want to.'

Kane cocked a brow. 'You don't want to?' he echoed.

'No.'

'It's a bit soon to be bored of us,' Viktor quipped from behind her.

'I mean it. I don't feel like … doing that. I just want to be ready to go. I want to get Sorin back.'

Kane took a step forward. 'We know what you want, Lana, better than you do yourself.'

Viktor caught her first. She gasped as his arm encircled her waist and he pulled her against him.

'You're very tense,' he murmured in her ear.

'Is it any wonder?' she asked as she tried half-heartedly to break free of him.

'Let us make you feel better,' he whispered, pushing her dress off her shoulders while kissing her neck.

She moaned in spite of herself and heard Kane moving closer. She opened her eyes to find him already in front of her. He jerked the dress down further, trapping her arms, his lips curving into a small smile as her breasts bounced into view.

'Are you sure you finally want to take part instead of just watching, Brother?' Viktor teased as he pinched her nipples gently.

'Oh, I took part plenty while we were on the road, didn't I, Lana?' He spun her around roughly to face Viktor. 'Why don't you speak to Viktor about some of the things we did out in the cold? How many times did you moan and beg me to fill you? Tell him how I rubbed ice over your nipples and suckled them warm again. You liked that particularly well, I recall.'

She moaned as she remembered Kane breaking an icicle

from a tree bough one night and making her lie still as he melted it on her – in her. Her nipples had been hard as granite and she'd almost found her release from his hot mouth on them alone.

Viktor's head descended and her muscles clenched as he pulled the tip of her breast into his mouth and sucked hard while Kane pulled up her skirts behind her. His hand delved between her legs as soon as it was able and, finding her already slick, he made a guttural sound of approval.

He kicked her legs apart. 'Feel her. Feel how wet she is,' he said to Viktor.

But Viktor ignored him, instead stepping back and pulling her dress down past her hips so it pooled around her feet. Then he took her other breast into his mouth, biting it while Kane's fingers twisted and moved in her. She arched her back, trying to get closer to both of them, and whimpered as she was held fast.

Something thicker than Kane's finger pushed at her entrance. He took hold of her knee and raised her leg high, opening her wide for him. She cried out as he filled her with one hard thrust.

Viktor's hand moved downward, finding the bud that was the center of her pleasure. He brushed his thumb over it again and again as Kane still pushed into her, and she writhed between them.

Then Viktor stopped and pulled away. She grabbed for him with a growl, but he simply grinned at her as his Brother lifted her, still impaled on his cock from behind, and carried her to the bed. He lay on his back and pulled her down with him, spreading her legs with his.

Viktor knelt between them and her eyes widened as he leant forward, pushing his hard shaft into her as well. She whimpered and moaned as they stretched her opening, thrusting into her channel together, both of them holding her in place as they drove into her. Her senses were overwhelmed, crying out for release as the pressure built up and up so intensely it hurt. Her body clenched, her legs spasming as she screamed their names. They spent themselves inside her, grunting and panting their releases.

They all collapsed on the bed. Lana in the middle, limp and satiated and aching pleasurably. She turned to Viktor and kissed his lips. He returned her caress, nipping her playfully. Kane, on her other side, shifted as if he meant to get up. She pulled him back, cupped his bristly jaw and kissed him as well. He looked surprised for a moment before succumbing to her and lying down once more.

They rested until the sun was low, and then it was time.

After they were dressed, Viktor produced a rope to tie Lana's hands. He hesitated as she held out her wrists.

'I'll have to do it properly, Lana. It won't be comfortable and there won't be any getting out of it. But once you're brought to the Collector you won't be mistreated. You're too valuable to him.' He cupped her face. 'That's the only reason we're letting you do this.'

She nodded and he secured her hands tightly. When he looked into her eyes to gauge his handiwork she smiled, not letting him see her unease. He drew her to him and kissed her. 'I'd be lying if I said the sight of you tied up didn't make me want you again, though,' he whispered in her ear.

'Stop that,' Kane said from the table as he slid a dagger from its scabbard and inspected the blade. 'She already doesn't look enough like a true captive. If the agent and his men sense anything amiss, they'll disappear and we won't get another chance. Bad enough that we're trying to pretend it's a coincidence that we're all in the same fucking town.' He looked up and swore again. 'This isn't going to work. Look at her.'

Lana scowled. 'What's wrong with how I look?'

Viktor drew back and scrutinized her face. 'He's right. Your lips are swollen and you have a look about you.'

'A look?'

'Well pleased.'

Her cheeks colored.

'Hit her,' said Kane absently as he continued to check his weapons.

'What?' they both asked in unison.

'Not hard, just enough to swell. Then the puffy lips, grazes and bruises on her neck can be put down to a few knocks to keep her in line.'

'No.'

The look on Viktor's face would have made her laugh at any other time.

'Do it,' she said.

'No!'

She clicked her tongue. 'Kane, you do it. This needs to work or Sorin is dead.'

Kane left his task and approached. He raised his hand and she flinched, her stomach in knots. He hesitated, his face inscrutable.

'Do it!' she barked.

And he did, the back of his hand hitting her cheek, the force turning her head, though she knew he pulled back at the last moment. The sound of it reverberated through the room and she gave a small cry, tears springing to her eyes and her skin smarting. He had done it exactly as he'd said, though. It would bruise and swell, but that was all.

She turned away to dry her eyes before Kane could see, but he came with her. He put his hand over where it hurt and wiped away the tears she'd shed with his thumb. He didn't say anything, but she put her hand over his and squeezed it to reassure him that there was no real harm done. The complete lack of emotion on his face was more telling than if he had actually looked upset, and it helped to soothe her as well. He did care for her. She could see that now. He just found it very difficult to express his feelings.

'Is that better?' she asked, showing her face to Viktor.

Teeth clenched, he nodded once.

'Good.' She looked out of the casement. 'It's time.'

KANE AND LANA stood under the bridge in the twilight. The agent and his men had formed a line not ten paces away as they waited for the last of their party to arrive. The tide was out and it stank, as water by towns usually did. The mud squelched as she shifted, threatening to suck the sturdy shoes Vie had given her from her feet. Viktor was hidden close by in case it was a trap or they were ambushed – and to follow them as closely as he could, as he'd lost them at the town last time.

Kane, dressed in black once more as part of their ruse that they were Brothers still, made an impatient sound.

'He will be here in a moment,' said the agent calmly – though Lana noticed that he kept glancing around surreptitiously for whomever they were waiting for whenever he thought no one was watching.

'He fucking better be,' Kane growled and pulled her forward by her rope for effect. She staggered in the mud, but he didn't let her fall. 'You aren't the only one interested in purchasing the witch.'

A man in long robes hobbled into view, looking at his surroundings in utter distaste and attempting to keep his clothes out of the mud.

'By the gods,' he exclaimed, 'could this really not have been done in a tavern?'

The agent rolled his eyes.

'A priest?' Kane spat. 'This is who we've been freezing our arses off waiting for?'

'*Former* priest,' the man huffed.

The agent gestured to Lana. 'Is she what they say?'

The man looked taken aback as if only just noticing she was there. Then his eyes widened. 'Gods,' he breathed.

'Well?' the agent asked impatiently.

'Aye.' He spared the agent a quick look, his eyes returning to her. 'Aye, she's a witch all right.' He breathed out hard. Then his eyes narrowed. 'What happened to her face?'

Kane shrugged. 'Just made sure she stays in her place is all. The goods aren't damaged.'

The priest spluttered. 'You would dare strike–'

'Spare me, priest, and let's get on with it.'

The exchange happened quickly. The money was handed over and the agent himself took the rope, leading her gently like a prize horse. He even helped her climb the slippery bank. She went with them docilely as they led her through the backstreets and over the threshold of a small temple. Down into the crypts they went, and at the end of a hall deep underground there was a passage. No wonder Viktor had lost them, she thought, as she was pulled gently through the darkness, their way lit by a solitary torch held by the first man. She hoped Viktor was following them closely enough now.

They came up from the floor in a stable yard, the horses not looking at all surprised by their sudden appearance. She was taken inside, down a corridor and left in a small but serviceable room. The priest cut her bindings, fussing like a mother hen over the wounds made by the ropes where they'd rubbed. He shook his head and grumbled that she had been treated most cruelly, and then he caressed her face, his eyes feverishly reverent. She stumbled back and he apologized profusely, bowing low in front of her as if she herself were a deity. Then he left abruptly and, in his haste, did *not lock the door*.

She couldn't believe her luck and wondered if Gaila was helping in some small way. Heart pounding, she waited until his footsteps had disappeared and then she bolted. She had to find Sorin and the Vessel. Once she knew where they were, she would be able to tell Viktor and Kane when they found their way inside. She walked quickly, hiding whenever she heard someone coming, before she saw some guards hauling a body through a doorway that led downwards. Her heart almost stopped, fearing they carried Sorin, but it wasn't him. She snuck in where she'd seen the men come from, down the stone steps. There were cells here. He must be close.

'Sorin,' she whispered. 'Sorin?'

Something rustled next to her and she almost shrieked, covering her mouth and throwing herself back.

'Who are you searching for, girl?' rasped an old woman's voice from the darkest part of the cell next to her.

Lana peered into the gloom and could just make out the shape of a person. 'His name is Sorin,' she answered the prisoner. 'He used to be a slave here.'

'The guards whisper of a slave. That one who escaped long ago.'

She let out a breath she didn't know she'd been holding. 'Yes! That's him. That's Sorin. Do you know where he is? Please. I have to find him.'

The person moved closer to the bars and Lana could see that it was a crone. She cackled. 'Vineri was very upset when that one went missing.' She sobered as she regarded Lana. 'You'll never escape this place, child. I should know. Vineri's had me here for years.'

'Who are you?'

'No one. Not anymore.' The crone sneered. 'Even the

guards forget I'm here. They gossip like fishwives in my presence. They say he is in the hole.'

'Where is that?' Lana asked, her stomach sinking.

'Just keep going down.'

'Thank you. I will free you from this place, I promise.'

The woman shuffled back into the deepest part of the cell and did not speak again.

Lana went back out into the hall and began to go down the steps, descending into the depths of the fortress until she came to a door. It wasn't locked, which she found odd in a dungeon.

She pushed it open. All of the cells were empty bar one. At the far end, she saw a man hanging by his arms. He was chained and badly beaten.

'Sorin?' she whispered, her voice breaking. The man's head moved slightly.

'Lana?' he croaked.

She rushed to the bars. 'Sorin! You're alive.'

One eye opened just a crack and he raised his head. 'Lana.' He smiled. 'They must have hit me harder than I thought.'

He didn't think she was really here. She wished she could get into the cell to touch him, but the door was locked and there was no key to be seen. 'Sorin, I'm here. Really, I am. And Viktor and Kane are coming. We're going to get out of here, I promise.' A lump rose in her throat as she saw how they had hurt him already. 'I'm going to make them pay for what they've done to you, Sorin.'

He just stared at her, a dreamy smile on his face.

'I have to go, but I promise you we are going to get out of this awful place. If you don't remember anything else I've said, please remember that.'

She turned away before he could see her tears, though he probably wouldn't notice them, and ran all the way up the steps and back to the room. She didn't look for the Vessel.

She'd been gone for too long, but at least she knew where Sorin was and that he was alive.

She was just in time. The door opened a moment later, and she hoped her heavy breathing was taken merely as a sign of panic, not of exertion.

The priest came in, along with the largest man she'd ever seen. He was bare chested and wearing leathers. He also sported a tattoo of two crossed axes on his chest. Her blood ran cold as she recognized what he was from the stories; one of the gladiators who fought each other like demons for the crowds of the northern arenas. What was he going to do? She shrank back, unable to mask her fear.

The priest was shaking his head. 'I've already told him I'm sure. There's no reason to test her. She's a witch. I'm certain of it.'

The big man regarded her, his chin jutting out as he looked closer. 'Well, I can't see a fucking glow, that's for sure. And orders are orders. So she goes to the pit for the night and we see in the morning. She'll be safe enough if she's what they said.'

The man grabbed her and she screamed. He ignored her and threw her over his shoulder like a sack of grain, marching through the stables and courtyard to another building. He opened the door and they were greeted by a barrage of sounds: steel on steel, grunts and shouts; the sounds of men fighting and sparring. When they saw her, the sounds quieted.

She was placed in a cage in the center of the room. It was locked securely. The priest was nowhere to be seen. Instead she was surrounded by other gladiators. Some were staring salaciously. Others simply looked puzzled by her appearance.

The big man snapped his fingers in front of her, getting her attention. 'They can't get in, but if I were you I'd stay away from the bars. If they grab you, they won't let go. See you in the morning.' He laughed. 'Probably.' And then he was gone.

She surveyed the room. There were at least twenty men, all as big as the other one. None of them spoke, but she noticed they wore only loincloths and many of them were hard just from looking at her. She remembered hearing that they were usually denied the company of women unless they won a fight. This must be a real treat for them, she thought wryly.

Two of them ran at the cage, putting their arms through the bars and grasping at her hair, her clothes – anything. One of them got hold of her cloak and dragged her back towards the side of the cage. She resisted, choking, as she fumbled with the clasp. She got it undone and it was snatched through the bars. The man who took it smelled it, breathing in her scent, and howled like an animal. More of them thrust their arms through the bars, yelling and making awful sounds. She screamed, wrapping her remaining clothes tightly around herself so they couldn't get her. If she stayed in the middle of the enclosure, they couldn't reach. Just stay in the middle. *Just stay in the middle.* She said it to herself like a mantra, as if that would keep her safe. She curled into a ball in the very center of the pen and began to sob, shutting her eyes and covering her ears as she tried to block them out.

The onslaught lasted well into the night, and at some point she fell into a fitful sleep to the sounds of them still grasping for her.

In the morning she opened her eyes, swollen and puffy from crying, and realised she was lying too close to the bars. Heart pounding, she shuffled silently back to the middle, where she was safe, before she saw that the gladiators had all given up. Some were sleeping peacefully against the cage. Others just watched her with an almost tranquil fascination. The fight in them seemed to have disappeared.

The door to the barracks opened with a crunch and the big man from the night before stepped inside. He looked around the room, disbelief evident on his face.

'Tell him to come. Now,' he whispered to someone behind him.

Moments passed and he didn't move, didn't venture into the room further. He watched her now with that same fealty she'd seen on the priest's face yestereve, and it made her skin crawl. Footsteps sounded and he finally moved to let someone through. Two someones. The first was the priest. He looked around in amazement.

'Calm as rabbits. You see? I was right.'

A tall thin man stepped around him and she got her first look at the Collector.

'So you're the witch.'

Lana wasn't sure what she'd expected, but the man in front of her looked ... unassuming regardless of his impressive height. His hair held more grey than not and while he definitely commanded the room, she'd expected some fearsome creature. This was just a man.

His fingers flexed as if he couldn't wait to get his hands on her, but the look in his piercing black eyes wasn't sordid in the least. She truly was simply a possession to him. He could and would treat her any way he liked and think no more of it than he would of a rare vase or jewel. She was relegated to a *thing* and it felt very much the same as being a slave. She wasn't having second thoughts, but she was terrified. What if things didn't go to plan? Kane and Viktor should be close, but if they were caught, if they couldn't find her, if they were too late. So much could go wrong and she would be trapped here. *No.* She would do whatever it took to save herself and Sorin, she vowed, even if the others couldn't get to them.

'Get her out of the cage,' Vineri said to the gladiator and turned to the priest. 'Well?'

The priest hadn't stopped looking at her, a disconcerting joy in his countenance. 'She's been bound by blood magick, but it can be undone. Then, I will bind her to me, with your leave.'

Vineri didn't take his eyes off her either as he continued to speak as if she were not there. 'And you can keep the witch alive?'

'Yes. But I will require the item you promised.'

'Done. I'll need her power soon.' He looked her up and down as she knelt in her small prison. 'She looks strong enough. You have my permission to breed her to get her with child.' Finally, he looked at the priest standing next to him. 'Take care of my investment or I'll have your head, Dugal.' He turned to leave. 'And collar her, or my gladiators and my soldiers will be fucking useless to me,' he called over his shoulder.

The gladiator from yestereve opened the door to the cage, reached in and grabbed her more gently than he had before. She didn't fight him, her mind reeling from what had been said. Somehow, they were going to break the bond she shared with Sorin, Viktor and Kane and insert the priest into their place. She had to work quickly.

They brought her to the main building, the gladiator carrying her over his shoulder while the priest shuffled along behind, all of his attention on her. They brought her to a well-furnished bedchamber; one without windows. The rugs were thick underfoot and the counterpane on the bed looked new; a nicely dressed-up prison cell. The fire in the hearth crackled merrily as the gladiator placed her gently on the bed. She leapt off immediately and scrambled to the corner, trying not to behave like a caged beast but feeling very much like one. The big man bowed to her, actually bowed, and left the room, walking backwards as if she were royalty until the door closed. The priest poured her some water and offered it to her.

'What's your name?'

When she didn't answer, he continued. 'I'm sorry about last night. I didn't want them to do that. I'll have some food brought.'

She took the cup from him gingerly. 'It's Lana.'

He looked pleased. 'Lana. Beautiful. Perfect. Just like you.'

Feeling uncomfortable under his unwavering stare, she muttered a thank you and drank thirstily.

'I'm Dugal. I was once a priest. That's why Vineri hired me. I advise him on matters of the gods. He's been searching for a real witch for a long time, you know.'

'What will happen to me?' she asked in a small voice, hoping he would see her as just a frightened girl and underestimate her.

'Well.' He rang the bell pull and sat himself down by the fire, facing in her direction. 'I'm to be your connection to this life. I will look after you.'

She approached him. 'But I'm already bound.'

An eyebrow quirked. 'Not for long. He will cut the link you have with the other and bind you to me instead.'

'But what if I don't want that?'

He regarded her in silence for a moment.

'I'm sorry, Lana,' he said finally, 'but you belong to the Collector now. You are his, and he has chosen me to guide you.' He leant forward in earnest. 'You don't understand, I'm sure, but you will die without him. You need to be loved and you must feel content because of your link to the gods. I can help if you'll let me, my dear.'

His face was a handsome one, but she disliked the vehemence she saw in it as well as his condescending explanations of her nature. His endearment turned her stomach. It wasn't her he wanted; not a friend or a real bond. It was power. Guide her, indeed! Be her lord and master, more like. He was no different from the Collector or any other slave-holder. In fact, he was worse because he was able to excuse himself from his cruel actions under the guise of piety.

How different Kane, Sorin and Viktor were from men like him. Her da, her stepfather, Ather – all of them had only seen her value through what she could give them, all the while ensuring she felt worthless. The Brothers weren't like them at all. They had done more for her over a few weeks than anyone had in her entire life. She would repay them however she could, though she knew they would demand nothing she wasn't more than willing to give.

'But I don't even know you,' she said, hoping her face had not given away that she did not actually wish to.

'You will. The artefact in the Collector's possession will help you to feel content by binding you to me and shaping your feelings. And, once it's done its work, I vow to you I will dedicate my every moment to you.'

Lana's brow furrowed as a dreadful suspicion took form. 'So it will make me care for you?'

'No, no, no. You don't understand, my love. Its purpose is to make you feel perfectly content by feeling the adoration you need. You'll thank me.'

She felt sick as she regarded Dugal. They were going to take her will from her – doing something far worse to her than even Ather ever had – as if it were a gift she should be grateful for. And there was something else Vineri had mentioned. 'The Collector said you were allowed to … breed me. What does that mean?' She was afraid she already knew exactly what they intended, but she hoped she was wrong.

'Well.' His face reddened slightly. 'It is hoped that you would get with child to produce another witch. But that will come later,' he added hastily. 'You need not worry about that now. When it's time, we will be devoted to each other, and I won't let the others mistreat you.'

'Others?' she asked.

'Well, yes. If you're to be bred, then there will be a few who will give you their seed so that there's a better chance … Vineri will decide who, but I'd assume you'll be a reward for the gladiators when they win in the arena.'

Lana's mouth fell open. 'You mean to say that you plan to take my free will and then let my body be given as a prize to rape in the hopes that I produce a babe?'

He looked chagrined. 'You will want for nothing, Lana. It's better than dying out there.' He stood and bowed his head. 'Everything I do is for you and the gods. I will leave you now. Food will be brought shortly.'

He put a hand on her shoulder. She tried to shake him off, but his fingers gripped her tightly, just shy of actually hurting. 'I'm sorry,' he said as something snapped closed around her neck.

She pushed him away, scratching at the contraption, but it wouldn't come off.

'What is this? You collar me like an animal?' she shrieked.

He put his hands up in front of him as if that would placate her. 'It's just to deaden the effect your presence has on those around you. It's only until we are bound and your power can be controlled.'

By him. She stepped forward and slapped him hard.

He cried out and gasped, holding his cheek as if he couldn't believe what she'd done. Then he flew at her, his dark nature suddenly visible in his eyes, making her stumble back. He grabbed her arms and held them at her sides in a punishing grip on her wrists that made her wince. Then he took a deep breath and took her hands gently instead, his face trying very hard to maintain its mask of serenity.

'I won't punish you for this,' he said with a small smile. 'I know the past days have been taxing. Truly, Lana, you will feel differently after we are bound together. I will prepare everything for sunrise tomorrow,' he promised, licking at a drop of blood forming on his lip where her blow had split it.

He bent his forehead to hers, closing his eyes as if trying to will her to be thankful to him as she stared wide-eyed at him. She had thought him odd yet harmless, but she had been so wrong. He was unpredictable and unhinged and very dangerous indeed. In truth, he scared her much more than the Collector did.

He kissed her head and left, remembering to lock the door behind him this time. A few moments later, food was brought, and she ate what little her churning stomach could take simply to keep her strength up. She paced the room, hands shaking. She had no doubt that Viktor and Kane would come, but what if they didn't make it before tomorrow? What if she was bound to the Collector's sycophant for her mind to be taken and her body ... *bred*? She shivered. Time was not on her side and she still had no idea where to find the Vessel.

She took the poker, the only thing in the room that might work, from the hearth and began to work on the door's large old-fashioned keyhole. She couldn't just wait here like a lamb for the slaughter.

CHAPTER 41

VIKTOR

The tunnels had been difficult. Viktor didn't care for enclosed spaces, but he had followed the men holding Lana as closely as he was able to this time for fear of losing them again. He waited in the darkness long after they'd climbed the ladder into the fortress until he was sure there was no one guarding the door. He had come out slowly and quietly, surprised that none of the horses had been frightened, though he supposed they saw men rising up from the passage all the time.

He made a quick survey of the cloister that followed the perimeter of the central courtyard, locating the buildings that they'd need later and realizing almost immediately that the fortress wasn't a fortress at all. It was an old monastery, though there were no priests in sight. And the soldiers he could see standing on the walls weren't the usual sell-swords, either. There were more of the men who looked like Brothers of the Dark Army. Kane was adamant that the only units on long-term secondment were in the capital city of Kitore. It wasn't possible and he wouldn't have believed it unless he'd seen it with his own eyes, but here they were.

Brothers' secrets were dangerous. They should not leave the confines of the Brotherhood and hadn't in a thousand years, so Sorin had told him once. Someone was breaking the most important laws by teaching these men, but who?

Drawing his gaze away from the guards, he caught sight of the answer walking nonchalantly across the square to what looked like the armory. Kilroy. What the fuck was he doing here? And if he was here, where were those mangy curs, Uth and Fen? He had to get Kane. Now. If nothing else, they hated Lana. If they didn't already know she was here, they would soon. He eased back into the stables and slipped down into the tunnels, feeling his way through the maze in the gloom and trying to ignore his unease.

Luckily the path was quite straight, though narrow in places, and soon he emerged from the small temple in the Forge. He walked quickly through the busy streets back to the room they'd taken and found Kane sharpening his knives, something he did when he was worried.

He didn't look up as Viktor closed the door softly. 'You didn't fail this time, then?'

Viktor felt his lip curl and bit back a retort, reminding himself that this was something Kane did to distract himself from his fears.

'They're in an old monastery just outside the town to the east.' He sat down heavily. 'I didn't see Lana, but there are more of those soldiers. The ones who look like Brothers.'

'How?' Kane murmured to himself.

'I saw Kilroy.'

Kane's head shot up. 'Fuck.' He stood and began to pace. 'They're fools, but they wouldn't be here without orders.'

'Greygor? Why betray the Brothers? If the Army finds out, he's as good as dead.'

Kane shrugged. 'He's old and weak. If someone challenges his leadership by combat, he'll lose.'

'If he's working with Vineri, that's why we were in the Islands, and that attack we watched in the forest at the exchange was a ruse.'

'If that's true, then he let at least one Brother and twenty soldiers died for nothing. Uth's unit has been teaching Vineri's men to fight like us. They're the weakest Brothers, but they're still part of the Army.'

Viktor rubbed his eyes. *What a mess.* 'Uth hates Lana. If he finds out she's within his reach, he won't care about orders. He'll kill her.'

'We need to move tonight.'

'Agreed.' Viktor hesitated. 'I know we aren't Brothers anymore, but …'

'Greygor needs to pay,' Kane finished, and Viktor nodded. 'I'll send Quin a bird once we have Lana and Sorin back.'

'Quin?'

'We'll still teach him a lesson for what he did to Lana, but he's Greygor's second now. He'll lead the Army well.'

Viktor made a dubious sound but said nothing more as he readied his weapons for that night.

Evening came quickly and they made their way into Vineri's fortress under cover of darkness. It was easier than they'd expected. Too easy. No guards were on the door to the stables and few seemed to be on patrol.

'This is a trap,' Kane muttered as they skirted the courtyard, and Viktor silently agreed. They turned back to the stables to regroup, but it was too late.

Something whistled through the air, hitting Viktor in the neck. He swore and pulled it out. A dart. His legs gave out and he fell to the ground just in time to see the same happen to Kane. He heard the sound of soldiers running towards them and then his eyes closed of their own accord.

CHAPTER 42

LANA

Lana wasn't sure how the lock undid itself. It certainly wasn't due to her ineffectual jabbing with the poker, but after a particularly hard shove into the keyhole, the door swung open silently, inviting her to escape.

She edged into the hall, finding it deserted, and wondered which way she should try for the Vessel first. She looked right. That was the way the priest had brought her and she hadn't seen any doors, so she turned the opposite way, silently slipping down the curving corridor and staying close to the wall.

She had to go slowly, frustratingly so, because she couldn't see what was coming. Luckily no one happened by and she came to a door. She listened at it and, hearing nothing, opened it quietly. Inside was another windowless bedroom, just like the one she'd been locked in. She shut it and continued. The rotunda began to slope down into long, shallow steps. The other side of the wall ended abruptly and became an intricate, short stone banister. Beyond it, she could hear a fountain. The walkway curved around and she was at the foot of what looked like a tower. There was an archway leading to stairs.

Lana climbed the winding staircase up to a small landing. There was a small door at the end with a barred window. She peeped through. Behind the door was a sparse room with a small bed and some books on a desk. A fire burned in the grate.

'Can't you read?'

Lana jumped at the voice. A young woman sat by the fire with a book in her lap. Her hair was black and she wore serviceable black woolen priest robes.

'Read?'

'There should be a sign.'

Lana looked around the door and saw it. 'Pestilence?'

'That's the one.'

She went back to reading and Lana knocked.

'Yes?'

'Are you a prisoner here?'

'I suppose I am.' The girl smiled. 'But it's not as if I can go anywhere.'

'Why?'

She sighed as if she was being disturbed. 'Read the sign.'

Lana frowned. 'I have. I don't understand.'

'Just don't come in, all right?' She looked up at Lana. 'Are *you* a prisoner here?'

'Yes.'

The girl looked out of the casement. 'Well, you should go. They'll be making rounds soon. You'll be seen if you aren't careful.'

'Thank you.' Lana turned away, bit her lip and looked through the door again. 'Can you help me?'

'I doubt it.'

'I'm looking for Vineri's collection.'

The woman got up and walked over to the door; she didn't stand within arm's reach, though, Lana noticed. In fact, Lana saw there was a line drawn on the floor. The girl didn't cross it.

'Actually, I do know where it is, though I've never been myself. He calls it his Gallery.' She rolled her eyes. 'It's on the lower hall on the rotunda corridor of the East Wing.'

'But that's where my cell is.' Lana frowned, wondering if the woman was trying to trick her.

She shook her head. 'No, no; the rooms are on the upper floor. The Gallery is below where they put you.'

Lana nodded. 'Thank you.'

'Good luck,' the girl called. 'If they catch you, he'll make you hurt awfully, you know.'

Lana grimaced. 'You have no idea.'

THERE WAS no one in the lower hall, so she ran as quickly and quietly as she could down the corridor. She almost missed it, the unassuming door, but there it was. She turned back and tried the handle, fearing it would be locked, but the door swung open smoothly without even a creak.

She walked into a substantial room and her mouth fell open. There were rows upon rows of shelves filled with objects, both wondrous and mundane. Her room was the closest to Vineri's Gallery, she realised, wrinkling her nose in distaste. He truly thought of her as part of his collection.

Some of the items were gold or encrusted with gems. Others looked odd and ancient, their uses long forgotten. She surveyed the vast space in awe. It seemed to go on forever.

She turned in a circle, perusing the closest shelves and hoping Vineri had just thrust it on the nearest one in haste, but it wasn't there. In fact, the more she looked around, the more there seemed to be a meticulous and mysterious order about the place, though she didn't understand it. Pieces were definitely grouped together, perhaps stored for their purpose, she speculated. She sighed. How was she ever to find the Vessel amidst these thousands of other artefacts?

She turned towards the door. She'd been gone too long already. But she was pulled back by some unseen force. She gasped and twisted away, but she felt herself being led, as if someone held her hand, down one of the many corridors. She walked for ages, past tall shelves of just … *things*. Big, small, round, square. Some of these artefacts looked interesting and otherworldly, but many were completely ordinary such as simple wooden spoons, small statues of the gods, and other trinkets she wouldn't look twice at on a market stall.

She slowed to a gradual stop and looked around her, spying it in one of the stacks just below eye level. Picking it up carefully, she examined it, wondering if it was Gaila helping her. It looked like a stone oil lamp without a spout, black and completely smooth. It was oddly weightless. She put it under her arm like a loaf of bread as she made her way back to the entrance of the room.

She cracked the door and, making sure the landing was deserted, sprinted back down the hall, up the stairs and back to her cell. She hid the Vessel under the monster of a bed, on top of one of the large girders that made up the frame. At least she had it now, even if she couldn't yet escape with it.

She looked at the door, still open, and wondered if she dared leave the room again. She'd be trying her luck, but it must be past midday. She was sure Viktor and Kane should have got in by now. She'd already been here a day and a night, and they'd promised it would be no longer than that. Pushing the worry to the back of her mind, she decided she'd try to get to Sorin again. If he were more lucid than yesterday, he might be able to help her think of a plan.

She poked her head out into the hall and slipped from the room again, this time going in the opposite direction, but as she rounded the corner, she bumped into someone who's footsteps she hadn't heard.

She looked up with a gasp into familiar eyes that made her stop dead. She turned on her heel as quickly as she could with a small cry, but it wasn't fast enough. A rough hand tangled in her hair and dragged her back, throwing her into the stone wall with a menacing growl.

'I knew you weren't dead,' Uth snarled, a nasty grin spreading over his face. He gripped her neck and squeezed, but luckily the rigid collar stopped him from crushing her throat. 'You're going to regret coming here, and you'll never get your unit out alive. You aren't going to last that long, you fucking bitch.'

'Lana? What are you doing out of your room?' Dugal asked from behind Uth.

Thank the gods. 'Dugal,' she croaked, trying to look as small and distressed as she could. 'Help me, please. The door wasn't locked. I was just coming to find you.'

'Find me?' He looked skeptical.

'Yes … to say sorry for what happened earlier. I'm very lucky to be here where I'm safe. I know that. But this man attacked me while I was on my way. Please, Dugal, tell him to release me. I'll go straight back to my room, I promise.' She whimpered, willing her eyes to fill with tears, which wasn't difficult after Uth's revelations that Viktor and Kane had been captured as well. She had no idea how they were going to get out of this.

'Let her go,' Dugal demanded.

Uth didn't budge.

'She is Vineri's. If you harm her, he will destroy you. I promise you that. No matter his arrangement with your Commander.'

But even the threat of Vineri's wrath wasn't enough to deter Uth. Lana could see it in his eyes. He had probably vowed to kill her if he was ever able, and he wasn't going to let this chance slip through his fingers.

'She is a danger to everyone here,' Uth ground out. 'I'm taking her to the dungeons. If you don't like it, go and tell your master, priest, and let's see if he really gives a fuck. Better be quick though. I think I'll start my interrogations with her.'

'Don't you harm a hair on her head, Uth!'

Uth smirked at the weaker man. 'You going to stop me?'

The priest threw up his hands in exasperation. 'Where is he?'

Uth shrugged and pulled Lana roughly along the hall, his grip on her arm painful as he wrenched her this way and that.

'He's in the hole giving that slave of his a good seeing to,' he whispered in her ear with a chuckle. 'Your precious Sorin loves it – moaning like a whore earlier, I heard tell.'

Fury coursed through her as she thought about what was happening to him. She flung herself at Uth with a scream, her nails biting into his neck. He swore and casually threw her down the stairway as they neared it. She cried out as she hit her head and shoulder on the hard stone and rolled until the momentum ran out. Luckily, they weren't steep, so it was only a few steps. He drew her to her feet by her hair and she gritted her teeth, trying not to make a sound. He wanted to hear her pain. Blood trickled down her face.

He pulled her across the yard and down the steps to the dungeons, running her face first into the wooden door that led to the cells and laughing as her head lolled and she fell to her knees. He grabbed her again and thrust her through the door. It was lighter than before. The torches were lit. She was in a daze as Uth pushed her forward. She stumbled into the iron bars and he grabbed her hair again.

'Look who I found.' It took her a moment to realize he wasn't speaking to her, but to Viktor and Kane, who sat on the other side of the bars. Neither of them made a sound, just watched. Then Kane shrugged and Viktor leant his back against the wall casually.

'Got yourself caught, eh? Thought you were long gone,' Viktor drawled.

'Do you two fools really think you can make me believe you don't care for her?' Uth smirked, grabbed her face and licked the blood that had tracked its way down her cheek, watching them. She struggled against him in disgust and he laughed as he pushed her into the adjacent cell, locking it behind her. 'I'll be back soon with Kilroy and Fen. Then we'll have some fun.'

He left, shutting the wooden door behind him with a bang.

As soon as he was gone, Lana slid to the floor of her cell. Unbidden, tears began to track their way down her cheeks. She tried to stop, but it only got worse, and soon she was sobbing.

'It's all right. He's truly gone,' she heard Kane murmur, and Viktor's hand came through the bars to take hers.

She clasped it tightly until her tears dried. 'I'm sorry,' she choked out.

'Come closer to the bars.'

She did as Viktor asked and felt him dabbing at her head. 'There's nothing to be sorry for. What happened? What did he do?'

She shook her head. 'Nothing, just threw me around a little. I'm all right.' She waved Viktor away, stood up on wobbly legs and held onto the bars beside her.

Viktor cursed. 'The first thing they'll do is use you against us if they think they can break us that way. And it will break us. We can't watch them hurt you, Lana.'

Kane nodded in agreement and she felt better except for her aching head and throbbing shoulder.

'What happened?' Kane asked, standing as well.

'I found Sorin. He's in the lowest dungeon beneath us.' She stifled a sob. 'Uth told me they're doing terrible things to him.'

Kane's hand came through and gripped her shoulder gently, pulling her around to face him. 'Remember, you're a prisoner, Lana. He's already using tactics designed to break you. It was most likely a lie.'

She nodded and wiped away more tears.

'I said you wouldn't escape from here, girl,' rasped the crone from the other side of the room.

'Who are you?' Kane growled.

Lana hushed him. 'She helped me find Sorin. What is your name?' she called to the woman.

'Xeta.'

'Thank you, Xeta. I found Sorin because of you.'

The old woman made a scornful sound. 'Lot of good it did you. Now you're in here with me.'

'Why did Vineri put you in here?' Viktor asked her.

'Because I knew him before he called himself Vineri, when his famed collection was nothing more than an old book and a useless amulet and his home was a one-room hovel by the docks in Kitore; one we shared with our da. I knew him when he was a lowly mercenary, fighting others for scraps from the high tables.' She cackled. 'I know where he comes from; I know him. That makes me dangerous.' She pulled herself up the bars, her gnarled fingers and long nails looking like claws. 'If you have a chance to escape, just go. You won't be able to kill him. He's too powerful now.'

As she came into the light, Lana saw that she wore a collar like the one Dugal had put round her neck.

'You're a witch,' Lana gasped.

'Once, but no more.'

Lana stared at the woman for a long time. Making up her mind, she turned to the Brothers.

'I – There's something I have to tell you. It's about what happened while I was with the wise woman.'

'What is it?'

'I should have told you before, but I was afraid.'

Viktor gave her a nod of encouragement and she smiled wanly at him.

'She's a born witch,' she continued. 'She performed a ritual and I woke up in the God Realm. I met two of them.' She shook her head at the memory. 'Two drunken idiots. But there was a woman there.' She told them of Gaila and the Vessel, and although they looked incredulous during some parts of her tale, neither of them gainsaid her.

When she had finished, she was silent, afraid they were going to laugh at her, but neither did.

'You found this Vessel?'

'Yes. It's in my room.'

Kane looked skeptical.

'It's the truth. Please believe me.'

'I do.' He sighed heavily. 'But even so, we still need to save ourselves, get Sorin, and now grab this Vessel and get that out of here as well.'

Lana straightened and lowered her voice. 'I know what Xeta said, but we need to kill Vineri.'

Viktor shook his head. 'Lana, thoughts of destroying that bastard kept us going for years. Then we met you and we realised that there's so much more to live for. What we need to do is escape with our lives. That matters more than anything.'

Lana smiled at his words. She agreed. 'But if you have a chance, don't hesitate.'

HOURS PASSED. Xeta disappeared back into the dark recesses of her cell. The Brothers, taking sleep where they could find it, were both settled against the stone walls with their eyes closed.

The door to the dungeon opened and Lana jumped up.

Vineri himself strode into the cell, Dugal hard on his heels.

'Why has he put my property down here? If she sickens and dies, I'll have his fucking head. When he returns, have him brought to me. He's taken me away from my associates for this, and they don't have the restraint to be left to their own devices.' He waved at the guard. 'Get her out of there and back to her room.'

She frowned. Uth hadn't told Vineri about her and the Brothers and, of course, the Collector wouldn't remember Kane and Viktor even if he'd seen them years before. Maybe they still had a chance.

The guard opened the door and beckoned her out. He took her by the arm and she glanced back at the Brothers, who were lolling in their cell, watching Vineri with calm detachment, their expressions not showing any of their absolute hatred.

As she passed Vineri, he took hold of her chin, forcing the guard to stop. Lana's hand brushed the keys at the Collector's belt and she eased them off his person, silently thanking Sorin for showing her some of his tricks over the past weeks.

'Next time stay in your room,' he advised. He glanced at Dugal. 'Clean her up.'

The guard led her past Xeta's cell and Lana stared into the darkness. She pretended to stumble and, as she fell to her knees, dropped the keys in the rushes by the bars, covering them as she stood.

'Forgive me,' she murmured to the guard, and he led her back to her room.

Dugal saw to her head himself and she tried not to let him see how distasteful it was for him to touch her. He didn't linger, and she was glad of it, though after locking the door, she heard him post a guard in the hall. She didn't dare try to pick the lock again, so she was forced to wait and hope that Xeta was able to free herself and the others.

She lay on the bed and tried to rest. It was only late afternoon, but she felt as if she hadn't slept in days. She hoped her body wasn't failing her already. There were still a few days until midwinter, when her time ran out. She longed to tell the Brothers, but they'd only fret, and they had more than enough to worry about, truth be told, without that as well – so she would keep it to herself until she didn't have to anymore.

There was a short cry from the hall and then a thud against the door. She scrambled up, grabbed the Vessel from its hiding place and tied it into a bundle under her skirts, as she'd done with the coins she'd stolen from Viktor. Gods, that seemed like a lifetime ago now. She secured the Vessel as high as she could so it wouldn't hinder her movements during their escape.

The door to her room opened and she caught sight of Kane and Viktor. She threw herself into their arms, hugging them both to her.

'No Sorin?' she asked.

Viktor shook his head as Kane answered. 'He wasn't there.'

'And Xeta?'

Viktor shrugged. 'She wouldn't come with us. She would have slowed us anyway. Come. We watched a servant disappear into Vineri's private wing where he entertains. We think that's where Sorin is.'

Lana felt sick. What were they doing to him?

CHAPTER 43

SORIN

They'd left him alone for the moment, Vineri and the others. Sorin remembered them all. Each of the men who had tortured him had had a hand in killing his mother that night and had hurt him many times. His lip curled as he thought of them. All five had seemed so much more terrifying then. Now he saw them for what they were; pathetic and small. He coughed up some blood and spat it onto the stone floor with a groan.

He wondered where the others were; far from here, he hoped, especially Lana. He smiled, though it hurt. He'd dreamed of her many times in this place; she'd come to him and smile and tell him she would free him and they'd escape together.

He heard the tell-tale sound of the door creaking. He couldn't see from here, but they were coming back. He couldn't help the panic that coursed through him, and he cursed. They weren't worth it, he kept telling himself. But still his body began to shake at the thought of what they might be planning next.

He steeled his mind. He would not show them fear. He

would meet their eyes, refuse to call them master and they could do what they willed. He would never again break for them. He looked up, intending to stare them down. They hated that, and they would lash him until he could no longer raise his head. He didn't care.

But the sight he saw made him question whether or not he was truly awake. Lana, Viktor and Kane were coming towards him. He blinked several times, but they were still there.

Lana gave a low cry, rushing to him as if she couldn't wait another moment and running her hands lightly over his bruised body. This was real.

His eyes flashed at his Brothers. 'I thought she was still safely with the witch far from here. How could you bring her?' he ground out, his voice low. He hoped they thought it was because he didn't want to draw any attention and not that he actually didn't have the strength.

Viktor raised an eyebrow. 'Told you he wouldn't like it,' he said to Kane.

'Sorin.' Tears filled Lana's eyes as she tried to reach where his wrists were tied above his head. 'What have they done?'

He chuckled as Kane cut his bindings. It sounded hollow even to his own ears.

'Nothing that won't heal, don't worry. Let's get out of here,' he mumbled even as his body threatened to collapse to the floor. He attempted a grin and knew he'd failed when tears spilled down her cheeks. He wanted to hold her, even just squeeze her hand, but his were numb. He shook them, willing the blood to circulate faster.

'Lana, I just need food and water. I'm all right.' He saw the other two exchange looks. They knew he wasn't, but he would live, and that was all Lana ever needed to know about what had happened here.

She wiped her cheeks, looking furious now. 'We need to kill them.'

He shook his head. Why weren't the others gainsaying her?

'No. We leave while we are able.' He looked beseechingly at Viktor. He still didn't know if he could count on Kane, but surely Viktor cared about what would happen to Lana if they found her here.

Memories of his mother flashed through his mind and he swallowed hard. 'We can't let them –'

The door creaked open and his words fled. They were coming. *Nowhere to hide.* He grabbed the closest weapon, a wooden mallet still splattered with his own blood. *Apt.*

Vineri, along with some of his false Dark Army guards, tore into the room. The Collector froze when he saw them, looking visibly relieved when his eyes landed on Lana.

He held out his hand. 'Come, girl.'

Lana shook her head, edging closer to Sorin. Anyone else would think she was frightened and searching for protection, but Sorin knew she was putting herself between him and Vineri's men. She was trying to shield him, not the other way around.

As she stood in front of him, she reached up to her neck, tucking some hair behind her ear, and her fingers brushed the necklace she wore. Except now that he looked at it closely, it wasn't a necklace at all. It was a collar with a lock. Understanding dawned. He shifted slightly and hoped all eyes were on Vineri as he reached slowly over to the table next to them – where his torturers had laid out all their instruments to scare him – and eased one of the needles between his fingers, thankful they'd left everything out on display. He began to work at the tiny lock through her long hair, his fingers tingling as he willed the feeling back into them.

Vineri was quickly losing patience, and it showed in the set of his jaw and the fingers clenching at his side. 'I don't know how you got caught up with these men, but I promise you that if you come with me now, I will not have you punished.'

Lana didn't say a word and, though he couldn't see her face, Sorin could picture her mulish expression. He almost smiled.

'So be it.' Vineri waved his hand. 'Take them all.' He turned his gaze on the rest of them. 'Gods, you're ridiculous. You don't even have any proper weapons.'

Vineri's soldiers advanced and Kane and Viktor didn't hesitate. They attacked first, rushing the guards for the element of surprise. Sorin tensed, but he could only watch as he tried to free Lana from the collar. His Brothers landed a few blows, but these soldiers were much better trained than the average sell-swords. His Brothers needed weapons, more men. They were soon overpowered. The guards forced them both to their knees.

Vineri's friends came back from their meal in the great hall, chatting and laughing, ready to continue their *entertainments*. This was a party, after all. Sorin's lip curled as he watched them. Gods, he wanted to tear them apart for what they'd done to him – both over the past days and years ago.

'What's this?' the portly one asked. 'A rescue attempt for our boy?'

Sorin snarled quietly at the pet name. It made his skin crawl.

'That's what it appears.'

'Oh, no,' his torturer grinned. 'We aren't nearly finished with him yet.' His eyes roamed over Lana. 'And who's this lovely? Has she come to join our fun?'

'This is … my newest acquisition. And, of course, you're

welcome to her, my friends. As long as our business arrangements stay intact, what's mine is yours, as always.'

Sorin's blood ran cold. What they'd done to his mother, it was going to happen again.

'You know what she is. You can't do anything to her,' Kane growled before Sorin could say the same. 'Not if you want her to be any use to you.'

'We shall see.' Vineri's eye caught that of a priest who'd just arrived. 'Dugal. You're going to perform your ritual on her tomorrow, aren't you?'

Dugal nodded and took a small stone disk from his robes. 'Yes. I was planning to do it at sunrise, but I have the relic here. I can do it now.'

Lana stiffened. What were they planning to do to her?

'Keep to sunrise. She won't remember anything that doesn't make her feel content afterwards anyway.' He smiled coldly. 'Kill the others.'

'No! Please!' Lana cried, but the swords raised and Sorin realized that nothing could save them.

No!

Vineri lifted a hand and his soldiers froze. 'So this wasn't happenstance. You do know them, girl. How?'

'I was part of the Dark Army. This is my unit. Ask Uth if you don't believe me. He knows the truth.'

Vineri looked stunned. 'The Brothers not only had a witch in their midst, but they made you one of them?' Without waiting for a reply, he began to guffaw loudly. 'I have a better idea,' he said between chortles. 'Chain them up over there. They can watch what is done to their Brother and their *Sister* before they die.' He shook his head and smiled disbelievingly. 'So, history repeats itself with another woman you care for, Sorin. Do you think she'll beg and plead as much as your pitiful mother did?'

He turned with a flourish to his friends behind him.

'Don't kill her. And no cutting her, Hektor,' he ordered the portly one. 'I intend to breed her once she's settled into her new life. Anything goes with our boy, though, as always.'

They all nodded, their gazes turning hungry as they looked at her; as they imagined all the things they were permitted to do.

Vineri directed his words to Lana. 'Sometimes a lesson needs to be learned.'

Lana pressed herself into Sorin. 'How will I learn the lesson if I don't remember it?' she asked insolently.

Vineri turned away. 'The lesson is for everyone else who would cross me, girl.'

He sat in a comfortable chair across the room – to watch, Sorin presumed. From what he'd heard, the Collector's tastes had changed in his older age and he wasn't usually interested in girls anymore. He'd make sure his friends followed his instructions, but the only things he wanted Lana for were her power as a witch and her womb to create more.

CHAPTER 44

LANA

The Collector's friends edged closer, but Sorin was still fiddling with the lock. She had a plan, but she needed this collar off and Sorin needed more time.

'Are you going to let them do this, Dugal?' She let a plaintive note into her voice. 'I thought you cared for me.'

Dugal shrugged. 'Now. Later. You aren't going to remember it.' He retreated to the wall and leant against it, watching the proceedings with a detached interest.

Her lip curled in disgust. So much for his virtuous loyalty to the gods and their kin.

The four men were closer now and it took all of her strength not to move. Every part of her wanted to at least try to flee – as if she were prey. Her body shook with her steadfast refusal to give in. She was no longer a slave. She was no longer a lone girl trying to survive. She had the others now. If only they could stay alive.

'What are you going to do to me?' she cried. She really was terrified, so it wasn't hard to show her fear, but she wanted to delay them with talk.

One of them picked up a crop from the table. 'I think we

should make our boy thrash her until she begs him prettily to stop. Or perhaps she should lash him.'

She swallowed hard as she eyed the whip. She made herself be still, though her knees shook. Sorin's arm snaked around her waist. The gesture was noticed of course.

'How sweet. They're like star-crossed lovers. Let's have the guards hold her. We can play that game. The one you were telling me about on the way here.'

'Yes! But we make him do it. And whenever she gets it wrong, *he* gives her the lashes!'

They laughed loudly.

'What game?' Lana asked, her voice faltering. She wasn't sure if she'd done that on purpose or if she was just that frightened now.

'Oh, you'll find we love games. It's simple. Our boy will put whatever object we give him inside you. You have to guess what it is. If you get it wrong, the crop is applied. Hard.'

Then, the collar loosened. She felt a sudden warmth fill a void in her she hadn't known was there and she gasped. Sorin had done it. Power. She could feel it now. She looked around. No one had noticed that the collar was slack. She closed her eyes and, with a silent prayer to Gaila that this would work, she threw herself to her knees in front of the nearest man.

'Please!' she cried, grasping his hands. 'Please let us go!'

She tried to let the power she felt *out*, willing it forth in a concentrated burst, her thinking being that if it was always trickling out and changing Brothers in the Army gradually, then a burst all at once would do the same but faster.

He looked amused and smug as he stared down into her pleading eyes. She thought for a moment that it had worked, but then he grabbed her and, in one swift movement, threw her to the waiting guards. They held her arms. Her dress was bunched up, exposing her lower half as she was pushed down, and she shrieked as hands delved between her legs. She prayed that the Vessel, still tied under the swathes of cloth, wouldn't be found. She dimly heard Sorin shouting as she was placed on her knees and her head shoved to the floor. A boot pushed down on her neck, anchoring her.

Why hadn't it worked?

She turned her thoughts inward and tried to ignore what was happening; the laughing and joking, their lewd comments, Sorin behind her saying he was sorry, Viktor looking on in horror, and Kane as well, but his face blank. She had only moments. Something nudged at her entrance. It was cold, and she knew at once that it was the handle of a knife. She realised what they meant to do. She hadn't understood before.

She gritted her teeth, refusing to give them the satisfaction of hearing her scream as it was forced into her dry channel. But her mind was in turmoil. This couldn't be happening. Was this really how it would end after all that had happened? After how far they had come?

Someone said something in her ear and she realised with utter revulsion that one of them was asking her to guess what they were defiling her with. She said nothing.

'She won't guess.'

'She's testing you. Show her her place.'

'Fuck her harder. Maybe that will loosen her tongue.'

The handle was removed and then shoved into her again with such force that a cry was driven from her throat. At the men's answering jeer, she began to sink, willing herself away from this nightmare. And as she did, she let go of something inside herself she hadn't even known she'd been holding. She felt that well of power inside her pulse; flowing out in an unexpected wave. The hands holding her went limp. The knife fell with a clatter and the sudden silence was palpable.

It took a moment for her to understand that it had worked. Her breath caught on a sob and she forced the tears back as she rose to her knees. She could cry later. She grabbed the knife from the floor. The man who'd been raping her was not Sorin, and she let out a small sigh of relief. Forced or not, she wasn't sure she could have forgiven him.

She stared at the soldier and he stared back, an empty grin on his face that, given what he'd just been doing to her, was disconcerting. Her anger bubbled to the surface and she shoved the knife through the side of his neck. She watched him slump over, gurgling, with satisfaction and turned her attention to the others.

All the rest of the men in the room looked the same, smiling stupidly and staring at nothing. Their bodies and their movements were slow and languid. It was as if they were happily and dreamily drunk.

'What did you do?' Sorin asked in awe.

'I'm not sure.' She turned back to him. 'But it worked.'

Then, she fell back to her knees and retched on the floor. Sorin handed her a rag and she wiped her mouth gratefully.

'Vineri's gone.'

'Fuck,' she heard Viktor mutter.

After Sorin freed him, Kane helped her up. Vineri's chair was indeed vacant. The coward had fled.

Dugal still stood by the wall. He smiled at her vaguely as she approached him. 'I told him you were strong.'

Her hands curled into fists as she thought of what he would have done to her; the things he would have let those men and probably countless others do, and she struck him in the jaw as hard as she could. He fell to the floor with an *oomph* that seemed to echo through the room, and Viktor appeared at her side.

He put his hand on her shoulder. 'Let's go while we can.'

'No,' Sorin murmured. 'After what they've done to me and to Lana and all the others, they need to die. They're blights on this world.' He drew one of the soldier's swords and slid it into the nearest one's abdomen. The man went down without a sound.

Kane grabbed a knife and did the same until every man in the room was dead.

Viktor tried to lead Lana away from the carnage, but she refused to budge. These monsters had done unspeakable deeds and, even in their helpless state, they deserved death a thousand times over. She'd heard the tales all her life of the Brothers being cold and ruthless killers. And it was true. They were. But she had blood on her hands too. She wouldn't shy away from it, nor from them.

But as she looked around the room, she couldn't help but wonder how much she had changed the Brothers. She'd been with them for weeks. Yesterday she would have said she knew these men well, but today, seeing the changes she had wrought so swiftly here, she wasn't sure. Were the Brothers she'd come to know, even love, real or had she made them?

'And Vineri?' she asked.

'Him too.' Sorin started for the door. 'He'll be hiding with his collection.'

Thankful to have something to do to take her mind off these worrying thoughts, Lana started forward. 'I know where it is.'

They left the room as a group, the Brothers following her closely as she led them down the halls and stairs to where the door to his Gallery had been. Lana wondered if she should go back to the tower and free the girl she'd found, though she hadn't seemed as if she wanted to leave this place. When this was over, she would try, she decided.

She found the door without too much trouble, only going

the wrong way once, and it wasn't long before they stood outside the giant room that housed Vineri's treasures.

She grasped the handle, but Kane pulled her back. 'He might be waiting for us. We'll go in first.'

She waited for him to let her go, but instead his grip on her tightened. She looked up at him and, for once, saw emotion in his face. He must have been very afraid for her, she thought as she looked into his dark eyes. She squeezed his arm and then wriggled away. After this was done.

'Ready?' Viktor asked.

They nodded and he opened the door. No explosions nor ambushes apparent, they stepped inside the mammoth room of the collection. The door closed behind them with an ominous click.

'What is all this?' Sorin breathed.

'My life's work, boy.' Vineri's voice echoed. But he was nowhere to be seen.

'Show yourself, you fucking coward!' Sorin bellowed.

Lana gave him a quick glance. He seemed a bit stronger, though he was covered in bruises and cuts and dried blood. She was sure he shouldn't be walking about, and definitely not fighting, but they needed to stay together now.

She saw a flicker of movement to the side of them. 'There!' She pointed, but there was nothing.

She huddled closer to the Brothers. Vineri had all of these objects because they held ancient power. If he knew how to use even a handful of them ... She shivered.

Kane darted down one of the long corridors of shelves, his sword raised. 'I saw him!'

'Wait!' Viktor yelled. 'He's trying to separate us, Kane.'

But Kane ignored him and when they rushed to follow, he was gone. Lana called out his name, but there was no answer. The three of them looked at each other, all trying to suppress their fear. They continued. All they could do was look for him as they did Vineri. They began cautiously walking through the room, down paths with dead ends and routes that looped in on each other, the high shelves on all sides always looming over them as if recording their course. They didn't find anyone, but they did realize that the room was much larger than it had appeared from the door, and the random stacks and paths made it a veritable maze, which they seemed to be stuck in.

There was a thud behind them and they all whirled around to find both men they sought standing calmly at their backs. They hadn't even known they were there, not until Vineri had wanted them to. The Collector held a small box in his hand. Kane stood at his side, not trying to kill him, not trying to escape. Nothing. A black cord was tightly wrapped around his neck.

'I thought you Dark Brothers were meant to be formidable.' Vineri tutted. 'But look at your leader, so easily subdued with the simplest of my trinkets.' He waved a hand in what Lana had come to see was his signature gesture of nonchalance. 'Kill your Brothers.'

Kane stepped forward and raised the sword he carried. He slashed at the air in front of him. His eyes were glazed.

'Kane?'

He turned towards Lana's voice but attacked Viktor immediately; his face contorted into a beastly snarl. Viktor rushed to parry, luckily stopping Kane's blade.

'I'll deal with Kane,' he muttered.

They began to fight, evenly matched, while Vineri spectated. He looked politely uninterested, as if he were watching a play he couldn't really be bothered with.

'I must say,' he commented to Lana and Sorin, 'I'm somewhat glad my friends' little games with you two were interrupted. They can last ages, and I do get bored quickly these days.'

'Your friends are dead,' Lana spat.

Vineri smiled. 'I thought they might be. You're so strong, my dear.' He licked his lips. 'A great investment if I can keep you alive. I hope you aren't feeling the effects of that little burst of energy back in my pleasure wing. It must have had its price.'

Lana didn't reply. What she'd done *had* cost her, though she hadn't said anything to the Brothers, of course. She was feeling weak, but Gaila had warned her this would happen if she wasn't careful. It would be worth it if they could defeat Vineri, if her Brothers could be free of him. She grasped for that power again, much diminished now, and tried to do what she'd done before. Vineri laughed at her.

'You're trying to use it on me. It won't work. I've been immune to all that for many, many years now.' He turned his attention back to Viktor and Kane, still fighting, and frowned. 'Too evenly matched,' he muttered.

Lana was suddenly very glad he didn't know about Kane's gift for bending people to his will. The things he could be commanded to make people do … She looked around them surreptitiously, searching for something, anything, that could help them. What if they just started smashing relics? She wished Vie were here. Considering her knowledge of ancient things, the witch would probably know what at least one of these objects did.

Vineri cried out, clutching his heart. He grimaced and slowly pulled out a small knife. He cast it aside with a look of annoyance.

'Learned a few more skills than sucking cock, eh, Sorin? I'm afraid the weapons of men can't hurt me either, but I commend you on the effort.' He yawned. 'Forgive me. As I said, I grow bored quickly.'

Vineri took out his little box again and began to fiddle with it. Viktor's and Kane's weapons could be heard clanging down one of the other corridors as they battled, but they were no longer in sight. Lana began to inch towards the Collector. Perhaps if she could get close enough, she could get that box, whatever it was, and use it to help them. As she shuffled forwards, she noticed a tiny movement out of the corner of her eye. Xeta was creeping slowly up the path nearest Vineri, her neck noticeably bare of the collar she'd had on in her cell. She was small and quiet and he hadn't noticed her. Lana stopped moving immediately. She wasn't sure what the old witch could do, but she was probably the best hope they had.

'You have amassed many artefacts. You can't know what all of them do,' Lana said, trying to draw his attention.

'I don't yet. I will soon. But you're trying to draw me into conversation to give your lovers more time. They will die, girl. And then you will be taken, your mind clouded and your body bred. You are mine, and so will your children be.' He opened his box and a black cord shot out of it and wrapped around Sorin's neck. He clawed at it with a cry, but then went silent and stood still.

'Hold her.'

Sorin grabbed her arm immediately. She tried to throw him off, but he had her. His eyes were glassy like Kane's. The clanging down the corridor stopped and she heard a groan. Kane walked out a moment later.

Lana sagged in Sorin's hold. *Viktor.*

Kane approached, sword raised and dripping with blood, ready to continue killing them.

'Stop,' Vineri commanded.

He came to stand on the other side of her, ignoring her completely now.

Xeta. Lana looked up just as she struck, tearing something from Vineri's neck and throwing it to the floor. Lana heard glass shatter and Vineri shrieked.

He fell to his knees, feeling for the pieces, and she knelt in front of him, grasping his head.

'Sister?' he whispered. 'How?'

'The girl freed me,' she rasped. She gripped him tighter and his arms came up to throw her off, but he couldn't move her. 'All those years, little brother, locked in that cell.' Her eyes turned red and began to glow like coals. 'You should have fucking killed me.'

Vineri's body began to smoke, then he began to scream. His flesh turned black and so did Xeta's. Objects on the shelves began to burst into flames. The woman turned her terrible eyes on Lana. 'Go.'

Lana knew what she had to do. Hoping her plan would work, she darted forward and grabbed the box from Vineri's blackening fingers.

'Kane, get Viktor and meet me at the door. Sorin, follow me.'

She made sure that they were doing as she told them now that she had the box. Then she ran as artefacts all around them started to explode. Shards of pottery, wood and metal flew through the air, showering them with debris as they fled. The fire burned red hot, engulfing the stacks at such a speed that it took all of their strength to outrun it.

Thankfully, Sorin was following her just as she'd ordered. They got to the door and she pushed it open just as Kane came sprinting down another corridor. He was pulling Viktor behind him. *Thank the gods he was alive!*

The room all around them was an inferno. She made sure the others were safe first, pushing them through the door. Only then did she go herself. She slammed it closed, leaving them in the hall smelling of cinders. The coldness and silence here was in sharp contrast to the raging fire and heat behind the door. She made a quick survey of the Brothers. They were burnt and bloody and bruised and cut, but they were alive and so was she.

'Lana –' Viktor began.

But she cut him off. 'Later. Can you keep up?' she asked, eyeing the slash across his chest, which was oozing blood.

He nodded.

'Come.'

She ran down the corridor, intending to get to the tower to free the girl, but the wall a few paces in front of them exploded, sending shards of rock in all directions. Lana skidded to a halt. The corridor was blocked completely, so she turned on her heel with a prayer to the gods that the girl in the tower would be all right and ran the other way around the rotunda towards the courtyard where the passage to the town was. The Brothers followed, Kane and Sorin still under the thrall of the box. She stopped short as they rounded the corner, and the men behind bumped into her, almost sending her sprawling. She pushed them back out of sight. There were guards all over the yard and it was the only way to the tunnel. How were they going to get through all those men without being noticed?

They stood there for a moment, catching their breath and trying to think of something. They were so close!

There was an indiscernible shout that echoed across the cloister, followed by another. She heard someone yell, 'Fire!' and when she looked around the corner again, everything was in disarray. Servants and guards scurried hither and thither, grabbing water from troughs in buckets and running. People were screaming; others stood frozen, just watching the drama with smiles on their faces.

'Follow me.'

Lana edged into the fray, keeping close to the wall, the others mimicking her movements. She was on her guard, ready to run as soon as they were noticed, but she needn't have worried. When they got across the yard, she glanced up and gasped. The whole of the eastern part of the fortress was in flames. They couldn't see the sky for smoke, and the fire was spreading fast.

She began to descend the ladder into the tunnel when Viktor stopped her.

'Let me go first.'

She nodded, thankful he was taking charge, and let him pass her.

At the bottom, he deftly lit a torch with a flint and they went quickly down the passageway. Lana shivered. The last time she'd been down here, she'd been so afraid. But as she looked ahead at Viktor's back as he led them to freedom and behind her at Kane and Viktor, plodding along as she'd ordered, she was filled with joy. It was almost over.

When they came up in the temple, Lana took the box out and turned it over and over. It was nondescript and there was nothing to show how it worked. She huffed. What had she expected, pictures?

'What do I do with it? How do we get Kane and Sorin back?' she asked Viktor.

He shrugged, threw the torch back down into the hole, and shut the hatch that led down with a bang. 'Want the Brothers' way?'

She nodded.

'If you don't know what it does, destroy it.' He grinned.

She chuckled in spite of herself and put the box on the ground. With a look at Viktor and another at the other two vacant-eyed Brothers, she crushed it beneath her heel.

The cords around Kane's and Sorin's necks fell away a moment later and they looked around, blinking dazedly.

Kane recovered first. 'What happened?'

Viktor gestured to his bleeding chest. 'You tried to kill me. I had to play dead so you'd leave me alone.'

'How did we escape?' Kane rubbed his forehead. 'My head aches like I spent all night at the tavern.'

'I'm free.' Sorin's voice was low and incredulous.

Lana took his hand. 'Vineri is dead.'

Sorin turned his head away, silent. 'I thought I was going to die in there,' he finally said. 'There were times when I wished …'He whirled back and took her hands, tears in his eyes. 'You saved me, Lana.'

She smiled at him. 'Viktor and Kane were there as well.'

He looked around at the others and grinned. 'It's done.'

Viktor rolled his eyes. 'I'm bleeding to death, and none of you look much better. Come on.'

He led the way. The other two went with him and Lana began to follow. She hadn't gone more than five steps before her legs gave way. She fell to the ground without a sound, her eyes closing.

'Lana? Lana?'

She looked past the concerned faces of the Brothers. She was back in the room at the inn. Groaning, she tried to sit up. One of them held her while another put some pillows behind her.

'What happened?' Sorin asked, fear evident on his face.

Lana looked apologetically at them all. 'I'm sorry.' She focused on Kane. 'I made you believe I was healed. We had to save Sorin, you see? I knew you'd never agree to my plan if you knew.'

None of them said a word, so she continued. 'I made an agreement. The goddess gave me until midwinter and, in return for getting this,' she pulled the Vessel out from her skirts, 'she said she'd help me.'

She put the artefact in Viktor's hand. 'Please can you take it to a priest? A real priest? I don't have the strength left.'

She began to drift off again and hoped Viktor would do as she asked.

'THERE YOU ARE. Finally succumbing, I see.'

Gaila stood before her. She tutted. 'You would have had another week if you hadn't wasted all that power.'

Lana frowned. 'It was hardly a waste.'

Gaila shrugged. 'Suppose so. Your man has given the vessel to one of my priests. I understand that you also killed my enemy. You did well. Much better than I expected.'

'It wasn't really me. It was the old witch, Vineri's sister. She burned him up and she destroyed his collection.'

'But you helped set her free. I saw you do it. No, my dear, I have you to thank. We all do.'

Lana looked around. There was nothing else here. Just them. 'Is this a dream?'

Gaila smiled. 'Yes. It's easier for me to speak with you here than trying to get you to the God Realm, as I'm sure you recall.'

'Am I dying?'

'You kept up your end of our bargain, so I will keep mine.' Gaila took Lana's hands. 'It is done.'

'So easily?'

Gaila shrugged again.

Gods.

The goddess turned away, but a sudden thought came to Lana. 'Wait. What if I have children? Will they be witches?'

She looked thoughtful. 'They may be. But if they are, they will be born to contain the power, unlike you.'

'And the Brothers. Will they go back to … the men they were before I changed them?'

Gaila rolled her eyes. 'No,' she answered impatiently. 'You never changed them in the first place; not with your power, at any rate. Any differences in them were your doing, not the Dark Realm blood. Now leave me be, girl. I have important, godly things to do.'

Lana's eyes opened. It was dark, but the sky was starting to lighten. The dawn wasn't far off. A lone candle burned in the corner. Kane, Sorin and Viktor lay around her on the bed. They looked clean and bandaged and in very deep sleeps. They needed the rest, so she didn't wake them.

There was water in a small tub in the corner. It wouldn't be warm, but she didn't mind. She'd brave it to be clean. She smelt of smoke still, and thinking back to what had happened in that room made her body feel dirty. She got out of bed, stripped and climbed into the bath. It was cold, so she washed herself quickly, shivering as she did.

'Let me attend to your injuries,' Sorin whispered in the dark.

She nodded in the dim light.

He helped her out of the tub and dried her. She stood in the middle of the room while he quietly rummaged through one of their packs.

When he came back, she hugged him. Unable to keep the smile from her face, she told him what Gaila had done.

'Are you sure it wasn't just a dream?' he asked gently.

'I feel better,' she said simply. 'Even better than after I was with the witch.'

He took her in his arms and sank into one of the chairs with her, not saying anything.

'Is all of this really over?' she whispered.

He breathed out. 'I hope so.'

'What are we going to do now?'

He chuckled. 'I don't know. I don't much care. After the past few days, I'm just glad we're all still alive.'

The dawn broke while they whispered to each other about plans and dreams and, as the room got lighter, she heard Viktor and Kane stirring.

Kane sat up first, his eyes flitting around the room when he found her gone. He met her eyes and frowned. 'You should be resting.'

She smiled at him. 'I am resting,' she teased.

Viktor, now fully awake as well, padded over to her and turned her face up to see her properly in the light.

'You look different. Better,' he observed.

'I feel it,' Lana answered. 'I believe I truly am healed this time. She told me I'm not a witch anymore. She took it.' Frowning, she glanced away. 'I'm just me now.'

Sorin took her by the shoulders and turned her to him. 'Without you, we'd be dead. Remember that. You're our Fourth and we'll never let you go.' He grimaced. 'Not unless you want to go.'

She kissed him gently, sucking his lip into her mouth, and he made a contented sound. 'Never,' she whispered.

Fingers wound into her hair and her head was pulled gently but firmly away from Sorin's. 'Are you telling the truth, Lana, or is this another lie?'

She pressed her body into Viktor's. 'No more lies. I promise.'

He pulled her hair harder, his face hard. He hated any kind of betrayal, and that included untruths, she knew. She whimpered, pressing her legs together eagerly.

'Good. You'll be disciplined for deceiving us, though. You know that, don't you?'

'Yes,' she said meekly.

Her hair was released, but he took her by the waist instead and plunged two fingers into her without warning. She gasped, kicking to dislodge him, but he wouldn't let her go.

'Are you feeling well enough for this, Lana?' Sorin's worried face appeared in front of hers.

She moaned in answer and pulled him to her. She kissed him hard, the sounds bubbling up from her throat muted as Viktor's fingers began to twist and work inside her.

Sorin began to knead her breasts, playing with her sensitive nipples. His lips stayed on hers, but he moved to one side, offering Kane a taste of her. The other Brother began to use his tongue on the tightening tips and she arched back into Viktor, whose other hand began to play with her mound, delving between her legs. His skilled fingers began to work her bud as well, squeezing it and rolling it. He kicked her legs further apart and she went over the edge with a scream, bucking against his hands as pleasure took hold of her.

As it ebbed, she realised that Sorin was now behind her.

Did you enjoy that, Lana?' he asked her, caressing down her arms to her sides and arse.

Lana nodded dreamily.

'By the time we're finished, you're going to be begging us to stop,' Kane rumbled from over near the bed.

She almost chuckled. *Never.* She craved their hands on her, and it seemed to have been so long since they were all together, she wanted everything they would give her.

'Bring her.'

Sorin pushed her over to where Kane lounged on top of the covers. She took his hard staff in her mouth, licking it up and down and suckling it gently the way she knew he liked until he moaned. He pulled her over him, kissing her, his tongue exploring her mouth. Then he lifted her up and plunged her down on his cock. She cried out, but her channel quickly adjusted and she began to move slowly.

Viktor knelt on the bed next to them and she took his

hard length in her hand, pumping it up and down in the same rhythm as she was using with Kane.

She was just wondering where Sorin was when she felt his finger prodding at her other entrance. She glanced at him and he put a hand on her back, telling her to let go and relax her body. She tried to do as he said, and he pushed a slippery digit inside her. She made a sound of discomfort as he began to move it in and out. She still wasn't sure about this sort of play. Then it began to feel nice. A second finger joined the first and he began to stretch her opening. She moaned and wriggled on Kane's cock. His hands began to play with her breasts again, just shy of painfully, twisting and tweaking them while she mewled and whimpered.

She took Viktor in her mouth, her hand kneading him gently as she licked the length of him, paying particular attention to the underside of the tip, which she knew he liked. He grabbed her hair and thrust into her mouth, filling it.

Sorin's fingers disappeared and she felt him kneel on the bed behind her. He lined himself up with her back opening and eased himself in slowly. She gasped at the sensation; it hurt and felt so different, yet it felt *good* at the same time.

When he was inside her to the hilt, he let her become accustomed to it, then he began to move – and so did Kane. As Kane pulled out, Sorin would thrust in. In. Out. In. Out. Lana moaned in pleasure as they held her, her mouth vibrating around Viktor's cock. She felt so full! Everywhere was bursting with pleasure.

Kane, Sorin and Viktor began to push into her faster. Her nipples were pulled hard and Sorin took hold of the swollen bud between her thighs, tugging it gently. Her body spasmed, her hips jerking as she screamed in the most incredible, intense pleasure. She was joined a moment later by all three of them, their seeds pouring deep within her. They collapsed together onto the bed, Kane's length still inside her as they lay intertwined.

Lana had never felt so content.

'I hadn't realised,' she panted.

'Realised what?' Kane asked her, caressing her cheek and tucking a strand of hair behind her ear.

She leaned into his touch and felt Sorin at her back, kneading the muscles of her shoulders. 'That we could do that all together.'

Sorin's hot breath was on her neck as he laughed at her, and she elbowed him in the ribs. He fell out of the bed with a mock cry and then began to get dressed.

Viktor gave her a look from across the room, where he too pulled on his breeches. 'We've only just begun, Lana,' he promised.

Lana frowned at him. 'Why is everyone leaving?'

'Sorin and I are going to get us all some food. We can't be expected to satisfy you all day and night without something to fill our bellies, little bird.'

'All day and all night?' Lana asked faintly.

He laughed and they both left her and Kane, closing the door with a soft click.

'I don't think I could do that all day and –'

Kane interrupted her with a kiss, rolling her over and bearing her down onto the bed.

'This is how I like you,' he growled. 'Powerless beneath me. I may shackle your arms to the bed, tie your legs wide so I can look at you and fuck you at my leisure while you beg me to pleasure you.'

She moaned at his words, hoping he would do as he promised, and felt his cock hardening within her. Soon he was plunging into her, bringing them both to pleasure again.

. . .

Sometime later, Lana lay on the bed trying to rest as they'd ordered. She and the Brothers would leave the Forge soon. A contingent of the Dark Army was coming with their new Commander to occupy Vineri's fortress and strip it of whatever valuables hadn't been consumed in the fire. It would be dangerous for her if she was still here when they arrived. Unable to sleep, she watched the three men attending to their weapons and packing their supplies. They would make their way north, in a roundabout way, arriving in the spring. The Brothers wanted to show her where they came from, but, in truth, she didn't care what they did as long as they were together.

She sighed in contentment. 'I can't imagine being without any of you,' she murmured.

'Good,' Kane growled without looking up, 'because we'll never let you go.'

~

Kane lurked in the shadows of the main gate to Vineri's fortress as Quin, the new Commander of the Dark Army, arrived with his unit. 'You got my bird, then.'

Quin nodded in greeting. 'I did. Didn't think you'd still be here, though.' He looked around. 'Where's your little witch?'

Kane eyed the other two Brothers. Mad Malkom, the quiet one, he knew, but who was this new member of his unit?

'Payn's dead, thanks to Greygor.'

Mad Mal spat on the ground at the mention of their General.

'This is Bastian,' Quin continued.

The new Brother grinned and dipped his head slightly. Mal ignored him for the most part, as he did everyone – unless he was killing them.

Quin chuckled at Kane's silence. 'You have nothing to fear. I don't care what she is so long as she stays away from us. My unit doesn't either.'

'Then why did you interfere in the Islands?'

Quin shrugged and didn't reply.

'Don't think we don't intend to repay you for leaving her defenseless in that fucking cave.'

Quin waved a hand in dismissal. 'It ended well, didn't it?'

Kane's eyes narrowed. 'She's gone. She and the others have travelled on ahead. I stayed to make sure Greygor is dead.'

Quin's lip curled in contempt for their old Commander. 'He was found guilty of betraying the Brothers' secrets and hanged from a tree. The bastard's dead all right. We let him wriggle around for a bit, then Mal put a bolt through his chest.'

'Commander.' A soldier came running up. 'They found a girl high in yonder tower.'

'So? Drag her out and put her with the other slaves and servants.'

'She's adamant she can't leave her room. She's makin' a fuss.'

A loud, feminine scream emanated from the tower followed by a man's yell.

Quin swore as he dismounted. 'This place is ours now. We'll do as we please. She'll soon understand who her new masters are.'

He gave Kane a mock salute. 'I look forward to your retribution, old friend.'

The End

IF YOU ENJOYED THIS BOOK, **it would be amazing if you were able to leave a review on Amazon.**

Reviews are so, so helpful to authors (especially new ones like me!) to get us noticed and, I'm not gonna lie, I love reading them!

Also, keep reading for the exclusive first chapter of *Kept to Kill,* Book 3 in the Dark Brothers series!

THANKS FOR READING! Not ready to leave Lana and her Brothers? Join my mailing list and receive an exclusive epilogue to find out what happens after they leave the Dark Brothers Army!

Use the URL below for your exclusive bonus scene:
https://BookHip.com/RZKFNVR

JOIN MY MAILING LIST

Sign up to my newsletter and receive an exclusive epilogue to find out what happens after Lana, Kane, Viktor and Sorin leave the Dark Brothers Army!

Members also receive exclusive content, free books, access to giveaways and contests as well as the latest information on new books and projects that I'm working on!

Use the URL below:
   https://BookHip.com/RZKFNVR

It's completely free to sign up, you will never be spammed by me and it's very easy to unsubscribe.

AND keep reading for an exclusive sneak preview of Kept to Kill, Book 3 of the Dark Brothers Series.

KEPT TO KILL (SNEAK PREVIEW)

Lily has been alone for most of her life. Held as a captive. Used as a weapon.

The mercenaries who 'rescue' her are as intriguing as they are brutal, but Lily is still a pawn in the games of men. They'll use her and cast her aside if she lets them. That's if she survives what comes next...

Quin, Commander of the Dark Army, has only one goal and will let Lily die if it serves his purposes, but he's also drawn to her in a way that makes him wish for more. No one is safe from Mad Mal, a monster who kills to satisfy dark needs. He will make her pay for tempting the other beast he hides within. And the playful Bastian seems harmless, with a taste for wine and women, but he might just harbor the darkest soul of them all...and the darkest secrets.

Each man has his own twisted torments and fierce desires that Lily cannot fathom after her years a captive. But as the days *and nights* go by, she begins to realize she needs something she never thought she'd have and it may not be the freedom she always yearned for at all.

Can she unlock the hearts of these men who care for nothing and no one to find the pieces of themselves they buried long ago, or will they decide their mission is more important than the woman who brings them to their knees?

Kept to Kill is the third standalone in the Dark Brothers Series of dark fantasy romance. If you like strong, but desolate heroines, antiheroes that make your blood run cold even as it heats up, and your Happily Ever Afters with some darkness before the light, you will love this book!

Read the next dark adventure in this amazing series today! More info at www.kyraalessy.com/kept2kill

Lilith

There had been a fire. That much she knew from the shouts and screams, the scurrying bodies she had seen in the courtyard below the barred casement of her small room. The topmost bower; the highest and most inaccessible prison in the Collector's fortress. He'd never called it that; told her prisons didn't have warmth, sunlight, food and all the books she could read from his great library. But a prison it was and it was where he had kept her since he'd brought her here from the north when she was still a child.

Priests left over from when this great estate had been a monastery had been her only companions here. They brought food, wood for the grate, and whatever books she hadn't yet read. Couldn't have Vineri's prize possession going mad from boredom, could they?

Though sometimes she wondered if she'd gone mad anyway.

When she'd first come here, the room had been small and stifling. She'd longed for the sky. She'd hated this place. But now, after so long, she loathed accompanying Vineri on his journeys, his little shows of power where she was the main attraction – or deterrent. Without fail, she was immutably glad when she was returned to her room's stone confines. Hearing the lock sliding smoothly into place was like a balm on her spirit. Vineri was right. She'd never have survived without his generosity, though like everything, it had its price.

She sighed as she craned her neck for some glimpse of what was happening below, but she couldn't see anything of merit. She threw herself down into her worn chair in front of the currently fireless grate and shivered as she wrapped her shawl closely around her, opening a book.

The wood had not been brought for two days. No food either. There had been yelling earlier, but it had stopped. Perhaps one of the priests would tell her about it later.

Lily began to read, quickly losing herself in the new story.

She heard boots clomping up the stone stairs, echoing through the hall. She canted her head she listened. They didn't sound like the –

A scraggly face appeared at the small window and she frowned. The bolt was thrown hard, making a loud bang that resonated through the tower. Still she didn't move as the door was flung open and a large man, unthinkably, stepped inside her room.

She was on her feet and shoving herself against the far wall by the time his eyes fell on her and he grinned – somewhat nastily, actually – and started forward, crossing the line. Her eyes widened in shock. No one crossed the line! Not unless she was cloaked and gloved and, even then, only Vineri. By the gods, her food was usually pushed through the cracked door on a tray with a long stick!

'Stop!' she cried. 'Don't come any closer!'

He didn't listen.

'Read the sign!' she screeched desperately.

'Can't read, woman,' he snarled, looking her up and down in a way that made her blood run cold. She'd never experienced a man *leering*. He didn't know. There were more men behind him, laughing and joking. None of them knew!

Lily screamed as he grabbed her, tearing off her shawl. She tried to bat him away with her arms, not touching her skin to his, but then he grabbed her by the throat with his bare, meaty fingers and the contact felt like a brand.

He yelled immediately and jumped back, glaring at his palm and then at her.

She stared back. 'You fool,' she whispered as he fell to his knees with a gurgle, his face turning an awful shade of purple as he gasped for breath.

He thudded to the floor. Already, he bled from his eyes, nose and ears as he twitched on the ground in front of her. Dimly, she wondered if this was one of Vineri's diversions or, perhaps, a test. It had never happened so quickly before. He'd be delighted, she thought as she sank to her knees, feeling as though she might retch. At least there was nothing in her stomach seeing as she hadn't been fed for two days.

The soldier in front of her breathed his last and she gave the others behind him a level look even as she felt the prickle of tears that she forced back. He had been intending her harm, she reminded herself. He was probably a terrible person. But it didn't ease the guilt. She stood shakily, giving the other soldiers a wary look. They'd all backed away at least.

'Get Vineri,' she ordered.

'Odd, I didn't think the Collector enjoyed women.'

A man cloaked in black pushed through the group of soldiers as they hastened to step out of his way. He was tall and broad, his hair a sable brown and his jaw, square. His nose looked like it had been broken at least once and his ear was missing a piece at the top, she noted. He also had an intricate, winding tattoo that began on the side of his neck and disappeared beneath his tunic. She'd never seen such a man. Her breath hitched and she hoped that, if her cheeks were colouring, he didn't notice.

She needn't have worried. He barely looked at her, his gaze flitting around the room, taking in the only home she'd ever really known and making her feel open, vulnerable. She didn't care for it. Not one bit.

'Your lover is dead.'

Her lover? She made a face at the thought. Wait, had he just said Vineri was dead? 'Dead?' she muttered aloud.

He finally glanced at her and then away again. 'Take her below to wait with the others.'

'But, sir, she killed Wron.' One of them gestured to the man lying on the floor.

'Doubtful. He was frequently seen overindulging in Faerie smoke. Looks like his body finally gave out,' sneered the man in black, their leader, as he toed the corpse, his eyes falling on her again. Whatever he saw made him bark a laugh and descend the stairs without a backwards glance.

The soldiers advanced, but she could see in their faces that they knew their friend's death had been her doing.

'Please. You saw what happened,' she tried, ready to beg is necessary. 'I can't leave the room,'.

But the nearest one shook his head. 'You're the Camp's now. You'll soon learn that an order from the Commander is an order best followed,' he said though he didn't touch her and, if there had been lust in his eyes before, all there was now was fear. But he drew his sword and used it to gesture to the door. The threat was clear. Their commander hadn't actually specified that she had to be alive when they took her below.

Lily took a step and then another, feeling as if she was walking to her death. Swallowing hard, she battled the dizziness that threatened to pitch her down the winding stairs. This couldn't be happening, could it? Where were they taking her? She reached the bottom and made herself loosen the death-grip she had on the railing, walking over the threshold until she was outside, in the square she could see from her window. There were a few others sitting in the frozen mud, a couple she recognised from the kitchens.

She was prodded in the back with a sword and stepped forward and the ones who knew who she was began to mutter to each other, their eyes scared.

She looked down as she walked, wishing she had some shoes or a cloak, or her gloves, but Vineri always had them taken away when they got back from their *excursions* in case she got a "stupid idea" into her head, he'd said. The man had been a permanent fixture in her life almost for as long as she could remember. Could he really be dead?

She was told to sit by the others, which she did, trying not to take it personally when they shuffled as far away as they could get. She was used to it. The mere's brush of her skin on someone else's was the touch of death itself. Sometimes it took minutes or days, or, in the case of the unlucky fellow upstairs, but a moment.

'Where is Vineri?' she murmured to the older woman next to her.

'Don't speak to me, you fucking witch,' the cook spat so vehemently that Lily drew back with a gasp.

Fighting a ridiculous urge to burst into tears, she

conceded that Vineri must indeed be dead. No one would have spoken to the pride of his Collection thus unless he was cold in his grave. She let out a breath she didn't know she'd been holding. So what would happen to her now, she thought as she looked around. She finally noticed that part of the monastery was burnt black and still smoking in some places. There were soldiers everywhere and she saw what they were doing here. Looting. They were taking everything not bolted down and sometimes even when it was!

Her gaze moved upward and she took in the sky. It weas so vast, so open. She took a long breath and closed her eyes, imaging she was still in her little room, closed off from the world. It would do no good to have an attack out here with everyone watching. It was just the sky. It was just outside. She'd been outside before. She was being silly, she thought as she forced the panic down mercilessly.

A new soldier appeared and ordered them up and she got to her numb feet with a wince. She didn't even have her shawl to keep the bite of the wind off her shoulders.

They were led outside the fortress and Lily gasped at the sight. Grey tents everywhere, some gargantuan and some clearly meant for one person to sleep.

There were rows and rows of them, all around her. Wrapping her arms around herself. She followed behind the others, keeping her distance from them, but hoping to the gods she didn't draw any attention. Thankfully everyone out here seemed to be very busy, all rushing about with purpose to their strides and no time for errant gazes.

They were led into a warm tent and told to wait and she let out a sigh as she began to defrost. It was bare in here. At a table in the middle of the tent sat two more soldiers in black. She couldn't hear what they were saying until she got closer, those in front being herded away, none of them protesting, not even the cook who'd snapped at her.

She got to the table and the one in front of her glanced at her once and wrote something in a large book.

He said something she didn't catch, sounding bored as he motioned for her to be taken from the tent.

She was ushered outside again and no one touched her, thankfully. She hoped that if she simply did what she was told quickly, no one would.

She followed one of the soldiers down a road of sorts and into one of the larger tents. Inside, she gaped at the colours. Everything was bright and beautiful. Coloured, sheer cloths hung from the ceiling, incense burned and there were cushions and … her eyes widened … *naked women*.

Pre-order Kept to Kill (Release date May 2021) at www.kyraalessy.com/kept2kill

ACKNOWLEDGEMENTS

A special thanks to everyone who read the original version of this story on Lit.

Without your feedback and comments, I would never have thought I could actually publish anything.

Thanks so much to all of you!

ABOUT THE AUTHOR

Kyra was almost 20 when she read her first romance. From Norsemen to Regency and Romcom to Dubcon, tales of love and adventure filled a void in her she didn't know existed. She's always been a writer, but its only now that she's started to tell stories in the genre she loves most.

She LOVES interacting with her readers so please join us in the Portal to the Dark Realm, Kyra's private Facebook group, because she is literally ALWAYS online unless she's asleep – much to her husband's annoyance!

Take a look at her website for info on how to stay updated on release dates, exclusive content and other general awesomeness from the Dark Brothers' world – where the road to happily ever after might be rough, but its well worth the journey!

- facebook.com/kyraalessy
- twitter.com/evylempryss
- instagram.com/kyraalessy
- goodreads.com/evylempryss

Printed in Great Britain
by Amazon